A Week in December

SEBASTIAN FAULKS

A Week in December

DOUBLEDAY

New York   London   Toronto

Sydney   Auckland

DOUBLEDAY

Copyright © 2009 by Sebastian Faulks

All rights reserved. Published in the United States by Doubleday, a division of Random House, Inc., New York

www.doubleday.com

DOUBLEDAY and the DD colophon are registered trademarks of Random House, Inc.

Originally published in Great Britain by Hutchinson, the Random House Group Ltd., London, in 2009.

9270

Book design Michael Collica

Library of Congress Cataloging-in-Publication Data
Faulks, Sebastian.
A week in December / Sebastian Faulks. — 1st ed.
p. cm.
1. London (England)—Fiction. 2. Christmas stories. I. Title.
PR6056.A89W44 2010
823'.914—dc22
2009030109

ISBN 978-0-385-53291-4

PRINTED IN THE UNITED STATES OF AMERICA

1 3 5 7 9 10 8 6 4 2

First United States Edition

Grateful acknowledgment is made for permission to reproduce lines from the following:

The Second Sin by Thomas Szasz (Copyright © Thomas Szasz 1973). Reprinted by permission of A.M. Heath & Co Ltd

"Business Girls," from *Collected Poems*, by John Betjeman © 1955, 1958, 1962, 1964, 1968, 1970, 1979, 1981, 1982, 2001. Reproduced by permission of John Murray (Publishers)

For David Jones-Parry

"As long as the music is playing, you've got to get up and dance . . . We're still dancing."

Chuck Prince, chief executive, Citigroup,
Interview, *Financial Times*, July 9, 2007

"If you talk to God, you are praying. If God talks to you, you have schizophrenia."

Dr. Thomas Szasz, psychiatrist,
The Second Sin, 1973

One

Sunday, December 16

I

Five o'clock and freezing. Piledrivers and jackhammers were blasting into the wasteland by the side of West Cross Route in Shepherd's Bush. With a bare ten months to the scheduled opening of Europe's largest urban shopping center, the sand-covered site was showing only skeletal girders and joists under red cranes, though a peppermint facade had already been tacked on to the eastward side. This was not a retail park with trees and benches, but a compression of trade in a city center, in which migrant labor was paid by foreign capital to squeeze out layers of profit from any Londoner with credit. At their new "Emirates" Stadium, meanwhile, named for an Arab airline, Arsenal of North London were kicking off under floodlights against Chelsea from the West, while the goalkeepers—one Czech, one Spanish—jumped up and down and beat their ribs to keep warm. At nearby Upton Park, the supporters were leaving the ground after a home defeat; and only a few streets away from the Boleyn Ground, with its East End mixture of sentimentality and grievance, a solitary woman paid her respects to a grandfather—come from Lithuania some eighty years ago—as she stood by his grave in the overflowing cemetery of the East Ham Synagogue. Up the road in Victoria Park, the last of the dog walkers dragged their mongrels back to flats in Hackney and Bow, gray high-rises marked with satellite dishes, like ears cupped to the outside world in the hope of gossip or escape; while in a minicab that nosed along Dalston Road on its

1

way back to base, the dashboard thermometer touched minus two degrees.

In his small rooms in Chelsea, Gabriel Northwood, a barrister in his middle thirties, was reading the Koran, and shivering. He practiced civil law, when he practiced anything at all; this meant that he was not involved in "getting criminals off," but in representing people in a dispute whose outcome would bring financial compensation to the claimants if they won. For a long time, and for reasons he didn't start to understand, Gabriel had received no instructions from solicitors—the branch of the legal profession he depended on for work. Then a case had landed in his lap. It was to do with a man who had thrown himself under a Tube train, and concerned the extent to which the transport provider might be deemed responsible for failing to provide adequate safety precautions. Almost immediately, a second brief had followed: from a local education authority being sued by the parents of a Muslim girl in Leicester for not allowing her to wear traditional dress to school. With little other preparatory work to do, Gabriel thought he might as well try to understand the faith whose demands he was about to encounter; and any educated person these days, he told himself, really ought to have read the Koran.

Some yards below where Gabriel sat reading was an Underground train; and in the driver's cab a young woman called Jenni Fortune switched off the interior light because she was distracted by her own reflection in the windscreen. She slowed the train with her left hand on the traction brake control and, just before she drew level with the signal, brought it to a halt. She pressed two red buttons to open the doors and fixed her eyes on the wing mirror to watch the passengers behind her getting in and out.

She had been driving on the Circle and Metropolitan lines for three years and still felt excited when she clocked in for her eight-hour shift at the depot. She felt sorry for the poor passengers who sat and swayed behind her. Sideways on, they saw only bags and overcoats, hanging straps and worn plush under strip lights with

2

suffocating heaters locked on max. They endured the jostle and the boredom, with occasional stabs of fear when drunken, swearing youths pushed on.

From her view, Jenni saw soothing darkness, points, a slither of crossing rails and signals that glowed like red coals. She rattled the train through the tunnels at forty miles per hour and sometimes half expected skeletons to loom out from the wall or bats to brush her face. Head-on, she saw the miracles of London engineering that no passenger would ever glimpse: the corbeled brickwork through which the tunnels had been cut or the giant steel joist that held up a five-floor building above the entry to the platform at Liverpool Street.

The week before Christmas was the worst time of year for people throwing themselves on the track. Nobody knew why. Perhaps the approaching festivity brought back memories of family or friends who'd died, without whom the turkey and the streamers seemed a gloomy echo of a world that had once been full. Or maybe the advertisements for digital cameras, aftershave and computer games reminded people how much they were in debt, how few of "this year's must-have" presents they could afford. Guilt, thought Jenni: a sense of having failed in the competition for resources—for DVDs and body lotions—could drive them to the rails.

Books were what she was hoping to find beneath her own tree. Her favorite authors were Agatha Christie and Edith Wharton, but she read with undifferentiated glee—philosophy or airport novels. Her mother, who had come from County Cork, had barely owned a book and had been suspicious of Jenni's reading habits as a teenager. She urged her to get out and find a boyfriend, but Jenni seemed happier in her room with 600-page novels with titles in embossed gold lettering that told how a Russian pogrom had led, two generations later and after much suffering and sex, to the founding of a cosmetics dynasty in New York. Her father, who was from Trinidad, had left "home" when Jenni was eight months old.

After her shift she would return to the novel that had won the big literary prize, the 2005 Café Bravo, which she was finding a bit thin. Then, after making something to eat for herself and her half brother Tony, if he was there, she would log on to Parallax, the newest and most advanced of alternative-reality games, where she would continue to create the life of her stand-in, or "maquette" as the game had it, Miranda Star.

Two years before, when she was still new to the job, Jenni had had a jumper. She was coming into Monument when a sudden flash of white, like a giant seagull fluttering from the platform edge, had made her brake hard. But it was too late to prevent her hitting a twenty-year-old man, whose leap had cleared the so-called suicide pit but not taken him as far as the positive rail on the far side. *Don't look at their faces* was the drivers' wisdom, and after three months' counseling and rehabilitation, Jenni had resumed her driving. The man, though seriously injured, had survived. Two months later, his parents brought a civil action against Jenni's employers, claiming negligence, because their lack of safety precautions had been responsible for the son's injuries. They lost the case, but had been granted leave to appeal, and the thought of the imminent second hearing—tomorrow there would be another meeting with the lawyer, Mr. Northwood—darkened the edges of Jenni Fortune's days.

At that moment in the wealthy inner suburb of North Park, "located," as the estate agent had it, "between the natural advantages of Heath and Green," Sophie Topping had just made a cup of tea for herself and her husband Lance, who was working in his study. He had done this every Sunday afternoon since becoming an MP in the recent by-election. Sophie wasn't sure how he could concentrate on constituency paperwork with the football blasting out from the television in the corner and she suspected that he sometimes nodded off to the excited yet soporific commentary. For fear of discovering him slumped with his mouth open, she always knocked before taking in his tea.

4

"I'm just finalizing the places for Saturday," she said, handing him a blue china cup with what he called "builders' tea" in it.

"What?" he said.

"The big dinner."

"God, yes. I'd quite forgotten," said Lance. "All under control?"

"Yes, I think it'll be a night to remember."

Sophie retired to her desk and looked at the list of names she had printed out from her computer. At first, she'd meant to have an intimate evening with a few powerful people, just so that Richard Wilbraham, the party leader, could see the sort of company Lance moved in. But when she got down to it, there seemed no end to the number of important people she and Lance knew—and wanted the leader to know they knew.

Looking down the names, Sophie began to sketch a table plan.

- Lance and Sophie Topping. The party's newest MP and his wife. It was still good to say those words.
- Richard and Janie Wilbraham. Richard, the dynamic PM-in-waiting, would be on her own right hand. He was nice enough, though tended to talk politics. But what could you do?
- Len and Gillian Foxley, Lance's local agent and his tiny wife. Sophie would put Len between two women who would have to bear his halitosis, while Gillian she buried midtable among the also-rans.
- R. Tranter, the paid leader of discussions at Sophie's monthly book club and professional reviewer. She wasn't sure what his first name was. He signed himself "RT" and the women in the group called him "Mr. Tranter" until he invited them to move on to RT.
- Magnus Darke. Probably not his real name, Sophie thought. He was a newspaper columnist and therefore dangerous, obviously, but could be entertaining. He had once said nice things about Lance, called him "the coming man" or some

such. Sophie dared to put Darke next to chilly Amanda Malpasse.

- Farooq and Nasim al-Rashid. Sophie sucked her pen. Farooq was a chutney magnate and a large private donor to party funds. He seemed a nice chap. But they both were keen "Allah botherers," as Clare Darnley put it. After some thought Sophie penciled each one in next to a Wilbraham, as a mark of respect for Farooq's contributions, and made a note to put no wine glasses at their places.

- Amanda Malpasse. Sophie had made friends with Amanda on a charity committee. She lived in a large cold house in the Chilterns and was beautiful in a dry, shut-down sort of way. Amanda already had Magnus Darke, so Sophie needed to find her someone tonier for the other side.

- Brenda Dillon. Sophie had only ever seen her on television, where she was an argumentative education spokesman. Her husband David was said by a newspaper profile to be keen on DIY and to carry his keys on the waistband of his trousers. This was a poser.

- Tadeusz "Spike" Borowski. Even more ticklish, this one, thought Sophie. Borowski was a Polish footballer who had settled with a London club. Arsenal, was it? No, another one. Lance had met him when his team were turning on some Christmas streetlights and had taken a liking to him. He thought it would make them look modern to have Spike there. But did he speak English? Would he behave? What did footballers like to do after dinner? "Dogging," was it, or "spit roasting"? She wasn't quite sure what either of these things was.

- Simon and Indira Porterfield. They at least were easy, and could talk charmingly to anyone. Simon was the billionaire owner of Digitime TV, whose reality shows, notably *It's Madness*, had saved Channel 7. Indira was a Bangalore-born princess of eye-watering beauty; he referred to her as his "mail-order bride," the first Mrs. Porterfield having been superannuated.

- Roger Malpasse, Amanda's husband. Sophie smiled. The thought of Roger always made her smile. He was a former corporate lawyer, now retired to farm and supervise his horses, which were trained at Lambourn. Sophie decided to put him near Spike Borowski, since, apart from dogs and horses, football was the only thing she'd ever heard Roger talk about.
- Radley Graves. Another tricky one, she thought. Graves was a schoolteacher at the coalface who was said to have given Lance the inside line on comprehensives during the campaign. The obvious person to put him next to was Brenda Dillon, but something about Graves's demeanor made Sophie doubt that either would enjoy it.
- Gabriel Northwood. He should be all right, Sophie thought, though it depended what mood he was in. He was a barrister, who could be melancholy and sometimes seemed to switch off from the conversation. After some consideration, Sophie placed him next to Mrs. Lime Pickle, Nasim al-Rashid.
- Clare Darnley. Another easy one. Clare was Sophie's favorite lame duck—elegant enough, but apparently condemned to loneliness. Perhaps it was because she was so outspoken and moralistic; it made people in the modern world feel uneasy to be told that certain things were "wrong." Clare worked in some appalling job in "care provision." Sophie put her on the other side of Gabriel.
- John Veals, the unsmiling hedge-fund man, and Vanessa, his long-suffering wife, who was also in Sophie's book group. John was a tough ask, there was no doubt about that. He had no small talk and was often late or jet-lagged or both. He spoke little. It drove Vanessa mad, Sophie knew. On the other hand, his lack of grace meant he was oddly

7

direct, if foulmouthed. He could be interesting. Sophie gave him half Indira Porterfield, and to Vanessa, poor thing, she dealt Len Foxley.

The remaining guests were Jennifer and Mark Loader, both in finance; two women drawn from Sophie's repertory company of singles; and three other couples she'd met when their children were at school together. One, the McPhersons, had bought and sold a chain of busy coffee bars, Café Bravo, before diversifying into other ventures; another, the Margessons, had invented an Internet site for lonely teenagers, called YourPlace; the third, the Samuels, had bundled up and sold on other people's debts. Sophie couldn't understand who the buyers for such things were—why would you *buy* debt?—but all three couples lived nearby and she "owed" all of them hospitality.

At her bedroom window, looking over the houses of North Park, Sophie felt a sudden shiver. She was so used to Christmas being hot and wet that the sudden Arctic winds were hard to deal with; she put on another sweater and settled herself on the bed. The book she needed to read for her book club was a typical Jennifer Loader selection; it was set in Chile and appeared to be written with all the sentences rolled into one.

Sophie didn't care about this man Javier and his life in Central or South America, whichever one Chile was in, she wasn't sure, it was sometimes hard to remember . . .

She snapped the book shut. She was sure that Jennifer had only chosen the book to impress R. Tranter, the professional reviewer; that was why she always picked books with haphazard narrators and unreliable punctuation. But, Jennifer had pointed out when her selection had been queried, this one had not only been short-listed for the Café Bravo and the Allied Royal Bank prizes, it had also been nominated for the Pizza Palace Book of the Year. You could barely see the photo on the jacket—a barefoot waif in a bomb site—for the prize sponsors' bright stickers. "Hmm," Lance had said, sniffing it briefly before tossing it back to her, "more endorsements than your driving license, Soph."

John Veals, the hedge-fund manager, was meanwhile looking at one of the four flat-screen monitors banked above his desk. His office was in a tall, blank building in Old Pye Street—the only such block in an otherwise quiet, residential road in Victoria—with a view over to the miniature Byzantine domes and piebald brickwork of Westminster Cathedral, where the bells were tolling for early evening Mass.

The weekends allowed Veals time to be alone in his office, without interruption. This was when he tried to let his market instinct find its true north, with no e-mail or telephone or colleagues to break the spell. It was not that it was ever a noisy office; even during the busy week, most visitors remarked on its calm. Veals himself spoke little because he was so aware of security risks. Although the office was regularly swept for bugs, he had trained himself never to say anything that he couldn't bear to have overheard. Much of his most delicate business was conducted in the Folger's coffee shop in Victoria station, in the Moti Mahal beneath a sooty bridge in Waterloo or through one of his six cellphones in an alleyway that ran off Old Pye Street, behind the Peabody Buildings. Marc Bézamain, his man in New York, told him that ninety-five percent of successful prosecutions brought by regulators stemmed from their reading of incriminating e-mail traffic.

Veals didn't do e-mail. To clients or counterparties too powerful to ignore, he offered the vague exec1@hlcapital.com as an address, but to make sure he couldn't reply even to the most provocative messages, he had had the back office disable his "send" capacity. There was one other ruse. The company which supplied the screens and their data also offered an e-mail service; and this was neither stored nor checked by the authorities.

The secretaries at High Level Capital were chosen for soft-footedness. The managers worked in soundproof offices with solid doors; Veals did the rounds each day, but avoided large meetings. The analysts came and went, then wrote their reports on silent keyboards. All of them were thin. Veals couldn't stand fatness; it riled the ascetic in him. The men wore charcoal gray suits, never navy, and he stipulated no pink shirts; the women's skirts were knee-length, their nylons black. In summer the air conditioning was turned up high; in winter the radiators were too hot to touch. Veals took thirty percent of his investors' profits annually; but he also took three percent a year of the value of funds (before leverage) as a management fee, so even by doing nothing, no new trades at all, he could make many millions a year. The electricity bill was not an issue.

In his twenty-seven years in finance, one thing remained constant in Veals's view: the only way to make money was to have an edge. No trader, however brilliant or intuitive, could outperform the market over a sustained period. Veals had read all the books on "rational" markets: he'd read the theories of Merton, Black and Scholes on the valuation of stock options; he'd weighed on the one hand their two Nobel prizes and on the other hand the trillion-dollar black hole left by the collapse and humiliation of the hedge fund for which all three had worked.

"Theory" was all, in John Veals's opinion, piffle. If you play blackjack every day for a year, the house will always win. Veals knew this for a fact since in his first experience of markets, at the age of fourteen, he *was* the house. His uncle was a bookmaker in Hendon and showed young John how to set the odds in a ten-horse race so that any outcome made a profit for the book. The keys, he taught John, were speed of reaction and constant recalculation. At the latter, John was a prodigious pupil. From the age of thirteen he could work out in his head what odds should be offered on an eleven-part yankee before his uncle could do it with paper and pencil. Horse racing taught him that the only way to beat the house was to have information. If you knew that Stardust Rosie had been held back by her jockey for three races till her odds were 18/1 for the next outing but on that occasion the jockey would give the horse her head, then you really could beat the bookie by backing her to win. No computer model, no algorithmic forecast, could outperform such knowledge.

Veals was viewed as old-fashioned by his peers in believing that the "real economy" of mills and factories and making things did still have a function—which was to generate a deal flow for the financiers. And these deals, he pointed out, did generate real revenue, which in turn generated tax (some tax anyway, depending on how efficient your tax-avoidance department was) for hospitals, roads, all that.

Where Veals gained an edge on most of his rivals was by knowing that the word "inside" in the phrase "inside information" had a surprisingly strict legal meaning. He had known many bankers who hadn't properly understood how much "inside" information they were legally permitted to acquire, and had thus unnecessarily handicapped themselves. He didn't tell them. They, too, could have studied the book if they'd chosen to. There was kosher inside and iffy inside. "Know the rules" was Veals's own favorite rule.

The second obvious step toward getting a sustainable edge was to stay away from regulation. In his years as a futures trader and a banker Veals had chosen to operate in areas where regulation was either minimal or nonexistent. It was only a matter of time in his own mind before he moved into the world of hedge funds, because here legal supervision was at its lightest: sophisticated investors needed flexible arrangements, not fussy inspectors.

Another obvious precaution, taken by most senior people he knew, was not to pay tax. When it came to running his own hedge fund, he naturally, therefore, based it offshore. He had chosen Zurich, because it was under the jurisdiction neither of the Financial Services Authority in London nor of the European Union. The large profits of High Level Capital were kept in the fund and rolled up abroad; it was structured so that it generated no taxable income. Vanessa, John Veals's Anglo-American wife, was for tax purposes not domiciled in Britain, and there were legal ways of making sure that the income they needed each year should be classified as foreign earnings in her name. A remittance of funds from abroad could alert the taxman, it was true, but the Veals family didn't need much income: John had no power boats or polo ponies; no collections of Sumerian stone tablets or early Picassos; no mortgage, no hobbies and no interests outside work. He hadn't even dug out the basement of his house to stick in a swimming pool. Petty cash could be also bled out of the fund through a web of trusts held in the names of his two children, Bella and Finn. Well, it wasn't his fault; he didn't make the laws.

He disliked the famous remark made by a New York billion-airess that taxes were for the "little people." It sent out the wrong signals. John Veals did, however, share the more elegantly phrased view of many of his senior colleagues in the London hedge-fund and banking world that "income tax is voluntary."

As the bells tolled, he closed his eyes and contemplated the magnificent good fortune of his life. The quiet in the office was wonderful. Two senior colleagues worked abroad, Duffy in Switzerland and Bézamain in New York, where how they behaved was their own affair (Bézamain wore espadrilles to work and sang French folk songs under pressure). But in the cathedral calm of Old Pye Street, Veals's partner Stephen Godley was the only person allowed to be voluble; he siphoned off the tension from the others: the billion-dollar sweats bloomed only in his armpits. Since the day they'd met at a New York investment bank in 1990, Veals had seen in Godley's open, sporting jollity something he himself was lacking: clients warmed to him in a way that no one ever warmed to Veals. He talked to them in sporting metaphors ("I think we'll put the other side in to bat first"), and he was the only Englishman in New York who seemed genuinely to understand baseball and gridiron as easily as he did golf and cricket. In the course of raising funds to start their hedge fund in 1999, Veals had learned to let Godley do the talking. Who cared what madman was in the attic so long as the door was firmly locked and the key was in smiling Stephen Godley's pocket?

The long association meant Steve Godley knew the details of

each trade made by John Veals for more than fifteen years, which allowed him to make unamusing jokes about bodies and where they were buried. On the other hand, Veals had seen Godley build his first personal £10 million at the bank by exploiting (first to his employers' advantage, then, through annual bonuses, to his own) the information that leaked through the bank's flimsy Chinese walls and by putting on his own trades a fraction before exercising identical ones requested by a client. This was regarded as simple exuberance, the fog of war; it was nothing like the distasteful insider dealing of the bond department. Everyone did it. Chinese people, as Godley remarked, tend to be short, and their walls are easy to look over.

Veals brought his mind back to the present. High Level had had a difficult six months. One of the fund's perennial problems was its sheer size (it had over £12 billion under management, of which about a quarter was Veals's own reinvested money): it was often hard to find market inefficiencies so glaring that they could make a real impact on returns. Then they had, frustratingly, not been able to profit from the mortgage market that was causing tremors in America. After much consultation with Marc Bézamain in New York, Veals had been convinced in 2005 that American mortgage companies had dangerously oversold mortgages to poor people ("subprimers") who would be unable to make the monthly repayments if anything—anything—went wrong.

High Level therefore bought hundreds of millions of dollars of "put" options on the relevant housing index, the ABX. The "puts" gave Veals the right to sell the index at a pre-agreed price in the future if he so chose; his profit was to be on the difference between that price and the much lower level to which he was convinced the market would fall. But the index didn't move. It seemed impossible. People were losing their jobs, defaulting on their payments; interest rates and thus monthly repayments were set to rise—but still the index wouldn't fall.

One of the marks of a good manager, everyone agreed, was to know when he is beaten, and in the summer of 2006 Veals had ditched the trade. It took another nine months for the index to collapse. He took no pleasure in being proved "right" eventually about the fall and still thought he had been wise to pull out: the market's ability to behave irrationally had outlasted his patience, and he had done the professional thing. He recouped some of his losses by short-selling two individual mortgage providers, but even here he closed the position and returned the borrowed stock with the price twenty points above its final nadir. This could happen.

Yet could he now be sure, in the cold December darkness, that he was not being influenced, even minutely, by a vestigial wound to his pride? He gazed from the window toward the cathedral and screwed up his eyes. This long introspection was a ritual. Not until he was sure that his motives were pure—driven in other words only by an unemotional and rigorous assessment of profitability— would he commit himself.

Somewhere in the passageways of John Veals's mind, beyond the thoughts of wife, children, daily living, carnal urges, beyond the scar tissue of experience and loss, there was a creature whose heart beat only to market movements. He couldn't be happy as a man if his positions weren't making money. For John Veals, the analysis of a potential position was therefore more than a business or a mathematical problem; it involved something painfully close to self-knowledge. His life depended on it.

II

In the rear carriage of Jenni Fortune's Circle Line train Hassan al-Rashid sat staring straight ahead. Normally, without a book to read, he would move his head up and down so that the reflection of his face in the convex window opposite would develop panda eyes, elongate like an image in a fairground mirror and then pop. But this was not the day for such frivolity: he was on his way to buy the constituents of a bomb.

Two white-skinned teenagers opposite him were kissing, sticking their tongues out and laughing when they touched. Although they were absorbed by one another, there was a challenge in their public intimacy. A black-skinned youth with feet in padded white trainers the size of small boats was leaning forward. From his earplugs came a hissing, thumping noise. Hassan could sense that this youth's eyes, though looking down, were ready to lock on to those of anyone who caught them, so he was careful to keep his own gaze somewhere to the left of the hunched shoulders.

To Hassan's left, in the standing area by the central doors, were Japanese and European tourists. It was Sunday, Hassan thought; most of these people should have been in church, but these days Christians viewed cathedrals as monuments or works of art to be admired for their architecture and paintings, not as the place where they could worship God. Their final loss of faith had happened in the last ten years or so, yet in the *kafir* world it had passed with little comment. How very strange they were, he thought, these people, that they had let eternal life slip through their hands.

Where Hassan had grown up in Glasgow, the Christians (he hadn't by then adopted the word "*kafir*") blasphemed and drank and fornicated, though most of them, he knew, still more or less believed. They were unfaithful in hotel rooms, but they got married in churches. They went on Christmas Day or when they buried a friend; they took their babies to be named there, and when they were dying they still sent out for a priest. Now you could read statistics in newspaper surveys which confirmed what anyone could see: that they'd given up God. And barely a *kafir* seemed to have noticed.

The conviction that the rest of the world lived in a dream was one that grew in Hassan each day. With the exception of those in his group and some of the more committed members of the Pudding Mill Lane Mosque, he viewed everyone he knew as deluded. It was perplexing to him that people paid so little heed to their own salvation; he was puzzled by it in the way he might have been by the sight of a mother feeding whisky to a baby. There might have been some short-term benefit in the respite from crying, but it wasn't something that a reasonable person would do. Yet the truth of life, and of life after death, was not exactly hidden.

Hassan licked his lips and swallowed. Although the individual parts that made up the bombs were easy enough to find and buy, he was aware that the grimiest corner shops these days had CCTV cameras. The purchase of even three or four bottles of soft drinks at once might be remembered by the man at the counter, then recalled from the digital memory of the camera. He was therefore spreading his custom right across London, one bottle at a time. The hardest thing to get his hands on had been syringes. Eventually he'd gone to the casualty department of his local hospital and feigned an acute pain in what he thought was the appendix area. He gave the triage nurse an invented name and address. After an hour, he was escorted from the waiting area into a more actively medical part of the building, with nurses, beds and stores; here he was put in a cubicle behind a curtain and told that a doctor would come. Then, ten minutes later, he peered out. There was no one in the linoleum-floored corridor. Ready to say, if challenged, that he was looking for a bathroom, Hassan set out to explore. Two large West Indian nurses rolled by, but neither stopped him. He could see a room with cardboard kidney dishes on a counter. In the cupboard over them, above boxes of antiseptic wipes, he found an open carton of syringes. He took a dozen, stuffed them in his jacket pocket and went quickly back to his cubicle. Nobody came to see him, so after twenty minutes in the airless, overheated little room, he retraced his steps to the waiting area and went unchallenged back into the world.

At Gloucester Road, Hassan stepped off the train and went up into the street. Batteries and disposable cameras were easy and cheap enough to find; the only thing he was having trouble with was hydrogen peroxide. But he had a plan for that.

In a first-floor flat of what had once been a railway worker's cottage in Clapham, Hassan's face in a photograph was being stared at by a young woman called Shahla Hajiani.

Shahla's father, an Iranian businessman, had bought the one-bedroom flat as an investment, and, rather than have the trouble of letting it out, permitted his daughter to live there for nothing. Shahla, who had previously lived in Hackney with three fellow postgraduates, wasn't sure she liked it. She sometimes felt lonely, particularly on a Sunday.

"Oh, you silly boy," she said out loud as she put down the picture of Hassan. It was just a snap taken at a friend's graduation party, but it showed him laughing, before he had become religious. Shahla herself was an atheist, having followed neither her mother's Anglo-Judaism nor her father's selective version of Islam.

The French professor had persuaded her to take a second degree after her success in the first, and now she saw a pathway into the academic world beginning to open up before her feet. She had agreed to do a Ph.D. on the poetry of the surrealist Paul Éluard, but felt wary of the idea of teaching and of institutions that would naturally follow. She liked parties too much; she liked traveling and big cities, and her fortunate knack with literature could also be a snare, she thought.

She had met Hassan when he was a dedicated left-winger at student rallies, and she had at once been drawn to his passion and his soft manner. Behind his rhetorical certainties, she saw someone who had at some stage in his life been wounded. It puzzled and intrigued her, while the way he would let no one come too close to him suggested to Shahla a degree of fear. Yet up to a certain line—an invisible but passionately defended boundary—he was irresistible. His large hands with their thin, hair-covered wrists, his humorous, deep voice, his eyes so candid and willing to engage until the moment they took fright . . . She saw all these things in the photograph, and she sighed, a broken exhalation, as she replaced it in a drawer and went to make her duty Sunday phone call to her mother.

At six o'clock Ralph Tranter was gathering his armful of Sunday papers from the Iraqi newsagent, his pulse rate elevated by the weight of newsprint as well as by the thought of what it might contain. He lived with a cat called Septimus Harding in a flat in Ferrers End, a suburb that straddled the North Circular. Traffic hurried through it on its way to places of importance—Tottenham, Edmonton, Harringay—or north to the open spaces beyond the crawl of blackened bridge, gridlock and speed camera. Tranter's road was called Mafeking Street and was occupied mostly by Kurds. A trip to the newsagent, Tranter told people, was like a walk through the history of the late twentieth century: here was the fallout of wars hot and cold; here was the collateral displacement of free markets and porous frontiers.

He had had a slow start to Sunday, finishing a book before going out late for the papers. His route to the high street took him through three near-identical roads of modest houses built for another London, a place long gone. He sometimes tried to picture those first tenants: manual workers who commuted to the smog-producing factories of Bermondsey or Poplar, then returned at night to their modest white enclave; but it was hard to imagine them now in these car-lined streets: that homogeneity was not in nature anymore.

R. Tranter was always known by his first initial only, though very old friends might call him "Ralph." Work colleagues and acquaintances called him "RT." It had started when he submitted some reviews on spec to a small magazine, *Outpost*, soon after he had left Oxford. Finding themselves short of material at the last minute, they had printed one, but he had signed it only "R. Tranter" and they had not been able to reach him by phone to find out what his first name was. When, a month later, a second magazine, *Actium*, rang to say they were also using an article by him and asked how he would like to be billed, he opted for reasons of continuity and superstition to go with "R. Tranter." He had never liked his first name anyway, and it had been the subject of a life-long confusion as to whether it rhymed with "Alf" or "safe."

He occupied the first floor of a two-story building, and, although the house was a sooty brick nonentity, one of a row that varied only in external paint color and size of TV aerial dish, his rooms were painted a pleasant magnolia and had simple furniture from a Finnish brownsite warehouse. To this clean modern look, the odd mahogany gateleg table or 1950s standard lamp from various secondhand shops had added, he felt, an original note.

Tranter logged on to the e-mail at his white PC. There was the usual Sunday horoscope from Stargazer. "Hi, Bruno Banks! A good week awaits you. Venus is in the ascendant, which means you are going to get lucky in love! Professional openings are abundant. Use your fabled charm to make the most of them. Have a good one, Bruno Banks! With best wishes from All the Team at Stargazer." Tranter envied Bruno his auspicious life. Unfortunately, Bruno was a fictional character Tranter had invented for a novel he'd abandoned two years earlier. As inspiration waned, he had looked to the Internet for help and hoped that signing up to a horoscope as Bruno Banks would give him ideas. It hadn't. Eventually, Tranter e-mailed Stargazer to tell them Bruno had died, been hit by a meteor, had met an unexpected—an unforetold— end, but to no avail: the predictions kept on coming.

The sitting room was entirely lined with bookshelves that Tranter had made himself, sawing up furlongs of dusty MDF, wearing a face mask from the hardware shop on Green Lanes, then propping lengths of undercoated shelf on the sport and finance sections of spread-out newspapers. His woodwork had won steady praise in his schooldays, more than thirty years before, and, when the shelves had been painted white and fitted to the wall, they were able to support, without sagging, Tranter's 2,000-piece library, ranged in alphabetical order from Achebe, Chinua to Zweig, Stefan. He sometimes regretted all the books he'd sold on to Bellswift, the sullen secondhand dealer in Lamb's Conduit Street, but he knew that it was the half price he got for them that enabled him to continue to live in Europe's most expensive city, albeit in Mafeking Street.

There was no television in the sitting room, merely a glass-topped coffee table with back numbers of the weekly papers, and a couple of armchairs upholstered in navy blue. One of these was usually occupied by the slothful Septimus, named after a character in *The Warden*, Tranter's favorite Trollope novel. The cat added a touch of warmth to a room that might otherwise have been intimidating in its single-mindedness: the size of Tranter's library meant there was no space on the walls for pictures or posters. The closest he had come to ornament was a wooden bust of G. K. Chesterton from a shop in Sicilian Avenue, which sat between the end of the *U*s (Upward, Edward) and the beginning of the *V*s (van Vechten, Carl).

In November, Tranter had invited Patrick Warrender, the literary editor who gave him his staple work as a reviewer, to come and have dinner. He had also invited a married couple he had known since Oxford and a woman novelist of his own age, who made her living by broadcasting in a vein both maternal and minatory that was favored by the radio, where she described *Moby-Dick* as "boysy" and *Anna Karenina* as "badly written." Patrick was gay, so there had been no need to find more women, and the conversation had continued successfully till one o'clock.

Tranter had written two reviews in the armful of Sunday papers he brought back from the newsagent. One of them had suffered the usual trimming, with some of his better thrusts cut back or modified; the other was untouched—usually a sign that Patrick Warrender, late back from lunch at his gentlemen's club, had miscalculated the space and so had been obliged to let Tranter run on to his full extent. In any event, both were satisfactory. Tranter felt he had not only explained why the books were flawed, but had also managed to demonstrate that both writers were, in some essential way, fraudulent.

He went through to the small kitchen that overlooked the backyards of the terrace. A woman in Muslim headgear (what was the word for it? Hijab? Burkha?) was hanging washing on a line. Were they allowed to do that? he wondered. At some level, Tranter was confused between Muslim women in traditional dress and nuns.

Was either group, for instance, allowed to ride a bicycle or play Ping-Pong? Would that be blasphemous, or merely comic?

In the next garden, the Bosnian war criminal was stripping down his motorbike, while from beyond him came the shrieking voices of the fast-breeding Catholic Polish family, as four boys attempted a football game on the tiny lawn.

Tranter took a mug of tea back to the sitting room and opened the third newspaper on his pile. He threw the sport and city sections into the recycling basket and turned to the book review pages. A history of the ballpoint pen was well received by a young novelist, who described Biro's invention as "iconic" and made reference to Roland Barthes and Eric Cantona. A life of Dora Carrington was given a guarded welcome by a biographer of Roger Fry. "Not vintage, but quaffable" was the verdict of the paper's diarist on a guide to New World wines, while the MP for a market town in Derbyshire dismissed the memoirs of an American Secretary of State as "Pooterish."

None of this stuff interested Tranter. His years in the business had trained him to go straight to the fiction pages, which he read with the eye of a fund manager scanning market prices. The difference was that Tranter had no investment and no favorite; he didn't want to see a modest growth, still less a boom. He was interested only in bad reviews. Crash was what he wanted: crash and burn—failure, slump, embarrassment. He liked it when acerbic youngsters teased established writers and he relished it when old pipe-suckers slapped down a lively newcomer. His own speciality was the facetious, come-off-it review which invited the reader to share his opinion that the writer's career had been a sustained con trick at the expense of the gullible book buyer. He dismissed equally the offerings of famous old men, heavy with honors, and those of photogenic young women. While he averted his eyes from other people's praise, he was generous in his enjoyment of like-minded reviews. Sometimes, he sent postcards in his precise ballpoint handwriting: "I thought you got the new _____ exactly right. RT."

Literary setbacks came in many shapes, and Tranter relished all of them: he was a connoisseur of disappointment, a voluptuary of disgrace. Alone among European reviewers, a young RT had found the agreed masterpiece of a Latin American novelist to be a "disappointment . . . tricked out with the sad old tropes of magic realism . . . meretricious." Of all the ways of failing as a novelist the one that Tranter relished most was the midcareer slide, because it freed him, retrospectively, from years of anguish. Foreign grandees were simple coconuts in Tranter's shy; firing off a bucketful of balls was second nature, routine stuff, and he doubted that it did much good in the face of universal fawning. But reading praise for the work of a British contemporary gave him a stomach pain as fierce as the cramps of gastroenteritis. Over the years he'd had to develop strategies for dealing with it, and the simplest was to write an anonymous review of his own at the back end of *The Toad*, a monthly magazine that was edited by an old Oxford contemporary. Here Tranter could place a powerful antidote to compliments that had appeared elsewhere. The savvy readers of *The Toad* were told that such praise had been offered in bad faith—by old Etonians, by former lovers of the author or by "poor saps" who were the victims of fashion. The truth was that the novel was full of "reach-me-down platitudes" and wasn't worth the time of unillusioned *Toad* readers. Sometimes Tranter had already reviewed the book under his own name in a newspaper, where, for plausibility's sake, he'd been obliged to mute his criticisms or leaven them with guarded praise; and then his anonymous *Toad* piece acted as a bracing corrective, even to himself.

Money was tight chez Tranter. Two book reviews a week generated £450, and a monthly *Toad* piece was worth a further £300. With other oddments, he had brought his year's income up to roughly £30,000, he thought. Then, eighteen months earlier, he had had a piece of luck. He received a letter from the headmaster of a famous private school near London, making him an offer. Although the pupils regularly came near the top of the national league of exam results, most taking home a full house of A-stars and A's, they had little idea of spelling or grammar, and neither had their teachers. The headmaster of the school had been sent a letter by an elderly parent, educated back in the 1950s, lamenting what he called the "basic errors of literacy" in his child's end-of-term report and suggesting that for £25,000 a year he was entitled to a teacher who knew the difference between "I" and "me" or "bought" and "brought."

The headmaster called a meeting of the staff, who shrugged. It wasn't their fault. Most of them had been educated by teachers who believed that spelling was at best a "fetish" and, more probably, just a way of trying to keep poor children out of university. Such things had long since been discounted by public examiners and it was far too late now, as the head of History put it, to "reinvent the wheel." And anyway, no one had ever complained about the teachers' literacy before.

One of the French staff, however, was married to a man in management consultancy who'd been at Oxford with Tranter and had kept vaguely in touch. She thought Tranter might be of an age and background still to have access to such arcana and she promised to dig out his address for the Head.

Tranter was intrigued to receive an approach from such a famous school and went in to see them, as requested. He crossed the cobbles that ringed the grassy quadrangle and thought how very different they were from the tarmac apron of his own old school. He went beneath a stone arch in which pupils had carved their names (Wm. Standforth 1822) and into another, smaller courtyard, ivied with age and bogus distinction.

"Very kind of you to come," said the Head, a tall, dynamic man with bushy black hair. "It's a slightly embarrassing request, really. I do personally recall the rudiments of spelling. Bit of a tyrant about it in fact. It's just that I don't have time to go through every single report and change 'Johnny appears disinterested' to 'Johnny appears uninterested' and so on. The current headmaster's life is largely one of conferences and administration, making speeches, marketing and so on." He coughed self-deprecatingly. "I can't pretend it's creative work we're offering you, Mr. Tranter, but we'd pay you decently."

Tranter smiled. "People'd be really surprised, wouldn't they, that you of all schools . . . I mean—"

"I know, I know," said the Head hurriedly. "Top ten of the league table and all that. But I also know for a fact that other illustrious schools do the same thing. No names, no pack drill. And obviously this must remain entirely between ourselves. It would be most damaging if it were to leak out into any . . . In any way."

Tranter thought of *The Toad*, and smiled again. "Well," he said in the higher, slightly reedy tone his voice took on when he was intrigued, "we could certainly give it a go and see how it works out."

The business part of the deal was quickly done. Drafts of all the reports were to be sent to Tranter on CD. He was not to change them or rewrite in any way, merely to correct the worst errors of grammar and syntax and all those of spelling. The school had 620 pupils, each of whom had roughly ten reports, most of them only a few lines. Tranter calculated that at the rate of three reports per minute, the whole task would take about thirty-five hours—or a working week. Based on annual earnings, his average pay per week was roughly £600, but this work would be more intensive. He had planned to ask for double, say £1,200 a term, or even £4,000 a year, but the headmaster's opening offer was £5,000 plus expenses and any secretarial help he wanted, so no bargaining was necessary.

Tranter's own writing style had long ago been sold over to journalism, with its "iconic images" and "cur's *cojones*," but he was just old enough to have been taught how to spell at school, had read thousands of good books and had once had the principle of hanging participles unforgettably explained to him by Patrick Warrender. He was up to the task. Five terms into the new regime, the headmaster was thrilled by the results. The complaining parent wrote a conciliatory letter, admitting the improvements, and the Head granted Tranter a £1,000 bonus. His nickname in the common room was Harry Patch, after the last surviving Tommy of the

Great War. "I've been Patched up," said the head of Geography, reading his corrected comments on-screen. "Me too," said History.

This success as rewrite man made Tranter see that there was still money in literacy. In fact, it was a simple demonstration of supply and demand. While graduates with first-class degrees from the best universities couldn't spell or compose an e-mail that made sense, the companies that employed them still had to write letters, put out documents and deal with law firms, banks and public companies. The counterparty didn't expect elegance, but needed at least to be able to understand what was on offer.

As someone educated at a grammar school before the towel was thrown in, Tranter had an asset: literacy. He could sell it. Then, a year after he began work with the school, he received an invitation to "moderate" the book-club discussions of a group of posh housewives in North Park. He could hardly believe his luck. Most of the women had university degrees in arts subjects, but they had no basic understanding of how a book worked. Even the vocabulary that Tranter had been taught at the age of sixteen was mysterious to them; they didn't know the difference between "style" and "tone," for instance. He was able to make £100 a time without exerting himself, as well as putting away a very good dinner and a bottle of wine. All the women were on diets, so Tranter was able to tuck in at will to a variety of dishes purchased at astonishing expense from local delicatessens and *traiteurs*. They also paid his Tube fares. After he had made a few observations about the book in question, they generally cut him out of the loop. What they wanted to talk about was whether the incidents in the book were "based on" events in the author's own life and to what extent his version of them tallied with their own experience of such things. Tranter tried to suggest that there were more fruitful ways of approaching a novel, a work of invention that aspired, albeit pathetically, to be a work of "art"; but although they listened patiently, they seemed not to believe him.

The book group met once a month and the school work came

in three times a year, so Tranter was still open to offers. In this hopeful vein, he had been intrigued one day in April to open his e-mail inbox and to see, after the usual spam for Bruno Banks, that there was one for him from Mrs. Doris Hine, or reception@ rashidpickle.org.uk.

Tranter had heard of the company, in fact had a jar of their aubergine chutney in his kitchen cupboard, and he could scent money in Mrs. Hine's message. He replied at once, and a date was set for him to visit Farooq al-Rashid, the founder and owner of Rashid Pickle, at home in Havering-atte-Bower with a view to advising him on a "literary project."

III

Jenni Fortune was on the final circuit of her Sunday shift. It was true she'd turned the light off in her cab the better to enjoy her privileged view of the city without her own reflection in the way, but that was not the only reason. She never looked at photographs of herself and spent as little time as possible looking in the mirror. There was nothing glamorous about the uniform, and for that she was grateful because it meant there was no choice; for the same reason, she had liked the blazer and skirt required by her school.

Being a Tube driver gave her power and responsibility. Almost all her training was in safety measures, the care she had to take with other people's lives; the train itself was controlled by a single lever and was easier to drive than a car. "We're paid," the older drivers in the canteen had said when she arrived, "not for what we do but what we know"—and this included how to get the forty-year-old rolling stock on the move again if it broke down, as, when the weather grew cold, it often did.

Jenni lived in a two-bedroom flat in Drayton Green, in the western suburbs between old Ealing and the new India of Southall. The second room was occupied by her younger half brother, Tony, who was out of work. Tony and Jenni had only known each other for a few years, though their respective single mothers had gathered from casual conversations with the father that there were other children too. Tony had been curious about his halves, said to be six in total, and had tracked Jenni down. Marie, Jenni's mother, thought Tony was a sponger, like his father, and that with Jenni he'd "latched on to a good thing." It was true that Tony looked at Jenni's payslip with awe, though in fact, after tax and rent at £250 a week, there was little left for much beyond the weekly shopping. Tony had lived off the jobseeker's allowance for the previous year. He was obliged to take occasional jobs to maintain a position on the benefit ladder, to which he returned when it was safe.

His room was at the back of the house, looking toward the athletics track. In his schooldays, he'd been a promising 400-meter runner himself, but it had meant training at weekends because the teachers wouldn't supervise sports in the afternoon, as part of some historic work-to-rule, and Tony found getting up at seven on Saturday to take the Tube from Tottenham to the club in Harringay too much to ask. He liked to think he'd kept in shape by playing Sunday football in Gunnersbury Park, but at the age of twenty-eight he was already carrying several extra pounds on his belly. The amount of weed he smoked made him hungry for food but not for exercise; in the evenings, he went to a pub in Harlesden and later on to various clubs, where he drank lager and bourbon.

He didn't understand Jenni. What would make a girl get up early every day and put on clunky shoes with rubber safety soles and drive a train through a dark hole in the ground? She had good holidays and steady cash, but so what? That canteen, that dick of a station supervisor, the social club, the smell, the darkness underground . . . And then when she got home she just read books. Or played that boring virtual-world game, Parallax.

Tony blamed Liston Brown, the man who'd taken up with Jenni when she was nineteen. Any man could see what Liston's game was. He was maybe thirty-nine, had three children with different women and too much money from developing property in North London. He played golf at a tolerant club off the M40 and was a member of a West End club notorious for its pole dancers and high prices. Jenni had been working as a catering assistant in a junior school in Islington when Liston picked her up. She'd never met anyone like him before. Nor had Tony, except once, when he'd been to buy some skunk and found his normal source off sick, and a man a bit like Liston—tall, imposing, in a black cashmere coat with a striped Italian scarf double-hooped at his throat—had done the deal instead.

As well as two cars and a house near Alexandra Palace, Liston had charm. Reluctantly at first, Tony had gone along for parties and Liston had treated him like a brother. He did near perfect imitations of people on television and had a fund of almost believable stories about them; he had a room with a private cinema and a bar at which you helped yourself to any drink you could imagine, as well as little pre-rolled joints in a glass jar. When everyone was high, Liston switched on the powerful karaoke machine and urged them to perform. He'd break the ice himself with a virile Marvin Gaye.

It had been shocking when he dropped Jenni. Afterward, she seemed to lose all interest in men. Her twenties passed. She was good to her mother and she was never out of work, though some of the jobs she did were things Tony wouldn't personally have considered. Then at the age of twenty-nine she had surprised them all by training as a driver; it was almost as though she was trying to hide from something, Tony thought, burying herself beneath the ground.

Jenni walked back from the station when her shift was finished and let herself into the flat. There was no sign of Tony. She made pasta shells with tomato sauce and opened a carton of orange juice; she ate quickly, eager to get on to the computer.

Sunday evenings were always busy in Parallax. People had been out clubbing on Saturday, got up late, spent the afternoon recovering and were now ready for a bit of fun before the week began again.

In the hallway there was a good-size flat-screen computer that

Jenni had bought from her savings. A colleague in the operations room at the depot had shown her how to cleanse the hard drive of Tony's weighty downloads, which caused the system to run slow. Jenni inspected the contents and removed, without opening, an energy-sapping item called "White Girls, Black Studs" and two games in which overmuscled men went through postnuclear cityscapes in battered army vehicles, carrying rocket launchers and gaining points for annihilating goons and half-naked women.

She had left Miranda Star in a far nicer place: on the banks of the Orinoco, where she had built a house. In order to pay for this, Miranda had borrowed 200,000 vajos from a mortgage lender called Points West and had engaged to repay it at a rate of five percent interest over ten years. With Miranda's new job as a beauty therapist, this was just about feasible. Vajos were on a fixed exchange rate with sterling in the real world, and Jenni had, cautiously at first, given her credit card details online to the Parallax Foreign Exchange, which was based on the island of Oneiros.

The economy of Parallax derived from that of the real world, but with a lesser sense of responsibility. The inventiveness of the traders was such that few people understood the securities they bartered, but the gains to be made were stupendous, while the losses, after a certain level, became either too complicated to compute or too subdivided by onward sale to pin on one person. If they were truly serious, they were absorbed by the Central Bank, and the resulting blip in the overall Parallax economy could be ironed out by raising game subscriptions, taxes and shop prices for the less sophisticated. The financiers' gains were theirs to keep, but their losses were democratically shared.

Most of the gamers, though, Jenni noticed, still preferred sex. She checked on the progress of Miranda's house and found that the builders had completed it overnight, a week ahead of schedule. The tiles in the swimming pool were slightly bluer than she'd imagined and there were rather more caged parakeets in the marble entrance hall than she remembered ordering, but otherwise it was perfect. Miranda's bedroom overlooked the river, and in the shining white bathroom were pink curtains with embroidered daisies on the hems. A breeze blew through the French doors that opened onto the balcony.

Round the new house was a thin tape, a bit like those used at a crime scene in reality, which said "NO ENTRY" at intervals. Some people left their houses open, unattended, but Jenni didn't want just anyone snooping round Miranda's bedroom.

When she'd finished her tour of inspection, she left the gated community on which the house had been built and went for a walk through some ruins on the edge of the encroaching and still gorgeously untouched rainforest.

She had not gone far before she encountered a man. He had cargo pants to the knee, bare torso and multiple piercings. His skin was light brown, though most of it was covered in tattoos; he carried a Uranium credit card (the highest rating) and a submachine gun in his right hand.

Jenni sighed. This was not the kind of man she would have chosen, but she had learned that it was pretty much standard dress for men in Parallax. Most of the maquettes were scary and you just had to remind yourself that they might in reality be women or children—you absolutely could not rely on appearances; you had to disbelieve your eyes.

She knew the man had seen her because she found herself being messaged.

"What your name?"

"Miranda Star."

An answering legend appeared automatically (you couldn't message and withhold your own identity) above his maquette's head: "Jason Dogg. Age 35. Pisces. Adventurer/Prospector."

"What you doing?"

"Looking at my new house."

"That your's? Then we are neighbors!"

Jenni noticed his English spelling. Most of the gamers were American.

"Great," she wrote, feeling a twinge of exhilaration.

"Can I visit your house?"

"Not til I know u better."

"Lets go clubbing tmw. I know a good place."

"Is it expensive? Only 15 vajos left," typed Jenni.

"Not if you do'nt drink. How long you in Parallax?"

"Two years."

"You'r so cool."

"Why u have machine gun?"

"Tell you when we know eachother more. Clubbing tmw?"

"Maybe. Must crash now. Am tired," Jenni wrote. "In TL, do you live in England?"

"Yes. London. Wot time u come on?"

"Working late tmw. Maybe Tuesday night?"

"See ya then."

Jenni felt excited at the thought that someone was going to take Miranda clubbing. She'd have to get some new clothes tomorrow—a dress at least—and she wondered what the stores were like in Caracas. In what the gamers called "TL" or True Life, she was on the second shift on the Circle Line, so she'd have time.

John Veals's wife Vanessa at that instant poured herself a large gin and lime. She was dreading her husband's return because he had said he'd take her out to dinner. Although half American herself, Vanessa retained an English deference toward waiters and restaurants, with their snooty manner and demi-French menus. She always asked politely for something listed and was quick to accept that her request had been unreasonable if told that it was no longer available.

John and his colleagues, with whom she was occasionally obliged to dine, didn't even look at the menu. They'd summon the waiter and tell him what they wanted.

"Right, we'll start with a plate of ribs in the middle of the table here. Then I want carpaccio of beef with a thin mustard sauce. What? No, I'm not interested in that. I want it very thin, with Dijon mustard in the sauce and a few green leaves, maybe rocket.

31

Then I want roast chicken. No, I don't want coq au vin. I want plain roast chicken, lots of salt on the skin, roast potatoes, not small ones, proper size and cauliflower cheese. That's it. OK? And some gravy. No, not fucking *jus.* Gravy. And my friend will have a cheeseburger."

"Sir, we do not have—"

"Yes, you do. You have filet mignon. Mince it up. Get a bun. You have a cheeseboard here. Look. It says here, £5 supplement! Get a slice off it. You can do it. It's what you do."

It was worse when the heads of American banks were with him. Even when one of them had been persuaded to try something that was actually on the menu he would change his mind after it had been delivered and send it away again. "Just bring me some clams." "Sorry, sir, we have no—" "Here's £50. Go and buy some."

John Veals hated holidays, but once, in the burning summer of 2003, Vanessa had told him that if he didn't come with her to an Italian villa for a fortnight she would leave him. It was an immense palazzo, the last cool building in the European heatwave, with a mosaic-tiled swimming pool, a small olive grove, eight bedrooms, silent icy air conditioning, a live-in couple and a view of poplared hills that might have brought a spasm of joy to Giorgione. Veals left three days early for an unmissable appointment in New York and discovered on his arrival at his Manhattan hotel that Vanessa had bought the villa for £2.5 million.

"How did you manage that?" he asked by phone from his room.

"I contacted the agent and they put me in touch with the owner. And I asked him how much he wanted for it."

"You did what?"

"You know you gave me access to the Bermuda accounts. You remember, last year when—"

"Yeah, yeah, it's not that. It's how you did it. Did you say you asked him how much he wanted?"

"Yes, I asked him how much he—"

"That's no fucking way to trade."

"Do you think it's too much, John?"

32

"I've no idea. It's just the principle of the thing. Asking him what he wants! For Christ's sake, Vanessa."

As the clock showed six, John Veals went to the bookcase in the corner of his office, removed a few volumes and opened a small safe behind them. He took out a brown envelope that contained three sheets of photocopied A4 paper. He sat down, tilted the back of his chair and put his feet up on the desk again while he examined the papers. It was not the first time he'd read them.

For more than two years, he had been watching Allied Royal Bank. It was a fine institution in many ways. Its roots were in the empire and its branches were in the high street. It looked after more institutional pensions than any other bank and it was laughingly said that the future happiness of one in three Britons over sixty-five years old depended on it. People joked that the four-legged runner of its logo, intended by a management consultant to represent "diverse synergy," looked like a walking frame. It was associated in the public mind with low-risk, traditional banking; one of its small branches had been in Edgware, and it was here that the eighteen-year-old John Veals had opened his own first bank account with £25 he'd earned in his uncle's betting shop. He had been with ARB in various ways ever since, and High Level used the Victoria branch for some of its day-to-day needs.

Allied Royal, however, wasn't altogether happy with the idea of itself as the old person's friend, the knitted cardigan of the banking world. It had therefore developed an aggressive investment banking arm which had generated most of its profits over the last two decades. Largely through its business in derivatives (many relating to commodities it had traded for real in empire days) the management had been able to deliver an average of twenty percent a year to the shareholders.

Veals had sensed, however, from the way the share price moved from day to day, that all might not be what it seemed at Allied Royal. He noted that when bank stocks fell, Allied Royal fell a fraction more than its competitors; when the other big banks returned to where they'd been, Allied Royal never quite clawed back all it had lost. These were only fractions, barely visible to the unfocused eye. Daily calls to the trading desks of large investment banks told Veals that to buy credit protection on ARB would cost a little more than those on any of its big British rivals. These insurance policies against a bank failing to meet its debt obligations were always cheap, because the chance of default was so slight; but to insure against an Allied Royal debt failure over the standard five-year period of the insurance, or "credit default swap," was just a whisper more expensive than it was for any comparable bank. This was what piqued Veals's interest. And then ARB's balance sheet publicly revealed how much money it had taken from the wholesale markets (or borrowed, in other words, from other banks): too much, in Veals's view.

In March 2006, Allied Royal surprised the world by buying a large Spanish bank. Veals's analysts looked hard at the deal and concluded that it was "testosterone-driven." The figures did add up, but everything was stretched. ARB had raised large quantities of debt secured both on the anticipated future cash flows and on the expectation that there would be cost savings in merging the two banks into one big new structure. Veals knew people always underestimated how much it cost in mainland Europe to achieve such savings and was surprised that ARB had managed to prevent the analysts from pointing this out. By now, however, he was definitely interested.

In April 2006, he fired his head of Compliance, a Scot called William Murray. In theory, such a person was meant to ensure that every deal made by the fund "complied" strictly with the rules laid down by the regulators. The word, however, lent itself to jokes; Steve Godley suggested that Murray had been fired for not being "compliant" enough. In the push-pull of dealings with Veals, Murray had pulled too hard: he seemed to have forgotten that it was Veals and not the FSA who paid his salary. The purpose of a compliance officer, in Veals's view, was to facilitate and to warn, in that order. If necessary, the third duty was to look the other way.

"I suggest you apply for a job with Shields DeWitt," Veals told Murray as he cut up his credit cards. This was an investment house of legendary rectitude, known to Veals as the Vatican. Its directors were often seen at Covent Garden, in black tie, or at dinners for charities to which they were willing and hefty donors.

Murray had been in place for only four years. For the first three years of High Level's life, the compliance officer had been . . . Well, there was only one person who knew the company intimately enough and who had done the daylong course required by the FSA; throughout its first prodigious growth spurt, the compliance officer of High Level Capital had been its founder and chief executive, John Veals.

In Murray's place, Veals offered the job—naturally enough— to someone from Allied Royal, a ductile young man called Simon Wetherby. Veals promised to double his salary and bonus package, provided he could stay in "lock step" with High Level's strategic ambition and not forget who paid him. Wetherby was amazed and delighted by the approach and joined High Level as soon as he could clear his ARB desk. The two men spoke every morning, and in the course of six months of doing little more than shooting the breeze, Veals had debriefed Wetherby on all he knew about ARB. It was natural that they'd want to talk about the most remarkable event of recent months, the purchase of the Spanish bank; rude not to, as Wetherby happily agreed.

Veals took no written notes during these conversations and never let it show if anything that was said was of particular interest to him. Veals was known to be a man obsessed by detail—one or two people had warned Wetherby that he might be driven mad by this—and Wetherby knew that the size of his first annual bonus would shortly be calculated. He told Veals all he knew about the debt covenants relating to the acquisition of the Spanish bank.

John Veals merely nodded; but somewhere in the thicket of Wetherby's detail, he had caught a glimmer of movement, as a sight-hound sees the twitch of a rabbit's ear across a field of grass. Pushed to the last fragment of his recollection by Veals's insistent

"And was there anything unusual?," Wetherby recalled a debt-covenant clause inserted late in the negotiation by a lawyer anxious to protect the group of other banks who had lent Allied Royal much of the cash necessary to make the purchase. The covenant stated that if, following the successful acquisition, the market capitalization of the enlarged Allied Royal should at any point fall below a certain level (a level viewed as impossible in normal financial weather) the creditors would have the right to call in their loans in full. Such a call would be impossible for ARB to meet without issuing yet more shares.

"Surely the middle office checked all this?" said Veals. "I mean the regulators are hot on all this, aren't they? You know, tier-one capital ratios and all that crap."

"Yes," said Wetherby. "But it was late. It was in a side letter, I believe. I didn't see it myself, it wasn't my job, but I was told about it by a friend in the leverage finance team. The FSA may never have seen the letter. And of course there was so much momentum for the deal at this point that—"

"Yeah, yeah, they'd all got wood by then."

"Exactly."

For some weeks, Veals had reflected on this information, and how to make it work to his advantage. If the market cap or share value (Wetherby was not exactly sure about the triggers) of ARB did fall below the agreed level, those who had lent the money—large investment banks and insurance companies—would not be legally obliged to call in their debts (indeed, they'd be better advised not to); but the mere emergence of the news would cause a panic—and a run on the bank's deposits.

Veals discussed his idea briefly with Stephen Godley.

"Christ, John," said Godley. "Talk about working the blind side. All those pensioners. You'll be attacked by an army of Zimmer frames. Savaged by—"

"By a toothless fucking army," said Veals.

The precedent of a failing bank was less than three months old.

In September, only three months ago, the British government had nationalized an overextended mortgage lender in northeast England as it was on the verge of going broke. The Prime Minister, like all politicians in Veals's experience, was childishly awed by cash—by the size of the contribution made to the economy by financial services. Though by instinct a state socialist, hot for high tax and interference, he was also a career politician, and he knew that his own life depended on the economy's continuing to grow. He had to protect the City's special interests and yield to the demands of its senior executives; he had no choice.

Veals believed the government would be loath to interfere with Allied Royal if it began to ail seriously, or plunge; it would show the PM to be a nanny and a fusspot who didn't trust the market. His party had spent many years out of office trying to convince the voter that it loved the market more even than its rival did; he couldn't afford to act like a socialist at this late stage. On the other hand, he would eventually calculate that he needed the combined votes of ARB depositors, creditors and pensioners to keep himself in power. He couldn't let it die; he would have to take it over.

High Level's reputation would suffer when it emerged that they had made a killing from the demise of a bank; the plight of the pensioners in particular would keep the story in the newspapers for weeks. However, Veals had ridden storms before, notably one about the repayment of an African debt; he could tough it out again, and he believed that in his own world his reputation for skill and ruthlessness would be enhanced. If he took care to ensure that the majority of the trading was conducted in nonregulated instruments, outside the jurisdiction of the Financial Services Authority, there wasn't much they could do to stop him. In any case, FSA fines were tiny.

First, though, before any of this could begin, Veals needed to know for certain that the debt covenant existed. He was preparing to put on the largest position of his life and wasn't going to do it on the anecdotal evidence of a wimp like Simon Wetherby. He needed to see the document itself, and for this purpose he had in the first week of June telephoned Vic Small at Greenview Alternative Investment Services.

They met at the Moti Mahal in Waterloo, and, over roghan josh and fizzy lager, Veals gave Vic Small an envelope full of cash. Two weeks later, a woman called Vera Tillman began to work as a cleaner at Allied Royal in Canary Wharf. She came with respectable references and a willing attitude; she was also receiving fat envelopes of cash from Vic Small to find and copy the relevant document.

She had been there almost six months. "Can't she work a photocopier?" Veals asked Small. "She must have worn out the fucking carpet with all that vacuuming."

"It's complicated," Small replied. "It's a very proper company. It has ID cards and iris recognition. All the bells and bloody whistles."

Then, on Friday, December 14, Veals had had an early Christmas present. Reception told him there was a gentleman outside who wouldn't leave until he'd personally handed over an envelope to him. A business card was sent through; it bore the Greenview crest. Warily, Veals went out to reception and took the envelope. The "gentleman" was not the usual motorcyclist whose offerings went through the post room, but an African in a blue suit with a knitted tie. There was no return address on the envelope and no signature was required for it. Back in his private office, Veals slid out the papers. There were only three sheets of A4, but they contained a well-drafted debt covenant, signed, executed and witnessed, relating to the Allied Royal takeover of the Spanish bank. He checked and rechecked to make sure it was fully executed, not just a draft. It was all right. Simon Wetherby's recollection appeared to be correct in every respect.

Veals checked his watch. Seven o'clock: home time. Contrarian in almost, though not quite, everything, he took the Underground from St. James's Park. Most hedge-fund managers were driven home from their Mayfair offices in German saloons. Some thought this added to their mystique, to be anonymous, disdaining City ostentation and overpriced champagne; one or two cultivated an academic look—tweed jackets, trainers—stressing the intellectual aspect of their mathematical day. There was also a practical reason for such men, each personally possessing hundreds of millions of pounds, to have a secure car and driver, and that was to avoid the possibility of kidnap.

John Veals did the opposite. For a start, he worked in Victoria. The herd was always wrong, he thought (except when it was right, and then he had an early position in the forefront of stampeding hooves). St. James's Park was a clean station and the travelers were kept well informed about the service as they waited on the hosed and swept platforms. It was the headquarters of Transport for London and no broken light bulb remained unchanged for more than six minutes.

On the train, Veals sat with a briefcase on his lap and watched the Sunday tourists with their wheeled luggage and their rucksacks. They chattered as they pored over guidebooks, glanced up at the Tube map overhead, trying to reconcile the two. What false picture of a city did these people have? Veals wondered. Their London was a virtual one, unknown to residents—Tower and Dungeon, veteran West End musicals and group photographs beneath the slowly turning Eye; but Veals believed it was important for him to be aware of other people, natives and visitors alike, however partial and bizarre their take on life. Since his own reality derived from numbers on a computer terminal, he thought it wise to keep an eye on flesh and blood; there might still be something he could profitably learn from them.

As John Veals made his way back home from Holland Park Tube station, a bicycle with no lights on shot past him along the pavement, making him leap to one side.

He swore briefly, then let himself into a white-pilastered house. It was in a quiet street, far enough away from the noise of Holland Park Avenue or the rowdy communal gardens of Notting Hill, where it always seemed to be firework night. For five years when his two children were still small, Veals and his wife Vanessa had endured the life of such a garden, where American investment bankers celebrated July 4, Halloween, Thanksgiving, Christmas, New Year's (always with that irritating possessive), Spring Break, Easter, innumerable bank holidays and—biggest explosion of all—Bonus Day, a movable feast of the patron saint of Mammon, usually sometime in January. Veals's breaking point had come when a series of Baghdad-intensity explosions woke his children from their sleep at midnight.

He went round and rang the bell next door. "What the hell's going on?"

"It's Bastille Day," said his American neighbor, perplexed. "Come in and have a glass of champagne."

"Ever been to Paris, Johnny?" said Veals, with grim restraint.

"Only for a meeting, once," said the American with the matches.

"You're like that cartoon in the sixties," said Veals. "Two astronauts approaching the moon. One's saying, 'Have I been to Paris? God, no. This is the first time I've left the USA.' Now put your fucking toys back in the box."

Soon afterward, the family moved to a dark but quieter street and installed the Filipina nanny in a small room, once the coalhole, with a glass roof, to the right of the steps as you went up to the front door with its brushed nickel fittings and "historic" paint color. It was peaceful here, and when Veals got to the half-landing, to a study that overlooked the small but mercifully private garden, he fired up the Internet to check the market news. Nothing disastrous. Vanessa had left a postcard from Sophie Topping on his desk: a "pour mémoire," Sophie called it, about her dinner on Saturday. Veals grimaced.

At that moment he heard his daughter's heavy footsteps going downstairs. He went out onto the landing in time to see Bella walking down the hall toward the front door with a small pink rucksack on her back.

"Where are you going?"

"I'm having a sleepover at Zoë's," she called up.

"Didn't you go there last night?"

"No, Dad. I told you. That was Chloë's."

"Have you—"

The door banged and Bella had escaped.

Veals went to find his wife, who was in the bath. "Where's Finn?" he asked from the doorway.

Finbar, their sixteen-year-old son, was up in his top-floor room watching a large flat-screen television and rolling a joint. He had bought £20 worth of skunk on Friday from a boy in Pizza Palace during a break from school, where he was in his GCSE year. Spread out on an atlas, he had three papers and the tobacco from a cigarette. The book was heavy on his knees and he envied his parents' generation, for whom LP sleeves must have provided an ideal surface. Most of his own music was digitized, and CD covers were anyway too small for the task—not that they were much good at the day job either, as the cheap hinges usually snapped within the week, leaving him with naked, scratch-prone discs of *Wind in the Trees* by Stefan Everson or *Forecasts of the Past* by New Firefighters. But rolling up on top of a picture of Neil Young's patchwork jeans or the Beatles' psychedelic uniforms ... That must have been something, he thought.

Finbar sat back against the end of the bed and fired up the joint. The flame from the disposable lighter showed up his smooth face with its half-dozen spots on the chin, a child's long-lashed eyes and a mess of brown curls. His bedroom was a twenty-by-twenty-foot den, lit by dimmed and recessed ceiling lights, with a tight-weave gray carpet and an en suite wet room with imported American fittings and a shower as forceful as a Yosemite cascade. Framed posters of Wireless Boys and Evelina Belle bisected the wall spaces. Through the windows Finn could see the raised stone parapet that ran along the back of the house. He flipped open his phone and hit the pizza number for a delivery. He wasn't hungry yet, but in forty minutes' time, post skunk, he would be.

Channel 7 was about to start his favorite program, *It's Madness*. Finn settled down to his solitary entertainment, easing back the ring-pull on a can of lager. He didn't really like beer, but he was trying hard to acquire the taste, since smoking made him thirsty first, before it made him hungry. He didn't really like smoking either, if he was honest, but he loved the effect of skunk: the sand-filled sock to the back of the head, the drying mouth, the sense of muscles in heavy motion, of a nervous quickening that couldn't be translated into action because everything was slowed down—as though time had ceased to operate, leaving him luxuriously alone to savor the last sound wave of the ringing cymbal or aching voice of Shoals, or Weir of Dunkeith—or, as now, the modern comedy of Channel 7.

The first patient on *It's Madness* was suffering from "bipolar disorder."

"Sounds like something you get in the Arctic," said Lisa, one of the celebrity judges. "Is it anything like frostbite?"

The audience began a long helpless chuckle as the patient—a red-faced, bedraggled woman in her twenties—explained her symptoms. "Sometimes it's like me 'ead's on fire, there's so much to say and do, like not enough time in the world to say all I've got on me mind and I can't sleep, I'll go like ten weeks without sleeping properly and I'll walk the streets at night at four or five in the morning, talking away to meself cos—"

"Because no one else is up at that hour, I imagine," interrupted Barry Levine, another of the celebrity judges, amid more laughter.

Finbar sucked on the joint and held the smoke in his lungs. Barry Levine was one of those all-purpose TV stars who cropped up on too many programs for his liking; they'd roped him into *It's Madness* when some writer woman turned out to be too long-winded; she hadn't really got the joke—the whole point of the program—which was that it was a comedy.

Lisa, who'd been lead singer with a successful but short-lived band called Girls From Behind, was better. She played the dumb-blonde part and was quick to get the wrong end of the stick—so quick, in fact, that Finn suspected it was thrust into her hand before the show began. Television was all a con—everyone knew that—but *It's Madness* worked because, in the words of the program makers, it was "there to make people think differently, to challenge their preconceptions."

The bipolar woman, who'd now been given the nickname Captain Scott, was explaining how at other times she was caught in a downswing that could last for months. "Then it's like I'm in a world which is only black and white before color had been invented and I'm like so tired I can't move, I just want to stay in bed for days and days."

"Yes, Scotty, we've all had days like that," said Terry O'Malley, the boss of the panel. "It's called a hangover." He waited for the laughter to subside before saying, "All right, everybody. It's time for . . ."

He stood up and opened his arms to the audience, who shouted back as one: "The Men in White Coats!!!"

Finbar didn't like this part of the program. Two psychiatrists (though he doubted they were really qualified) gave an assessment of what treatment the patient needed, how much it would cost and whether she should be admitted to a hospital. While the debate roared, there came a buzzing, relayed from the front door. Finbar went unsteadily to the stairhead to go down and let the pizza man in.

He had heard his parents come and go half an hour before, but didn't bother to leave his room. Talking to them was an ordeal. His father never knew what to say and seemed anxious that he might betray some ignorance of Finn's life; neither had quite recovered from the moment the year before when John Veals inadvertently revealed that he thought Finn had already taken his GCSEs. Finn presumed his parents had gone out to their usual Sunday evening dinner at the Simla Rest House, a maniacally overpriced Indian place in Mayfair.

Back in his room, he opened the pizza with extra sugar-dusted dough sticks, Italian dressing and a liter and a half of Coke. The smell of white dough and tomato paste made him salivate as he tore the first slice from the half-yard-wide disc. He'd gone for the margherita, because although he pretended when in company to prefer the American Hot with extra chili, he really still preferred the simple cheese and tomato he'd first encountered as a toddler. He wondered in his ravening, post-skunk hunger whether even a family-size pizza would be enough.

Chewing avidly, he let his gaze drift to the screen. He fast-forwarded a bit, then hit the resume button and sat back. A new contestant had come on. He was a schizophrenic of about fifty, called Alan, who had spent twenty years in psychiatric hospitals but had been released into a "care in the community" scheme when his asylum, one of the original Victorian ones, had been closed by the government, bought by a property developer and turned into "luxury apartments with state-of-the-art gym and sauna facilities." The prospectus described the place as having won "two architectural design competitions," Alan said, without mentioning that the first had been for a county lunatic asylum in 1858.

For the last fifteen years, Alan had been without a permanent home. He said he hadn't liked the hospital, it was loud and dirty, but at least he'd felt safe there.

"So," said Terry O'Malley, "as far as your accommodation's concerned, it seems you're in two minds about it."

The audience laughed. "Schizophrenia . . . in two minds . . ." O'Malley underlined his joke for the slower ones.

"That's not what schizophrenia means," said Alan. "That's a misunderstanding. It's nothing to do with a 'split personality' or—"

"Sorry," said Barry Levine. "Which one of you said that?"

Finn drank some of the Coke. The huge bottle was unwieldy and some of it washed back over his chin and down his T-shirt.

Beneath the knockabout surface, the program got to grips with important issues. Its premium-rate phone lines allowed the public to interact democratically, their opinions counting every bit as much as those of the "self-proclaimed experts." The climax of a series came when the contestants were dispatched to spend a weekend together in a remote but well-appointed one-story house (the so-called Barking Bungalow) whose exact location was kept secret. Hidden cameras followed them, watching them sleep and eat and clothe themselves, scrutinizing their attempts to communicate with one another.

Alan, the schizophrenic, was losing his way as he tried to explain to Lisa how the voices in his head both mocked and instructed him.

"It's like being nagged, all the time, by four or five people," he said.

"Can't you just ignore them?" said Lisa.

"No, the voices are too loud."

"Blimey, love, you should try being in a girl band. It was like that all the time with Girls From Behind. Lee and Pamilla were the worst. Nag, nag, nag!"

Finn relit the last inch of his spliff, not wanting to waste it. The pizza had done the business in the end, leaving him happily bloated. He left *It's Madness* on in the background while he listened to some music he had downloaded onto his compact, gunmetal gray player. "A First Step in Dying" by Shanghai Radio Gang came through the earpieces and fizzed across his cortex.

Fetching his laptop from the window seat, Finn went to the Dream Team website to see how his virtual eleven were doing. He had read good reports online of a new Polish striker, Tadeusz "Spike" Borowski, who had just joined one of the big London clubs, and wanted to register him before his price became prohibitive.

One of his strikers had suffered a knee injury in the first match of the season, and although he was back in action he seemed to have lost his edge. This guy Borowski looked quick and lethal—like Carlton King with a first touch, the buyers' guide said, or Gary Fowler with an IQ.

Finn dragged the names of players from his subs' bench onto the numbered icon on the pitch. It was time for a major rethink, a shake-up before the January window. The best players in his shadow team came from clubs that in reality he detested. When he watched Arsenal or Liverpool, he naturally wanted them to be whipped by the Turks or the Spanish in Europe; yet without the steady income of virtual points from their star players, his fantasy eleven would have dropped to Division Two of the Dream Team league.

Finn closed his eyes for a moment as Shanghai Radio Gang sang the dreamy, robotic start to "People of the New Frontier" before the Alternative smash-and-grab began. The skunk had sharpened his deep appreciation of the sound. The synapses in his brain were charged with electronic joy and solitude. He fell asleep, leaning back against the bed, his face adopting the seraphic look his mother had so loved when he was two or three years old, watched over in his cot by toy bears and monkeys.

In the background, now unseen by him, the first night at the Barking Bungalow was being played out on the plasma screen.

Somebody was crying.

Two

Monday, December 17

I

At about nine o'clock, after the morning rush had subsided, Hassan al-Rashid took the Piccadilly Line to Manor House. He had received an address on a piece of paper sent from Salim, the head of his group, Muslim Youth Coalition, which was based in Bethnal Green. Salim believed the post was a safer way of contacting the members of the cell than e-mail. "You might just as well write a letter to the local newspaper," he told them. "The spooks intercept all that stuff. Also, they can get your computer IP number from the websites you visit and they can track down your phone line and then your address, so if any of you have visited jihadist sites you'd better ditch your hard drive right now. If that means getting a new computer that stays completely clean, so be it. I have funds. I'll show you how to get rid of the old one."

Following Salim's instructions, Hassan first downloaded some software called Drive+Nuke and selected "Total" from the "Level of Erasure" menu. He then took a hammer to the casing of his computer and extracted the hard disk. Rather to his surprise, it really was a disc, like a shiny CD and about the same size. In his father's shed he mixed fine-powdered iron oxide and aluminum, both of which he had taken from the lab at college, poured them through a funnel into an empty drinks can, then stuck a magnesium strip in the top. He took this, along with the hard drive, up onto the common at night, put the can on the disk, lit the magnesium strip and retreated. The drive was eliminated, as was the earth to a depth of more than a foot below it. Thermite, Salim told

47

them, could reach a temperature of 4,000 degrees Fahrenheit. Hassan kicked some loose earth over the hole in the ground and made for home. Salim certainly didn't like to take chances.

His new machine, unfouled by Internet and e-mail history, remained in its box for a week. He couldn't find any legitimate use for it. Eventually he thought he'd better download some songs, go on YourPlace or do a few of the things young people were supposed to do, so that if the police did come calling it would look normal. YourPlace was one of the most boring things he had ever seen. Pictures of millions of grinning *kafirs* whose lives were so empty it was fun for them to know that someone had "jabbed" their photograph. Dear oh dear. It was almost a relief to know that the main practical use of the site was for sex; at least it had *some* function— for pedophiles to cruise, for teenage boys to rope in likely-looking girls for sex parties or for older *kafirs* to find "fuck buddies." Hassan visited the site daily, but left the room while his Internet record clocked up some plausible hours in this parody of a human world.

Today, he was going to meet for the first time the people with whom he was to wage jihad. The most famous group at this level of activity, boasting that it had precipitated coups in African states as well as fighting in Bosnia and Kuwait, was Hizb ut-Tahrir; but the alliance to which Hassan now belonged claimed to talk less than Hizb and to bomb more. It was called Husam Nar (which translated roughly, he knew from Arabic studies, as Burning Sword), though it rarely referred to itself by this or any other name; it was an organization with no headquarters and no records. What it did have was money, and this, Salim told Hassan, came mostly from Saudi Arabia. This news was comforting to Hassan; to know that the money came from the country of Mecca and Medina reassured him in his new identity. Hassan's gradual progress from local mosque through youth organizations of gradually increasing extremism had been typical enough. The distinctive factor had been the single mentor, Salim. Most young men left behind their early guides in the course of their ascent, but Salim had been with Hassan from the beginning, like a wise uncle.

48

Having looked up the street name in the *A to Z*, Hassan memorized the route from the Tube station and ten minutes later found himself turning into a street with rusty Japanese cars along the curb and a busy outdoor life—children, men and women of all ages talking in their front gardens, despite the cold, or smoking on the pavement. The house he was directed to looked as shabby as the rest, with one windowpane boarded up and thick gray net curtains on the ground floor. There were three bells by the front door, each with its own wire drilled through the jamb. Hassan pressed "Ashaf," as instructed, and heard heavy footsteps on the uncarpeted hall. It was Salim.

"Come in, brother. You're the last to arrive."

The others were gathered in the back room on the first floor. First, they knelt on the bare floorboards and prayed, facing Walthamstow.

One of them, Hassan noticed, seemed ill at ease. Although he bent low, he didn't seem to know the words of the prayers.

"All right, brothers," said Salim. "This house is ours for as long as we need it. We will all leave at different times, just as we arrived at twenty-minute intervals today. Don't speak to anyone in the street as you walk away, but don't be unfriendly. If someone asks you for a light or says hello, just smile vaguely. Do nothing anyone might remember. Now, I want you to introduce yourselves to one another and pick a *kafir* name that will be yours from now on. When you pick a name, it must be something easy to remember, something that's connected with where you come from. For instance, I'm from the East End so I'll call myself Alfie. It's an old cockney name."

He nodded at a boy of about Hassan's age with the remains of acne showing through his sparse beard. He cleared his throat, but his voice caught nervously. "My name is Akbar," he said. "As you can probably tell, I'm from Yorkshire."

"Aye. 'appen." This was said, in imitation of the Yorkshire accent, by the man who seemed not to know how to say his prayers properly; he was tall, about twenty-five, with a yellowish skin color and a gold tooth. "'appen we'll call thee Seth, lad," he said.

Salim looked at the youth. "Is that all right? Seth?"

The boy nodded, though he didn't look happy about it.

"Where are you from?" Hassan asked the man with the gold tooth.

"My name is Ravi. I'm from Leicester." He looked at them challengingly.

"That doesn't sound like a Muslim name," said Hassan.

"I was born a Hindu. I converted," said Ravi. "Do you have a problem with that?"

Hassan shook his head. It did seem odd to him that someone not born Muslim should be engaged on jihad, but he couldn't explain why. "No," he said. "No problem."

"I don't suppose you can think of anyone famous from Leicester, can you?" said Ravi.

"Gary," said Hassan.

"Who's Gary then?"

"A footballer," said Hassan. "Their most famous ever player."

"Gary's good," said Salim. "Now you." He nodded at Hassan.

"My name is Hassan," he said. "And I'm from——"

"Och aye," said Gary, né Ravi. "I think we all know where ye're frae, MacTavish."

"There's a name that I was called once and it really angered me," said Hassan. "Someone called me 'Jock.' If I'm going to die, I'd like to take that name down with me."

Salim nodded. "All right. We'll call you Jock."

The last of the five said, "My name's Hanif and I'm from Watford." He was bald and thickset, unlike the others, all of whom looked hungry. "I bet you can't name a footballer from Watford."

"Bet I could," said Hassan, "but why don't we call you Elton?"

"Elton?"

"Elton. He's the chairman. Or he was."

"It's good," said Salim.

"You seem to know a lot," said Elton.

"He's the brains," said Salim. "He's our college boy."

Gary the Gold Tooth Hindu, thought Hassan. Seth the Shy

One. And Bald Elton. It was easy enough. What would be harder was to remember to call Salim "Alfie" from now on.

Hassan had a sudden and terrible desire to laugh—at the thought of roly-poly Elton John with his diamanté glasses and his boyfriend and his platform heels having unwittingly given his name to a solemn would-be terrorist . . . Salim had occasionally had cause to rebuke him for his descent into laughter: it showed spiritual immaturity, he said. Hassan did believe in purity and truth with all his might; but he had been brought up in a godless country where television and newspapers mocked the social structures night and day . . .

"And we'll call this place 'the pub,'" Salim was saying. "So if you hear someone say, 'I'm meeting Alfie down the pub' it couldn't sound more normal, more everyday *kafir*."

"When do we get our instructions then?" asked Seth.

Salim coughed and walked round the unfurnished room. "In a couple of days. For security reasons, it's best if you don't know in advance."

"Why?" said Gary. "It's not as if we're going to—"

"For heaven's sake, didn't you learn anything in Pakistan?" Hassan hadn't seen Salim impose himself like this before. "It's rudimentary. All knowledge is potentially a leak. You are told only what you need to know and not one thing more. The only reason you're meeting together today is that you'll need to recognize one another. I also think it's a good idea to form a bond. But this is as far as it goes. I don't even know the real name of my superior. I meet him in different places—cafés, parks, even in a pub one time. I just know him as Steve."

"And what are we going to do on the day?" said Elton.

"We are going to wage jihad. Each of you has a task. Jock is doing the shopping. Seth and Elton will assemble the ingredients. Gary will help me plan the route and the timing. We'll all plant the bombs. Today is Monday. We need Jock to have brought everything here by Thursday morning so that Seth and Elton can put it all together."

"Do we know where we're going?" said Gary.

"Yes. I've already been there and had a good look. But I won't be telling you until we meet on Friday."

"What time on Friday?" said Hassan.

"I'll let you know the day before. Why?"

"It's just . . ." Hassan stopped. "It's difficult to explain. My father is . . . is . . ." He felt his throat constrict. He was frightened of Salim's anger.

"What is it?" said Salim.

"My father is going to Buckingham Palace to get the OBE," said Hassan. "And my mother and I have to go with him."

There was silence in the little upstairs room. Hassan sensed that the others were not sure whether they should laugh or be indignant. They looked to Salim for a lead.

He spoke very quietly. "The work of the Prophet will take place at its appointed time. And you will be there. I shall give you the exact timings on Thursday, not a moment before."

Hassan nodded. He quickly considered the various excuses he could offer to his parents. "Sickness" wouldn't work: his father would compel him to come, however ill he claimed to be. He would simply have to go out the night before to Pudding Mill Lane and not return. He would later have to claim a loss of memory, an accident with a car or something. His parents would be so pleased that he was safe that they'd forget their disappointment at his absence from the palace.

"How will you be in touch? Still post?" said Elton.

"Have you heard of steganography?" said Salim.

Elton shook his head.

"It's a way of embedding text in a computer file so that it can't be seen unless you have the right kit for decoding it. I'm going to give you an Internet link and I need you to check it daily. As you know I've preferred the post till now, but it could be that in the last forty-eight hours things will move too fast for the Royal Mail. So we need a fallback. There's a *kafir* porn site called babesdelight.co.uk. It's not hard filth like most of them. It's just naked girls, that's all, the kind of thing they sell in their most famous high-street family stationer. You get a choice of lots of pictures—sets of pictures in fact. There's a box called 'Search for your girl' and in that you type 'Olya.' She's some Russian hooker. Anyway, the main picture of her, the big money shot, is the tenth, the last on the page. Click and open it up big. Embedded in that, in a particularly intimate place, will be any last-minute instructions. You'll need to check it hourly from Wednesday at noon. It's the last place the spooks would expect people like us to be communicating."

"How do we get to read the hidden message?" said Seth.

"You can download the tools. Dead simple. The program you want—and you must remember this—is called Stegwriter. You need the Gamma version 16. Got that? Some of the instructions for encoding are in German, but that's OK. I can handle that. Of course it's more complicated using an image already on the Web rather than one from my own photo collection, but I have a great little geek to help me. Anyway, decoding is easy for you guys. You download your program. What's it called again? Seth?"

"Stegwriter, Gamma version 16."

"Good man. Then, basically, you follow the prompts. Open the photo of the girl on—what's the site, Elton?"

"Babesdelight.co.uk." Elton didn't relish saying the words.

"Right. Then open up Stegwriter. Click on File Manager and then Decrypt. Follow the prompts. My problem was that in order to hide data of any size I had to find a file that was proportionate. Eventually I found a 650-kilobyte WAV file would carry a five-byte text file. Stegwriter has the whole kit."

Seth coughed. "Is it right to be looking at these pictures? I know that in the name of the Prophet . . ."

Salim looked at Seth sorrowfully. "There is nothing in life that is moral or immoral, there is only the command of God. If Allah has forbidden something, then it is wrong. I am not aware that he has forbidden us to look at women. In fact, there is an early scriptural source in which devout men look at the reflection of a naked woman as she is preparing to bathe. Another authority tells

53

us a man may inspect his wife before marrying her, to make sure she is without blemish that might harm their children."

"But I don't intend to marry Olya," said Elton.

"But you can still look. Some scholars of Arabic have argued that the word means very much more than 'look' in English."

"I think I'd feel uneasy."

"Islam does not recognize 'feeling uneasy,' it only cares about what God has commanded. You're talking like a Christian, some ridiculous Catholic. In any event, Seth, the important issue is not whether your eyes have rested for a moment on a naked woman, but whether you can play your part in ushering in the new caliphate."

When it was his turn to leave the house and walk back to the Tube station, Hassan also felt "uneasy." There were a large number of Muslim girls at his college and when some of them took to wearing the hijab, he supported them, as did the other serious male students. What he didn't dare admit was that he found the black covering attractive, particularly with girls he had previously seen in Western clothes. Rania, for instance, used to wear gray skirts and leather boots, so her dress was modest, revealing only her knees, shiny beneath navy blue tights, when she sat down in the lecture hall. On her upper half she wore a white blouse, buttoned high, and a cardigan or jacket. There was nothing to distress her parents in all this. But in her eyes . . . She applied a thin line of black and a trace of mascara in the Ladies after she'd arrived in the morning, and her lashes were long. The gray skirt, though knee-length, did cling to her hips, and if Hassan happened to be watching when she innocently crossed her legs, he glimpsed for a moment the deep blue thighs and the darkness beyond. He had the contours of Rania's body so deeply etched in his mind that when she took to wearing the hijab it wasn't, to begin with, any hardship for him. He saw through it. The clean white bra and underpants that he could picture beneath, the thighs presumably still in the same navy blue nylon, the curve of the hips and the smallish, firm breasts . . . Now the eyes had no trace of liner or mascara, but when the long lashes were lowered over the dark brown iris there was still a message of invitation.

The scriptural reference to "looking" was one that had been popular among his friends, as it seemed to excuse so much. One of them pointed out to Hassan a passage from a Koranic scholar that read: "The dual nature of what is shown and what is concealed is fundamental to the understanding of God; and this double aspect is explicitly linked in at least one place to sexuality, where the female genitals are identified with the concealed aspect of the divine. There are no Islamic monks. The Prophet had many wives, and we are urged to copulate and procreate. Many scholars have seen orgasm as a foretaste of paradise, where the sensation will not be brief, but eternal."

One of the boys at college, who had a large collection of top-shelf magazines, told Hassan it was fine if the girls in the pictures were *kafirs*. Hassan thought this was making a virtue of necessity, since Muslim women simply didn't pose nude. His own aesthetic taste was always for dark-haired women of his own background; leaving aside his sinful thoughts about Rania's body, he simply liked the elegance and coloring of these women, their femininity.

It was a torment that seldom let up. At the age of nineteen, before he became religious, he had had a *kafir* girlfriend, a white Londoner called Dawn who was in the same year at college. It seemed to be just his luck that he had found the only sexually reticent *kafir* in London. Parts of the West End were no-go zones on Friday and Saturday nights with drunken girls in tiny skirts showing their breasts to passers-by before they threw up in the gutter. Friends of his at college told awed tales of the licentiousness of ever-willing *kafir* girls. But Dawn, for some reason she couldn't properly explain, allowed Hassan only limited access. He could put his hands beneath her clothes and touch her between the legs, but that was all. She refused to reciprocate. It was only when he (to his self-admitted shame) suggested to her that her reluctance was due to some atavistic racial prejudice that she tearfully relented.

It was in a flat she shared with three other girls in Stamford Hill, with the thump of noisy dance music coming from the lounge. Dawn was rigid with resistance, then with cold, in her unheated bedroom as she lay naked at last beneath the duvet. Hassan was scared they might be interrupted by one of the flatmates, all of whom, this being a Friday night, were stupefied with drink. It wasn't at all how he had hoped it might be. Dawn insisted on turning out the bedside lamp, depriving him of the stimulus of sight. When he lay down on top of her, she seemed to shudder a little; he thought perhaps she was crying. He told her that they didn't have to go ahead, but she replied that now they had got this far he might as well finish it off. Hassan felt the pent desires of seven years since puberty compressing to a hard explosive point. Then as Dawn's cold hands stroked his back without enthusiasm, the moment seemed to pass him by. After twenty minutes or more of fumbling and apology and desperate measures, he managed something—a sort of end point without any preceding sensation. He was too ashamed of himself to see her again.

A few weeks later, he found his attention increasingly focusing on a tall and amusing Iranian called Shahla Hajiani, and it seemed to him that his interest was reciprocated. But by then he'd found religion, or a political version of it. When, after a student party, Shahla placed a modest but flirtatious hand on his arm, he explained to her that he must lead a pure life. She looked at him with sad eyes, in which there was still laughter, but also a little hurt and bafflement. "I'll be your friend, then," she said. "If that's allowed?"

"Of course it is."

And she had been a good friend, too, he had to admit. Shahla's father was a Westernized Tehran businessman who had left the country with the fall of the Shah; her mother was English, of part Jewish descent. Shahla, though nominally Muslim, didn't understand or approve of Hassan's mosque life; but she had been solicitous and kind at college, generous with her time and company, swinging through the canteen on her long legs, shoulder bag flying, to settle down beside him over lunch. Sometimes Hassan thought he could still see a glimmer of hope, or lust, or something, in her deep brown eyes. Mostly she asked him innocent questions or told him what play or film she'd been to see and gave an animated account of it.

Thinking of the eternal fires that waited for the unbeliever, particularly an apostate like Shahla, Hassan felt he should ignore her. Yet her friendliness was so unassuming that he found himself, against his better judgment, absorbed by what she said.

Although his understanding of Islam forbade Hassan physical contact, no amount of prayer could quell his twenty-one-year-old desires.

The *kafir* press and media were degraded by images of sex. On quiz shows, talk shows, game shows, the most highly paid and respected presenters, with millions of taxpayers' pounds in their back pockets, talked of masturbation, genital size and sodomy. They did so with a twinkle, with a laugh, slapping their guests on the thigh, as though that made it all right.

On the commercial channels, products were sold to the credulous *kafirs* in the ad break by women mimicking fellatio or commenting with breathy voiceovers. A cheap shampoo was flogged to the sound of a female orgasm; so was a breakfast cereal, with a series of *kafir* women howling on their backs, and this was supposed to be "fun" or "saucy" or something. In a way, Hassan didn't mind; it merely convinced him that he was right.

What troubled him more were the subtler insinuations of girls and women into his consciousness. There was a half-breed, perhaps Eurasian, presenter who seemed to crop up on almost all channels at about eight o'clock. She didn't go in for the filthy talk, but her skirts were short and Hassan found her wholesomeness unsettled him. Sometimes he felt the world was just too full of women, girls, females of every kind who'd been put on earth by God to test his resolve. The black-haired waitress in the Italian café, Barbara, whom he saw having her cigarette break when he went past, puffed insolently, returning his stare. Or take the young

57

mothers at the school gates in Walworth, chattering as they waited for their children to come out: he could sense the hormonal activity coming off them, their marriages now eight or ten years old, love handles swelling gently at the hip, but so alive and keen and not wanting to let their youth go by. Notice me, their body poses said, I'm married but you can still want me.

In April, Hassan's father, Farooq al-Rashid, had received a letter in an envelope marked "On Her Majesty's Service." Assuming it was from the taxman, he opened it cautiously. He had to read it several times before he understood its astonishing contents. From 10 Downing Street, someone who was his "obedient servant" told him "in strict confidence" that the Prime Minister had it in mind on the occasion of the forthcoming list of Birthday Honors, to submit Mr. al-Rashid's name to the Queen for . . .

For what? He had to start again, blinking. Queen, Empire, Prime Minister . . . He thought for a moment that he was being crowned king. At last it became clear: he was, if it was "agreeable" to him, to be appointed an Officer of the Order of the British Empire. Surely, he thought, this was something normally given to TV comedians or Olympic winners. He had seen their pictures in the newspaper, holding a medal on a ribbon and wearing a top hat. And the great British honor was to be granted him for . . .

"Lime pickle," he said. "Who'd have thought it?"

Nasim stood up and kissed her husband on the cheek. He hugged her close.

Farooq al-Rashid had started his first factory at Renfrew in Scotland twenty-two years ago, in the month of Hassan's birth. He himself had come to Britain as a thirteen-year-old in 1967. His parents had left the Mirpur Valley in Pakistan-administered Kashmir when their smallholding was flooded during the construction of the Mangla Dam, and, like many others from the region, they had at first found work in the textile mills of Bradford. After leaving school at sixteen, Farooq had studied for a diploma in business studies and decamped to Glasgow, where he found a clothing company run by the grandfather of a Mirpur friend. Farooq was called "Knocker" because in his early days in the city he would go round people's houses, knocking on their doors, looking for fellow Muslims with whom he could pray at the Oxford Street Mosque.

His business interest, however, was not in textiles but in provisions, and he quickly saw that food from the subcontinent might be sold not only in cheap restaurants but through supermarkets to a population becoming interested in strong-tasting foreign dishes. It took him more than ten years of hard work and saving to assemble the money, the staff and the ideas. At the age of thirty-four, he left the clothing company, where he was second in command, bought a lease on an old factory in Renfrew, then borrowed money for industrial weights and scales, giant cauldrons and sterilizing equipment. He had alterations made to the production line so it could carry cartons of glass jars instead of boxed vests, and traveled to Mexico, Brazil and Iran to find the best fruit. He devised, in consultation with three local chefs, a recipe in which the taste of ginger, chili, salt and garlic was eased into the savor of lime with the aid of brown sugar. It fired up the blandest dish; the citrus skins remained soft and digestible while the sweetness mitigated the heat. He could hardly produce it fast enough for the Glaswegian palate. Within ten years he was a millionaire. He had married the most beautiful girl in Bradford, sticking to Mirpur traditions by choosing a bride whose parents were from the same village as his own, and they had a dark-eyed handsome son—the apple, or the lime as Farooq put it, of his father's eye.

Farooq al-Rashid made friends in Glasgow; his demeanor appealed to the old Scots. He couldn't join them in the pubs, where the true intimacy was forged, but he wasn't squeamish about their profanity, their football or their godlessness, and they found his devotion to Islam easy enough to ignore.

"Does this mean we have to call you Sir Farooq?" asked Nasim, looking up with worried eyes.

"No, don't be silly. You just call me Knocker like before."

"But on letters, do they—"

"That is if you're a knight. Then I would be Sir Farooq al-Rashid. But as it is, I am Farooq al-Rashid, OBE."

"It's quite ironic, isn't it?" said Hassan. "That you should be an officer of the empire that conquered and partitioned your homeland."

"That was a long time ago, Hassan. As you know. We are friends now."

"The British have their pet dictator in power, who—"

"Stop it, for goodness' sake," said Nasim. "Don't spoil your father's day."

"Do I have to wear a penguin suit?" said Hassan.

"I shall buy a new dress," said Nasim.

"And I," said Mr. al-Rashid, "shall think of something to say to the Queen. Do you think she reads many books?"

One of Knocker al-Rashid's secrets was that he himself could barely read. His family had been illiterate on both continents and had no books in the house. At the secondary modern school he had attended near Manningham Lane, the Yorkshire boys were destined for manual jobs in factories or in building trades, so didn't care about lessons. The children in the small immigrant class in which he was placed were too busy learning how to speak English to have much time to read it. A teacher called Mr. Albrow gave him books by Winifred Holtby and Emily Brontë, but he couldn't understand them. Farooq left school with exam passes in math and science only. At night school, he forced himself to read the newspaper and found he could understand balance sheets and company reports, but their language was specialized and, because there were relatively few terms, easy to grasp. When at about this time he first heard of something called "dyslexia," he wondered if that was a condition he might be suffering from—as well as from the natural difficulty of working in a foreign language. But once he'd gained his diploma, with distinction, he worried less about reading and concentrated wholly on business, for which he seemed to have a talent that needed no words.

The thought of meeting the Queen, however, reawoke some old anxieties. Knocker al-Rashid imagined he would have to spend some time with her in the throne room and that once they'd talked about his journey—"Have you come far?"—and the weather, she would ask him, conversationally, if he'd read any good books lately. That's what smart English people always asked. Had he, the Queen would inquire, read the winner of the latest book prizes—the Allied Royal or the Pizza Palace, for instance? He hadn't; he'd just seen the names in the newspaper. Or she might ask if he knew Sir V. S. Naipaul or Sir Salman Rushdie; but he'd never read a word of either, not because he didn't like the sound of them, but just because he couldn't read properly.

He might have a quiet talk with the imam at the mosque in Chigwell. He was a wise man and would give good advice. If he was tongue-tied, Her Majesty would consider him dull, which would be wounding to his family and his faith. From what he understood, he had two months before the announcement and then it could be another six before he went to the palace, so he had time enough to do a crash course in English literature. No one—not even Queen Elizabeth—should say that Knocker al-Rashid was not a cultured man.

All day long he found himself picturing the scene that must have prompted the letter from the "obedient servant."

Her Majesty, on the occasion of her approaching birthday, sat upon her throne, raised on a platform. Below her, also seated, the Prime Minister pored over a sheaf of papers.

"We come now, Your Majesty, to the case of Mr. Farooq al-Rashid."

"Ah yes, indeed," the Queen replied. "It is high time we recognized his services to our country and ourselves."

"An Officer of the Order of the British Empire, perhaps?" The Prime Minister looked up over his spectacles.

"At the very least," said Her Majesty. "Send for the Obedient Servant and command him to dispatch a letter."

Knocker's pleasure at the thought of the OBE was tempered by his anxiety at looking foolish when he came to meet the Queen. He had very little time in which to get an education. Sitting in the back of his car one day on his way to Dagenham, he had a sudden, clever thought. A year earlier, at a political fund-raising dinner, he had met a man called . . . What was it? Knocker may have had trouble with what was written down, but spoken words and names lodged easily in his sober memory . . . Tranter. That was it. Sophie Topping, the hostess that night, whose husband was hoping to be elected an MP, had given a party to show off potential donors like Knocker to the party grandees. Among the guests had been this man Tranter. He was a book reviewer or critic (Knocker was not certain of the distinction) who once a month was paid to "moderate" the discussions of Sophie Topping's book-reading group. Tranter was neither a politician nor a potential backer, just someone Mrs. Topping was proud to know and who, she clearly thought, would raise the tone of her gathering.

In the course of the evening, Tranter had revealed a wide knowledge of books, talking confidently about living and dead authors (he seemed to prefer the latter). So far as Knocker could understand, he was someone who was able to exist by reading books and having views on them. A newspaper hired him to give his opinion and others paid to read it. This was so far from any way of earning a living Knocker had previously encountered that he had to talk himself through the logistics of it a few times to make sure it all made sense. In the end, he decided, the cash flow and productivity, the supply and the demand, didn't really matter; what counted was that this man Tranter was the one to help him in his destined meeting with the Queen of England.

At the Dagenham factory, he asked Mrs. Hine, his secretary, to track down Sophie Topping and find out how to reach Tranter. Before long, Mrs. Hine had sent an e-mail to rgt34@easinet.co.uk. "Dear Mr. Tranter, please forgive this message from out the blue, my employer a very distinguished gentleman is desirous of making a business connection with you in regard of a Literary matter and would be most obliged if you would telephone the above telephone number in the strictest confidence and ask for Mr. al-Rashid. Yours truly, Mrs. Doris Hine."

II

John Veals walked down the steps of the sixteen-seater PetJet at Zurich airport. He had a rental share in the plane, and if he booked ahead and filled it up—two families going on holiday, for instance—it was no more expensive per head than buying good seats on an airline. His last-minute travel decision, however, meant there were only three other passengers, so the flight was expensive. Sometimes you had to spend to earn. After immigration, he found the modest gray car that was waiting to take him to Pfäffikon, a discreetly drab town that might have been invented to help people like him make large trades away from prying eyes.

There was gray snow along the edges of the streets, neatly shoveled by municipal workers in the early hours. Veals met Kieran Duffy, the head of High Level's trade execution team, at the usual coffee shop, well away from the insipid food and high prices of the restaurants designed for their kind. Veals had first met Duffy in New York, where Duffy had worked for twenty-five years for a rival bank. Duffy was one of the few competitors they had really feared; what he didn't know about shafting the client could be written, according to Godley, on the sharp end of a golf tee. Despite his name, Duffy was Jewish and had always been known to Veals as O'Bagel, O'Shlo or even once, when he'd messed up, as O'Kike. (There had been an awkward moment early in Veals and Godley's partnership when Godley had wondered whether Veals, being at least nominally Jewish, if irreligious, himself, would mind the banter of the office. "Don't be fucking feeble, Steve," Veals told him. "Most of my best friends are anti-Semites.")

At the age of forty-nine, Duffy had retired from Wall Street to stare at his millions in Connecticut. Veals gave him nine months to get bored, then offered him a job as chief of his own "buy side": to be the man who no longer sold opaque products for an eye-watering commission but who had the power to decide when, what and from whom to buy. Duffy decamped to Zurich six weeks later. His wife was to join him "in due course," and meanwhile he had set up house with a twenty-eight-year-old Italian girl he'd met in his last days on Wall Street.

Over dry croissants and strong coffee, Veals began to outline to Duffy his thoughts about Allied Royal Bank. He told him as little as was necessary for Duffy to begin to design the positions. Even in his own man, handpicked, and with a strong record with High Level already behind him, Veals saw only risks. High Level's trades generated tens of millions in commission for the brokers and investment banks they dealt with; this meant everyone wanted to know Kieran Duffy and that he was the target of "cash rebates" and other under-the-table favors. Veals knew that Duffy had banked enough not to be prey to such clownish temptation; that was one reason he'd hired him. Still, he had thought it wise to pay all of Duffy's annual salary and bonus in the shape of shares in High Level. Veals trusted Duffy all right, but—just to be sure—it made sense to lock him in for more than any bribe could match. "Making certain our interests are aligned" was how Veals put it; "Not throwing out a hospital pass" was Godley's term.

Veals was ever thrifty with details. "I think silver's likely to get hammered," he might tell Duffy on his orange cellphone from the alleyway off Old Pye Street. "Put us in for five percent of the fund by Friday." It was up to Duffy to decide what market instruments to use; it went without saying, ever, that listed markets should be avoided. With what Veals had in mind for ARB, however, he needed face-to-face time with Duffy. It was going to take the lightest and most ingenious of touches by both men; it would involve all their experience and guile. If Duffy had started work in London or New York, the compliance officers would have asked if the amounts at stake were not in breach of the fund's own published risk-tolerance statements; in Pfäffikon he was more likely to be asked whether he fancied another glass of the fruity local Malvoisie.

The simple, but perhaps too simple, thing to do was to short-sell the stock. This meant first borrowing a vast number of ARB shares from an insurance company or some other registered owner who specialized in lending stock; then selling it at whatever the market would offer; and, finally, repurchasing it at a much cheaper price when the market had collapsed and returning it to its owner. The profit was in the difference between the price at which they'd sold and the lower one at which they had rebought. The exposure, the risk—if the stock price rose—was almost limitless. "Shorting takes rugby-sized balls," as Godley was fond of saying. But the ARB price wasn't going to rise, not in the long run—not with what Veals knew about the debt covenant.

The second obvious thing to do was to buy "put" options on ARB stock. These gave them the right to sell the stock at a pre-agreed or "strike" price. If the strike price was fifteen but the market price had fallen to ten, you bought a million at ten and sold them to the party who'd agreed to buy them at fifteen. Easy. The price of buying these "puts" was determined by the strike price (and the further that was from the current price, the cheaper it was to buy the option); the "time value" before the option expired; and the volatility of the underlying market. Each was given a Greek letter, and the relationships between them further Greek letters, so that some of the quants ended up with worksheets that looked like a page from the *Iliad*.

It was mostly, in Veals's view, absolute piffle. A trade was a trade, and it was driven by two things only: greed and fear. Gamma for Greed if you insisted on talking Greek, said Veals; but, well, "The Greeks had no letter for F," he had more than once remarked.

For two hours they discussed the virtues of "puts" and "calls." Traditionally such instruments had existed as insurance: by limiting their exposure to future price fluctuations, companies could use them to smooth out their forecasts and their cash flows. But turn a safety mechanism upside down and, hey presto, you have a gambling instrument. Through "calls," High Level could trade with people who took the view that the ARB price would rise, or were at least prepared to name a figure that would reward them if it did; through "puts" High Level could express their own conviction that the price would fall. The danger in the dual strategy Veals outlined was that they were not using one position to "hedge" against the other; on the contrary, the success of both trades relied on the same thing: they were simply doubling their bet on the chosen outcome.

"Shit." Duffy seldom swore. "Do you know something I don't know, John?"

"Trust me," said Veals.

Duffy stared into his coffee, saying nothing for a minute. Eventually he lifted his head. "OK, John. It's not my fund. It's your baby. I'll do what you ask."

Veals nodded. "But I'm worried that we might blow out the counterparty. I don't want one of them to collapse and default on the trade."

"We have to spread it across the whole industry," said Duffy. "It's time we called in a few favors. You've got every prime broker in the world as well as half the hedge funds gagging for a bit of the action. I can get some special terms. Then people will see the banks' names not ours listed on the trades. They won't know it's us they're dealing with."

Veals ordered more coffee. "If ARB goes down," he said, "it's possible the amount of bad debt in all the other banks will make their share prices plummet too. The whole banking sector could be in trouble. There'd be panic on the high street. Mrs. Smith's £10,000 life savings. Queues round the block. The government would have to guarantee the savers. And to do that, they'd have to increase their own borrowing by half overnight."

"And that would have a huge effect on the price of government debt," said Duffy.

"Yes it would," said Veals. "On gilts. So we take a position on gilts."

Duffy smiled slowly. "And then," he said, "there's the currency. The extra government debt would mean that sterling gets hammered—even against a shaky dollar."

"Well," said Veals, putting down his cup. "I think we have the makings of something."

He almost smiled. The reason he particularly liked the sterling aspect of the trade was that the currency market was almost completely unregulated.

"Do you want lunch?" said Duffy. "We could go to that Spanish place I'm always telling you about."

"What? And be seen by a whole lot of hedge-fund managers? For fuck's sake, Kieran. I'm not hungry. My car's outside. I'll get him to take me back to the airport. I'll call tonight at five. On your cellphone."

"All right. What are we going to call this trade, John?"

Veals and Duffy always had code names for sensitive trades, just as an extra protection.

"I suppose," said Veals, "in view of all the pension business we could call it . . . What about 'Rheumatism'?"

"Fine. Rheumatism it is. So long, John. Been nice seeing you."

Kieran Duffy stood outside the steamed-up coffee shop and watched the lean figure of John Veals crunch a homburg onto his head and climb into the gray saloon.

Some hedge funds had narrow specializations, but Veals and Godley always intended to deal across the whole financial *carte*. Veals dreaded boredom and he feared missing any opportunity.

To begin with, until they found their feet, they did some easy deals in his old bank speciality: debt. This seemed an obvious way of "getting our eye in," as Godley put it; there was the further attraction to Veals that bank debt was not regulated. You could pass on market-sensitive information without a problem; what would have got you three years in prison for insider trading if you dealt in equities was quite permissible when discussing bank debt, and here was Veals's preferred position: the kosher edge.

An early coup came when he noticed that one of the Eastern European countries was owed £30 million by a former French African colony. Veals discovered that the Slavs expected little or no return on what they'd rashly lent the Africans and they were delighted to get the whole debt off their hands to Veals in return for £5 million.

When the Jubilee 2000 movement for the cancellation of debt persuaded the G7 countries to write off the African debt, Veals at once sued the African government in the London High Court for repayment of the £25 million shortfall. The judge expressed distaste at the action, but said his hands were tied by law. Veals owned the bonds; the Africans were obliged to reroute the G7 refund straight into Veals's recently opened private Allied Royal bank account in Victoria Street, London SW1. It was a happy result for High Level Capital in its infant days.

There was a large industry in London which existed to exploit the "rights" of junior debtors in companies on their deathbed: it involved taking extreme legal positions of doubtful morality. Veals viewed it as a boring and mechanical trade, with irritating lawyers' fees, but admitted it was a dependable revenue earner; it was, as Steve Godley put it, "a club we need to have in our bag. A handy seven iron."

In New York, Veals had given Marc Bézamain carte blanche to do such trades whenever he saw fit. Veals knew that Bézamain had the kosher edge in this area because of his friendship with people in the ratings agencies. If a troubled company's bonds were downgraded, some mutual funds were obliged to shed them for what Bézamain called "noneconomic" reasons: pensioners' representatives could be just too fussy—the bonds hadn't lost any real value.

Bézamain had come into Veals's orbit in New York, via Paris and a *grande école* or two, but originally from a poor village near Cahors in southwest France. His parents were smallholders— "fucking peasants," as Veals put it to him at interview: his aunt worked stuffing grain down the throats of geese in an industrial foie gras plant. But the young man was good. He was very strong on risk limitation; he had a rustic smallholder's caution, and Veals and Godley both privately believed he kept his annual bonus ($8 million this January) in cash beneath the mattress.

To John Veals the staffing of High Level Capital was a matter of frantic delicacy, and the most valuable to him were the consultants. They included two East Europeans, whose utilities he had bled white on behalf of his bank in New York in the course of their post-Communist denationalizations. They had gone from being treasurers and chief financial officers to being politicians: finance ministers for their respective governments. Their days of being "entertained" by Veals and Godley with the limitless expense account of the bank in New York had given the men a taste for the exotic which they couldn't fund themselves. Veals and Godley had made available a few "founder shares" in High Level, then hired them as research specialists on "economic trends." Their job was to deliver inside information on their respective countries; they were paid a retainer, but also on results that accrued from that information.

In the course of the African debt venture, Veals had addressed himself to the British Embassy, where the commercial attaché, a well-spoken young man called Martin Ryman, who was bored with making car-parking arrangements for visiting dignitaries, had been excited by the plans that Veals laid out to him. Ryman showed a commercial acumen and a flexibility that had impressed Veals. He kept an eye on him over the years and, one day, when he sensed that he was bored, offered to double his salary if he would come to High Level as a consultant. Ryman brought to High Level Capital connections in a world that Veals knew he could never penetrate—a place where diplomacy met government and even "the arts" in a kind of fraternity of the educated. His best introduction had been a former Israeli prime minister, who became an "undisclosed" consultant and was paid to inform Ryman of any impending action in the Middle East that was likely to affect the price of oil.

Veals made it a condition of employment that all his consultants had an interest in the fund. This kept them honest. It wasn't just "the Vatican"—Shields DeWitt—who were straight arrows in Veals's experience: most people he had met in his life in finance were essentially law-abiding. For many of them the lack of regulation meant that they didn't need to break the law to make surreal amounts of money. There was also, he'd discovered, a snobbery about being honest: people who believed themselves to be unusually gifted were proud of the fact that they could make millions in a legal way. The distinction between "legal" and "ethical" was of no concern to him—or to anyone he'd ever met.

In the mid-1990s, Veals had been impressed by an exchange with a senior director of an asset management company that had emerged from inside a bank, then been so successful that it bought its parent. The new entity was subsequently sold for more than $3 billion to a huge American brokerage, and each of the asset management company original directors personally made £83 million on the sale.

The happy director gave Veals this information as they strolled round his large estate, where Veals had been trying unsuccessfully to shoot game birds. "Still," a momentarily nonplussed Veals countered in a rare excursion into humor, "after tax, it hardly comes to anything." The director looked at him in disbelief: "We didn't pay *tax*."

The profit had been capital, not income; it had been deferred, rolled over, swallowed by a specially created vehicle and tapped off only when the coast was clear.

"And the glory of it is," the strolling landowner concluded as he raised his shotgun, "that it was all quite kosher."

Eighty-three million tax-free and kosher. Fuck me, thought Veals. Even he was impressed.

III

For her Monday lunch, Jenni Fortune took a plate of vegetarian lasagne with garlic bread and green salad to a corner table in the depot canteen.

"Orright, Jen?"

She looked up at Liverpool Dave and nodded. Although he was one of the good guys, she didn't want to talk to him. She preferred to spend her lunch break with a book. She had made her own path into literature. Reading hadn't been encouraged at her school, where the teachers had been too concerned with crowd control and the nondiscriminatory management of the children to have much time for education as such; it was enough to get them back on the bus without offense.

As a teenager, Jenni liked books that took her into unfamiliar worlds, but didn't differentiate between them. She had read *Jilly Jones Gets Married* and *Almayer's Folly* in the same week; she was drawn in both cases by the title. Joseph Conrad's jungle and hidden treasure appealed to her, and she was intrigued by the way he dealt with the question of sex between different races, which made her think of her own parents; but Conrad's sentences, if she was honest, had really been a stretch.

For dessert, she had a chocolate biscuit and a cup of tea. She could feel Liverpool Dave's eyes fixed on her from the other side of the room, where he was eating his steak pie with chips and peas. She pushed the hair back from her face and sipped the tea beneath the bright strip lights. She should have let him sit with her: it had been unkind. But there was just too much of Dave—too much person, too bulky, too real.

Jenni remembered the first time she had been to see the lawyers, two years ago now. She had been nervous. She wore a navy blue dress, her best coat, black tights and new leather boots, then took the Tube to King's Cross. She went to the station supervisor's office and was led back across the concourse by his assistant through a locked "Staff Only" door, down a brightly lit corridor full of fire doors and lined with flame-retardant tiles, until she came to a small kitchen that smelled of curry. Here Margaret from Human Resources was waiting with Barry Gaskell from the union.

"Hello, Jenni love," said Barry. They shook hands. "Don't half pong in here," he added.

"Yes," said Margaret, "one of the control room assistants on night shift has his meal here. He likes curry."

Barry Gaskell, a red-faced man in a suit with a small enameled union badge on the lapel, looked at his watch. "Now look, what's happening today is we're going to see Mr. Northwood, who's our brief. Got that? He'll want to go through a few things with us, make sure he's got it all off pat."

"Is he a barrister?"

"Yes. Just like Mr. Hutton. But he's the junior. He's the powder-monkey who gives Hutton the ammunition for when he gets up on his hind legs in court. Hutton's the big gun."

"OK," said Jenni. "And what about Mr. McShane?"

"He's the solicitor, love. He's the middle man. He's in our control room at the moment. We thought it would be a good idea for him to have a look and see how everything works. But I think we'll go and fish him out now, we need to be on our way."

The four of them made their way to the dark control room, where McShane was receiving a lesson from the duty assistant. In the twilight, a row of screens showed images from CCTV cameras. The control assistant pointed his pen at one of the pictures, which showed the interior of a stalled lift. He spoke into the microphone to a trapped passenger.

"Please don't swear, sir. We're getting help to you as soon as we can. Please, sir, there's no need for that language . . ."

Barry Gaskell chuckled. "It's the raspberry switch, innit?"

"What?" said Margaret from HR.

Gaskell coughed. "Raspberry ripple. Old-fashioned term for . . . disabled. It's really called the 'mobility-impaired alarm button,' and it has to be set at a height where a wheelchair user can reach it. But what happens is, some bloke with a big arse leans back and sets it off by mistake. But the knob can't be covered up to stop this happening because of the Disability Discrimination Act. All right, Mr. McShane, we need to go now, please."

Jenni took her Oyster card from her bag and made for the ticket gate.

"Oi, Jenni," said Gaskell. "This way." He pointed to the exit stairs. "Union business. We're taking a taxi."

They were met in the foyer of the chambers of Eustace Hutton, QC, by Samson, the clerk.

"Mr. Hutton is in court, Mr. Gaskell. He asked me to give you his regards. The conference, as you know, will be with Mr. Northwood, who will be the junior in the case. A specialist in this area. This way, please."

Jenni followed down a warmly heated corridor over an oatmeal carpet. On the walls were hung prints of old lawyers—cartoons, she thought, caricatures or whatever they were called, from long ago—the time of Joseph Conrad, or even earlier perhaps. The men in them looked frightening, full of words and learning. It was odd, these old pictures in the modern offices: pictures of great men. Were they what today's barrister wanted to become? Perhaps in their wigs and gowns they were already like that—a throwback.

The man inside the office, when they'd been shown in, was modern, though. Jenni smiled momentarily to herself, a little laugh of relief suppressed. He was ever so thin, she thought; his ragged hair was in need of cutting; he wore a dark gray suit and a maroon tie, but it looked all right, not too olde worlde; in fact he looked a bit like one of the available "ur-maquettes" in Parallax for "lawyer."

Jenni looked all round his room while he spoke to them; she didn't take in what he said. There were no photographs, and that was odd. Surely he would want to have pictures of his wife or kids—or if he wasn't married, then of his mum and dad. Jenni herself longed for an office she could make her own, with photos and plants and a proper coffee machine. There were hundreds of books on the shelves, of course: gold titles on scarlet and calfskin with roman numerals—and someone, she supposed, had read and digested every word inside.

One thing was odd about this lawyer, Mr. Northwood's, room, Jenni noticed: some of the books seemed not to be law books, but to be novels or stories. There were at least a dozen by Balzac, whom she'd heard of but never read, and then there were some very thin paperbacks which she guessed would be poetry. There was a sandwich bag peeping out of his wastepaper basket under the desk; she could see the rim of a styrofoam coffee cup and a rolled-up newspaper covered in scribbles where he'd been working on the crossword. He was human.

Jenni sat back in the modern chair and folded her hands in her lap. Gabriel Northwood had a low, cultured voice—"BBC," her mother would have said—suggesting layers of knowledge and unvoiced jokes at her expense.

Barry Gaskell seemed to be taking it all in OK; he was nodding and making notes. McShane, the solicitor, did most of the talking, handing Gabriel some papers and asking Barry for others.

When he wanted to read them, Gabriel put on black-rimmed glasses, which made him look older, Jenni thought. She wondered if he was shortsighted and what a nuisance it must be; she herself had almost perfect vision, her instructor had happily noted.

Where would someone like Mr. Northwood live? she wondered. Although she covered so much of London every day, Jenni knew little of the streets above her head. She went up West occasionally, to Piccadilly Circus, Leicester Square; she knew a few of the smaller streets and clubs in Soho from hen nights and birthday parties; but if someone said to her "St. James's Park," she just thought "shiny floors"—which you'd expect, as it was TfL headquarters. Gloucester Road meant a giant panda head between platforms, and Sloane Square was merely little shops under green arches and the rumor that once, not long ago, there had been a bar on the platform where commuters stopped for beer and cigarettes on their way home. Of its streets and houses she knew nothing.

And Mr. Northwood? Marylebone? Hampstead? Or maybe he lived in what they called the "chambers." Perhaps the man Samson was like a butler, who took them food upstairs and put them all up in bed at the end of the day, in a dormitory, like in a boarding school . . . Jenni found herself having to bite the inside of her lip again.

"We could always arrange for you to have a ride with one of the drivers, if you liked," said Barry Gaskell. "To give you a sense of what it's like as the train comes into the station—how little time you have to react to a determined jumper."

Gabriel looked surprised by the suggestion. He took off his glasses. "All right," he said. "I will. I suppose I ought to go with Ms. . . . er, Fortune herself."

Jenni appreciated the pause he put before her surname.

"Would that be all right, Jenni?" said Margaret.

Jenni shrugged. "Whatever."

She saw Mr. Northwood flinch a little at her surliness, but it was a first defense that was too deeply ingrained to change.

"We'll have a look at the shift rota when we get back to the depot," said Barry, "then I'll give you a call with some possible times."

There were another ten minutes in which Gabriel went through more paperwork, writing in a blue foolscap notebook. His questions were about training and recruitment of drivers as well as the obvious detail about safety precautions. Eventually, he showed them to the door.

He held out his hand to each in turn. Jenni couldn't quite meet the candid, slightly anxious look in Gabriel's brown eyes and kept her own on the floor as she briefly offered, then withdrew, her hand.

In the course of the first trial, Jenni had come to know Gabriel, and also Eustace Hutton, QC, his "leader" as they called him.

Hutton's room, where they next met, was piled with boxes and files, some of them on porters' trolleys.

"Sorry about the clutter," said Hutton waving his hand. "The price of success, I'm afraid. Upcoming briefs. Worst of all is I have to read the wretched things."

"We could go to my room," said Gabriel. "It's certainly uncluttered by success."

Hutton ignored him. "Take a seat, Miss Fortune." He left no tactful pause between the two words. "Right. Let's see. We'll have to ask you a few questions in court, I'm afraid."

This was what Jenni had feared: being on trial.

Hutton looked at her over the top of his glasses. "You do understand, don't you, that there is no question of your having done anything wrong? The plaintiff's action is against your employer. They allege that the safety precautions were inadequate."

"They're no different than what they ever were," said Jenni.

Hutton beamed. "Indeed. The core of our argument of course is that the transport provider is required to take reasonable precautions to ensure the safety of its passengers—or clients as, alas, I think they prefer to call them. Such precautions have been in place for many years and have not successfully been called into question before. However, that doesn't mean that they're perfect. I'm sure you remember the fire at King's Cross in 1987, which—"

"Of course I do," said Jenni. It was the worst day in the history of the Tube: thirty-one people had died when a lighted match fell down the side of an escalator into an area that had not been cleaned since the thing was built in the 1940s. As well as a lot of mechanical grease, there was a nice bit of tinder supplied by sweet papers, discarded tickets and—the bit that stuck in Jenni's memory—rat hairs.

"The fact that fire precautions had previously been thought adequate doesn't mean that they actually were adequate," said Hutton. "And more importantly from a legal point of view, it doesn't mean that the subsequent public inquiry found that they were adequate either. Are you with me?"

"Of course."

"There is a second difficulty, and that concerns the provisions of the Human Rights legislation which our government chose to bolt onto our existing legal system."

Mr. Northwood coughed at this point. "I can probably explain that at some other—"

"Nonsense," said Hutton. "Miss Fortune is clearly a highly intelligent young woman. The Human Rights Act derives from the European Convention on Human Rights, which was drawn up by the Allies in the wake of the Second World War. It was intended to help occupied countries with slightly less sophisticated legal systems than our own to make sure they observed certain proprieties when bringing Nazis to justice. A good idea in principle. Then our own government, fifty years later, fancied trying to graft it on to our own legal system, which has evolved quite satisfactorily on its own. It was like recalling all modern Aston Martins and fitting them with running boards and squeeze-horns. Are you with me?"

"I think so," said Jenni.

"The government loved legislation, and especially if imported from Europe. More the merrier. And of course anyone opposing something as pleasant-sounding as a human rights act risked appearing a bit of a cad. We tried to warn them that the two systems wouldn't sit well together. I predicted that the only people who would profit from the mess would be the lawyers."

"And have you?" said Jenni.

"Enormously!" boomed Hutton. "And the contradictions are such that many cases get heard three times. At first instance, in the Court of Appeal and in the House of Lords. I have three bites of the cherry."

Gabriel coughed. "I wouldn't want Ms. Fortune to think—"

"My conscience is clear," said Hutton. "I wrote to the Attorney General and the chairman of the Bar Council, warning what would happen. I wrote two articles in legal journals and one in a national newspaper. Moreover—"

"What it means in your case," said Mr. Northwood, looking at Jenni, "is that quite a large amount of the argument will be what you might call hypothetical, about duties of care and who is responsible for what. And a lot will be about what previous judgments tell us. Not much will be about what actually happened. And I'd like to repeat that there's absolutely no criticism of what you did. So when we ask you about the events, it's just to establish the nature of your training. It's not to suggest that you did anything wrong. You're not on trial."

He smiled at her encouragingly, and Jenni nodded.

Gabriel Northwood disliked his reputation for being melancholy and did what he could to undermine it. He sent humorous e-mails to Andy Warshaw, his tireless friend in Lincoln's Inn; he made sure he didn't subscribe to the Eustace Hutton view that the modern world, with its short-termist, ignorant politicians, was something to be mocked. He was careful not to slip into the Inner Temple way of talking, with its clubbish phrases, mispronounced Latin tags and unvoiced conviction that its members were cleverer than the rest of the world. Most of the barristers who lunched on the wooden benches in the dining hall seemed to view nonlawyers as willful children, fit for an amused reproof; even solicitors, the "junior branch" of the profession, were really more like accountants or management consultants, out there in modern offices and shiny suits. Gabriel made sure he read tabloid papers as well as ones with the law reports; he watched television, he saw new films and went to galleries where they showed video installations of a homeless naked man sitting in a chair for twenty minutes on end. He learned how to cook modern food from bestselling books and didn't sniff at them because their authors had been on television; he liked the taste of chili, ginger and garlic, with organic vegetables and flame-seared meat.

Even with all these efforts, he never found his spirits lift to meet the day. The call of the alarm clock didn't fill him—as he was pretty sure it filled Eustace Hutton, Samson the clerk, Andy Warshaw or even that train driver Jenni Fortune—with pleasurable anticipation and a desire to get things done. The day never looked like a challenge he could deal with, but more like a blankish stretch of time in whose margins he would seek small intellectual pleasures to get him through till home time and a bottle of wine in his cramped rooms in Chelsea.

Partly, he supposed, it was because he seldom slept well. The undersheet, when he stood up from the bed, was corrugated from his night-long turning. Blister packs of pills curled on the bedside table—mild over-the-counter, risky prescription, useless homeopathic or American depth charges shipped by an online supplier in Tampa, Florida. He had looked with incredulous envy at the side of the bed occupied for five years off and on by Catalina, now gone. When she rose to make tea, the sheet and duvet bore almost no imprint of her passing—any more than a vellum envelope might be ruffled by the insertion and removal of a stiff invitation.

Catalina . . . there was a story or a reason in itself, Gabriel thought. Perhaps the loss of her had made him miserable forever. She was married to a diplomat and Gabriel had met her when they'd found themselves next to one another at a charity dinner. He'd tried to entertain her as he believed he was charitably required to do, making routine conversation about the cause and why he supported it, the crumby bread rolls, the immigrant waitresses and what was in the news that day. Catalina's wide eyes stayed on his face throughout; she seemed to listen, which was always encouraging, and told him about her childhood in Copenhagen, her American father, her Danish mother, her three sisters—whatever, as Jenni Fortune might have said. Gabriel did some conversational time with the woman on his other side, sat back and waited as the speeches began, to be followed by the silent auction and the quiz game hosted by a TV impressionist.

He was surprised when Catalina tried to engage him further; the convention was that once you'd done a stint to right and left and the "entertainment" had begun you were off the hook. But this woman, intent and humorous, seemed to want to go beyond politeness. Surely, Gabriel thought, no one he'd met at a public function could really be interested in his thoughts about local authority liability or the invasion of Iraq. So he started to listen more carefully to what Catalina herself was saying, to its harmonic line. She had a faint accent, a contralto voice that lifted into laughter of an unexpectedly girlish kind. He estimated she was about three years older than he was, maybe thirty-six. What struck him most, though, was her determination to tell him her story and the elegance with which she did so—amused by her own failings, it seemed, as well as fond of all those sisters. She also had two children, though they featured less in her conversation. This surprised Gabriel, who had generally found young mothers keen to share tales of nursery or school. Her husband was with the German Embassy in London, though he spent much of his time traveling. At the end of the evening, Catalina made Gabriel write down his phone number on the back of her place card. And then she rang it.

A year later, when they were lying in his bed one winter Saturday afternoon, she said, "I knew from the moment I sat down next to you. I just knew I had to have you, that I couldn't rest until I had you in my bed."

He called her names that marveled at her daring, but she replied with dignity that he was only the third lover she had had, the first having been a student, the second her husband; she was not the *grande horizontale* of his imagination, just a woman who had met her perfect lover and had had the wit to recognize him when chance placed them next to one another on cheap gilded banqueting chairs. Gabriel had felt uneasy about adultery, but Catalina told him emphatically that that problem was hers, not his, to wrestle with. She referred to her husband as she might refer to the day of the week or the Tube map, something given that had to be consulted; she neither disparaged nor repined over him, but told Gabriel when he would be in London and when she was required to be with him. Gabriel stopped asking for information about him, feeling that until the other man's name (Erich) crossed his lips he had no true existence. He did wonder how Catalina, a rather transparent person in many ways, managed her double life, but she only said something about Chinese walls, compartments, and repeated that it was not for him to fret about.

Love grew slowly in Gabriel until he saw, one day in the course of a tearful phone conversation, that it was too late; there was no way back. It felt as though the reserves he'd held in various accounts had been drained, electronically, without his knowledge, presenting him with the paper statement—the first he knew of it—that all he owned was now vested in Catalina. In some ways he was glad of this development, since the other holdings had been in largely trivial matters, the emotional equivalents of National Savings. On the other hand, wasn't the conventional wisdom for diversification? Eggs/baskets?

What it meant was that he wanted to be with her all day long. It wasn't enough to look forward to Friday night, when Erich was invariably away, and to maybe one other meeting snatched excitingly in the course of the week. He counted all the time he wasn't with her lost. He wondered at what point he'd forfeited control. She had seemed to outrun him by so much at the beginning that he'd felt uneasy about an inequality of passion, not believing he would ever feel as much, though happy at the same time that he seemed less exposed to harm. He viewed her with a detached amusement that seemed both to frustrate and charm her. "It's as though you don't quite believe in me," she said once.

"I'm not sure I do," said Gabriel. "Someone like you doesn't happen to someone like me. The norm of life is a sort of qualified failure. And I was quite happy with that. I've learned to live with it, like everyone else. You don't expect your perfect woman to sit down next to you one day. And then to ring and come round to your flat in beautiful clothes bringing wine and flowers and—"

"I am real," she said.

"But still hard to believe in."

When he went to his mother's Hampshire village at Christmas he felt he wasn't present in the bare garden where he tidied up the last leaves and the broken flowerpots for her. He was peeling back his padded glove to see his watch and work out what Catalina was doing in Copenhagen, in the family house near St. Frederik's Church, ringed by verdigrised statues. The pie his own mother heated for supper on Christmas Eve became in his imagination the feast of sweet-cured fish, roast goose, fried apple slices and "glögg," a red-wine punch Catalina had lovingly described to him. He could barely spare a glimpse for the choir in church, needing both eyes to scrutinize his mobile-phone screen for the promised text, in case one eye alone might miss the season's greeting, the only one he cared about: "1 message received."

Catalina made anything seem possible, or more than that, irradiated. Since almost every aspect of their love affair, beginning with its beginning, had been improbable, so her later miracles, such as making the evening appear worth living for, the day worth rising to greet, were accepted by him as mundane stuff, well within her compass. When he tried to work out where he'd lost himself, yielded control or whatever it was he had surrendered, the answer didn't seem to relate to himself or to his past; it seemed only to be about her. He was enslaved by it now, as a criminal client in his early days as a barrister had once told Gabriel he was enslaved by heroin; whatever in their inner landscape had predisposed them both to dependency was now beside the point.

To be that much in love was not good for you. It wasn't healthy. The likelihood of what doctors called a "good outcome" was slight, and this much Gabriel recognized even at the time. There was a flaw in the heart of most of the Western books he'd read, the plays he'd seen, and it had shaped the way he'd come to think about himself. Centuries of occidental culture seemed to suggest that the greatest emotions were the best: this love for another, this desperate passion, was the earthly happiness that you should aim for, and those who never found it had in some way failed in life; the minority who'd known, and the even smaller number who'd secured it, or together watched it develop into something less exhausting, were the ones who had done best. At the sound of the Last (secular) Trump, theirs would be the laurels and the crowns.

Yet was it really such an enviable way to live, always at the edge of panic, desperate for a facile cellphone bleep, all your judgments skewed? Even in the grip of such a passion, wanting only to see his lover again, Gabriel allowed himself to enter what the Appeal Court would have called a dissenting judgment.

And yet the loss of such a woman might be enough to make anyone unhappy—for the rest of his life, thought Gabriel. Why would you look forward to tomorrow, when it, like all the other days, was going to deny you the one thing you most wanted? But it wasn't that, he felt. He'd been able to be philosophical in a way about losing Catalina. He concentrated on remembering and reliving the intense joy he'd known with her. To ask for more would have been unreasonable. He had a photograph of her on his mobile phone, just one, taken in a café in Stockholm where they'd been for a last-minute weekend. But he'd changed phones since then and couldn't find a USB cable that would fit the old one to download the picture. In any case, the battery was kaput and they didn't seem to make replacements. Sometimes he held the old phone in his hand, throwing it gently up and down, feeling the weight of loss in his palm.

In any event, he thought, perhaps his problem was not so much the loss of Catalina as a failure of engagement—or rather an incongruity. Here was this world—London, the park and trees and the people in his chambers and the precedents he studied, the case law, paperwork; there was the culture it threw at him in cinemas, in galleries and in the self-devouring press and television with all its horrifying "reality" programs; and then the weather, chance of travel, other people, going out. That was what was on offer, out there. And then on the other hand there was him—the sum of random mutations among his ancestors, one outlying bud of an unstable species. Why would you expect *b* to like or enjoy *a*? What, really, were the chances of an overlap, a rough fit, let alone a congruence? The odd thing wasn't that his spirit—if that was what it was, the flickering of electrical charge and spill of chemicals through a synapse—failed to lift to meet this world; the more remarkable thing was how many people did seem to like it, slotted into it and felt right at home there. Lucky them.

Gabriel put his day together in slabs of time. If you could break it down into smaller parts, it became easier. Denial helped—not going to the Corkscrew at lunchtime so that his daily ration of wine was still untouched when he got home. Working, just pushing himself through papers passed on to him by busier colleagues. Talk in the clerks' room with Samson and Jemima, the junior clerk, known to everyone as Delilah. The cryptic crossword. The announcement of the latest international football squad with player assessments in the evening paper. Tea. The ping of e-mail with a wine offer from Rhône Direct or a joke from Andy Warshaw with a link to a risqué video clip.

He didn't much like Internet porn, which was odd, because he didn't consider himself to be prudish. The arrangement with Catalina had been that she was shameless, yet they never lost the sense that what they did was also forbidden. He looked into her brown eyes, and they didn't flicker from their diplomatic politeness as he described what he would like to do next, or was already doing, and she agreed, or volunteered for something more. There was always a sense of borders crossed—never a Nordic wholesomeness, but shame and trepidation.

He had had no lover since Catalina. He did look at women who came in for conferences, black-stockinged junior solicitors in court, bankers in the Corkscrew or secretaries at the sandwich counter in Alfredo's. He appreciated their pretty hair or eyes or legs, but that was all. Then he went back to his room and thought of something else.

His father had died when Gabriel was seventeen and this had given him an early awareness of the immanence of death, its bulk invisible behind the empty static of the day. The white nights that normally came to people in middle age, he'd been told, brought on by the weakening and death of parents, had been known to Gabriel from an earlier age. At twenty, he was familiar with 4 a.m., and what it brought. But he was reckoned to be the more levelheaded and the more sanguine of the two brothers (Adam was the elder) and he tried to live up to this billing. His reputation (a volatile stock since it was made up in equal parts by those who knew him well, those who didn't, and those who misunderstood him) was for being melancholy, not easy to approach, but essentially kindhearted.

The case of Jenni Fortune and TfL was the first one Gabriel had had for almost twelve months. He was at a loss to explain the trough in his fortunes, but it made life tense in chambers, where the rent arrangements were such that the more successful subsidized ("carried" was their word for it) those less in demand. It was sometimes hard to meet the eye of Eustace Hutton or of Jerry Sanderson, the senior silk who'd billed over a million the previous year.

The conference or "con" on Monday was what Barry Gaskell called a "heads up," by which he seemed to mean a chance to go over old ground and summarize where they were before the Appeal Court hearing in January. It wasn't in Gabriel's view a necessary meeting, but he could bill Gaskell's union for it and he could also conduct it himself, since Hutton was in court.

Gabriel first tried to put Jenni Fortune at her ease, though this wasn't easy. As they were settling themselves, he saw her eyes slide down his bookshelf over the spines of some novels by Balzac.

"Have you read any Balzac?" he found he had said, without thinking.

Jenni shook her head in silence.

Gabriel cursed himself. "I . . . I just saw you looking. Are you . . . Are you a big reader?"

"Nah. Not really."

He saw a glimmer. "But a bit."

"A little bit."

There was a pause, but she offered nothing more. Gabriel felt he had just about got away with it. Over the many months that he had known the Tube team, he had often seen such flickers from Jenni. He was fairly certain that she followed the legal points more clearly than any of the others, including McShane, the solicitor, but any attempt to bring her into the conversation resulted in her shaking her head and disowning any interest.

Once or twice, usually when Barry Gaskell was giving a leisurely *tour d'horizon*, Gabriel found himself wondering about Jenni's background. There was something unusual about her, something unresolved. Her skin was quite dark, but her features didn't look fully Afro-Caribbean. Her voice was London, but without West Indian inflection. Her manner was offhand to the point of being rude, but he sensed, or hoped, this gruffness was partly a defense.

He gathered himself and refocused. When it came down to it, Jenni Fortune's life was not his business.

After she had gone, Gabriel started thinking about the evening ahead and at what time he might allow himself a glass of wine. To

85

celebrate, in advance, the check that would eventually come his way for the conference, he could have a glass of the house red in the Corkscrew.

As he looked out of the window, he found a garbled quotation trying to reassemble itself in his mind. "Man comes and drinks the wine and sits below . . ." Something like that. *Omar Khayyam*, was it? He looked online for the quotation, but without success, then went on to refresh his memory of the *Rubaiyat*. Odd, he thought, that such a glorification of drinking should have come from Persia, a country where alcohol was now banned. There had long been a theory that the Shiraz grape, backbone of the northern Côtes du Rhône and other wines he favored, had even originated in the Iranian city of that name, but DNA tests had lately shown that this was not possible . . .

Such news, along with much else that was pointless or untrue, can be discovered, Gabriel knew, by a man with a mouse in his fingers and time on his hands.

The Shiraz question reminded him, via Iran, of the Koran. Before the Leicester schoolgirl case had made it urgent, he had long intended to read it. He suspected that some demagogues wanted to inflame and some to soothe, but probably neither told the truth of what was really in the book. He had wanted to know, for instance, how strict it was on the alcohol question. How much of a problem anyway had liquor been in Medina and Mecca in A.D. 630? It seemed odd, also, that Jewish and Muslim dietary laws—pork, shellfish, milk—seemed to follow the logic of hygiene in a hot country, but on drink the religions so dramatically diverged, with Muslims going dry and Christians giving their Messiah the supply of top wine as his very first miracle, at Cana . . .

IV

In Ferrers End, in his book-lined sitting room, R. Tranter was posting an early opinion of a new novel on a popular bookseller website. He had found that the first review could set the tone, so that whatever later bouquets were offered by newspapers or online readers, the prompt and mocking disparagement of Cato476, Lollywillowes or makepeacethack1 (he had any number of e-mail accounts) could linger like a floating Chernobyl cloud, blighting the praise that followed. He usually hadn't read the book in question, but it was easy enough to piece together a plausible critique from the summary in the publisher's catalog, and it was vital to be first up.

On this occasion, however, he was distracted from his routine task by a familiar anguish. It wasn't only novelists who made Tranter miserable. For many years he had also been tormented by the work of a reviewer called Alexander Sedley. From nowhere, or possibly from Oxford, this young man had appeared at book launch parties, introducing himself to his elders, then following up next day with obsequious letters. ("It was a privilege to meet you last night. I have long admired your pages as almost the last remaining forum for serious discussion in our depleted culture . . .") Tranter had seen one such letter lying around when he'd stopped by Patrick Warrender's office to deliver a review. Surely no one had written like that since the 1930s?

To anyone with space to fill, young Sedley offered long reviews, unpaid, on any current or forthcoming book. He even volunteered to deliver something over the weekend on the 600-page Canadian magic-realist novel that had sat for six weeks on Patrick Warrender's desk, catching the poor man's eye when he forgot to screen it from his gaze with the covering of that day's paper.

Sedley's combination of private-school manners and iron tenacity had eventually broken the reserve of even the most world-weary. Somebody had to review *The Treasury of Eighteenth-Century Anecdotes*, and here was a piece from Sedley sent in on spec; if he set aside an hour's labor after lunch to remove the self-congratulation, Patrick Warrender told himself, it would exactly fill the space at the bottom of the page.

Sedley was as tireless as Tranter, but with better connections. To Tranter's irritation he turned up at parties in a charcoal gray suit of expensive-looking cloth, while most male reviewers wore egg-stained trousers and brown shoes. He looked ridiculous, like a partner at a family bank, but what was annoying was that no one else seemed to think so. It was frustrating to see one paper after another begin to print young Sedley's contributions. There was a time when the sharpest young newcomer had been one RT, but now this youngster was making him look old hat—or *vieux chapeau* as he would doubtless have put it (Tranter didn't speak French and thought it affected to use phrases from another language: "*Nostalgie de la boue*, my aunt Fanny," as he'd told the readers of *The Toad*).

In the whippersnapper Sedley's journalism there soon developed the prematurely weary voice of one who appeared to believe that, since the death of Lionel Trilling, it had fallen to him alone to uphold the purity of Literature. It sounded like hard going. The young man so recently scrabbling for work now appeared bowed down ("the finest life of Belloc that we have") by the gravity of his own significance. Yet more and more work seemed to flow his way.

Eventually, the gods relented. Though the seas threatened, as Prospero might have put it, they were merciful. After some years of successful self-promotion as the Leavis of the new millennium, Sedley made what Tranter could see straightaway was a schoolboy error: he proposed to publish a novel of his own.

As soon as he heard word of it, Tranter rang Patrick Warrender's office, but of course he was out, and his posh secretary made it sound unlikely that he'd call back even if he did get back from lunch before five o'clock. Then Tranter e-mailed Warrender about a review he was doing ("Just checking the word length on the Updike") and dropped a casual P.S.: "I gather A. Sedley is venturing into fiction. It might be interesting? Happy to have a look if you have no one else in mind. RT." There was no reply to that either, and he was forced into a daily blitzkrieg of telephone and e-mail. Eventually, he cornered his man.

"Yes," said Patrick, "I thought I'd let Peggy Wilson have a riffle through it. She's a great enthusiast for first-timers. Charming woman. D'you know her?"

Tranter stuttered at the other end. Peggy Wilson was the softest touch in town. Her group "roundups" were like a nursery teacher's first reports: all were "special" and all must have prizes.

"Oh, I think it's a bit more of a big deal, actually, Patrick. We wouldn't want to lose it in some sort of group thing. I'll probably be reading it anyway. Just out of interest."

"OK, I'll think about it. Is the Updike any good?"

At a party the following week, Tranter was appalled to see a young woman reviewer with a finished copy of Sedley's book in her shoulder bag.

He rang Patrick again the next day. Finally, his luck was in.

"Thank God you rang, RT. I'd completely forgotten about young Sedley. Peggy Wilson's having her hip done. She had a fall at the weekend and she's going to be out of action for a month at least. I'll get the publisher to send it straight to you. Let's do it for next weekend. Five hundred words."

The next day R. Tranter received by motorcycle courier the parcel he had long been wanting. The padded bag fell open to reveal a slim but expensively produced hardback from one of London's snootier publishers. The title alone gave him grounds for hope: *A Winter Crossing*. Inside was a compliments slip from the publicity department. "We're all very excited about Alexander Sedley's wonderful first novel. We publish on March 1st. I do hope you like it. Rachel x."

Tranter took the package upstairs to his flat, where he opened it carefully and sampled a sentence. He was too agitated to take it in properly. He flipped open the jacket at the back, where he hoped to see the face of his tormentor, but no: it was stylishly minimal. Sedley had supplied no photograph, and the two-line biography had no reference to his elite private school or even to his university. Good call, Tranter conceded. But even in the restraint, was there not smugness? "Alexander Sedley is chief literary critic for . . ." Who was he kidding? He's a penny-a-line reviewer like the rest of us, thought Tranter, not Sir Arthur Quiller-Bloody-Couch.

Tranter opened the book and tried another sentence. It wasn't *terrible*. It added up; the words were in a syntactical order; it made sense. How hard would he have to work to find a fault line in this novel—something he could get the end of his knife into and start levering? The guy was nearly forty now, a ridiculous age to be making his first venture into fiction. But suppose it had been, as his bum-chums were doubtless even now preparing to say, "well worth the wait"? God.

Tranter repaired to the kitchen, made a cup of tea and poured some dried food into a bowl for Septimus Harding. He went to look at his e-mails on the white PC, but found it unable to connect to the Internet. This often happened.

"SoftWare Works," as Patrick Warrender had irritatingly pointed out to him when he'd had trouble before. "A classic oxymoron. A palpable untruth. An actionable breach of the Trade Descriptions Act. Get a proper machine, Ralph."

When my biography of Alfred Huntley Edgerton wins the Pizza Palace prize, thought Tranter, that's the time to upgrade.

Then, for no clear reason, the egg timer suddenly unfroze and Tranter's functional inbox was revealed. "Hi there Bruno Banks!"

"Oh, piss off," said Tranter and hit delete.

"Are you sure you want to del—"

Delete. God, life was complicated sometimes. The virtual world consumed more time than the real one: much more, in fact, since his connection with the real one was—to borrow a word he'd come across in a sci-fi magazine—asymptotic.

When he had deleted the junk and replied briefly to an invitation to the launch of a war memoir ("Out of London that day, sadly"), Tranter felt strong enough to sit down and tackle Sedley.

With a cup of tea on the table next to him and with Septimus Harding on his lap, he licked his slightly trembling finger and turned to Chapter One.

For forty-five minutes there was no sound in R. Tranter's sitting room apart from the rustle of a woody page going over at two-minute intervals. The Bosnian war criminal revved his motorbike unheard; the Polish boys whooped and shouted through a full first half in their back garden. Tranter's eyes moved steadily, hungrily, from side to side. Inside his head, the neurons went silently about their business, the axons and the dendrites dutifully fired and received.

But after twenty minutes, a brain scan would have shown, in the part of Tranter's cortex that registered pleasure, some signs of activity—slight at first, then intermittent, then growing after half an hour to a row of pulsing alpine peaks.

At page forty-six, he dropped the book with a whoop of incredulous delight. Sedley's novel was not just bad; it was embarrassingly, deliciously lame. Tranter threw back his head and laughed out loud; it was worse, far worse than he had even dared to hope. He shivered with pleasure—then had a moment's doubt.

He reread a few sentences to reassure himself he hadn't just imagined it. But no. It was that bad.

He fast-forwarded and read a paragraph from page 219. All clear!

Tranter felt tears of mirth in the corner of his eyes. Sedley had not invented *anything*. He had had the whole world—all of history, all of time, to say nothing of fantasy and other worlds—to choose from: people of all ages and both sexes in every country of the earth. But with the cornucopia of material at his disposal, Sedley had chosen to write up . . . a few episodes from *his own earlier life*. It was a posh young man's coming of age; it even ended with his twenty-first birthday party—in dinner jackets!

But that wasn't all, Tranter thought. He'd written it in a style that was meant to be "poetic" or something. There was phrasemaking; there were descriptions that begged to be admired; and these purple bits weren't just intrusive, they were inept. Eye-catching similes were made from items that bore no resemblance to one another. It was arch, it was self-loving, it was impotent; it was so idiotic that Tranter felt a shiver of compassion for poor Sedley when he pictured the critical Culloden, the firestorm of derision that awaited him . . .

He took up *A Winter Crossing* again and settled back into his chair. Phrases began to form in his mind. His review would write itself; it would strangle Sedley's career at birth; it would be a cause célèbre—if that was the term he wanted.

And if only that had been the end of Sedley; if only Tranter's review had finished his career. But enough of Sedley's old school friends had gathered round; although the reviews had been "mixed" (mostly poor) there had been a couple of good ones; the book had not died of shame. Sedley still haunted him; over the intervening time, their lives, in fact, seemed to have become more and more entwined.

And now, Tranter reflected at his desk that Monday evening, the stuck-up little bastard stood between him and the Pizza Palace Book of the Year award.

At six o'clock, Gabriel said goodbye to Samson and the other clerks, then crossed the Temple to the Underground and took the Circle Line to Victoria.

At the other end of his short overground journey, he had to walk fifteen minutes from the suburban station to the hospital. He knew the way from five years of visiting his brother Adam in Glendale. He barely noticed the bookmaker's garish temptation, the pizzeria, the low-cost supermarket and the clothing chain; the surprisingly numerous pubs, some with Thai food and karaoke but most unregenerate and drab; the park, the dual carriageway, the famous red and gold burger outlet, once a single stall at San Bernardino racetrack; and then the forest of roadside warnings: camera, speed limit, hump and restriction. The bare chestnut trees were the first he saw of Glendale, their leafless branches dripping on the rusted iron rails. There was a porter's cabin with a raisable pole inside the main gates, where Gabriel was no longer asked to sign the visitors' book, but was simply waved through by Brian or Dave.

He held a cheap umbrella over his head as he walked up the tarmac drive, between the lime trees and the lawns beyond. Glendale was a relatively modern place, built mostly in the late 1960s, and its architect had avoided any suggestion of its famous Victorian precursors. There was no Italianate bell tower or home farm;

no sound of locking doors and footsteps fading into half-mile corridors. Its first building had been planned as a unit of a still-functioning but older general hospital, to which it remained connected by a corridor.

The brick buildings were many and low, with bright orange or scarlet curtains. Double doors swung freely under fierce strip lights. Most of the houses were single-story, double at the most, and took their friendly names from benefactors of the hospital: Collingwood, Beardsley, Arkell . . . In the rainy darkness, the whole complex might have passed for the barracks of an unconventional tank regiment or the headquarters of a government listening post, had it not been for the signs at the mini-roundabout, with their NHS logos, and then the smaller arrows on the buildings: X-Ray, Long-Stay Unit, Secure Wing, Rainbow Room (for the terminally ill, Gabriel presumed) and Electroconvulsive Therapy.

Adam was in Wakeley, a low house toward the back of the plot in the shade of half a dozen pine trees. Gabriel made his practiced way through the staff parking and the canteen delivery area with its giant cylindrical dustbins. The door was open onto the steamy kitchen behind, and he caught a whiff of a long-boiled gravy dinner as he passed.

Rob, the muscular charge nurse, was in the glass booth by the door of Wakeley when Gabriel went in.

"Evening, Rob. I called ahead. Did you get the message?"

"Yes, Dr. Leftrook told me. If you'd like to come with me . . ."

Gabriel followed Rob down a short passage and into the dining area of Wakeley. One or two patients sat in chairs round the edge of the space; these were people who had wanted to escape the television that played constantly in the dayroom beyond.

At one window was Violet, as she had been every time that Gabriel had ever visited: a thin, hunchbacked old woman, her skirt folded over at the waistband to keep it up, who stood gazing out into the darkness with her right arm raised in permanent greeting— or possibly farewell.

She didn't notice Rob and Gabriel as they went by. In the dayroom, the television was showing a celebrity competition with the sound turned up loud. There was a scuffle taking place for possession of the remote control between an elderly man, who wanted to change the channel, and a loud young woman with blond hair showing black roots who wanted to stick with the celebrities. The central heating had made the room so hot that most of the patients were in T-shirts. It was too dark to read; a single table lamp lit up a level, surging fog of cigarette smoke, through which Gabriel was just able to see his brother.

He crossed the room and stood in front of him. "Hi, Adam. Fancy a chat? Come into the other room?"

Adam showed no sign of recognition. He was eighteen months older than Gabriel, though looked more. He had developed a large belly and his uncut hair was shot through with gray.

"I've got something for you, Ad. Come on."

Adam followed Gabriel out of the fug, back a short way down the corridor and into a glass-walled room that was used by day for group therapy.

They sat down, alone in the room, where Gabriel opened a window onto the dark lawns behind. Wakeley was a low-security building and there were no extra locks or bars.

"How are things?" Gabriel held out a box of dates and a packet of cigarettes to his brother, who took them wordlessly.

When he was with Adam, Gabriel behaved toward him as though there was nothing wrong. There were a number of reasons for this. He thought Adam might appreciate it, might prefer not being talked down to or addressed as though insane. It made Gabriel feel better, too, as though the tragedy was contained and his brother was not ruined, wrecked. And how else was he supposed to carry on, in any case? What better form of speech might there be than the normal and respectful? And finally, most irrationally, he hadn't quite extinguished the hope that Adam might "snap out of it"; that since the corporeal shell remained his brother's, even if it had grown fat and shabby, somewhere inside it, like a thin flame still flickering in a deep, protected crevice, the man himself might still exist.

"Have you been able to get out at all? Have you been for walks? You should try and play some squash again. You used to like that."

Adam pulled a cigarette from the pack and lit it with an old gas lighter he kept with him at all times.

"You used to be too good for me," said Gabriel. "Remember how you thrashed me when we played at that club in London once?"

Adam inhaled greedily. When smoking had been outlawed in public places, banned outdoors and deemed unacceptable in every house in England, when cigarettes had been removed from sale in shops, Gabriel sometimes thought, the schizophrenic population would still find a way to light up.

"Are you married?" said Adam.

"You know me. Not one to rush things," said Gabriel.

"You can marry. You can take up to three wives. But then you must be faithful."

"Of course."

"If you are unfaithful, if you sleep with another man's wife, that means you'll be punished."

"I wouldn't do that."

"You'd be punished for all time. In the flames."

"Have you been receiving more instruction?"

Adam ignored the question.

"Who's been talking to you?" said Gabriel.

In the early days of Adam's illness, before anyone knew how ill he was, Gabriel had believed him when he spoke of meetings, visitors, instructions. When the details of the stories contradicted one another or became far-fetched, he had at first thought Adam was just exaggerating. Then, when it became clear that his brother was delusional, Gabriel had tried to get to the bottom of his private mythology, on the grounds that this imagined world must have a structure, and that by first knowing, then interrogating it, he might better understand and help him.

Over the long years, however, the hierarchy of Adam's control had remained elusive; what was beyond doubt was how real the people in it were to him. Whatever Eustace Hutton or Samson the clerk, whatever landlord, taxman, police and Parliament might have been to Gabriel, they didn't organize his life or bear down on his waking thoughts with such powerful and compelling credibility as the figures of authority in Adam's world. Gabriel sometimes felt that, in comparison, his own existence lacked conviction.

"The Messenger told me," said Adam in the same flat, affect-free voice he might have used to say "The nurse told me."

"I see," said Gabriel. "And on what authority?"

"You know," said Adam.

Gabriel didn't know. The ultimate self-grounded truth holder in Adam's mythology had been given various names at different times over fifteen years, but lately had shed them all in favor of something ineffable—yet inevitable: something just There.

"He destroyed your cities. He destroyed Sodom and Gomorrah. He killed the Jewish people because we told them what they believed was not lawful."

"What does all that old stuff matter, Ad? We're living here in Britain in the twenty-first century, in the here and now. We can't go on worrying about the cities of the plain and whether they deserved what they got. There's a lot of good stuff going on now."

Adam's eyes held his. "Be careful you don't burn. You can change your ways."

"Are you two all right?" Rob was standing in the doorway. "Would you like some tea?"

"Ad?" Adam didn't respond. "Well, I'd like some anyway. Thanks," said Gabriel.

When Rob came back with two cups, Gabriel said, "So how's he been?"

"Pretty good," said Rob. "Dr. Leftrook's still trying to get the balance absolutely right with the medication. It's a delicate thing."

"Yes, I know," said Gabriel. "She explained to me once."

"You can control the delusions, but at a price. How does he seem to you?"

"Well . . . I don't know. How you feeling, Ad?"

Adam lit another cigarette. "It's better to shed blood than not to believe," he said. "You have your chances to believe. You make the choice. And if you choose not to . . ."

Adam's fingers made a gesture of rising flames.

In Holland Park, Finbar Veals was having another evening on his own. His father was at a business dinner and his mother had gone out to a Japanese restaurant with the members of her book group—not for a discussion, she said, just for some sushi.

Finn stood up unsteadily from the floor. The skunk had not had the usual effect. There was a cold sweat on his forehead and a dryer than usual taste in his mouth. The joy of weed was the feeling of time dislocation that spread from the belly; the sense of the body being too heavy to register the speeding beauty of thought; the failure of words to express the depth of music, when the jaw grew too weighty to move.

What he felt was none of those things. It was more like a severance. He had moved into the alternative reality the drug provided, but had somehow become detached from the original world. So there was no joyous, comic interplay between the two ways of being—just a sense of separation.

He was shaking a little and he knew his face would be ultra-pale. He was undoubtedly doing what his best friend Ken called "throwing a whitey."

"Shit," he said, and went downstairs to the kitchen, where he struggled with the security locks on the French doors. Eventually he made it out into the garden for some air. Teenage wisdom didn't go so far as to recommend any cure for a "whitey" apart from just waiting for it to pass. There was nasty sweat on his forehead and in his palms, which the cold night air did nothing to dry.

He breathed in deeply as he walked up and down the lawn, glancing up at the big expensive houses all about him. He felt an odd sense of envy for their inhabitants—people he'd previously pitied. They were in their boring rooms, watching television or washing up after dinner, reading books or entertaining neighbors with their mind-numbing chat about schools and business and dreary people that they knew in common. But at least they were attached to the physical world.

To Finn, the piled brick courses of his parents' £10 million house looked of doubtful solidity. When he glanced up, he saw the giant idle cranes on the Shepherd's Bush skyline where they were building a monument to greed and possession—Europe's biggest shopping center, slap in the middle of the shop-lined streets of the world's most well-provided consumer city—and he saw above them an airliner dipping down through the clouds, wing lights flashing, as it descended toward Heathrow.

He felt a clutch of panic in his abdomen. He imagined himself in the tight little tube of the plane's fuselage, strapped in, going down to hit the ground. He tilted his head back quickly to find a bigger view, but found that the sudden movement made him feel sick, with blood raging up behind his eyes. He sat down on a stone step that led up to his mother's small rose garden. He put his head between his hands and squeezed his eyes shut. It was no good. There were too many images of light and furious color. He was better with his eyes open. He leaned against the trunk of a pleached hornbeam that separated the two parts of the garden and trained his gaze up toward the restful infinity of space.

Something about the light pollution gave a color-flattening gray to the lower sky, but made the upper reaches seem not infinite but obviously domed. His world was a sphere, inside another sphere, whose curvature was clear to him. He felt a wave of cosmic claustrophobia.

Shit, this stuff was strong. He just wanted to escape, to un-take it, un-smoke it, go back to what as a child he'd called "true life." Did his mother have tranquilizers? Probably she did, but how would he know which ones they were? And would they help?

The boy in Pizza Palace had promised him a "massive high," with no bad effects, but it had been a lie. His hands were shaking as he lay down on the cold grass and curled himself up into a fetal ball. He saw images of Alan the schizophrenic and Terry O'Malley leering down at him. He wrapped his thin arms round his T-shirt and felt the wetness of the grass on his smooth cheek. For once, he wanted his parents to come back—even for his father to be there. But they were out, away, and he was alone, trying with all his childish might to keep a grip on a reality that he could no longer properly inhabit.

Three

Tuesday, December 18

I

Amanda Malpasse said goodbye to Roger at the front door of their Chilterns farmhouse. She liked Roger well enough, she was truly fond of him, but since he'd been eased out of his job in a City law firm at the age of fifty-one she did see the old fellow pretty much round the clock. Both their children were at university, and there was only so much she could find to say to him about their numerous dogs and neighbors. London, on the other hand, reminded her of being young again, when she had lived in a flat with two girlfriends near the Fulham Road and had been, in the phrase of the time, a bit of a goer.

"Don't drink too much, darling." She always said this when she left him alone.

"Would I ever?" And he usually said this in return.

"And I'll be back at teatime tomorrow. We've got the Manns coming over."

"I know. Drive carefully."

By eleven, Amanda was in a café in North Park, where she had arranged to meet Sophie Topping, who wanted reassurance about her big dinner party that Saturday. Amanda didn't know Sophie well, but was happy to do what she could to help if it gave her an excuse to hit town. The café was also a *traiteur* and deli, where North Park women could buy precooked dishes of astonishing expense and quite edible quality.

Sophie was in the back room with another woman, whom she

100

introduced as Vanessa Veals. They were in midconversation about children and schools.

"Vanessa's daughter Bella is such a sweetie," Sophie explained to Amanda.

"I hardly ever see her," said Vanessa. "She's always off with her friends."

"That's because she's so popular!" said Sophie. "She really is a dear."

Vanessa looked unconvinced—more than that, thought Amanda: she looked unhappy.

Sophie prattled on. "And Finn's so clever, isn't he? I'll bet he'll do brilliantly in his GCSEs."

"He seems to have stopped working lately, though," said Vanessa.

"Doesn't John read him the riot act?"

"He used to push him like mad. He made a terrible scene when Finn didn't win a race at the sports day a couple of years ago. He was swearing at him, you know, saying, You effing this and effing that. But lately he seems to have lost interest."

The waiter brought three milky versions of coffee, but had no takers when he offered them food.

After half an hour talking about who was coming on Saturday and who would be sitting next to whom, Amanda said: "I know Roger's looking forward to it a lot. He loves parties. Don't give him too much wine, though, or he gets a bit overexuberant."

"You're lucky," said Vanessa. "I find it hard to get John to come to anything."

"He is coming, though, isn't he?" said Sophie anxiously.

"Oh, yes. It's a three-line whip. He just regards social life as a waste of time."

"What does your husband do?" said Amanda.

"He works," said Vanessa. "That's what he does. Work. He has a hedge fund. Most hedge-fund managers work hard, I know, but most of them have fun as well. They own a boat, they have a glider pilot's license. I know one who has a climbing wall in his house. There's another one who lives near us who plays the piano beautifully and plays chess for a club and goes to the theater twice a week and takes his wife to the opera. But John . . . I don't know."

"But he's very loyal and—"

"I tell you what I would like more than anything in the world." Vanessa's voice suddenly deepened against the chatter of the café, and the effect was odd, as of a sudden key change. Sophie and Amanda leaned forward. "I could forget the lack of fun," said Vanessa, "or his dread of parties or holidays or romance, I could forget everything if I could just once see him laugh."

There was an embarrassed pause. Although Sophie and her friends talked about little other than their families when they met, they were seldom indiscreet and never raw.

Sophie said, "He must sometimes laugh. I'm sure I've seen—"

"Never," said Vanessa. "When we were going out together, at first, in New York, I thought it was charming in an odd way. I could make him smile back then, and I think I was the only person who could. But laugh? Never. It has never been seen."

"Well," said Amanda, "I'll make that my special task on Saturday. To make your husband laugh."

"Good luck," said Vanessa, a more normal tone returning to her voice. "But I should warn you, that road is paved with the bodies of those who tried and failed."

When she got back to Holland Park, Vanessa found Bella on a rare visit home. She was making pasta in the kitchen.

"Hello, darling. How was Katie's?"

"Great, thanks. Would you like some pasta?"

"Is it lunchtime?"

"Yes, it's nearly one o'clock."

"No, thanks. I'll have . . ." Vanessa poured herself a glass of white burgundy from the fridge. "I had an apple earlier."

Bella took her bowl to the table and opened a carton of orange juice.

"What are you doing this afternoon?" said Vanessa.

"Going to a movie with Zoë. At Whiteleys. I can't wait till the new shopping center opens up. You know. Westfield."

From the kitchen window they could see the top of one of the giant red cranes that lowered over the site.

"Where I grew up in Wiltshire," said Vanessa, "there was only one cinema within a twenty-mile radius and it had only one screen."

"But that was in the Dark Ages, Mum."

"I suppose that's why I was always bolting up to London. Do you ever wish you'd been brought up in the country?"

"No," said Bella. "I like animals. I wouldn't have minded a pony. But that's about it."

"Don't you sometimes feel all the people you meet in London are a bit the same?"

"Yeah, but I like that. Gotta go now. See you later."

"Yes, darling. Have fun."

All of Vanessa's family were mysterious to her, though none more than her husband. She often wondered at the way John seemed so exactly suited to the modern world. It was something to do with tunnel vision, she thought, of being unaware of contingency.

She herself had read psychology at university, trained as a lawyer in London, then worked for a petroleum company in New York, before finding a position with a charitable foundation; this was what she had been doing when she met John Veals with his then colleague Nicky Barbieri on Long Island. So for a time in the late 1980s and early 1990s, Vanessa Whiteway had been on the edge of the financial world and had seen how it transformed itself.

The essential change seemed to her quite simple: bankers had detached their activities from the real world. Instead of being a "service" industry—helping companies who had a function in the life of their society—banking became a closed system. Profit was no longer related to growth or increase, but became self-sustaining; and in this semivirtual world, the amount of money to be made by financiers also became unhitched from normal logic.

It followed, Vanessa thought, that the people who could flourish here must themselves be, in some profound and personal way, detached. They could have no qualms about the effects of what they did; no cares for the collateral impact—although, to do them justice, they did take precautions to minimize the possibility of any contact with reality; indeed the joy of the new products was exactly their magical self-sufficiency, the way they appeared to eliminate the risk of any final reckoning. However, it remained necessary for these people to have—or to develop very quickly—a very limited sense of "the other"; a kind of functional autism was the ideal state of mind.

And in addition to this, there must be a passionate faith: they had to believe that theirs was the true system and that earlier beliefs had been heretical. Where there were doubts, they had to be excised; where there were qualifications, they needed to be cauterized. A breed of fanatic was born, and Vanessa saw them with her own blue eyes. She met them at off-site bonding sessions in Florida, at charity dinners and—dog-tired and windburned—at the end of golfing weekends in Scotland. Although she wasn't there for the lectures or the golf or the drinking, and glimpsed them only at the lobby or the airport, she could tell that these loners had reinforced one another's beliefs over the three days away; that by the end of their exhausting rituals they were reinvigorated in their faith—convinced they needed nothing and nobody beyond their own fantastic circuitry.

What intrigued Vanessa about John was how easily he had fitted into the required psychological profile. To hear him talk of his North London childhood, you would have foreseen nothing so extraordinary; his school performance was unremarkable and his family had neither "spoiled" nor bullied him. There were no "formative" incidents that made him set his face against the world, no early loss or trauma for which he needed to compensate.

In fact, when she thought about John, Vanessa found the whole toolbox of her undergraduate psychology classes to be useless. There was no "compensation," no subliminal desires or reenactments. What there was, in her view, was a simple and unmotivated collision of two things: the way these new financiers were by nature, and the way the world, for the first time ever, had indulged them.

Some people thought the crux of it was the invention of some credit derivative products by a few people at J. P. Morgan; but in fact, in Vanessa's mind, the key was that society as a whole in London and New York had so lost its bearings that it was prepared to believe, with these analysts, that cause and effect could be uncoupled. To her, this social change, the result of decades of assault on long-accepted norms, was far more interesting than the quasi-autistic intellects of the people, like John, who worked in the new finance.

Very occasionally, these individuals were compelled to interact with society—most notably when it looked as though politicians might regulate them; then for a moment they were required to leave their cloister and dirty their hands in the world. The largest check that John Veals had ever written was to a political lobbying firm in Washington when he, and the bank for whom he was then working, feared that credit derivatives might be the subject of government regulation. They had contributed $3 million to the fees of the key lobbyist on Capitol Hill.

One other moment came to Vanessa's mind, one other instance when her husband had collided with the old world of obligation and debt that he had outgrown. It came when she accompanied him to a function addressed, quite recently, by the British Prime Minister. What had it been? A Lord Mayor's dinner? The opening of a bank's offices in Canary Wharf? She could no longer remember. What she could recall clearly was the way the Prime Minister lowered his voice with the stagey vibrato that politicians used to convey "sincerity" and, congratulating the assembled financiers, had said words to the effect that: "What you have done for the City of London, we now intend to do for the entire British economy."

She looked at John and thought he was going to faint. All color had left his face and he was holding hard to the edge of the table. She put her hand on his. At first she thought he was appalled at the idea that his own circle's understanding of the world was about to be stolen and made public by a man who was not really of their faith. Later, she understood that the loss of blood was, paradoxically, his way of blushing: of betraying shame.

She had never seen a trace of it again—of shame, or doubt, or the embarrassment of reconnection with the world; it was all over in that moment.

And when little Sophie Topping asked her if she still "loved" her husband, it was not a question that Vanessa felt she could answer. How could you "love" such a man? "What makes him tick?" "What does he enjoy?" "When you're alone, what does he . . . ?" None of these were questions to which Vanessa could give an answer, because her husband had long ago migrated to a place where such matters had no meaning.

II

Growing up in Glasgow, Hassan al-Rashid was aware from an early age of the differences between people. His family was richer than average and he had things other children didn't—better toys, more pocket money, newer clothes. He went to the mosque and prayed, while few of the "Christians" bothered with religion, unless you counted a weeklong alcohol binge at Christmas. Hassan felt lucky to be well off, anxious about being different, and angry that his family didn't seem to have the respect it deserved. Surely his father, such a good man and so hardworking, should at least have been the Mayor of Renfrew.

At home, his father sang him traditional songs and read to him from the Koran. Knocker's version of Islam was musical and poetical. Although he had never actually read the Koran, he was a fair scholar of the parts that appealed to him—the nice bit in "The Bee," for instance, which suggested that in emergency you could even eat pork, and, so long as you meant no harm, God would turn a blind eye; and as a motto for daily life, Knocker thought, you couldn't do much better than the verse in "The Night Journey": "Do not walk proudly on the earth. You cannot split the earth, nor can you rival the mountains in stature."

In truth he would have preferred it had the book carried fewer angry assurances about the eternal punishment that awaited every nonbeliever, but he tended not to listen when the most spiteful of these were recited in the mosque. At the end of every such recital, he would happily intone the words: "In the name of God, the compassionate, the merciful." These were the qualities of Allah that Knocker al-Rashid was interested in. He was like a Church of England Christian who paid lip service to the Bible as a whole, but only believed in the New Testament because the Old, while full of good stories, was ancient Judaic stuff, of chiefly anthropological interest.

The pith of Islam was likewise to be found selectively, Knocker thought, not so much in the hellfire-for-infidel Koran as in the gentle teachings of many generations of wise and kind old men. Knocker's spiritual belief was secure: he had trust in the omnipotence of Allah and no doubt that a place in paradise awaited him, so long as he remained strong in his devotions and pure in his behavior. His faith enabled him to ride over financial turbulence and local hostility, because he knew there was a truth that lay beyond cash flow and VAT, deeper than the prejudices of some of the people he dealt with. He could always detach himself from them; and most business associates found that his soft answers turned away their suspicions.

As a child, Hassan had songs and verses, stories and prayers embedded in his memory, and perhaps because they were offered to him in an atmosphere of affection and calm, they lodged there like the first marks in wet concrete, never to be erased. He had a pure voice, and under an imam's guidance became adept at *tajwid*, the art of Koranic recital. This could be emotional and competitive, with the reciters wanting to see who could produce the biggest reaction, but when at the end of the service the congregation would stand and sing greetings to the Prophet, Hassan felt secure enough in who he was.

The world outside his home, however, was more troubling. He was made aware that his skin was of a different color from that of his pasty classmates. By the age of eleven—a slight, black-haired child with wide brown eyes in a Dundee-woven school blazer—he knew a fair amount about the planets and the solar system, but almost nothing of the earth. He was astounded when a prematurely developed Scottish classmate punched him in the solar plexus at break time. As he lay gasping in the corridor, the pain that seeped from him seemed to crystallize into a small certainty. It was a moment he never forgot. The world was not fair, or reasonable, or loving. You could therefore either fight within it like the others, or you could look for a better explanation and a superior way of life.

There were prayer groups and special trips up to the Highlands or down to the Lake District with others of his faith, but while Hassan was thrilled by the stories of Noah, Joseph and others in the Koran, he didn't want to be a special case, in a gaudy coach with wailing music and a devout driver. He watched the same programs on television as the rest of the children in his class; he went to the same films at the ABC and even supported a football team (Kilmarnock: choosing between Rangers and Celtic had been too fraught). While his father's Punjabi accent was overlaid with a West Riding inflection, Hassan spoke Glaswegian English like the native he was. Much as he liked his parents, he didn't want to make a fetish of them and their culture; he didn't want to be singled out and stared at, in the way he and his friends gawped at the Jewish children who left early on a Friday in order to be home in Giffnock before dark.

Hassan tried on different disguises. At fourteen he was all Scottish and atheistic: he exaggerated his interest in football and girls; he drank cider and beer from the off-license and was sick in the park. He derided the women in hijab, calling out insults after them: "Bloody penguins!" "Daleks!"

He enjoyed the sense of release and belonging, but the specific boys that he was obliged to spend his time with all repelled him. At least he was putting on a front, he thought; he was being perverse with the knowledge that a solid cliff of learning and culture lay behind him. But for these boys, the swearing, the bravado and the sex talk was everything: the foulmouthed emptiness was all they had. By the time he was seventeen, Hassan had come to despise these friends and was looking for another cloak to wear.

It was at this time that his father announced that the family was heading south. He had opened a new factory, in Dagenham, and wanted to supervise its early days himself. The Renfrew operation no longer required his presence and he had installed reliable men in Leicester and Luton, where he had smaller units producing a range of pickles and sauces. He had hired a culinary scientist at Cambridge to try to develop what he viewed as the holy grail: a microwaveable poppadom. The ready-cooked ones in sealed packs lacked flavor, while the old-fashioned sort, which needed deep-frying, tended either to burn or to collect fat in their folds. Either way, they were too much work for the modern person.

Meanwhile, Nasim, Farooq's wife, was tired of the rainy streets of Glasgow. She was still young enough to yearn for the shops and theaters of London, where she pictured herself lunching with elegant friends in Piccadilly, then meeting Knocker in the foyer of the National Theatre. There were not enough spending opportunities in Glasgow for her to dispose of the generous allowance her husband made her, but London . . . Her idea of it was based on television programs and newspaper supplements with pictures of boorish chefs and thin models with brand names coming off the pages in a flickering, subliminal staccato. This year's go-to, must-see, gotta have . . . She didn't know why there was such urgency about a "raunchy" musical or a shiny handbag but she wanted to find out, before she was too old.

Havering-atte-Bower wasn't what Nasim had had in mind. It was almost in Essex. Knocker pointed out to her that in Knightsbridge or Notting Hill they couldn't have had such a lovely house, with an acre of garden, in sight of Edward the Confessor's old hunting lodge. They were at the highest point of Greater London, 110 meters above sea level, surrounded by three parks, with open country to the north and extended views in all directions. It was convenient for the Dagenham factory; and for Nasim, Knocker pointed out, it was a short drive to Upminster station, from where the District Line could take her straight to Sloane Square.

"Do I want a view of Purfleet?" said Nasim. "Or the M25?"

"Yes," said Knocker. "You may grow to like them both."

"And who was Edward the Confessor?"

"I think he was an English king, or perhaps a monk. A good man anyway."

Hassan was pleased to make the move with his parents. He'd been arrested in Renfrew during a scuffle outside a club. After a night in a police cell, he'd come before the magistrates and been given a lecture and a conditional discharge. He told his parents he had stayed the night at a friend's, and the local paper's court reporter didn't connect his name to that of his father, so no account of it appeared.

So that was the law, thought Hassan, as he left the court. He wondered how many people had criminal records that they had concealed from their families. He certainly felt no obligation to tell his.

Running with the non-Muslim gang hadn't helped his work, and neither did the move down south. He caught the second year of sixth form in a new school and did well enough in his exams only to squeeze into the University of South Middlesex, a clumped aggregation of prestressed concrete and multiple fire doors in one of the wider streets of Walworth. He put his name down to study social policy.

One night after lectures in his first term, Hassan found himself by chance at a meeting of the Left Student Group. One of the third-years was giving a talk called "Multiculturalism: The Broken Dream" and something in the title appealed to Hassan.

The speaker was a scrawny white Londoner with a fluent manner.

"The advertisement read as follows," he said, leaning forward to the lectern and adjusting his glasses as he looked down at a piece of paper. " 'We are trying to recruit from all sections of the community. Because of the specific nature of the work, the number of self-confessed Jews we can appoint will be subject to certain limitations.' "

He lifted the piece of paper and shook it at his audience. "And this," he said, "is not the product of some neo-Nazi dictatorship, this is from a local council in our very own capital. Yes. Think about that."

The audience thought about it, and didn't like it.

"And yes," said the speaker, "the wording has been modified by me, with 'self-confessed Jews' instead of 'gay men,' but, it should be stressed, that is the only amendment. Not good, is it?"

There was a murmur of assent.

"What was the advertisement for?" said Hassan.

"Not sure," said the student next to him. "Some sort of youth team leaders, I think."

"Have these people already forgotten who went into the gas chambers at Belsen and Auschwitz?" said the speaker. "Not only the Jews, but tens of thousands of gypsies and what the local council in question would doubtless call 'self-confessed homosexuals.' We must fight homophobia wherever it appears. It is a virus as vicious as racism. In fact, homophobia *is* racism."

Hassan had given little thought to homosexuality. No one he knew in Glasgow had admitted to being gay, and the teaching of the Koran on this matter hardly encouraged debate. Meanwhile, the speaker's voice was rising: ". . . and such views are symptomatic of a much wider and deeper hostility and intolerance of otherness. Only last week, a London evening paper felt able to sponsor a debate entitled 'Is Islam Good for London?' Do another substitution here and imagine the reaction if Judaism had been the subject. Are Jews good for London? You just can't picture that question being posed in a civilized society. Yet there are still those who claim that Islamophobia can't be racist, because Islam is a religion not a race! They're fooling themselves. A religion is not only about faith but also about identity, background and culture. As we know, the Muslim community is overwhelmingly non-white. Therefore Islamophobia is racist—and so is anti-Semitism."

Hassan was aware that a kind of slip of logic had taken place in the last two sentences—perhaps that a part and a whole had swapped places, or that an implied "moreover" had become a "therefore"—but he couldn't put his finger on it. What he could see was that the flapping dove had been pulled from the conjuror's top hat and so, like the others, he applauded. He was against racism, and homophobia and Islamophobia. He didn't see how he could not be.

Soon, Hassan became a regular at the LSG meetings. They talked about things that had previously troubled him in a peripheral, unformed way; but what was most attractive to him was that the LSG seemed to have an answer to all these uncertainties—a unified explanation of everything. In this way, he thought, it was itself a bit like a religion. When you went to the imam, he could answer all your questions; that, for believers, was the point of him. Presumably it was the same with the Christians and the Jews: no religion would offer partial solutions or offer help on only *some* of the big issues, while admitting that on the others it hadn't a clue. So it was with the LSG. Once you'd got into their way of thinking, there was nothing it couldn't explain: everything could be seen as the wish of the powerful to exploit the weak. As a template for understanding the world, it drew its strength from the fact that it was grounded on the basest part of human nature—the only thing that defined the species: power. Power expressed through money. But really just power. The other attractive thing about the LSG view of the world was that, once you'd cracked it, it was instantly practicable. It was as though after a one-week correspondence course you could sight-read all music, from "Frère Jacques" to Scarlatti.

Hassan felt ready to try his new skill on an audience, and began with his parents. They disagreed with him, as he'd expected, but what impressed him was how easily he was able to counter all their objections. The LSG model told him that any international situation could be seen as imperialism and its descendants manipulating the less developed, while domestic issues were always about economic exploitation. Abroad, there was a hierarchy of ownership and race that could not be bucked (it was like a card game: spades always trump diamonds; white always exploits black), while at home the ownership of property and/or employment conferred powers in exact proportion to the value of the item owned. Rich, Western-backed Israel was the source of all stress in the Middle East; America, being the biggest and wealthiest country, was by natural logic the worst offender: the embodiment of the power principle.

There were in this system no variables or abstracts, nothing fickle, unpredictable or unquantifiable. Here were the simple laws of physics, before any uncertainty principle. To suggest that people acted for any reason other than economic or cultural self-advancement was willfully to ignore the evidence; you might as well believe in Creationism. And with these rules of caste and behavior in mind, you could impute motive with certainty. You knew what drove decisions, because only one motive existed.

"You've become very cynical," said Nasim. "You sound so disillusioned with life."

"Not disillusioned," said Hassan, quoting an LSG speaker. "Unillusioned. There's a crucial difference."

For at least a year, the certainty of his understanding gave Hassan a new confidence. It made him feel better able to talk to his fellow students and more at ease with his parents, whom he could see in a clearer, if smaller, perspective.

It was a kind of joy. He no longer felt brown-skinned or alien or different; he felt enfranchised into a brotherhood of the wise. The many new friends he made through the LSG came from a variety of families, but they had a common intelligence and a bond of knowledge: they had the keys to the kingdom, and Hassan was pleased to be in their number.

What he had found, he told himself, was identity, and an international one at that; what he had stumbled across was nothing less than himself—and such a discovery was sure to be exhilarating.

Two years after he had first chanced across the LSG, there was an emergency meeting about the American and British occupation of Iraq.

Hassan was standing at the back, next to Jason Salano, a confident third-year whose grandparents had come to London from

Jamaica. The second speaker of the evening was a guest from outside the college, an angry woman from a race relations advisory board.

"Let there be no doubt," she said from the lectern, "the West wishes to have a base in the Middle East so that if and when its ally Saudi Arabia undergoes a revolution and a new fundamentalist Saudi government is hostile to the West—as Tehran, remember, once kicked out BP—then America and its friends can still have guaranteed access to cheap oil. Did it ever occur to you when the American military was slaughtering Iraqi civilians that Iraq, far from possessing dangerous weapons with intent to use them on the West, was in fact very easy to subdue? Did you ever pause to think that this was precisely *why* Bush and Blair selected Iraq—not because it was strong and threatening, but for precisely the opposite reason: because it was weak and cheap to invade?"

She paused rhetorically. "It makes sense to the United States to invade countries where it can first use overpowering force to win the war at minimum cost to itself, and then award long-term business contracts to its own multinational companies for decades afterward to rebuild the devastated country in the American image. Cue Dick Cheney and Haliburton. I'm not saying Saddam Hussein was a blameless leader. But I am saying that Iraq under his leadership had one of the more enlightened regimes in the Middle East, particularly in regard to women's rights and religious freedoms."

It was an odd thing, Hassan sometimes thought, that although all the LSG people were atheists, they were often concerned for the religious freedoms of others. The Mormons of North America were Creationist bigots, but the Shias of Mosul, it seemed, had their rights. The Protestants of Bogside used their brute numbers to suppress the Roman Catholics—whose kitsch little shrines, on the other hand, being all they had, were entitled to protection. Sometimes Hassan worried that this was a perverted kind of colonialism—little better than the French Empire which, long after it had ditched religion at home, was concerned to send nuns and missionaries to the people it colonized in Africa and Indochina.

It wasn't that hard to explain, though, this apparent inconsistency. Religious belief, he thought, was always subservient to the power motive and therefore . . .

At this moment, Jason Salano jabbed him in the ribs with his elbow. "Stick your hand up, Jock."

"What?"

"Stick your hand up, Jock. We're voting for immediate withdrawal."

Dazed and a little bruised, Hassan raised his arm and made himself one with the crowd.

"What did you call me?" he said, as the applause for the speaker and the carried motion died down.

"What do you mean?" said Jason Salano.

"Did you call me 'Jock'?"

"Don't get like that, man. It's just a friendly term. You know. It's like the way you talk, man. Like the Welsh guy, we call him 'Dai' Thomas."

"I see," said Hassan. He felt the sudden, icy recoil of cultural loathing that he'd felt toward the foulmouthed Glasgow boys—a desire for higher ground, with cleaner air. "And does that mean I call you Rasta?"

"Aye. Ye can gi' me a wee nickname anytime ye fancy, Jock." Jason laughed. "Come on, man. Let's go. I'm hungry. It's time for my tea."

As he walked away from the college and toward the Tube, Hassan felt his belly grow acid with anger. He had tried as a boy to find a place of safety and light where he could be a good, true thing. God knows, it hadn't been easy, what with his different-colored skin, the complication of his parents' relative wealth—to say nothing of their religion and of being always in a minority. And then in the LSG he had found people of like mind to whom these superficial things were of no interest because they were all just citizens of a multicultural world. And now . . . *Jock*.

He spat the word out as he walked up Walworth Road in the icy rain toward the Tube station at the Elephant and Castle. Well fuck *them*, he thought. He was close to tears. The truth was that for a long time now he had been dissatisfied with what the LSG was offering, and Jason's crude intervention had served only to make him confront the fact that he had been avoiding: that politics alone were not enough.

A bicycle with no lights on shot past him along the pavement, making him leap to one side.

A few days later, he began a blog on YourPlace.

Blog blog blog blog feel a bit funny doing this. blog blog blog. OK what am I trying to say?

The thing is I feel confused. I guess most guys of my age are trying to find what they believe in. I see it at college, I saw it at school. I liked that about college at first, the passion. Of course I didn't go for the same things as everyone else like folk dancing or astronomy. But I had principles, I had passions and I knew what was right. Trouble was I just couldn't put it all together, I couldn't find a scheme that explained everything. Then I thought I'd found an answer in politics. We had some very good meetings and I caught a glimpse of how there could be a unified explanation.

My father was a religious man, he still *is* a religious man. When I was a kid I used to recite the Koran in public. I learned enough Arabic to recite well at the mosque. When I was eleven, *tajwid* was my thing. That's a special way of recitation. Blog blog blog. Who on earth will read this? I'm talking to myself, aren't I?

God I'm like a fifteen-year-old locked up in his room wondering if he EXISTS! You can see from my "doormat" how old I really am and what I look like.

I lost interest in religion when I was at school because I felt it was divisive. It was pushing me away from my friends and making a foreigner of me. My experience of politics at college underlined this. It made religion look kind of tribal and a drag on progress which was to get people to understand how exploitation works, how economic systems are geared, how the U.S. runs the Middle East, etc. How the wretched of the earth toil for the rich.

Then I had a sort of road to Damascus—road to Mecca, more like—moment. I saw that identity was more important than economic power and that till we've got that sorted out we're going nowhere fast. Is this back to square one?

Hassan stopped typing. He'd in theory been a "member" of Your-Place for two years but hardly ever logged in. His "doormat," or welcome screen, gave little away and he wasn't much interested in what had happened to the children he'd been at school with, even though one or two of them had graffitied his bulletin board.

Blogging was the last resort of the loser, he thought, as his eye ran down the accounts of going to the pictures, trying out new restaurants, arriving at airports to visit far-flung aunties. They were like an end-of-year round robin sent by a cousin so boring he'd been exiled as a penance to Patagonia. The videos were worse: shaky travelogues filmed from the back of taxis on mobile phones, or music promos of women thrusting out their groins.

Most of these people just seemed to be asking for confirmation that they existed, thought Hassan. The answer was, they did. Unfortunately. Now millions of them could show each other just how empty their existence was.

But he still resumed his typing, two-fingered and accurate.

Within the week his homepage had a "jab," as YourPlace called it, from someone called Grey_Rider, who said he was very interested in what Hassan had written and thought perhaps he could help. It would be better to meet in person and he suggested an Internet café at the top of Tottenham Court Road.

Hassan thought about it for a few moments. It was the sort of thing your parents warned you against, but he was no longer twelve years old. What could go wrong? At the worst, the man would be a pervert, in which case he'd just walk out. From a life in Glasgow and London he'd at least picked up some street nous.

Seated in a booth, with a takeaway cup of tea from the next-door Café Bravo, Hassan passed the time by connecting to his e-mail server. Grey_Rider, it was agreed, would recognize him from his YourPlace photograph so there was no need for any red carnation in the buttonhole of his bomber jacket.

"You must be Hassan."

He hadn't noticed the man in the next booth. How long had he been there while Hassan was going through his webmail?

"Aye."

Hassan stood up and found his right hand warmly clasped.

"My name is Salim. No need for this pseudonym nonsense anymore."

Hassan found himself shaking hands with a man of about thirty, taller than he was, of African parentage, Ethiopian maybe, with a candid, friendly expression and a London accent. He put his arm briefly round Hassan's shoulder. He had an earring in his left lobe.

"There's a juice bar not far from here. We could go and have a chat there if you like."

"All right." Hassan was aware of how guarded he must seem and regretted not being able to respond more openly to Salim's friendly manner, but the way they'd met had after all been pretty strange: from the hypothetical reality of pseudonymous e-mail to the warmth of human touch.

In Grafton Way, Salim led him into a juice bar/café with light-weight metal chairs and circular tables. It was the kind of place Hassan liked—modern, teetotal and one of a dwindling number not owned by Café Bravo, Folger's or some other U.S. monster with sour, expensive coffee, glutinous muffins and a long queue.

He ordered mango juice and noticed Salim did the same.

"I saw your thing on YourPlace," said Salim. "I use this, like, powerful search engine that picks up a lot of keywords. Then, when I read what you'd written I couldn't stop laughing."

"I know it was a wee bit teenage, it's just—"

"No, no, I didn't mean that. I laughed because it was so right. Me and you were meant to meet."

"We were?" Hassan felt himself smile a little, despite his caution. Burly Salim reminded him of Baloo the Bear in the *Jungle Book* cartoon.

"We were." Salim smiled. "I run a discussion group at a mosque not far from where you live. Near Pudding Mill Lane. We meet after prayers once a week and we discuss our faith and our lives, how we can bring the two together. A lot of traditional Muslims, I think they pay lip service if you know what I mean, and when they've said their prayers they think that's it. But we share our thoughts on how the Koran's a program for all you do. Islam's for life."

"Not just for Christmas," said Hassan.

"What?"

"Silly joke. Like a dog. It was an RSPCA advert. 'A dog is for life, not just for—'"

"Do you make a lot of jokes about religion?"

"No, no. Not at all," said Hassan quickly. Shit.

"Are you from Scotland?"

"Yes," said Hassan. "Is that relevant?"

"No. Not to our purposes." Salim smiled again.

"Good."

"Well, do you think you'd like to come along and try it? You obviously know the scriptures and you're looking for something more meaningful in your life."

Hassan thought. It was a little disappointing, just to be called back to the old faith. But in another way, he felt it was time. There was something attractive about going home, returning to the fundamental things, when politics alone had let him down. "Jock." God.

"All right," he said. "On condition I don't have to give any speeches or public declarations."

"Sure," said Salim. "We're perhaps a bit more fervent than people of your father's generation. You know. But we're traditional too. It's all based on scripture, not on interpretation."

119

"But no public speaking? You promise?"

"I think you'll find you want to. But it's entirely up to you."

Salim paid the bill and gave Hassan a booklet to read. "Our next meeting's on Wednesday. Will I see you there?"

"Maybe. Probably."

III

Gabriel Northwood was staring through the window of his barrister's chambers at the warm drizzle that was starting to fall on Essex Court. He had finished the Tuesday "brutal" sudoku and had fallen back on the "Testing." He tossed the puzzles into the wastepaper basket and picked up a copy of the novel he was reading, one of Balzac's slower ones, which he'd borrowed from the library since he no longer had enough money to buy books. The pace didn't bother him. He didn't care for too much narrative in novels, and he liked the solidity of the Master's specification: the stone flags, lead and verdigris; the inky writs and rent books. He held it in his left hand and, with his feet up on the desk, he used his right to click the mouse over the e-mail icon and watched the inbox unfurl from the dock.

There were two new messages. His accountant. Subject: Your VAT return. Then, sophie@thetoppings.com. Subject: Dec 22: pour-mémoire.

He had forgotten he was meant to go to dinner with them. Perhaps he had meant to forget. In the human mind, the French psychologist Pierre Janet had claimed, nothing ever gets lost; it was merely a question of whether the route to finding it was blocked by other traffic or by a hidden desire to forget—as Janet's one-time colleague Sigmund Freud maintained; for in our thought processes, the old Moravian dream-reader had believed, nothing is ever accidental.

By this reasoning, Gabriel was a contributor to his own failure. His lack of work couldn't be ascribed only to chance or to the judgments of solicitors who didn't brief him—or even to his own performances in court; there must on his part have been at least an element of volition.

Perhaps, thought Gabriel. He didn't remember how he'd met the Toppings in the first place—probably through Andy Warshaw, his friend in Lincoln's Inn; then all it had needed was one attendance at their house, reasonable manners, and he was forever listed as a solitary man who could be summoned to sit between female strangers.

Yet the thought of dinner was attractive to Gabriel. The food at lunchtime in the dining hall was no longer the bargain it had once seemed; he disliked sitting on long benches with other barristers and he disapproved of the way they called the dining hall "Domus," to rhyme with "comb-us," as though they could rewrite Ovid's scansion in their own dog-Latin. The Toppings would doubtless have caterers who'd be obliged to provide a minimum of three courses. Most of the other guests would probably spend the evening trying not to eat, pushing the food round the plate while offering insincere compliments. Someone had to put the stuff in his mouth, and Gabriel was thin enough to eat three dinners single-handed; a week before, he had bought some braces (from the Oxfam shop, he couldn't help noting) to keep up the trousers of his suit.

Samson put his head round the door. "Tea in Mr. Hutton's room, Mr. Northwood."

"Thank you," said Gabriel.

The Thames was just visible from the window of Eustace Hutton, QC's room, where members of the chambers stood among the boxes of documents and the towers of lever-arch files from which curled yellow gummed-paper markers. When Hutton walked over to the Royal Courts of Justice, the clerks preceded him with railway porters' trolleys on which they wheeled the weight of papers his Appeal Court appearances necessitated. "If I might request your lordships to start the day with a little housekeeping," Hutton invariably began, speaking from within his piled redoubt of cardboard boxes, while identifying for the judges the system by which he would refer to documents he wanted them to see.

Equally invariably, their lordships, however scintillating on matters of jurisprudence, grumbled about the paperchase. "Box four, file two, appendix three, page forty-four, paragraph seven . . . Is this not something of a record—even for you, Mr. Hutton?"

Gabriel rested his teacup on a ziggurat of his head of chambers' upcoming briefs and looked out of the window, down toward the river. Swollen with December rain, it was gliding on beneath the lights of the Embankment, under Blackfriars Bridge, above the embedded railway underpass, below Southwark Bridge and over the buried Cannon Street commuter lines—under, over, under, like a liquid weave, thought Gabriel, as it made its way through the old slums of Limehouse and Wapping, where watermen with lanterns in the bow had once pulled bodies from the water, and on toward the sea—or at least to the tidal barrier at Woolwich against which the swollen oceans were rising.

After tea, back in his room, Gabriel took off his jacket and loosened his tie. He put his feet on the desk and picked up the crossword. "Butcher has ox tongue." It was the last clue, and if "boxcar" going down was right, which he was sure it was, it began with an "X." And since there was also an "X" in the clue, this suggested an anagram. He looked away, out of the window, then looked back, and, as though by itself, the word formed in his mind. "Xhosa." The African language, or "tongue." "Butcher" was not the man it had seemed, but a verb—a command to cut up "has ox." Purists preferred that anagram indicators be verbs, and an imperative was even better. Every word worked its passage, yet the surface meaning was fluent, unimpeachable; it passed the ultimate test—that it could be read not as a cryptic clue but as a normal statement.

He wasn't quite sure which part of Africa the Xhosa tribe inhabited. Was Nelson Mandela perhaps a Xhosa? Well, he wasn't a Zulu, he was fairly sure of that. Zulus no longer made him think of Michael Caine at Rorke's Drift, but of Saul Bellow, who, when defending the teaching of dead white male writers to university students during some multicultural debate, had declared himself open to authors from other countries, and happy to teach them, but unsure about who they were. "Who is the Proust of the Zulus?" he had asked. "I should like to read him."

Gabriel typed the words "Bellow" and "Zulus" into his search engine. It turned out that the actual quotation was "Who is the Tolstoy of the Zulus? The Proust of the Papuans? I'd be glad to read him."

Bellow, as a Canadian-Russian Jewish immigrant to Chicago, could say things like that because he was himself the human outcome of persecution and upheaval. This gave him an advantage and an immunity. When he revealed a new character to be the dean of an arts faculty it was as good as saying that the tragedy of the century would run through his veins; he was Everyman as much as Bellow's creature, and the stresses and desires of his campus life in the broad-shouldered city would have a global relevance that could be sensed equally in Minsk and Tokyo. Philip Roth likewise, Gabriel thought: the more fiercely he focused on the making of gloves or luggage in Newark and the minutiae of sexual desire, prostate surgery or coming death, the broader, paradoxically, seemed the resonance. For German-Protestant Updike it had been harder, since he was by birth aligned with a majority; but something about his detailed love of America, itself so diverse that it was barely an entity, had periodically at least allowed him to present his characters as representatives of something that reached beyond their native Shillington, PA. Culturally, it had remained impossible for a realistic British novelist to transcend Leicester or Stoke; the place names alone seemed to laugh at the idea.

Gabriel found his thoughts turning to Jenni Fortune, another result of human migration. What a frightened little whippet she had seemed when first she came in for a conference. He guessed that the panoply of law, the threat of Latin and long words alarmed her. Yet she drove a train. People entrusted their lives to her. As the months went by, he'd come to see that it wasn't intelligence she lacked and it wasn't character; it was confidence. He supposed her education in the local state school hadn't done much to supply the missing quality. He could tell from the way her eyes were always straying to his bookshelves that she was a reader, but when he'd first tried to draw her on the subject of her favorite authors, she clammed up.

What was this thing with women and confidence? he wondered, not for the first time. Catalina had had more of it than Jenni, though even she at some deeper level found it difficult to believe in her own value. Imagine Eustace Hutton ever doubting himself. Even Terry the junior clerk thought the world should move across and make room for him.

In Old Pye Street, meanwhile, it was a lethally quiet morning. John Veals spoke to no one. Those who knew him well—Stephen Godley, in other words—recognized that this meant a trade was being put on. The words that stayed furthest from Veals's closed lips were "Allied Royal Bank"; even to put the name into the air was to chance it being inadvertently repeated outside the office before Kieran Duffy could get to work.

Veals was confident that Duffy could take the positions in gilts and sterling without arousing too much suspicion, but as he sat at his desk with the door locked, trying to think how else he could exploit the collapse of Allied Royal, he did what he sometimes did at moments of quiet introspection: he looked to Olya for inspiration.

John Veals's desk had a small rectangular table set at right angles to one side. On this he kept a laptop, whose screen was a modest 15.6 inches; it was a negligible affair when compared to the four flat-screen terminals with their jagged graphs and instant price movements that lowered over his main desk on a chrome gantry. On the laptop, however, he would flip through various websites— the BBC news, a horse-racing site and, more and more often, a soft-porn place he had recently discovered. It was called babes delight.co.uk and featured naked young women who were mostly, to judge by their names and cheekbones, of Slavic origin. Having read of the proportion of Internet traffic devoted to porn, Veals had vaguely wondered if there might be money in it. He was un-embarrassed by sex, as by anything else, and didn't bother to turn off the pictures if someone came in. The girls were clearly over age and weren't engaged in anything more than showing their bodies to a camera; there was nothing here that was not on knee-high offer from the country's favorite family high-street stationer.

The girls at babesdelight were laid out like an exotic stamp collection, twenty to a page. If you clicked on one, it offered you a series of a dozen poses, many on a beach or by a waterfall, some in the jagged mountains of what might have been Slovenia. Occasionally when you clicked, the first image didn't lead to the next page of the album but prompted something cruder, which Veals snapped shut. Usually, however, it was just naked girls in bedrooms, naked girls on farms or naked girls on a hike.

There was one in particular who had taken his eye. She was called, allegedly, Olya and claimed to be keen on tennis and cooking. She was slim, as were almost all the girls at babesdelight, but she had large breasts which she held coquettishly in her hands as she grinned out from her Transylvanian background. Her hair was black, her eyes brown and, unlike the majority of the girls, she had not undergone total depilation. She reminded Veals of a real girl, not a pinup; he could imagine himself talking to her, as well as stroking her rear when she knelt on all fours and glanced back over her shoulder.

Olya awoke in him a feeling other than lust. He couldn't put a name to it and didn't try; it was a soft and unfamiliar sensation. He just liked looking at her, almost every day. He felt a fraction guilty if he left it more than a week.

Hello, Olya, he almost said. Hello, John, she almost replied.

Veals suddenly sat up straight in his chair. He had had an idea. Olya had cleared his mind.

Thanks to its empire roots, Allied Royal still had strong connections in Africa, where the commodities export markets had long relied on its finance. If ARB suddenly found itself short of money it would look for quick savings. It couldn't hammer its pensioners or its U.K. mortgage holders because that would cause a riot; but who would care about a few Third World farmers? If ARB decided to suspend its credit lines to distributors, exporters and shippers, then the producers of cocoa, coffee and so on would find the value of their crops plunge—they would wither in the field; but by contrast the price of what they had presold, of what was already in the warehouse, would rocket—and the profit from that could go to John Veals. He could get Duffy to take long positions in warehouse receipts for all the commodities financed by ARB.

He had suddenly remembered what fun trading could be.

There was a knock on the door and Veals went over to unlock it. Young Simon Wetherby was standing outside.

"I was just going through some papers, John, and I had a couple of queries. Is this a bad moment?"

"No. It's a good one. Quiet day."

"Yes. So I'd noticed."

"Come in and take a seat."

Veals followed Wetherby's eyes to the laptop computer, where Olya was in close-up. "Charming girl, isn't she?" said Veals.

"Yes. Pretty." Wetherby sat down and looked across at Veals, his innocent face shining with concentration. "It's about our activity in the American subprime market last year."

"What about it?"

"There's just something I didn't understand. All these credit default swaps. The insurance things. How did that work?"

"Aah . . ." Veals put his feet up on the table. "That was fun. That finally opened the door. Do you want to hear a little story?"

"That's what I was hoping for."

"It's a little bit tough. You may want to take a deep breath at this point. Gather your forces. It won't take long, though."

"I'm sure I shall be equal to the task, John."

"OK. Here goes. You know we screwed up on subprime. I could see it was a disaster waiting to happen but we just couldn't make it work for us."

"Yes. I saw the positions we liquidated."

"OK. Bézamain calls me from New York. This is sometime in April. He's had a weird visit from this banker."

"Why's it weird?" said Wetherby.

"He's offering us a way of us shorting his own market."

"What? I've never heard of that before."

"Me neither," said Veals. "So I got on the plane to New York and met this guy, Johnny from Moregain or Goldbag, I forget which. We knew the subprime market was rotten but it was too expensive to short the stock of the mortgage lenders and the builders and so on. And anyway the market was still holding up. But Johnny says: Look, forget the stock, you can short the actual mortgage bonds—the ones that are backed by the subprime loans."

"You can short the actual security?"

"Yes."

"The useless ones?" said Wetherby. He looked a little shaken, Veals thought.

"Exactly. These original subprime mortgage bonds, a boxful of iffy mortgages, were mostly rated overall BBB. Fair enough. But when the banks bought them, they turned them on their side and sliced them like a loaf of bread. Then they asked for different ratings for the different slices. And clients could buy the slice of their choice, according to their appetite for risk. At this point of course it ceased to be a simple mortgage bond and became a synthetic bond. And then the bank asked the agencies for a rating for all the different slices, because some loans were naturally riskier than others—even in a crock of shit, some shit smells worse than the rest. So the agencies give them a range of ratings, and in a way that was fair enough. But the problem was that while the ratings may have reflected the internal differences between the tranches, the whole lot was overrated by comparison with other products."

"But why were the agencies so bullish overall?"

"Because they had the wrong computer models. They just couldn't get their heads round the fact that many of these loans were worthless. Their computer model simply misweighted the possibility that house prices could fall. Ever."

"So now you had dangerous product with a safe rating," said Wetherby.

"Yes, but it's even better than that, Simon. Even the AA tranches which you'd expect to pay out modestly are giving the investor the high return he'd normally get from risking his cash on a BBB. So Goldbag has for a moment actually squared the circle. It's exciting. They're selling respectable-sounding instruments with disreputably high returns. And don't forget that because all the loans are basically subprime, the house owners, the unshaven hobos, are having to pay a penally high rate of interest. And it's that rate of interest that gets passed through to the new investors, who are therefore getting a massive B-style yield from an A-rated risk."

"It sounds as though the banks were flooding the market."

"No, they were responding to a demand for shit. A ravenous demand from their customers. Many of whom, incidentally, were credulous Europeans who trusted the ratings agencies."

"Then what happened?"

"They ran out of stock. No more houses, loans or buyers to be found." Veals laughed. "It was a fucking Klondike and there was no gold left."

"So what did they do?" Wetherby grimaced. "Do I want to know?"

"They created more stuff. Even dodgier stuff. Now Goldbag and Moregain cut out the mortgage-lender people, Out West or whoever, and send brokers out like door-to-door salesmen. Find a wetback or a hobo. Offer him a giant loan with a teaser rate or an introductory payment holiday. Get it back to Wall Street. Slice it up. Secure the dodgy rating. Sell it on. By now they've got a lot of these synthetic bonds on their books. But they've got one problem."

"What's that?"

"It's costing Goldbag a lot to pay out the shit holders, the people with the worst tranches of the worst bonds at maybe ten percent interest. And that's when little Johnny comes knocking at Marc Bézamain's door and says, 'Would you like to short my market?'"

"But how could you borrow it and sell it and—"

"You couldn't. It wasn't like shorting a normal stock. What

Johnny was suggesting was that we entered into a credit default swap on one tranche only of the bond. The worst part."

"So they sold you insurance against one section of the bond defaulting." Wetherby seemed to be struggling, Veals thought; perhaps he feared where this was heading.

"Yes," said Veals. "Our bet was that it would default. They bet that it would hold up. Because it was the dodgiest slice, they charged a lot up front to buy the swap. The premiums to insure a paper house in a forest fire are going to be expensive. But they were still less than what it would have cost us to short the stocks in the usual way. And when the penniless sharecropper couldn't make his repayments anymore, the upside was huge. The full insurance payout."

Wetherby shook his head. "But how did you pick which mortgage bonds to work on?"

"The banks helped us. Johnny from Goldbag gave us a list of mortgage bonds from all over the U.S. You'd look for the worst lenders in the dodgiest states—Nevada or Arizona were particularly shit if I remember rightly. There'd be some kid who'd swum the Rio Grande and was earning fifteen grand a year pumping gas, couldn't even speak English, and they'd lent him three quarters of a million bucks to buy a house with a pool. We were doing the kind of research the mortgage lenders should have done themselves but never did. Bézamain had three guys on it full-time. We found the worst tranches of the worst bonds and took on a bet with Goldbag or Moregain that they'd default."

"But what was in it for the banks now?" Wetherby said.

"Easy. The premiums I paid to buy the insurance pretty much covered the bank's outgoing interest payments to the BBB holders. Then the bank was laying off its own risk anyway. And they still had plenty of buyers for this shit, some of whom were happy to take it in derivative form. So for the bank the dodgy part is now cash-neutral *and* risk free."

"This is a fantasy," said Wetherby.

Veals's lips twitched, as though they wanted to smile. "That's not all. Now this is the tricky bit, Simon. Concentrate. Get through this and you can go and ring Susanna Russell from HSBC and take her out to lunch. After this bit, it's all laughs. OK. The thing is that every time Johnny wrote me or others like me an insurance on a triple-B bunch of shit, he effectively created a new security. Then he put all these securities—the credit default swaps—into a new synthetic bond, which he could then trade on! More commission, more profit, and the market goes on. It's fantastic."

Simon Wetherby was starting to grow pale. "But surely these new securities didn't have any reference obligations? There was no additional house, no actual new loan, no actual mortgage involved."

"You got it," said Veals. "They replicated the original mortgage bond, but with one crucial difference. There was no house. The only asset backing this synthetic bond was my side bet with the bank. Trouble was, there seemed to be no liquidity in these synthetic CDOs. They stuck to the banks' fingers."

"Christ, John," said Wetherby. "It sounds like this fantasy football game my son plays. Does your son do that?"

"I don't know," said Veals. He looked thoughtful for a moment. "But I think you've got the point, Simon. This is Fantasy Finance. It wasn't enough to have poor people borrowing money they couldn't repay to buy houses they couldn't afford. By writing credit default swaps, the banks could leverage the real market many times over. That's why the overall losses are going to be so much greater than the losses on the actual mortgage loans they reference. And of course that's how we hedgies could make a killing on the losses."

Wetherby had turned white; tiny bubbles of sweat stood in a line on his freshly shaved upper lip. Veals smiled inwardly when he noticed: this was the younger man's way of showing shame.

"But surely," Wetherby said, "this can't have been signed off by the accountants. When they inspected the balance sheets?"

Veals snorted. "Ah, the Big Five . . . Big Four nowadays. No, they were happy to sign it off."

"But why?"

"I don't know, Simon. I'm not a chartered accountant. Perhaps they didn't understand. Or perhaps they did."

"Well, I certainly don't understand," said Wetherby.

"Think about it. If Lemon Bros. or Bare Stern goes down with billions in complex instruments needing to be sorted out, who are the liquidators going to call in? Pricewaterhouse or one of the other four. They get tucked into the carcass from day one. They can bill north of £4 million a week to go through the books. It would probably take two years minimum. By the time they've finished there'll be nothing left on the skeleton for the investor. But why should the accountants care? They've trousered £400 million."

Simon Wetherby was swallowing hard. "But we're all right in all this, aren't we, John?"

"Of course we are, Simon. We were able to exploit one or two market inconsistencies for the benefit of our investors. It's what we do."

"Yes, I know, but by shorting the banks' own market, by buying the swaps, weren't we creating the liquidity to keep the whole terrible thing going?"

"Yes," said Veals calmly. "At the invitation of the banks."

"Knowing it would blow up in their faces?"

"Not their own faces, Simon. Johnny Dickhead, age twenty-eight, he doesn't care. He'd get his commission and his fat bonus on the mortgage bonds. Then he took commission for selling and managing the synthetic bonds. Anyway, by the time it blew up, he'd have moved on."

"But couldn't it bring down his whole bank?"

"Conceivably. Look here." Veals typed the abbreviated name of one of the investment banks into his keyboard and turned the screen to face Simon Wetherby's pale, traumatized face. The graph was sinking.

"But what about the investor in all this?"

"Oh for Christ's sake, Simon." Veals was beginning to tire of this interview. "The bank doesn't give a fuck about the investors."

"But why did they do it?" Wetherby was now growing plangent. "They must have known it could only end in disaster."

Veals had had enough. He stood up and went over to where Wetherby was sitting.

Then he leaned over and spoke slowly: "They do it because they can. They do it because the government encouraged it. They do it, Simon," he said, gripping Wetherby tightly by the forearm and lifting him to his feet, "because it's what they do."

"I see," said Wetherby uncertainly, as Veals ushered him to the door.

At the threshold, he rallied a little and tried to bring the meeting to a dignified conclusion. He coughed and pulled himself up.

"They do it," said Simon Wetherby, "because they're bankers."

"No," said Veals, pushing him out into the overheated corridor, "they do it because they're a bunch of cunts."

IV

For Shahla Hajiani, Tuesday was just another day in which she couldn't see the world for the obstruction that lay so close to her face. When she awoke, before she remembered who she was, everything seemed possible—daylight, friends, work—as she felt the first stir of hope quickening her limbs; but in a second it had all returned: the knowledge that she was stuck headfirst in a narrow tunnel, unable to turn back.

Oh God, she thought, as her vision was once again blocked. Hassan. She knew that through the day there would be small somatic signs: a headache that by teatime would need the relief of pills from the corner shop, a tremor in the hand, a rash on the inside of her elbow. None of these, admittedly, amounted to much in itself; none of them compared to the continuous twist of anxiety in her gut, but all of them served as reminders—as if she was likely to forget.

Why on earth, she thought, as she dressed, drank coffee and made her way onto the street, did people imagine that such a state of mind was elevated or desirable? What was to be commended in going through a day quite blind to the lives of others, deaf to the news on the stand, merely blinkered by the narrowness of her own dead end? Oh, Hassan, you silly boy. They called it "love," but it felt more like confinement. Even Paul Éluard, the subject of her Ph.D., as radical and clear thinking as a poet could be, had found himself locked up by it, his breakthrough book of love poems even called *The Capital of Pain* . . .

On the top deck of the bus, Shahla pushed her long hair back from her face and put on the reading glasses she wore for an astigmatism. Ah, well. Enough of this, she thought, her lips mouthing the words in her determination. She plowed on through a morning in the library, lunch in the canteen and an afternoon meeting in which she outlined her plan for the French Society's proposed trip to Verdun. No one would have known, she believed, from her bright and practical manner, that her mind was wholly occupied elsewhere.

After an early shift on the District Line, Jenni Fortune went home to Drayton Green. She whisked through the flat, straightening and tidying, then texted Tony to see when he would be home. "6.30. 2 late 4 t?" he replied. "No. fine. Pie?" "xx☺." She set about cooking. Twice a week, Sunday dinner and one other time, she tried to do proper cooking with fresh food. She'd collected steak and kidney from the butcher on the way back from the Tube and now set about making pastry while she listened to drive-time radio. She got the pie in the oven and peeled some potatoes to go with it; she'd given up making greens for Tony, but there was a packet of salad in the fridge that she could have.

The furnishing of the flat meant a lot to her. She looked at celebrity magazines, not at the faces of the soap stars or weather girls but at the background of their houses, to see if there was anything she could copy or adapt. She even bought specialist monthlies, though she didn't like the pictures with stainless steel and toneless color schemes that looked like a factory; she preferred a cozier look with bright fabrics that suggested somewhere you'd actually want to live. The look of a room through a half-open door and the way the light fell were more to her than housekeeping; they suggested stories and lives: they awakened a longing in her.

That was almost as much reality as Jenni wanted. She ran a bath, lit a scented candle and slid beneath the surface with the winner of the '05 Café Bravo. The novel was still very thin to her way of thinking. The words didn't seem to make any sort of music, they just told you facts, like a manual; but she didn't like to give up on books once she'd started and she plunged once more into its watery gruel. The characters were called Nic and Lilli. The whole thing was, like, tinny. Couldn't one of them just be called Jake or Barbara, she thought, something with a different sound? Even that would have helped.

After tea with Tony, Jenni did what she had been looking forward to all day: she logged on to Parallax. She knew that Jason Dogg wouldn't be online till later, but there was a lot to do first.

She loved being back in Parallax. The game's owners and regulators (a syndicate of twelve Chinese Californians, Jenni had read) seemed to have solved one of the persistent problems of such worlds: the so-called "uncanny valley" effect. People can identify with humans photographically reproduced; they could also be interested in stick figures or cartoons. But as representation of humans moved from rough toward complete there came a sudden loss of empathy: the graph started and finished high with stickman or photo, but dipped badly in the middle. Most manufacturers lacked power to push onto verisimilitude, so pulled back toward the crude, thus reclimbing the empathy line. The Parallax geeks, however, had managed to harness something close to the technology used in epic cinema; their coup was to have done it at real-life speed and at a reasonable cost.

So when Miranda went for a walk or met her neighbors or did some shopping, it was like interacting with people from the movies, real people, if a little smaller. She could bring their faces into extreme close-up and see the pores of their skin. It wasn't like playing a children's computer game; it was like being a star in your own improvised film.

134

Miranda herself looked almost like one of the three entry-level female maquettes. This was deceptive. While she dressed in off-the-shelf jeans and T-shirt, Jenni had in fact incorporated features from a large number of different True Life actresses, singers and models. Her eyebrows, for instance, were based on those of Pamilla, a cute singer in Girls From Behind. She had a "celebrity walk" that was a fusion of the Hollywood star Juliana Richards and the Ethiopian model Zhérie, who had recently married the footballer Sean Mills. Her eyes were the shape of Evelina Belle's and the color of Jennifer Cox's famous dark hazel/chocolate glow lamps.

Much of this subtlety, expensive to buy, was wasted on the muscle-bound, gun-toting warriors she encountered in the shopping malls. But Miranda, like Jenni, didn't really dress for men or male maquettes; she dressed for fun. Now, what would Miranda like to wear to a night of clubbing and a first date?

After a couple of hours wandering up and down the virtual emporia, Miranda emerged with a black dress of mid-thigh length, with pink high heels and a pink leotard from Mary Lou's Fashion Girl Boutique in Porta Cascarina. By Parallax standards, it was restrained (many girls danced topless or with miniature tigerskin thongs), but it was much riskier than anything she wore in TL.

She had only been in the new outfit for a minute when she received a message asking if she wanted to be airlifted. It was from Jason. "You bet," she said, and a few moments later she was by his side in Purgatorio, one of the newer clubs. The guest DJ played techno, hip-hop, trance . . . a variety of stuff streamed from illegal Internet sites in TL. The setting was spectacular, with a kind of indoor cascade lit from underneath by purple lights; people were actually swimming in it! Jenni bought drinks for her and Jason with 100 vajos she'd transferred in from her credit card and they danced on a floor that was open to the stars.

You could begin by clicking on a few buttons beside the dance floor, but what they offered was a bit like what your gran did, so Jenni had bought a number of moves, such as Cover Girl, Saturday Shake, Caramel Poison and Hip Shiver; with these Miranda did look cool. When she swung and twirled, the dress rode up to show her shiny pink gusset and she thought it looked sexy, but also proper, like a ballet dancer. Jason had no money left, so Jenni bought him beer, and liter after liter of fresh springwater for herself.

At about eleven, Jason suggested they go to a strip club. Here, in a bright overhead light, various females were gyrating on poles. There was a "tip jar" next to the stage, and Jason said, "Will you put in some vajos?" As a result, the dancer took Jason into a large red room behind the main stage and Miranda followed, uncertainly.

The dancer performed gymnastic actions in front of Jason Dogg, who had now taken off his clothes.

The dancer messaged Jason, "Last man had forgot to buy dick."

"Lol," Jason replied. Laugh out loud. The basic maquettes were not provided with genitals, though they could be purchased at a price. Jason Dogg, Miranda noticed, had equipped himself with a doughty black one, which didn't go with the color of his other skin, though it stuck out tenaciously as the dancer attempted to maneuver herself into a position to accommodate it.

Moving Miranda back out of the room with the D and C keys on her computer, Jenni got her onto the terrace, where she pressed the E to fly away, high above the city of Caracas, through the beautiful moonlit night and back to her sparkling new house.

In reality, or True Life as his fellow gamers called it, Jason Dogg was a thirty-five-year-old schoolteacher called Radley Graves. He taught English at a comprehensive school in the Lewisham/ Catford overlap.

He stared at the screen of his computer, from which Miranda Star had so rudely vanished. Bitch. His flat was in a modern development that overlooked the Thames near Kingston Bridge. Though small, it was bright and well looked after. When he'd been for his run on a Saturday, Radley vacuumed it and made sure his books and DVDs were in order; once a week, a man came in to give it what Radley called a "deep clean."

When he discovered that Miranda Star had logged off, he was angry. He was hoping that she'd be impressed by him and would want to see him again; he'd meant no harm by having sex in the nightclub: it was just a bit of fun. He sensed Miranda was a prude, and this made him more intrigued by her. Most of the women in Parallax had breasts the size of cantaloupes, held in place by strips of bright material; they favored rings through every visible cartilage. Radley had never looked at the female ur-maquettes, but he guessed this one was pretty much off the shelf: an entry-level model barely improved by her real-life godmother. She excited him.

Why had she vanished? Most people he'd met online were blasé about sex, which—apart from hard-core pedos or whatever—was something gamers pretty soon grew out of, once they'd tried it a few times. Also, the other people in Parallax admired his bespoke genitals, which had cost 300 vajos; Miranda hadn't even commented.

Although it was late, Radley went out to take a night bus into town. The double-decker was empty apart from a few fifteen-year-old drunks. They didn't frighten him. Radley's regular visits to the school gym had layered muscle onto his back and shoulders. He could bench-press more than any of the other teachers, including Paul Watts, the PE man. He didn't smoke, and although he drank a fair amount to help him through the day, he jogged in Bushy Park three times a week with a twenty-pound pack on his back.

Teaching wasn't a career that Radley Graves had foreseen when he left school with a handful of exam passes and a desire to travel. An only child, the by-blow of a sales rep on a one-night encounter, he had been brought up by his mother in a pebble-dashed house in Malden. His natural father made small, rare contributions to the housekeeping, as did his mother's live-in lover, a Scotsman called Colin who ran a "self-storage" warehouse off the A3. For weeks at a time Colin would ignore Radley. When he came home from work at about five, he sat in the lounge in front of the only television, smoking efficiently and drinking tea. On Fridays the adults went to the pub and Radley was able to watch a program of his own choosing; sometimes on a Saturday Colin dragged Radley to see Crystal Palace at home and bought him a pie and a scalding cup of tea at the ground.

The night bus took Radley to Southwark, where there was a pub he knew that stayed open. It had once been a haunt of lightermen and dockers from downstream; then, when that world had ended, they'd tried to make a feature of its waterside position by opening a dining room that sold fish and chips. The restaurant failed and the natural clientele remained the same: nightbirds who fetched up on the cold stone flags of the public bar when they'd finished their nocturnal business. Some were criminals and some just worked unsocial hours; porters from Borough Market went there from four in the morning. The room smelled of damp straw and hot animal, like a stable; customers endured the vindictive landlady and her husband because in defiance of the new law they allowed their regulars to smoke.

Among the bedraggled clubbers, burglars and nightwatchmen, Radley Graves stood out in his neat sports-casual clothes. He sat with a pint of bitter and thought about his life.

The problem with it was that the effort of living it—the early trains, the 8:30 roll call, the jammed timetable, the trying to protect his back, the weekend preparations—left him no time to climb outside and take a look at himself. He couldn't think about a better job, a different life, because the alarm was always dragging him from sleep, the deadline for half-term reports was always yesterday. As for the drag of "coursework" . . . The "C word" they called it in the staffroom.

His Tuesday had started well. He had an off-lesson and was able to prepare his other periods in the Communications Team staffroom. Anya, the new woman, had brought in some almond biscuits (they'd given her £10 each at the start of term to keep supplies up) and he made a mug of instant coffee, black. The departmental staffroom was strip-lit, small and gave off the kids' computer suite, so privacy was minimal. Radley had preferred the old, gigantic all-staff place with carpets and a television, but it had been required for indoor sports facilities. The outdoor playground stretched as far as a twenty-foot-high wire fence; on the other side of it were the extensive playing fields, both Astroturf and cropped grass, of the local private school. Days passed with no child of any kind seen on them, but their use was forbidden to the comprehensive, whose pupils could only gaze at them through their retaining mesh.

Radley Graves taught the lower years mostly, though he had a Year 11, GCSE, set as well. English had been fused with modern foreign languages and media studies under the banner of Communications, and this was something Radley felt he knew about. His training had focused on the politics of race, gender and class, with hardly a mention of pupil management or lessons. These things had to be learned on the job, and initially Radley had found it difficult. At his first school, he'd twice been suspended and sent to anger management courses. Eventually a senior colleague took pity and explained the principle of control. "Never lock on. Never engage one-to-one. You can't win a battle of egos. Speak softly. Stay respectful. Answer without sarcasm, and if they won't cooperate, don't rebuke them. Never, ever raise your voice above a four out of ten."

It took some practice. Radley didn't approve of the system because he felt it admitted that the teachers had ceded control to the pupils. The kids were allowed to come in late to lessons; and, after having once been threatened with a sexual harassment suit, Radley never again asked a girl pupil what had kept her. They were allowed to talk pretty much unchecked throughout a class, though if you could quell the noise by a soft and a generalized appeal, that was all right; what was not permitted was to single out the talker by name. They were allowed not to work if they didn't fancy it, though they could be gently reminded once. Swearing was permitted, unless it had racial or sexual overtones: Abir could call Radley himself a bastard but couldn't call Mehreen, who sat next to her, a bitch.

The corridors between lessons were a hard-hat zone, best avoided. The tiny first-year girls of barely four feet tall clung like shadows to the wall as raging fat six-footers of both sexes surged past them, heavy bags swinging, shouting down the length of the yellow and blue corridors. A bell rang, and Radley waited for the fireworks to stop going off in the stairwell before he made his way to the classroom. The molded plastic chairs were set in twos at wipe-clean Formica-topped desks; only the carpet tiles, with brown mysterious stains, showed signs of the restless human traffic. The GCSE class came in, as it willed: Aaron, Abir, Alex, Arusha, Ben, Darryl, David, Ezra, Ian, Jasmine, Jordan, Ladan, Laila, Marcus, Mehreen, Michael, Nathan, Nawshad, Nooshin, Ocado, Paul, Pratap, Rubina, Ryan, Sangita, Sherin, Simon, Zainun.

Radley wrote the names of the missing three on a whiteboard under the halfhearted word: Warning. He joined in the universal talking, then began to dominate—and slowly it became a lesson. He breathed deeply in order to keep his voice at four or less on the volume scale. This trick he'd borrowed from Anya, who did yogic breathing in the staffroom before class; Pat Wilder just took tranquilizers—little yellow ones from a rattling bottle.

That afternoon the school was playing football against St. Michael and All Angels, "St. Mick's"—one of the few fixtures to have survived the work-to-rule that banned teachers from staying after school. This meant that Ocado, the most brutally effective midfielder in the school, was allowed not to take his medication. Usually this caused him to become uncontrollable and he had to be taken outside to a secure location before kickoff. So far today he'd been all right, Anya reported, though he'd used the internal window that divided all the classrooms from the corridor to expose his genital piercing to the Year 13 French revision class.

"Sir, you're such a dork," said Sangita as Radley placed a photocopied sheet on her desk.

"Really?" he said, the model of mildness. "And what's a dork?"

"You know. Like a nerd?"

"Dick more like," said David.

Radley didn't allow himself to hear, as "dick" was arguably a sexual word. He went back with calm slow steps to the laptop at his desk and made a few lines of text appear on the whiteboard.

"Why aren't you writing, Aaron? Is something wrong?"

"To be quite honest wiv you, sir, I got writer's block."

"Sir, is that a love bite on your neck?"

"No. Now listen up, everybody. What can you tell me about Billy Elliot? Sherin?"

"Is he like gay, sir?"

In the break Anya discovered her mobile phone had been stolen, but was unable to search the suspect's bag because it would be a "violation of his rights," he claimed. A loud noise was heard coming from Pat Wilder's classroom, where Ocado was banging Jordan's head against a metal locker. Radley telephoned the gym and asked Paul Watts, the PE man, to take Ocado under his wing until kickoff at 2:30.

"Can't do that, mate," said Watts. "He's only just back from a three-day exclusion."

"What for?"

"Having sex in the toilets with Sophie Rees. It was five days but they got it down to three because it was only oral. Sorry, Radley. Your kid."

When Anya volunteered to watch Ocado, Radley made himself another cup of instant coffee. "What happened to your neck, Pat?" he said. "It's all black and blue."

"I was taking the Year 10 French group on the Tube to a French film," said Pat Wilder. "They said Tony had disappeared at Tottenham Court Road station, so I stuck my head out to check and they pressed the 'Close Doors' button and they trapped my neck."

"Who was it?"

"I couldn't see. My head was stuck. There's a note for you by the way." He stiffly handed Radley a piece of paper.

"Dear Sir, I am sorry I behaved like I did. I was disrespecting you. I interrupted you and I should not of said what I said about sucking Ocado's cock. I am tuely sorry. I don't blame you that you walked out. I will show you I am better than this, sir. I am really sorry. You are a good teacher. Yours Selima Wilson."

The lesson before lunch was quiet and Radley escaped school

141

briefly to the Lion's Head, which he entered via the car park and the toilets to avoid being seen. He drank two barley wines and ate a chicken pie with gravy and frozen peas. He had only one more class, a cover for an absent colleague of a Year 12 group.

The alcohol in his blood helped him to stay calm and he ate several strong mints on the way back to school. Two boys whose names he didn't know had already locked horns by the time he arrived in class.

"You're gay," said one repeatedly.

"Enjoyed your mum last night," said the other.

This made the others, mostly girls, snigger. Radley had heard this taunt before; it wasn't confined to children with young or tarty mothers, he'd noticed. In fact it seemed more effective when it wasn't.

"Gay."

"Your mum."

There was an explosive noise as one boy grabbed the other round the throat. The girls screamed in fear and enjoyment as the two boys rolled on the ground, punching and kicking. Radley hauled one off and slammed him back against the wall. Then he marched him to the back of the room and sat him down alone. The other boy, the mother-enjoyer, had a thin trickle of blood coming from the corner of his lip.

"You sit over there," said Radley.

"Sir, I need to go and—"

"Do what you're told," said Radley, his voice nearer to an eight than a four.

The boy went.

At the end of the lesson, Radley made them both stay behind.

"I don't want you doing that again," he said.

"Mind your own fucking business."

"Yeah, that's right. We know where you live."

"I don't think so," said Radley. "And in any case, I wouldn't recommend it."

There was something in his voice the boys responded to; the air went out of them.

"Anyway . . ." said one.

They tried to find a surly way of leaving without losing face.

"Yeah, exactly. To be honest wiv you . . . Anyway," said the other.

They shambled off.

"Yes. Exactly," said Radley, loudly, so they heard.

He felt a sense of power and determination. That Miranda tart, she'd disrespected Jason Dogg as well.

V

In Ferrers End, Ralph Tranter was busy knocking out a review for *The Toad*. It was of a book he'd already reviewed under his own name in *Vista*, a new monthly magazine, and he was keen to put the record straight for *Toad* readers, to sweep up any crumbs of comfort the author might have taken from his signed piece.

He enjoyed reviewing, and over the years had developed a facility for it. One of the secrets was to allow your view of the book to color your account of it, so that rather than have a schoolboy précis bracketed by an evaluation in the first and final paragraphs, the whole thing was a compound of description and judgment. Sometimes, of course, you had to stand back to make your points more firmly; such, for instance, had been the case with *A Winter Crossing* by Alexander Sedley. The derision that Tranter felt then couldn't be contained within the usual framework. He felt obliged to draw the reader to one side to let him into the full horror of the con trick that was Sedley, A. He had given it both barrels, then sent out for another gun. "Provincial, narrow Englishness . . . garlanded with praise from all the usual suspects of the metropolitan snob brigade . . . workaday psychological observations . . . unintentionally hilarious juxtapositions . . . embarrassing purple passages."

Unfortunately, it hadn't worked. While one or two other reviewers agreed that it was disappointing that Sedley seemed to have made nothing up, most of them had enjoyed the book and looked forward to more from a "promising first-timer." Tranter wasn't surprised by this supine response; it merely goaded him into further action. His *Toad* piece a fortnight later went through the reviewers one by one and pointed out that they were all Sedley's old university chums (there was no need in an anonymous review to mention his own college connection to the editor of *The Toad*) and suggested that those Sedley hadn't actually bribed were members of a loose homosexual coterie. The fact that Sedley, so far from being gay, was married to a notably good-looking consultant oncologist and was the father of four meant nothing to Tranter, since Sedley's type were always on for some queer stuff; it was part of their education.

But nothing, it seemed, could stop the bandwagon. A few weeks later, the wretched book made it into the preliminary list of six for that year's Café Bravo first-novel prize. This called for more intense guerrilla action, Tranter felt. From a listings magazine, he saw that Sedley would be reading from his "highly acclaimed" novel at a bookshop in Hampstead at 5:30 on a Friday, and by 5:10 Tranter had placed himself on the end of a row of chairs in the center of the aisle with a glass of free Rioja.

Sedley arrived late, looking flustered. The traffic had been terrible, he explained to the bookshop manager, as he quickly downed a glass of wine before facing the dauntingly full bookshop.

"Hello, Alexander," said Tranter, sidling in to where the author stood preparing himself behind the travel section. "How's things? You're a bit late."

Sedley seemed to gasp and swallow. "I . . . er . . . I didn't expect to see you here. You know . . . A . . . er, a fellow professional, as it were. It's normally just, you know, readers."

"Oh no, I really wanted to drop in. I only live just up the road." The A1 anyway, he thought.

The strangest thing that Tranter had discovered over the years was that if at a party or a literary festival you accosted someone whose work you had slagged off in print, he didn't punch your nose or pour his drink over you. On the contrary, he always wanted to be your friend. Presumably he felt that by kneeing you in the groin he might lose face; and for these "poor saps," keeping face, or trying to recover what he'd tried to strip them of in print, was all that mattered.

"Anyway, good luck," said Tranter and went back to his position in the aisle.

Sedley went to the lectern and began nervously, with an explanation of why he wrote and how he had come to write *A Winter Crossing* in particular.

Tranter began to yawn, aware that he was in Sedley's eyeline. Then Sedley began to read in his posh, slightly tremulous voice, a description of his relationship with his stern father or something. Tranter raised an incredulous eyebrow and looked round the audience to enlist their fellow feeling. This chap had to be joking, didn't he?

Sedley took an admiring question from a sturdy woman in a bobble hat, then launched into a "party scene" in which the bloodless hero proved unaccountably attractive to some willowy girl.

During this sequence, Tranter upped the volume of his yawns so that they became more like groans of incredulity. Half the audience turned to look at him and he noticed Sedley's eyes also lift from the page. There was an embarrassing hiatus when he tried to find his place again. As he resumed his reading, Tranter glanced round again and this time spread both his arms out wide in a gesture of "I mean, come on, what *is* this already?" There was a slight answering titter from behind, and the reddening Sedley once again glanced up from his book.

He took another softball question from someone Tranter assumed to be a plant from the publicity department of his publisher, and then with a very solemn look began to read the passage in which his alter ego was jilted by the willowy girl. Tranter remembered the sequence from the book, but it was only now that Sedley was reading it that he saw that it was supposed to be emotional—"moving," perhaps.

Leaning back in his chair, he let out the loudest yet of his yawns—a sort of roar. Then he flung his arms wide and looked all round him, making urgent gestures at his wristwatch, as though to suggest that some people had jobs to go to, lives to live, thanks very much, rather than listen to any more of this.

Then he pushed his chair back so that its feet squealed on the wooden floor, stood up and walked slowly down the aisle to the doors onto the street. He pushed them open violently and allowed them to swing unchecked behind him, allowing in the greatest possible noise of rush-hour taxis and lorries as they labored up Rosslyn Hill.

John Veals was on the Tube, going home, thinking with some surprise about how dismissive he had been that morning in his talk with Simon Wetherby about "Moregain Sucks" and "Goldbag Lunch." He had once loved banking. After ten years trading futures, he'd been headhunted, in 1990, by a New York investment bank that viewed itself as the smartest on the planet and had statistics to support its claim. Others of the big banks might dispute the title; Veals did not, and he felt the time was right to move.

The American brokerage for whom he had been selling futures in London had had a rogue trader and had called in management consultants. In the New York office, young men in rimless spectacles rose unspeaking in the bank of elevators that lay beyond the security gates. Their pale faces and watery eyes reflected their hours of study; box after box of paper documents were wheeled into stripped offices by porters dressed like the old Red Caps on the Chattanooga Express. Veals had been glad to leave.

Like everyone else who worked there, he referred to his new employer simply as "the Bank." Started by three Latvian Jewish refugees in 1885, it had in its early days brought together investors and capital, enabling businesses to grow and new merchant ventures to be undertaken; but by the time John Veals joined it in 1990 it had become, in all but name, a hedge fund that thrived by trading its own capital. Veals was slightly contrarian at this time in that he still believed the client had an important role. And the function of the client in Veals's view was a simple one: to provide a flow of information on which the Bank could more efficiently trade its own money.

In theory, Chinese walls were intended to separate those trading on behalf of the Bank from those acting for clients, and this usually worked. While one arm of the Bank was underwriting a rights issue for a cash-strapped company, the "prop" desk was short-selling the same company. But the rights issue was public knowledge and no one had had to breach a confidence; it was simply considered by some outsiders to be "distasteful." No one at the Bank cared about "taste."

At other times the Chinese walls were too thin. Veals and everyone else at the Bank knew that if two men met for a drink after work it was impossible to police everything that was said. It was laughable, really, Veals thought: it was too easy. On the other hand, it was against the law, or against the SEC rules. The fact that everyone knew what went on didn't mean to say that it was all right, that it was risk free, and Veals preferred at this stage of his career to take his edge in a way that was, in the jargon of the Bank, completely kosher.

His first job at the Bank, on the energy desk, coincided with the time that many East European and African governments were denationalizing their energy supplies. The fledgling private organizations that emerged all wanted to buy protection against future price fluctuations. They could do so on an open exchange, but Veals preferred to steer them toward the "over the counter" method, where deals were made privately, between consenting adults.

He loved it. It was like playing poker with a guy whose hand was all faceup on the table. With these ingénus, Veals had found an edge again, but more valuable than anything he'd enjoyed on the market floor. On listed markets there were algorithmic trading engines that kept prices boringly close to fair value at all times; but over the counter, he could act like a tailor's master cutter, providing for Messrs. Mbungwe and Radninski a bespoke product so complex and precise that they had no idea of whether or not it was fair.

At the peak it seemed that every day would bring a new wide-bodied jet full of clients to New York, serious men taking their first uncertain steps in the capitalist world. After taking their money, Veals taxied them, with Steve Godley to do the small talk, to lengthy dinners at overpriced midtown restaurants and afterward provided hookers. These men were desperate for the Bank's expertise; its name alone was a guarantee of financial sophistication and power: they wanted to be able to take it home and show their bosses and their governments. They took off from Kennedy on the Saturday night and went back to their countries with a smile on their faces, dreamily grateful to have been shafted by such an august name.

In his own mind, Veals wasn't really trading CDS's or other fancy options: he was trading Polish credulity; he was trading Czech naïveté; he was trading stupidity.

Yet still he was not quite satisfied. It was like going to one of the famous bankers' whorehouses in Geneva and finding the prime hookers, the prettiest girls from Prague and Vilnius, all bent over naked in a row for the visiting fund managers. Veals yearned for something with a bit more challenge and a bit more edge.

In London, in the second part of the 1990s, the Bank asked Veals to concern himself with the question of debt, and Veals responded enthusiastically. Debt could be traded as bonds, on an exchange, but bank debt was not subject to insider trading rules. One of the tasks of Veals's department was to raise money that was not seen by the credit rating agencies as debt, and to achieve this they invented new instruments, with deceptively sunny or simple-sounding names. Who wouldn't want to buy a Fiesta or a High Tider? ("Tider" stood for Tertiary Interest Deposit-Enabled Revenue. "High" referred, in an extremely private joke between Veals and Godley, to the Bank's margin. "Still a fucking debt, though," as Veals admitted to Godley.)

Later, they immortalized the private joke in the name of their hedge fund, High Level Capital. "Twenty fucking percent of the client upside, plus two percent management fee," said Veals. "The industry norm! What an industry! What's Latin for twenty fucking percent? We should put it as the motto on our coat of arms." *Viginti copulantes per centum.* Godley looked it up, but didn't send it to the printer.

Then they decided to go for three and thirty anyway. It showed they meant business.

The compliance regime in the Bank emphatically met the modern requirements. What this meant in reality was one hour a year training, largely concerned with money-laundering precautions similar to those used by a high-street clerk when taking on a new customer: photocopy of passport and recent utility bill. Veals had once sat a compliance "exam" in which the first question was "In what year did the Singapore Stock Exchange open?" He and others at his level were required to go on a further one-day course each year in a country house hotel. After they'd signed the register, most of the "students" spent the morning trading or e-mailing as usual on their mobile devices. Veals liked to take bets on his own arithmetical prowess. He would bet one of the young tigers that he could get an answer to a complex sum before his opponent with the palmtop computer and made thousands this way in quiet moments.

In his bright, clean office in Pfäffikon, Kieran Duffy had had a long day. He was a man of strong carnal appetites and a naturally short attention span; for many years his weekends in New York had involved Long Island, much golf, some cocaine, French wine and as many girls as he could manage without alienating Mrs. Duffy.

When a large trade was on, however, Duffy could think himself into a kind of trance, in which he would stay for as long as it took. After a vigorous morning encounter with his Italian girlfriend Marcella, he showered, dressed, told her he might not be back till the following day and drove his blue German sports car at speed over the freezing roads to Pfäffikon. He had told his trading assistant and his secretary the night before to be at work by eight, and when he opened the office door he could smell espresso and croissants.

He fired up the four large flat-screens at his desk and rubbed his hands.

The markets opened at nine, Swiss time, and he spent the morning on the phone to the main option market-makers in the London banks. One by one, the bids and the offers came back to him, and one by one Kieran Duffy agreed the transactions, over the counter, by a simple phone call. After each trade was agreed he wrote a ticket and gave it to his assistant, a tall, elegant Englishwoman called Victoria Gilpin, who entered it via computer into High Level's back office and risk systems.

As Victoria went to work (she had an old-fashioned touch-typist's style in which the wrists were static and only the long fingers moved quietly over the keys), Duffy received in turn: an e-mail request for confirmation from each bank he had traded with; a notification from High Level's prime broker in London (the shiniest American investment bank) that each trade had been accepted on their books; and an adjustment to his own onscreen trading position. This figure was made up from a constant recalculation of all High Level's many positions. Because of the size of the trades he had done in the course of the morning the slightest variation in ARB's share price was causing huge movements in his own trading figures. It was exciting.

At noon he had a conversation about risk limitation with Teddy Robinson, the deceptively relaxed Californian who looked after most of High Level's business at the prime brokerage in London. Then, after a tomato sandwich on rye bread at his desk at one o'clock, Duffy turned his attention to gilts: loans to the British government, in return for which it issued "gilt-edged," or guaranteed, bonds. If British banks got into trouble to the extent that John Veals believed they would, the government would have to borrow huge sums of money to refinance them and the tradable value of British debt would consequently fall to sub-Italian levels.

The London office of First New York bank contained a gilt specialist Duffy had had his eye on for a while: a young man who had made money throughout the previous twelve difficult months and was beginning to believe himself infallible. Duffy rang and asked him to make a two-way price in ten-year gilts for settlement in seven days' time. As he waited to hear back, Duffy rechecked his calculations, and when the spread came down the line to him, he sold short $10 billion worth of U.K. debt.

Victoria entered details of the gilt trade into the system and watched as they departed for their numerous electronic locations. None of these involved a proper exchange or a regulated forum of any kind. While the people with whom Duffy spoke by phone understood that High Level was the "end client," the actual counterparty they faced in the market was the legendarily strong American investment bank that, as prime broker, managed all the trades.

Problems began to arise midafternoon. The market in Allied Royal shares was too thin for Duffy to be able to trade further: there was simply not enough activity in it for him to put on positions of the magnitude he needed, and at four o'clock he called John Veals's cellphone to report his decelerating progress.

"OK, Kieran. Leave it with me. I'll see what I can do."

That evening, in his mezzanine study overlooking the garden, John Veals was scrutinizing a screenful of figures. He thought he could already see the faintest trace of O'Bagel's fingerprints.

So far so good, but Veals was worried. Anxiety was the staple of his work: night after night. His immediate problem was that the markets were so skittish, so nervous of financial collapse, that even the minimal movements he had seen might be noticed by others. The financial world was in a kind of suspended animation. On October 31, only seven weeks earlier, financial firms on Wall Street had lost $369 billion in a single day. The writing was smeared in letters ten feet high across the wall, but still people were trying to ignore it. The party was still on; the hard core, drunk on risk, unable to believe the gold rush might ever end, would not go home.

In this atmosphere, Veals doubted he could make the end of the week without a keen analyst somewhere spotting that simple U.K. health indicators—currency and gilt values—were down, and then making a connection with ARB.

The second problem was the one Duffy had rung about at teatime: that the market, as it stood, was too thin for him to put on a position of the size he wanted. Veals needed to spark some buying that he and Duffy could then sell into; before the ARB stock crashed, it must first therefore rise. The only way both to insure against others cashing in on ARB before he did and to create the market activity he needed was to do a Rothschild.

During the Napoleonic Wars, the Rothschild brothers had the fastest communication system in Europe: a pigeon post. Everyone in Lombard Street was aware that Nathan Rothschild would be the first to know how the Battle of Waterloo had ended, and this made it impossible for him to trade on his knowledge; his competitors would copy him and no one would want to be on the other side. So, with exaggerated furtiveness designed to draw attention to itself, he began to sell small amounts of government bonds. The herd followed, and the bond market crashed. Unknown to his rivals, Rothschild had, by using intermediaries, accumulated huge long positions in government bonds. When victory at Waterloo was announced, the patriotic rally in bond prices delivered him the largest fortune the City had ever seen.

Veals discussed the position at length on the phone to Stephen Godley. There was no sound from the other end, apart from the occasional grunt. After twenty minutes, Godley said, "OK, I've got it, John. We've built up a decent first-innings lead, but the next session's going to be crucial. I leave it in your capable hands. I'll make sure everything's fine in London tomorrow. Give O'Shlo my love."

Upstairs, Veals's son Finbar was settling down to watch the latest live episode of *It's Madness*.

He was feeling fully recovered from his whitey. A deep sleep with two strong ibuprofen tablets seemed to have done the trick.

His hand was steady, there was no more cold sweat and he felt sure that he was back in the real world. Only a frightening little twist of anxiety remained in his belly when he thought about what had happened—so he tried not to.

As a measure of respect, or something, he had decided not to smoke for a couple of days, so was sitting back with nothing more than a can of Pilsner in his hand.

The contestants were in the Barking Bungalow, where the celebrity panel could watch them go about their business. In addition to Scotty, the bipolar woman (whose real name, Valerie, had been forgotten) and Alan, the schizophrenic, there was a chronically depressed woman in her thirties called Sandra, an old man called Preston, whose diagnosis was unclear, and a youngster called Darren with severe antisocial personality disorder who claimed he was not mentally ill.

Sick or not, he certainly added something to the mix, as the newspaper reviews had pointed out, with his forthright aggression and willingness to take off his clothes and expose his lightly pixelated genitals to the camera.

Terry O'Malley now filled the screen, his red cheeks shining in close-up beneath the lights in the studio, which was dressed to look like an upmarket dinner party, with bottles of wine on the table, bowls of nuts and celebrity fruit—mangoes and kiwi.

"OK, ladies and gentlemen," said Terry, "we're coming to the business end of the evening. Are we ready for this? Lisa?"

Lisa nodded over her glass of wine. "Count me in, Tel."

"Let's do it," said Barry Levine.

With a theatrical gesture of his right arm, Terry pointed out emphatically. "Camera three, it's all yours. Take it away!"

The dinner-party set dissolved, and with it any sense of jollity. Instead, a steadicam showed the interior of a bare surgery, filmed in black and white, into which, one by one, the contestants were called for their daily "consultation." They were asked to sit in a chair by a desk, while the large leather seat on the active side of the desk, the "doctor's" side, remained empty. Every day the consultation contained a new "therapeutic challenge"—or "TC," as it was known. Usually, this was something quite unthreatening: telling the group an anecdote from childhood, or trying an all-fruit diet for a day.

First in was Alan, the schizophrenic.

"Good morning, Alan. How are we today?" The disembodied voice—a man's, portentous—was relayed through a concealed speaker.

Alan, a thin, half-bald man in middle age, tossed his head back and forth as though against invisible restraints. The camera moved in closer on his distracted eyes and their black sockets, cavernous with fatigue. He was clearly not well enough to play, and before the details of the daily challenge could be outlined to him, the light was switched off while someone went to pull him out.

The scene switched back to the celebrity dinner.

"Well what did you make of Alan, Lisa?" said Terry O'Malley, swiftly on top of the situation.

"I don't think Alan's really given us the best of himself since they've been in the bungalow," said Lisa. "You know, he's like such a nice guy, really supportive and that. And I think he's let himself down a bit."

"Thanks, Leese. Barry? What do you think?"

"To be honest, I think Alan's got to give a lot more of himself," said Barry. "He's got to show more commitment. He's got to really *want* it."

Finn went down to the kitchen for another can of lager, and when he rejoined the bungalow, the contestants had gathered in the living room for a karaoke session. This was one of the most popular elements of the entire show, the so-called Loony Tunes evening, when Lisa was delivered by helicopter to the secret Barking Bungalow location. A handheld camera caught her ducking beneath the rotors and running to the front door, accompanied by a security man. A second camera filmed the first cameraman in a blur of day-for-night vérité.

"... judged by our very own music specialist," Barry was say-

154

ing, dragging out his introduction as he watched Lisa being let into the house, "lead singer on no less than six top-ten hits and three platinum albums with the fabulous Girls From Behind, yes, it's L-i-i-i-i-s-s-a-a-a!"

Lisa clattered down the two steps inside the Barking Bungalow, expertly balanced in high heels and tiny skirt. She greeted the assembled contestants with loud bonhomie and tested out the karaoke microphone with a few bars from Girls From Behind's best-known hit, "Between You and I."

All seemed to be working well as the elderly Preston crossed the floor to have the rudiments of the machine explained to him by Lisa.

"So you take this in your hand, love," she said, giving him the microphone, "then you look down at this little screen and sing the words you can see. No don't hold it down there, not in front of your trousers like a . . . No, no, Preston, you naughty boy . . . Hold it up to your mouth . . . Now what have I said? Stop it, Barry. Now, what are you going to sing, love?"

Preston, a Londoner in a gray cardigan with heavy-rimmed glasses, was an experiment for *It's Madness*. Normally they liked the contestants to be no more than thirty-five years old, so that there was more likelihood of "chemistry" in the bungalow. The introduction to "You've Lost That Loving Feeling," the Righteous Brothers song, played loudly while Preston gazed at the screen by his feet.

"Where's Mandy?" said Preston. "I said I'd take her to the pictures. Why haven't you brought the car round?"

A cut to the celebrity studio showed Barry Levine saying, "Maybe we should give him the lyrics of 'Mandy' if that's what he wants to sing."

In a moment, a scuffle had broken out in the bungalow, with big Darren trying to force Preston to sing into the microphone, and Preston lashing out with his arms while Lisa, in exaggerated alarm, hid behind the sofa, peeping over the edge from time to time to wave to the camera.

"She's a natural, that girl," said Barry in the studio. "What a talent."

155

Four

Wednesday, December 19

I

Hassan al-Rashid was sitting on the Dover to Calais ferry, where he was surprised to find himself almost the only passenger. He'd imagined throngs of thirsty *kafirs* going to stock up at discount alcohol warehouses in time for their "religious" festival. As he came onboard down the covered companionway and stepped through the first available door, he found himself at once in an outsize alcohol-vending lounge; it was apparently called "Le Pub." He'd walked round both decks available to passengers, but there was no escape: every seat was in a licensed area. He placed himself as far as he could from the bar and stared through the window. The low, gunmetal sky met the high pewter sea at a smudged horizon; the world was wrapped in gray.

He'd risen with the alarm at six in Havering-atte-Bower to be in time to catch a train from Victoria. He found a seat in a quiet compartment and opened his book. At home he was reading the seminal *Milestones* by Sayyid Qutb for the third time, but didn't want to be seen with it, so had brought along one of the many new books that had recently been arriving in his father's study since the "literary gentleman" had been visiting. It was a "thriller" about horse racing, though not that thrilling. His concentration was disturbed by a raised voice. It was a youth who'd been evicted from first class by the ticket collector. The boy, though white, tried to sound black. He was accompanied by a man who actually was black: a tubby old-timer with a leather cap perched on top of graying dreadlocks.

They settled next to Hassan, and the youth occasionally stood up and shouted. He swore in his too-loud, fake-black voice, still angry with the ticket man. Next he tried to catch the eye of others in the carriage, but all were suddenly engrossed, even by giveaway newspapers. Hassan knew the type: attention-deficit and destined for a life in and out of prison; the old black man was presumably his probation officer or social worker.

At Faversham, the train divided and Hassan used the excuse to switch carriage with a dumbshow of having only just noticed that he was in the wrong section. At Dover station he waited for a bus to the port, but there was no bus. Then he saw a taxi and climbed in. They went past Dover College and down to the front with its dilapidated hotels; it was gone to seed in the mysterious way of all seaside towns. One hotel had an old red phone box in the forecourt, filled with flowering plants; the cliffs to their left looked less white than gray: grubby and tired in the winter light.

In the travel center, Hassan could choose between two ferry lines and picked the one with the first sailing.

"Name?" said the clerk behind her computer. "And first name?"

Why on earth did you have to give your name to buy a foot-passenger ticket? But Hassan was too surprised to lie. Worse was to come. A loudspeaker announcement directed him and his five fellow passengers to a coach. They drove smartly through the dock area, down white-edged lanes, and were nodded through by the man at the frontier post. As Hassan was starting to relax, the coach was suddenly waved into a shed. Everyone got out and had to put bags and coats through a scanner, then walk through a metal-detecting machine, exactly as at an airport. He hadn't foreseen this, and it was a setback, perhaps fatal, to his plan.

So as he sat encased in his gray world on the ferry, Hassan tried to work out how, assuming the scanning arrangements were the same in Calais, he might be able to get his cargo of hydrogen peroxide back through security without arousing suspicion. He hoped to buy the chemicals piecemeal in different pharmacies, to make

157

himself less remembered, but had also found, after only twenty minutes on the Internet, the address of a hairdressers' supplier in the outskirts where he could buy it all at once.

He had used Shahla's knowledge of French to prepare himself. She was always pleased, if a little surprised, to hear from him and, when he told her that he needed help, she'd asked him to her flat in Clapham. She made Persian kebabs with rice and salad; she had bought orange juice for him.

"All right, mister, what's it all about?"

He told her he was going on holiday to France in the summer and wanted to practice his conversation. Shahla clearly disbelieved him, but was too pleased to have his company to ask difficult questions. She'd visited friends of her father's in Lebanon and learned to speak French from a young age.

"I may have a slight Lebanese accent, Hass," she said, throwing back her long black hair as she leaned over to struggle with the cork in the wine bottle. "But they won't mind that in Provence."

Hassan was able to turn the conversation to the general topic of how similar many words were in the two languages.

"Exactly," said Shahla. "It's easy to have conversations about science or philosophy because the words are all the same. What's hard is when they talk about . . ." She glanced round the room. "You know, concrete things—windowsill, fender, poker, mantelpiece, castor, latch."

It was easy then for Hassan to have her confirm the pronunciation of oxygen, for instance, or hydrogen.

"*Hydrogène*. You'd say it 'eed-row-gen.' Try and gargle the 'r' a bit."

Later he slipped in peroxide.

"'Pay-rock-seed,'" said Shahla. "No, let me check. It may not have an acute." It didn't. "So it's 'pe-rock-seed.' Sorry about that."

He watched her as she reached up to put the dictionary back on its shelf. Her gray skirt rode up to show for a moment the navy blue tights above the brown leather boots. How long were those legs from ankle to hip? he wondered. The funny thing was that Shahla wasn't coltish on them, but moved quickly and with such balance.

Then they did some general conversation about shopping and getting into a bus or taxi.

"You're brilliant, Hass. I thought you said you couldn't speak a word."

"Aye, well we did study French at school. The Scottish system, you know. Hadn't quite packed up yet."

"So you did a GCSE or something?"

"Yes, but you didn't have to speak it to pass."

He didn't like to use Shahla in this way, but it was easy enough to explain it to himself. It was a question of priorities. The minor deception of a friend would be forgiven in the long perspective of establishing justice on earth and gaining paradise afterward. God would look well on Shahla for having helped him; he might even overlook her irreligion.

Hassan's conviction that he was right was troubled only by an aching sense of how lucky he was to have a friend who questioned him so little, who seemed to like him just for what he was. If everyone could have taken this view of him, he wondered, would he be planning to go to Calais at all?

He couldn't tell anyone of what Husam Nar was planning, but if there was one person in whom he might have confided, it was Shahla. There had been moments over the past two years when he had been tempted to tell her what path he was traveling, but he had always pulled back.

It was not that Shahla would have been unsympathetic; on the contrary her brown eyes glowed with concern for him. No, the reason he couldn't tell her was that he felt she would laugh.

She wouldn't call Special Branch or MI5 or even the local plods; she wouldn't tell his parents or his tutors, but he could just imagine her holding her face in her hands and shaking with laughter while her long black hair tumbled down over her breasts. "All this, Hass, for a disembodied voice in a desert?"

Every month he saw a magazine called *The Toad* on the news-stand and it seemed devoted only to showing how fake and dishonest the public world really was. On radio and television, he felt bombarded by cynicism about current affairs, about politics and, within certain limits of correctness, religion.

This low-minded national skepticism was part of what he wanted to leave behind in his devotion to what was pure and eternal. No *kafir* or Jew would ever understand just how spiritual and how demanding Islam really was; in the marrow of its being it meant that every breath and every thought you had was touched by the divine. Hassan's difficulty was that as a native Scotsman, resident there or in godless London all his life, he was saturated with British culture; his difficulty, if he could have been truthful to himself about it, was that he found *The Toad* quite funny.

Shahla was a Muslim and a friend; she shared the outlines of his identity; but she was also a danger because she had balanced things in such a different way. The more he was drawn to her, the more he had to keep away.

On the ferry, Hassan noticed that most of the conversations he overheard were about money—or rather, about price and value. The chips, the beer, the duty-free drink . . . They were obsessed by it, and it made him long for cooler, more spiritual air. His father had often told him as a child that their religion had sprung up because the Prophet was shocked that the people of his tribe were so mercenary. The backbone of Islam, in Knocker's version, was the need for generosity, almsgiving—for sharing with the weaker members of the group.

Hassan remembered coming in his parents' car to France when he was eight or nine, when the ugly materialism of his fellow countrymen, and their drunkenness, had not particularly bothered him. Now everything he saw affirmed the Prophet's words. Every crude action and word of those around him made him more convinced that he alone on the gently heaving ferry had access to the truth. It was exhilarating—the way that everything, every detail,

160

every observation, played into his heady conviction. It was almost, he imagined, like being in love.

At Calais docks, he boarded the shuttle bus, then saw a taxi draw up ahead and drop its passenger. He went to the front of the bus and asked the driver to release him. She opened the double doors with a pneumatic hiss and he was in time to catch the taxi and instruct him, "*Center ville*." ("Not 'sontruh vee.' You sound the 'l': 'sontruh *veal*,'" Shahla had stressed.)

Just outside the dock area were bars called Le Pub and Le Liverpool, where Hassan pictured busloads of vomiting English fans on their way back from a match.

The driver began talking to him conversationally, so Hassan said "*Pardon*," pulled his phone from his pocket and feigned a call. He had wondered whether he should perhaps pretend to be deaf, to wear an obvious hearing aid, but then wondered how many deaf Pakis took a taxi into Calais. Be normal, always normal, Salim had said.

He was deposited near the huge town hall. The driver gave him a card with his number and told him, so far as Hassan could understand, to ask in a shop and anyone would call the cab for him. To gather his thoughts, Hassan went to look at the statue of *The Burghers of Calais* by Rodin. The dejected men in their robes and chains had outsize flat feet; some of them looked more like bronze apes than town councillors.

It was three o'clock and growing dark already. Hassan had forgotten to bring his gloves, and his hands were cold. They always were in winter; it was presumably a genetic weakness that harked back to his ancestors in the warm Mirpur Valley. Or was that an impermissible thought?

Hassan walked down the Boulevard Jacquard with its halfhearted Christmas lights. He looked into a pharmacy on the left, advertised by its large and flashing green cross. It was forbiddingly empty, with a serious bespectacled woman behind the counter. "Edith Dumont. Pharmacien" it said on the glass door. He could imagine her saying, "And why exactly do you require so much hair dye?"

He had the answer. "*Je suis coiffeur.*" "Zher swee quaff-urr." He had got Shahla to spell it out for him in a conversational game of what might be said to him by people he met on holiday. He'd also taken a few business cards with the blessing of the local hairdresser in Havering.

The eye of Edith Dumont, however, was too forbidding. He tried the shop across the road, then the one in the Boulevard Gambetta, without ever feeling he could manage it. How odd it was they all sold so much homeopathic stuff and "*produits vétérinaires*"—dog food—as well as skin tonics advertised by naked women with golden skin. Finally, he tried the supermarket at the far end of the Center Commercial, the indoor shopping center. At least he wouldn't have to speak to anyone there, but could just load a trolley. His eyes scanned the ceiling for CCTV cameras; none were visible, but perhaps they were just better hidden than at home.

The "*Cheveux*" section of the supermarket was huge, but the amount of hydrogen peroxide in a bottle of proprietary coloring was so small that he would need to buy up the whole place and all its reserve stock. The hardware section had variations of something called Javel in large enough bottles, but its active ingredient was chlorine; it was bleach, but of the wrong kind.

Hassan walked swiftly back down the overheated mall, with its tinny music and sweet smell, past a shop selling women's underclothes where a *kafir* poster girl in scarlet suspenders pushed her breasts against the glass, and out into the freezing air.

He found an alley where he was unobserved, then bent to say a brief prayer.

In a twenty-four-hour brasserie on the Boulevard La Fayette, he ordered something easy to translate—"*Une omelette*"—and gave the waiter the taxi driver's card.

"*Pouvez-vous—*"

"*Oui, oui.*" It was clearly not the first time the waiter had been asked.

Ten minutes later he was in the back of a sickly-scented people carrier on his way to the out-of-town hairdressing supplier whose address he'd printed off the Internet and now handed without speaking to the driver. The shop was a fifteen-minute drive away on the edge of an industrial zone, and had a counter in front with stockroom shelves behind, like a builders' merchant in London.

On the counter Hassan placed a piece of paper, on which he'd written his order, and one of the cards from his local hairdresser, in case he needed proof to qualify for the cash-and-carry discount.

The shopkeeper was a man of about sixty in denim overalls with greasy gray hair and thick glasses. He fetched a cardboard box, about the size of a case of wine, from the back of the store and placed it on the counter with an effortful grunt. For the sake of realism, Hassan handed over a second piece of paper requesting twenty liters of conditioner. He paid in cash.

With the boxes in the back of the people carrier, Hassan said to the driver, "OK, *maintenant vin. Supermarché.*"

It was dark by the time they reached the wine warehouse, which was on the edge of a different industrial zone, apparently on the other side of Calais.

The driver looked reluctant to wait a second time, but Hassan showed him the large roll of euros in his pocket and the man nodded.

On the concrete slab inside the warehouse were thousands of different wines and vintages displayed in open wooden boxes. Rhône, Roussillon, Alsace . . . The places and the chateaux meant nothing to Hassan, who wanted one thing only: screw tops. Had the French ever heard of such things? he wondered, as he went from one primly corked burgundy to another. Eventually, among the rosés of Bordeaux, his search was rewarded. He put a case in his trolley and took it to the checkout.

A young man passed a handheld bleeper over it and the price rang up on the electronic till.

"*Pouvez-vous,* er . . . ?" Hassan mimed lifting the case with one hand and the young man nodded. He tied some hairy string round the carton in such a way that it made a primitive handle.

"*Merci,*" said Hassan, parting with more euros from his roll. "*Toilettes?*"

The man said something he didn't understand, but Hassan followed his gesture clearly enough. He carried the case in the direction indicated, through the door, and secreted it under the sink. He went quickly back to the taxi, held up three fingers to the driver, saying "*Trois minutes,*" and carried the carton of hydrogen peroxide back across the floor of the warehouse to the lavatory. He took both boxes into the cubicle and locked the door.

There was something profoundly satisfying about pouring away alcohol, then refilling the wine bottles with a purer liquid—something closer to the heart of the almighty God. Hassan gargled with some of the wine and spat it down the seatless lavatory; then he splashed some down the front of his clothes to make himself smell like a *kafir* on a Christmas outing. He resealed the wine carton carefully with the brown tape so that it appeared unopened.

The taxi took him back to the passenger terminal of the ferry, and he tipped the driver, though not so generously that it would stay in his mind. The next departure was not on the line he had come over with, but left in only half an hour; he bought a single ticket, disclosing his name again, then took the carton of hair conditioner to the Gents and dumped it in a cubicle.

He was ready to go. He said a brief prayer, opened the lavatory door and made for the security area to which he had been directed by the ticket clerk.

Two bored young men stood by the scanner and the metal detector. Hassan hoisted the wine box onto the conveyor belt and placed his jacket in a plastic tray behind it. In a moment of inspiration, he left his mobile phone in his trouser pocket, so that when he walked through the metal detector, it let out a screech. In the ensuing body search, the finding of the cellphone and the repassing of the detector, nobody took any notice of the case of Bordeaux rosé as it chugged slowly on the runners down to the end of the ramp.

Hassan made male drinking noises, laughed and breathed fumes on the younger guard as he hoisted his "wine" up and made his way over to the brightly lit waiting area. There were only three other foot passengers, and he expected a quiet crossing. He recited a few *surah* of the Koran silently to himself as he waited for the gates to the shuttle bus to open.

Hassan al-Rashid knew the Koran very well. Scriptures you take in as a child, his father told him, are with you always; they provide the landscape of your life. So when he went to his first meeting with Salim at the Pudding Mill Lane Mosque he quickly saw that he was among people who either hadn't read the book or who'd moved on from it. This surprised him. He'd expected the group to be scripturally based.

The atmosphere, though not really religious, was collegiate and warm. Salim introduced him to the others—about twenty-five, all men—and they went to pray. Afterward, they had fruit juice and cigarettes while they listened to a speaker in the meeting room. The speaker referred to a famous book by Ghulam Sarwar, and Hassan remembered it from comparative religion classes at school in Renfrew. It was a basic text read by British schoolchildren of all faiths; its central claim was that in true Islam there was no distinction between religious belief and political action. Islam contained everything that was necessary for men to run and build their own societies. The only problem was that there was not yet a truly Islamic state anywhere in the world: kings, generals, dictators or Westernized democracy got in the way. It followed that, since religion and politics were coterminous, the task of the believer was a practical one: to build the true state—the pure Islamic model that had been absent since the last caliph.

"That's my simple proposal for you today," concluded the speaker, a softly spoken man of about thirty. "And it's a more inviting life task than that available to the Christian or the Jew. They believe their political structures are separate from spiritual beliefs. They also believe they have already achieved civil perfection. Their idea of this is . . . the United States of America."

There was some low satirical laughter.

Hassan was not impressed by the speaker. When at the age of sixteen he'd first told his father about this idea of an Islamic state,

Knocker had ridiculed it. "It's not in the Koran," he said, "it's a pure invention. Who's filled your head with this nonsense?"

"A book they teach us all at school."

Knocker was appalled. "And who wrote this rubbish?"

"His name is Ghulam Sarwar."

"That joker!" said Knocker. "He's not an imam, he's a business management lecturer! How come they pass that stuff around?"

"I don't know, but that's what's given out. To all the children. Of all faiths."

Shamefaced, Hassan had not mentioned the Islamic state again: he had readdressed himself to the central message of the Koran, which was to devote oneself to Allah or risk hellfire in all eternity. Of course, there was also practical advice: be kind to orphans, pay the alms levy, go to Mecca if you can, sleep only with the servant girls of your own house and not with other men's. But the overwhelming, overpowering message of the book, which Hassan knew from back to front and of which he could recite large sections in Arabic, was that Allah was the true and only God; that, while Abraham, Noah and Jesus were decent men, the Jews and Christians were wrong in their beliefs; and that if you did not believe in Allah and Islam then you would be tortured for all time after death.

There was nothing in the Koran about the politics of building an Islamic state; the Prophet had not concerned himself with such things. So, as the discussion grew heated around him, Hassan found himself become detached from it. These young men reminded him of the members of the Left Student Group at college; there was a competition going on among them to see who could be more radical in his alignment. At college it had been a contest between the International Marxist Group, the Socialist Workers Party or the mysterious Red International. Here the name-drop of Muslim Youth International was finessed by World Islam League; Mid-East Forum was trumped by Jamaat-e-Islami. He also had misgivings about the way they referred to all non-Muslims as *kafirs*. It was all right for Jews to refer to non-Jews as "Gentiles,"

166

but less so to call them "goys." To Hassan's ear, "*kafir*" had a slur of assumed racial superiority about it.

He sighed. At least the Pudding Mill Lane Mosque had a prayer area for women. That seemed an advance on some of the places he'd visited, where row upon row of battered men's shoes were lined up outside with never a female slipper. After the political debate, matters moved into calmer waters as they read out news of football tournaments, youth camps and fund-raisers.

Afterward, Salim put his arm round Hassan's shoulder as they walked toward the station.

"Did you enjoy it?" he said.

"Up to a point," said Hassan. "I don't agree with the political agenda. There's no basis for it in the Koran."

"Religions move on," said Salim. "Even the word of God evolves through human interpretation. That's what theology is for. Other religions are the same. Christ had only male apostles. Now the Church of England even has female ministers."

"I wouldn't take the Church of England as a model for anything," said Hassan.

Salim laughed. "Of course not. But you can look at it like this. True Muslims need to live in a society that respects their beliefs and gives them every chance of enjoying paradise when they die. Whether the Koran contains instruction to the last letter for making this new society is something the textual scholars can dispute. But meanwhile is it such a terrible aspiration to want to live in such a good place on earth or to want to help to build it?"

"If you put it like that, then—"

"I do put it like that," said Salim. His deep voice was reasonable and reassuring; he seemed to have reserves of eloquence he'd kept hidden at their first meeting in the juice bar.

"Can I give you a lift? That's my old banger over there by the fence. Where do you live?"

"It's OK," said Hassan. "I'll take the train."

"It's a DLR station. It's probably not open at this time of the evening. Come on. Hop in. It's no trouble."

* * *

As the ferry was leaving for Dover, a strange thing happened: it began to fill up rapidly. Several coaches must have caught it just in time, Hassan thought, as he tried to find a seat away from the slopping of alcohol. He was pushed out of the way by a fat woman in her sixties making for the food court. "Look at 'er go! Like a bloody grayhound!" her jovial companion shouted. Amongst the crowd of new passengers was a sense of hilarious relief at being homeward bound; a day on foreign soil had been enough. They carried pyramids of pale chips from the servery and ate them with their hands.

Next to the food court was a club lounge, though you had to pay to go in: £15 to escape the rabble, read free copies of the tabloids and have "complimentary" coffee. Hassan didn't want to stand out from the crowd; he found a seat among the beer drinkers downstairs and noticed that the woman opposite was the one who had sat next to him on the shuttle bus to the ferry: young, Indian, quite well dressed, reading a middlebrow bestseller—typical, he thought, of the new MI5 recruits.

He looked down the deck to see if he could plausibly escape. There was a Café Bravo concession at the front of the ferry, but its queue had at least thirty people in it. At the other end of the deck was—of course—a giant bar. It was a nuisance to lug his heavy wine case down there, but he wanted to see if the suspicious woman followed.

"Any spirit. Double it for an extra £1," said a notice behind the bar, where Hassan positioned himself, with a good view of the whole room.

Some of the *kafirs* were so fat they could barely manage to get the trays full of lager and crisps back to their tables; many of them used sticks to help the knees that had given way beneath their weight. The younger ones sprawled on the red seats with their pierced bellies showing as they rolled down in lard layers over their low-cut jeans. Hassan noticed how many of the people in the bar were misshapen or deformed, though felt a slight unease at do-

168

ing so, not sure at what point religious righteousness became a kind of racism. Above their heads came the fizzle and thump of a music video on a screen where a woman with dyed hair mimed fellatio on a microphone.

Hassan thought of the Prophet's life and of how in his religion God was immanent in all things, as he had been in the Sunna—the everyday actions of the Prophet; there was no disjunction between the sacred and divine because to a true believer all was holy, all was pure.

But suppose the afterlife was not as the Book described but a low-ceilinged, strip-lit hell like this? Not a garden of peace but a *kafir* ferry?

Hassan smiled as he placed his foot on top of his wine carton in a proprietary and confident way. He had no real concerns. His belief, at moments like this, was adamantine.

At Dover, he had to wait on the cold, deserted platform for an hour for a train to Charing Cross. There was a security announcement about unattended parcels.

With his own package tightly in his hand, Hassan walked up and down to keep warm. Through the glass door of the station manager's office he saw bored men waiting for their cold shift to be over. How few human beings lived life as if it mattered, he thought; to most of them it was just a case of passing time.

Eventually, the train came and he found an empty carriage. It was nearly nine o'clock and he had been on the go for fifteen hours. With his feet on the wine box, Hassan settled back against the headrest and fell asleep in the fug.

Above his head was a picture of a lone red suitcase with the words "Increased threat to your security."

II

Spike Borowski had arrived at the Worcester Park training ground at nine-fifteen that morning and parked his small German saloon. His customized large German saloon was on order from Bavaria

169

and the dealer had lent him the embarrassing two-liter, two-door job in the meantime. In his kitbag he carried two pairs of boots, underwear, sweatshirts, gloves, a selection of crucifixes and two dictionaries. Max, the bootman, had told him on the phone there would be fluorescent bibs and a selection of team kit at the ground. Borowski looked up "bib" in his Polish-English dictionary, where it offered "*śliniaczek*." His English-English dictionary defined bib as "child's food guard"; though "bib *v*" was also defined as "drink alcohol to excess." He'd heard a lot about English footballers' habits, but he didn't think the manager would kick off a training session by drinking to excess. Afterward, maybe.

At first, Spike thought his bossy German satnav had brought him to the wrong place. This was not what he understood by "training ground," which had always been a hectare of rough grass with iron railings and a single-story building with an outside urinal. This was something else entirely. For a start, there were seven football pitches, one with stands for spectators and one, Astroturf, under cover of a giant tent. The building was painted white over three floors with a pillared portico; it reminded him of the country club in Connecticut he'd seen in an American comedy film. However, the security man on the gate seemed to recognize him and nodded him through with a smile.

Inside the main building, on the first floor, was a canteen, where some of the first-team squad were eating a late breakfast. Spike had met a couple of them at the ground when he posed on the pitch after signing his papers and they nodded in his direction. One was eating toast with some sort of chocolate spread smeared on it, the other was spooning in cereal.

Spike took a tray and pushed it along in front of the servery. He took a cup of tea. He had already eaten eggs and rye bread in the hotel in Chelsea where he was staying till they'd found him a flat, and they were lying heavy on his stomach.

"Fancy a smoothie, love?" said the woman behind the counter.

"What?"

She picked up a bottle and showed him.

He shook his head and moved off. "'Fancy a smoothie, love?'" What did it all mean? The way these people spoke was not in the books; he was already aware of that, and had taken steps to understand them. Using the computer in the "office suite" at his hotel, Spike had found a website called interbabel.com that linked into numerous thesauruses and colloquial translation engines. Inter babel.com certainly had the dope. It had so many possibilities, in fact, that he was spoiled for choice, overinformed. This didn't stop him pursuing all the links and meanings, all the definitions and re-translations: he'd graduated in politics and economics before taking up football professionally; he owed his degree to his willingness to study thoroughly, and he carried the habit through to all parts of life. "Stubborn" ("*przymiotnik*") or "dogged" ("*uparty*") were words the press in his own country applied to him.

After breakfast, Spike went down the corridor, past numerous carpeted offices with shimmering flat-screen computers, including the private lair of the Turkish manager, Mehmet Kundak, to the team room. In sweatshirts and shorts, sipping glucose drinks, the first team lolled on rows of padded luxury-leather recliners. Kundak came in from a side door and told Archie Lawler, the coach, to start the video, which showed film of the last time they had played that evening's opponents. Occasionally Lawler would pause it and point out the shape of the opposing midfield, the triangles they played.

After about five minutes, Spike began to panic. Although the score had apparently been 1–1, his team had never won the ball. Had he joined them on false pretenses? Were they really that inept? Wave after wave of opposition attacks came crashing down on them, but as they watched it the players looked unembarrassed and Lawler much less alarmed than he needed to be.

"Why we never have the ball?" Spike asked an African sitting next to him.

"We know how we play," he said. "The film just shows their moves. It's cut."

Spike laughed. "Is big relief."

171

The African ignored him. After some brutal exhortation from Lawler about the evening game, Spike followed the other players downstairs through a huge carpeted vestibule and into a corridor from which led numerous treatment and changing rooms. He got ready, took one of the club tracksuits, size XL, crossed himself and trotted out onto the pitches.

The first-team squad numbered thirty-eight, but without the nine on loan and the chronically injured there were twenty-five at the training ground. Seven reserves went off to train with the youth teams, leaving the eighteen-man squad, including Spike, for the evening league game. They gathered by the side of one of the pitches and bent themselves into postures like figures in a medieval depiction of hell. They locked hands round their ankles; they pulled one foot up into the buttocks until they could bear it no longer; they reached for the sky and laid their hands flat on the ground while standing. Spike joined in, though not wholeheartedly. After forty minutes, when every muscle fiber had been tweaked, expanded, rested and stretched again, they were thought ready for some action.

"We're going to be working on set pieces," said Archie Lawler. "Spike, get on the far post."

For half an hour, Spike found himself doing things he hadn't done since the youth team in Gdansk. He was marked by the reserve center back, Charles Watiyah, a giant Liberian, who was keen to force his way into the first team. Every time Spike went to head the ball, he found himself pushed in the small of the back; it was nothing violent, just enough to unbalance him. On the occasions he became airborne, he found the Liberian's head in his mouth. The crosses were provided by little Danny Bective, one of the few English players in the squad, a midfielder with what Archie Lawler had described to a television interviewer as an "unbelievable engine." He kicked the ball over a wall of life-size plastic players in bright red shirts that Lawler had wheeled up and left only eight yards in front of him. There was no point in moving it

172

back the mandatory ten, because that never happened in a professional game.

"All right, Vladimir, you get on the far post now," said Archie. "Spike, you take a blow."

Vladimir Stoev was a Bulgarian who had been at the club for two seasons and had scored eighteen goals the year before. He had once been banned for three months when a drug test found traces of something he claimed had come from an anti-asthma medicine; this, and his origins, had got him the nickname Vlad the Inhaler. Spike watched how Vlad dealt with Charles Watiyah, by jumping up and down like an excited child, moving around so he was not in one place long enough to be fouled, then making sure he jumped early, as soon as Bective had begun his three-pace run-up to deliver the cross. Sometimes Vlad was already on the way down by the time the ball arrived, but he could often maintain his height by leaning on Watiyah's shoulder. Finally he elbowed him in the face and managed to head the ball past the stand-in goalkeeper.

"The beautiful game," said Spike to the Egyptian left-back, Ali al-Asraf.

"Fuck off," said al-Asraf.

Spike wondered whether he'd said the right thing. "Is what Pelé say," he explained. But had something been lost in the translation from Portuguese to Polish to English? "The beautiful game. The . . . lovely play?" He felt the links of interbabel.com clicking uselessly in his head.

Al-Asraf spat at his feet and trotted off to run through some cones with Danny Bective and Sean Mills.

The next part of training was "One-Touch-He." The players assembled in a circle with one, a small African Spike didn't know, standing in the middle. When they were ready, Archie Lawler threw a ball to one of them and he hit it first time to another, who sidefooted it first time to a third, who chipped it to Spike, who nodded it on toward Vladimir. At that moment, Vlad turned and moved away, so the African in the middle was able to nip in and take the ball.

All the players began laughing, and the one next to Spike came up to him and flicked his ear, hard, with the thumb and forefinger of his right hand. Then every player in the circle came up and did the same thing. Seventeen stinging flicks were administered by seventeen laughing millionaires before the game resumed, with Spike as "he." He was sweating and panting before a slightly underhit pass enabled him to dispossess Sean Mills with an ugly lunge. When Mills had stopped swearing, Spike enjoyed flicking his ear along with the others.

After showering, Spike explored the ground-floor warren further. There was a resident doctor in a small office of his own and, opposite, a glass-paneled door with the words "Nutrition Team" stenciled in black. In the treatment room afterward, Spike was offered a rubdown by Kenny Hawtrey, the chief physio. He saw that two of the other players were already stretched out on the green and white couches having their calf muscles worked over and thought it would be the right thing to do. On the table next to him was Danny Bective.

Spike tried to remember what the assistant manager had said about him on television. Yes. "Archie say you have incredible motor," said Spike.

"Yeah, it's a Sherman Pathfinder."

"Er . . . And you do much running."

"Yeah. They like that."

"What happens now?" said Spike.

"Normally we have dinner upstairs and go home. But because there's an evening match we'll have a big meal at teatime in the hotel near the ground."

When they had had their showers and were in the car park, nineteen men climbing alone into nineteen large cars, Danny said, "By the way, mate. Word of warning. Don't let Kenny Hawtrey rub you down."

"Why?"

"Shirt lifter."

"What?"

"Iron hoof."

"Sorry?"

"Fuckin' bummer, innit?"

"Aah . . ."

Something about Danny's pose made Spike understand. As he was about to climb into his car, one of the press liaison people took his elbow.

"Tadeusz, do you mind giving a quick autograph? Young lad over there, he's bunked off school to come and see you."

"Sure, I meet him."

Standing by the exit from the car park was a youth of about sixteen, slightly built, with curly brown hair and a few pink spots on his chin. He wore a T-shirt, jeans off his hip and a blue hooded top.

"Hello. I am Spike Borowksi." He held out his hand to the young man.

"Finbar Veals," he said softly, looking down at his new white trainers.

None of the three syllables sounded like a name to Spike. English people didn't seem to be called John Robinson anymore; but linguistically it had been a bad day all round.

"You want I sign your book?"

"Yeah, thanks." Finn held out a battered school notebook.

"How long you support the team?" said Spike. "Since you a kid?"

"No, I . . . er, I don't. I . . . support a different team."

"What?" Spike laughed. "Maybe you support Chelsea!"

"No, I . . . It doesn't matter. I wanted to meet you because I'm thinking of signing you in my Dream Team eleven. Do you know that website?"

"No. You tell me."

Finn blushed. "The Buyers' Guide said you're like Carlton King with a first touch, or Gary Fowler with an IQ."

Spike laughed. "Is very rude. Your newspapers too. They say

something like I play like Orlando if he stop being a girl. Is not kind to Orlando. Just because he wear earrings."

"No, I think it's because he dives. Do you think you are going to score a lot of goals? Are you feeling confident?" The meeting was important to Finn, and he found his natural shyness ebbing.

"If I get picked by the boss I will score. But we have four strikers, so is not easy."

"But he won't play Vladimir Stoev now you're here, will he? He hasn't scored for months."

"Is strong player." Spike was thinking of the elbow to Charles Watiyah's face.

"They say he only scores if there's a full moon," said Finn.

Spike laughed. "OK . . . Finbar? That your name?"

"Finn."

"OK. Finn. You also go to training ground of team you support?"

"No."

"But here you come."

"It was important for me to see you in the flesh."

"For a place in your team which is not in flesh."

"Yes," said Finn. "I know it sounds weird, but all the guys in my year have teams in Dream Team and I don't want to be relegated."

Spike looked at him oddly. "I think you live in dreamland. Like Disneyland, yeah?"

"Well, no, I think it's the real thing."

"And who else in your special team?"

Finn went through his current eleven. There were two England international center halves, a Congolese enforcer in front of them, a Brazilian show pony on the wing and a giant Dane in goal. They were his big-money signings. The rest had been squeezed out of the budget that remained to him; they included a psychopathic Guinean with a dyed white goatee, a Welshman on a short fuse and a one-sided Colombian. He had sold a French striker and needed a steady supply of goals.

"I see," said Spike. "You make some good choice and some bad ones, I think. Now you meet me, what you say? Think I can score goals on the Internet?"

"You have to score them on the pitch, then they can be counted on the—"

"I know, I understand," said Spike. "But did you think I was good enough in training? You watch?"

"Yes, I saw." Finn felt suddenly shy again. How was he to tell this man he needed to watch out for Sean Mills and Danny Bective, how they'd shafted the prospects of the last expensive striker?

"I must go now," said Finn. His encounter with reality had left him drained.

"You want I take you somewhere in the car?"

"No, no, thanks. I'm fine. Thank you for the autograph."

Finn turned and jogged off, out of the car park and down the pavement by the suburban street.

Spike watched him go and frowned. Why wasn't the kid at school?

Finn was already in the back of a black taxi. It was useful that the training ground was in the right direction for his second point of call on his day out: a pet cemetery in Esher.

He'd set his alarm for 8:32 that morning and called the direct line to the school office while his voice was still sounding fogged by sleep. Registration was at 8:40 and the form teachers were in the classroom by 8:30 so he had every chance of getting Peggy, the friendly school secretary. His luck—or timing—was in, and it was easy to convince Peggy that he felt "terrible." He did: he always felt awful when he first woke up. His father had long since left the house, while his mother, he guessed, would be drinking milky coffee in one of the larcenously priced delis on Holland Park Avenue. Finn went downstairs in his T-shirt and pajama bottoms and made himself some hot chocolate and a toasted bagel with crunchy chocolate spread. He nodded to Marla, the Brazilian cleaner, as she passed the fizzing iron over one of his father's shirts in the laundry room. Marla spoke hardly any English and never got to the end of the few words she did know. "Good mor" was as far as she went in greeting; she thought Finn's mother was called "Vaness."

It was a big day ahead. As well as checking out a striker for his virtual team, Finn was going to a place recommended by Ken, his best friend at school. Ken wasn't really called Ken, he was really called Leo, but when you typed Leo as predictive text on your mobile, it came out as Ken.

Ken told Finn he was mad to score his dope in Pizza Palace from a runner working for that king of rip-off artists, Liston Brown in Muswell Hill. He should go to the main supplier—to a farmer. So, at Esher station, he gave the taxi an address near West End Common. Paying for cabs was easy for Finn, as he always had cash, thanks to his Allied Royal debit card. His balance was kept permanently topped up by a trickle-down from one of his father's accounts; John Veals fiercely resented high-street bank charges and had set up the arrangement so that Finn could never overdraw.

The taxi pulled up outside a large low villa with a gravel forecourt and a waist-high brick wall. Next to the wrought iron gates was a signboard, like those announcing bed and breakfast or a two-star hotel in Bexhill. In blue letters on a red background, it said "Snoozetime Pet's Rest." Finn rang the bell by the locked gates, wondering vaguely what his English teacher had said about apostrophes.

The front door of the house opened, and a slightly hunched man came toward Finn over the gravel. He wore an anorak over tracksuit bottoms with brown leather shoes, had smudged spectacles on a long cord round his neck and gray hair sticking out under the sides of a purple baseball cap. There was something wrong about old people wearing baseball caps, Finn felt; and this man looked as though he'd slept in his clothes for a few days.

"I've come about a cat," said Finn, as instructed by Ken.

"I see. And is Pussy still with us?"

"Er . . . Yes, but it's kind of on its last legs. Can you show me some, like, you know, what you do if I bring it."

The man unlocked the gate. He held out his hand to Finn. "Simon Tindle," he said. "This way please."

"Yeah, right, er . . . Finn, yeah," Finn mumbled.

"Now then," said Tindle, "I can begin by showing you the Garden of Remembrance. We have a special position here, backing onto the common. Would you like to tell me a little about the beloved? I hope you don't think I'm being rude."

"Rude? No. Why?"

"I'd hate it if you thought I was being rude. People can take things the wrong way and I don't want to cause offense."

They were walking beside the house down an alley, through a gate and out into a large grassed area of perhaps an acre, crisscrossed by gravel paths.

"Most of my friends," said Tindle, "prefer to take the departed home with them but one or two are buried here. You can see all our different stone memorials."

"When you say 'friends' . . ."

"I call them friends because I don't like to think of them as clients. You'd be my friend if you decide to leave Pussy with us."

"I see. So I, like, bring the . . . like, the body . . . and then what?"

"I give you a special heat-sealed thermabag now. You pop Pussy into it when she passes, then you bring her down here on the train. Or in the car. It doesn't matter, so long as it's within twenty-four hours. After that, it can get a little . . . I hope you don't think I'm being—"

"No, no. Not at all. Bring him down here."

"Oh. Pussy's a boy is he?"

"Well, whatever, bring her down and then?"

"We have a crematorium. You see over there? With the chimney."

Finn followed the direction of Tindle's pointing finger to a large outhouse.

"Looks like Auschwitz," Finn said, without thinking. They were always doing the Holocaust at school. That and climate change.

"Oh dear."

"I'm sorry," said Finn, "I didn't mean to be—"

"No, not to worry, it's very upsetting when the dear one is ready to pass. I can show you inside the crematorium if you like. It's very humane."

"No, that's all right. I believe you. Then what?"

"Then I give you the cremains."

"The 'cremains'?"

"Yes, the ashes if you prefer. I think that sounds rather coarse, though. Cremains is more dignified, don't you think?"

"OK."

"And we choose a casket. I can show you a selection when we go indoors. We can do that now, if you like. And most of my friends like a cup of tea after the cremation. And then you take Pussy home."

They were now standing outside the aluminium-framed French doors at the back of the house.

"What I really wanted," said Finn, following the formula Ken had told him, "was the full deluxe service with grass covering."

Tindle stopped. "Oh, I see. Aren't you rather . . . I hope you don't think I'm being rude, but aren't you rather young?"

"Eighteen," said Finn, pulling himself up to his full height.

"All right. Come on then. This way."

Finn followed Tindle down some crazy paving, past a bronze bust of an evil-looking German Shepherd with the words "Ever Faithful" on a plaque beneath it, round the back of the crematorium and into a dropped level of garden, where there was another low shed, this time without a chimney. Tindle took a bunch of keys from a purse in his anorak pocket and fumbled with the two heavy padlocks on the door. He held the door back for Finn.

It took Finn's eyes a moment to adjust to the overhead lights.

"Ah, methinks I see the metal halide blink!" said Tindle. "The 1,000-watt bulb can put out your eyes if you're not careful. But they put out ever so much more light than your old fluorescent."

"Heat, too," said Finn.

"It would be a lot hotter without the fan up there. But it has to be pretty hot. And humid."

Now that Finn was standing next to Tindle in the germinating

180

atmosphere, he could tell his guess about the old man's clothes was right.

Marijuana plants filled the shed from wall to wall. They were potted on wooden trestles at about waist height, while the lights, in long galvanized metal shades, were suspended on chains from the ceiling, drenching each plant, forcing its growth, so that the room was filled with an odor that made Finn's mouth go dry and his stomach tense in reflex.

"This is a hydroponic system," said Tindle. "That means no soil. It's cleaner, quicker and you get more weed. Instead of getting the nutrients haphazardly from the soil, the plants get it in exactly the right amount through what we put in the water."

Finn inspected the array of tubes and pipes that fed the flourishing plants in their plastic containers, sweating under the lights. They had woolly buds around the top, the promise of power, of great synapse-blocking and reality adjustment.

"This is Aurora Indica, very potent," said Tindle. "This little madam is my version of Super Skunk, which was an attempt to beef up the famous Skunk Number One. I've crossed it with a strain of Purple Haze for quick effect."

"Sounds great."

"Let me show you through here," said Tindle, opening a locked door at the end of the room. "In here we use the sea-of-green method."

In the second area, the plants made a denser, lower canopy. The idea was to pack the space with smaller plants that matured earlier and force a continuous year-round harvest, Tindle explained. "We're concentrating all the effort in the main cola, this bit here at the top of the plant," he said. "It gets so heavy that we have to support it with chicken wire. When they get nice and tall, we tie the top back down on the stem, like here, leave it for a week and then let it go—and hey presto, it's got twice as bushy. It's a year-round harvest festival."

"Yeah, great," said Finn. Something about the room made him uneasy. It was all so unnatural. When he'd first read about marijuana he'd pictured it as a mild weed that grew beside the road in sunshine and was smoked by laughing girls in California. This shed looked like a factory, where everything was forced, intensified.

"Well, anyway, that's enough horticulture," said Tindle. "Now let's do some business. Shall we go to my office?"

"All right." Finn felt nervous. He knew how much he paid at Pizza Palace to Liston Brown's runner for half a sandwich bag of weed and he knew it ought to be cheaper if he was cutting out the middle man, but he wasn't sure he'd know the jargon. If he was confused, he'd be too embarrassed to reveal his ignorance.

Tindle locked the grow shed and led him over the crazy paving to the French doors at the back of his house. With his foot, he cleared away a tortoiseshell cat that was in the way.

"That your cat?" said Finn.

"No, it's next door's," said Tindle, pulling back the doors. "I haven't got pets. I don't like animals. I'm allergic."

Indoors, he pulled the flap down on a walnut bureau, raised his greasy glasses on their string and opened a notebook. "Now," he said, "what can I do you for?"

"I want something that'll give a great high. Big, powerful, but you know, no ill effects."

"And what quantity are we talking about, young man?"

"I . . . Er, what, you know, what do you, like, deal in?"

"Half a kilogram is the minimum I do. I could do you half a kilo of Super Skunk Two, cut with Aurora. That's a popular mixture. It's good value, too, because you don't need much of it."

"What's it feel like?"

"I don't smoke myself because of my allergies. But I believe it's as good as anything you'll get in London."

"How much is it?"

"Hang on. Let me have a look at my little book of rules. Right. Here we are. The street price would be about £45 an ounce—if you could get it. But you can't get anything of this quality on the street. But let's just say for the sake of argument you could. One kilo is thirty-five ounces. Now let me see." Tindle tapped a calculator. "As a very special offer, I could let you have it for £700."

"Do you take debit cards?"

"Yes, of course. Here's my little johnson. You give me the card. Now you put in your number while I go and get the goods."

Finn keyed in 1991, the year of his birth. PIN ACCEPTED.

Tindle returned with a giant zip-sealed polyethylene bag full of skunk and tore off the receipt from the PDQ machine. The slim curl of paper said "Snoozetime Pet's Rest. 700.00 Received With Thanks."

Some big coffin, thought Finn.

The first-team players were driven by coach to a modern hotel about a mile from the ground of the team they were playing. In a private dining room they helped themselves to food from the sideboard. There was pasta with tomatoes, pasta with spinach, pasta with peas and sweetcorn, pasta with more pasta and shreds of chicken, baked potatoes with pasta on the side, risotto and pilaf with pasta salad. Spike felt like a few pork sausages or a beef goulash with sour cream, but there was nothing like that on offer. He took a piled plate of pasta with bits of bacon and chicken and tried to pick the meat from the rigatoni. There was rice pudding to follow, with yogurt and bananas. It was a bit like being in hospital, Spike thought.

What the players ate was carefully overseen by a young man called Gary Foskett, the senior club nutritionist. He had pale red hair, white flaky skin and a slight tremor in his hand.

Toward the end of lunch, the manager finally joined them. Mehmet Kundak had done well in his native Turkey and less well in Italy; his appointment had been a surprise, but he managed to carry with him an air of superior knowledge, intensified by the fact that he seldom spoke. Kundak left the set pieces, the cones and the stretching to Archie Lawler, while he chain-smoked over videos of the opposition. His substitutions were sudden and contrary, but often successful. It was known that he sometimes took against players for no reason. He had paid £9 million for a Serie A striker the year before and picked him only once, in a Cup match away to a third-division side. His loyalty to players like Danny Bective and Sean Mills, cannon fodder of an English kind that hadn't changed since Agincourt, endeared him to traditional supporters who naturally distrusted the Australian private-equity company which owned the club.

Kundak greeted some of the senior players with a friendly hand on the shoulder. He had large rings round his heavily bagged eyes and their darkness was intensified by the sensitive transitional lenses of his glasses, which seemed to count even a 60-watt bulb as a cue for blackout.

"How you like it?" he said to Spike.

"Yes. OK," said Spike.

"You like the food?"

"Yes. OK. It stuff you up."

"It make you run. Run all day like Bective. Eh, Danny?"

"Yes, gaffer."

"Tell the truth," said Kundak, "is shit English food. If you play well Saturday I take you to my best restaurant. OK?"

"Thank you," said Spike. "So I play for the team on Saturday?"

"Too right you play for the fucking team. No prima donnas here, mate," said Sean Mills, and everyone laughed, except the small African and Ali al-Asraf.

After eating, Spike was sent to room 416 with Vladimir and told to relax. Vladimir stretched out his six feet four inches on the bed and scratched his heavy, week-old beard. He was a frightening prospect, even prone. From his bag, he took out a small double-screened games console and began to play something in which baby dragons collected gold coins to the accompaniment of bleeping sounds.

Spike hated lying down on a bed during the day. It reminded him of being a child, when his mother would make him go up and have a rest every afternoon in their flat overlooking the shipyards in Gdansk. Tadeusz, as he was called then, lay and watched the cobweb that joined the flex of the suspended light to a piece of cracked plaster in the ceiling. He looked out of the window, then closed his eyes and wondered at the way that he could still "see" afterimages of what he had glimpsed through the glass.

He went and turned the television on, but Vladimir protested. "I try to concentrate, you fool," he said. "I have nineteen pieces. One more and I go up a level."

Spike lay down on the bed and flicked through the Gideon Bible. He'd know better another time: get a different roommate, bring a book. This Bulgarian was a jackass. Spike let his mind turn to his girlfriend, a Russian called Olya he'd met at a sponsored event when he'd first come to sign with his new club. Just thinking of her made Spike happy.

He dozed a bit, picturing Olya naked in the hotel bathroom. She had that happy accident of a small ribcage and breasts that seemed disproportionately large: not in any freakish way, but just as though they belonged to her older sister. She was a little shy of them, he thought. She had dark, almost black hair, and naughty brown eyes; although her legs and hips were slim there was something not quite perfect about their proportions: they were touchingly, credibly flawed and when she took her clothes off he didn't feel that he was looking at a model but as though he'd surprised a fellow student in the changing rooms at university. Her English was as good as his, perhaps a little better, and she'd known who he was as soon as he went up and introduced himself at the club on Piccadilly. She worked in "event management," though she was keen to move on, and Spike had agreed to make a few inquiries on her behalf at the club's headquarters. He wasn't sure what she'd done at home in the Ukraine, then in Moscow, before she came to London and she didn't seem to want to talk about it. Privately he thought it was a ridiculous idea to set such a girl loose among the old women who worked in merchandise and admin at the club; they'd just stare at her and wonder why she wasn't modeling. But maybe that was how you got started, he thought. Anyway, if it kept her happy, he'd ask around.

Spike dozed, and dreamed of Olya coming off the bench with ten minutes to go and scoring against Man U at Old Trafford. He didn't like it that all the other guys were staring at her, and she should have been in the club away kit, not topless.

He was awoken by Kenny Hawtrey knocking at the door. "Wake up, sleeping beauties. Time to go to the ground."

III

John Veals had also had a busy morning. He had a breakfast meeting with a man called Alan Wing, who worked for Vic Small at Greenview Alternative Investment Services. Veals's chosen meeting place was the Oasis Coffee Bar on the top section of Kennington Road, where it runs down from Lambeth North Tube station toward the Imperial War Museum. It was about as anonymous a stretch of road as you could find in central London: a straight strip of asphalt that joined nothing much to something else. The coffee wasn't even from an espresso machine but from a clouded glass jug, and tasted of acorns; Veals, who'd eaten at home, treated Wing to a toasted cheese and tomato sandwich from a sizzling waffle iron.

Wing handed over an A4 buff envelope that contained the fruit of two weeks' work. He had been following first the chief executive; then, when the CEO had taken an unexpected flight to Madrid, the chairman of Allied Royal Bank. There were several photographs of the two men at work and in transit, accompanied by Wing's diary of events in which the chairman and chief executive were respectively Charlie and Eric. "Charlie arrived for work at 7:42 by his usual car which was then parked in his reserved slot. He took the lift to the seventeenth floor. His PA was waiting. See attatched photo. Eric had breakfast meeting at Connaut Hotel with Unknown Lady (see pic). He ate kejeree, she ate bran flakes and orange juice."

Alan Wing's photography was better than his spelling, and

186

Veals could identify the Unknown Lady without too much trouble: she ran the bond department of one of the larger investment banks. The meeting could be for any number of reasons, but none of them suggested any particular cause for alarm to John Veals, even as he entered the most gut-wrenching hours of his trade.

What was worrying Veals was a strange, almost neurotic anxiety: suppose the rumor that he was about to start turned out to be true. He had weighed up the situation and decided that the way to boost the ARB share price was for people to believe that it was about to be taken over by First New York. If John Veals, in his bath at midnight, had concluded that such a marriage for ARB was highly credible, why would no one at either bank, people who were paid to think of little else, have concluded something similar? There would be something of Sod's Law, of almost unbelievable irony if this turned out to be the case; but in Veals's ever-turning calculations, the worst outcome was always the one on which to focus longest.

"All right. Keep at it," he said. "You have my mobile number. Call me if anything with the faintest whiff of the American comes up. Understand?"

Wing opened his mouth to let a piece of scalding tomato drop onto the plate. "How do they get these things so hot?" he spluttered.

Veals flicked through the wad of yellow expenses sheets that accompanied the report. "Don't like to go hungry, do you, Wing?"

"There was sometimes two of us. I couldn't be in two places at once."

"I'll get the cash biked round later today. Here's something to keep you going." He peeled six £50 notes from a roll in his back pocket.

"Thanks, John."

Veals stood up and looked down to where Wing was still scooping up the remains of the melted cheese. "Well, get a fucking move on," he said, and went out onto Kennington Road.

His next meeting was in a tennis club in Chelsea. Stewart Thackeray was a considerably more polished character than Alan Wing, though, in John Veals's view, stupider. He was a partner in an executive recruitment agency, whose offices were in Mayfair, but he was a keen tennis player and liked to mix sport with business among the potted palms of his club lounge overlooking the river.

A few pearls of sweat stood out on his forehead and receding hairline as he ordered fresh orange juice and sat back in the wickerwork chair.

"Sure you won't have anything, John? Not even a mineral water?"

"All right. Water."

"Gosh. I think I'm getting too old for singles," said Thackeray. "Little bugger I just played, ten years younger, he ran down everything. I hit winner after winner and there'd be a scampering sound and the bloody ball came back again."

"Did you win?"

"Just about. In the end."

Veals, having done small talk, said, "Right, Stewart. What did our friend have to say?"

Thackeray dabbed a towel against his forehead; although he'd showered and was in a suit ready to go to work, he couldn't turn off the sweat. "Well, it was a fairly standard exit interview. He was mightily pissed off about being fired."

"What did he do?"

"Shagged his secretary on the boardroom table."

"Aren't you allowed to do that?"

"Not unless you're the Deputy Prime Minister."

"I see."

"No. I mean, Allied Royal is a proper, old-fashioned place. They have a rite of passage when you reach a certain level that you have to do this, you know, shag her on the table, but if you're caught in the act then that's it."

"So he's pissed off with ARB."

"Yup. It's not a great time to be looking for a job in that world. Not at his level. The situation may get better and—"

"It may get worse."

"But in any event the climate's tense. All the big banks have toxic assets, and they haven't been quite candid about the extent of them."

"You're teaching your fucking granny here, Stewart. But will he work for us as a consultant? Is he worth it?"

Thackeray drank some fresh orange juice and wiped the back of his hand over his lips. "He knows a lot. He sat in on all the meetings when they took over the Spanish bank. You remember, the—"

"Yeah, yeah. So he knows all about that. What about ARB's underlying strengths and liabilities?"

"I believe so. You know, to some extent that's his pitch to future employers. He's had experience at a high level. He's selling himself as someone who's a calm head, a steady hand."

"With a stack of inside dope."

"Well obviously he can't work for a competitor for a hell of a long time. At least twelve months, I think."

"But he could do some freelance."

"You could ask him."

"No I couldn't. I can't possibly be seen with him or anyone else from that bank."

Thackeray raised an eyebrow.

"And you didn't hear that," said Veals. "Otherwise—"

"John, I never hear what you say. The acoustics in here are terrible."

"You fucking bet. Otherwise—"

"Take it easy, John. It's been five years since we met. Five leakproof, hermetically sealed years."

Veals fiddled with his water glass. "I just wish he'd shagged the secretary in the spring. I could have used him then. I think it's too late now."

"I've never seen you like this before, John. You look really stressed."

Veals took in a deep breath, then spoke through clenched teeth. "I'm just covering all the options, Stewart. It's what I do. What I

189

want you to do is this. Get this man back into your office this afternoon. Tell him you may have something. Get him interested. Then chat a bit more about ARB. Shoot the breeze. Now in this envelope I'm giving you there is one question I need to know the answer to. Make sure you ask him, then text me tonight on the number I gave you. Yes or no, that's all I need. It's belt and braces but I really want to have it. I'm shitting paving stones here."

"Am I going to be able to work the question in?" said Thackeray.

"Of course you are. It's what you do. Old-boy chat. What did we pay you last time?"

"Twenty."

"OK. Thirty."

"I'll see what I can do."

Outside, in a cold, deserted street near Chelsea Harbor, John Veals pulled out his blue cellphone, the one he used for intra-office calls, scrolled down to Martin Ryman's name and pressed the green icon.

"Martin? Meet me at the sushi conveyor belt in that Knightsbridge place at twelve noon. Don't expect to eat because you're going to Saggiorato's for lunch. Book for two. Take someone with you. Maybe Susanna Russell from HSBC. You like her, don't you? Pretty *and* clever: just your type. And ring Magnus Darke. Tell him you've got something for him. Arrange to meet tomorrow. Lunch. Anywhere. Throw money at it. One of those places with a psychotic chef who charges two hundred quid a head. Got it?"

Veals liked the sushi conveyor belt because it naturally threw strangers together. Although Ryman was on his "office" phone list, he didn't actually come into Old Pye Street, and the fact that he was retained by John Veals as a consultant was known only to the pair of them; even Stephen Godley was unaware of the contract. In return for his large honorarium, and a small stake in the fund, Ryman had to drop everything when Veals called.

He was already sipping water at the chugging conveyor belt when Veals arrived at 11:55. Of the three people Veals had dealt with that morning, Ryman was immeasurably the classiest act: just as well, since he was being paid the most.

"Internet chat rooms," said Veals. "Know how to use them?"

"Yes, I think so. I'm going to take a bit of salmon here, John, just for appearance's sake."

Veals knew this was a prompt for him to take some food too. One of the things he liked about Ryman was that he didn't waste words; another thing he liked was that Ryman wasn't frightened of him, not like Alan Wing or, beneath his tennis club bullshit, Stewart Thackeray.

"On your way to Saggiorato's," Veals said, "go to an Internet café. Get yourself half a dozen instant e-mail addresses. Get into a financial chat room. Pretend to be a nineteen-year-old waiter. Say, 'I was waiting at a dinner party in Chelsea last night and I heard the head of First NY's London office talking about their decision to buy ARB. Their historical roots across much of the developing and former colonial world were the answer to First NY's aspirations as a truly "global" bank . . . blah blah.'"

"First NY?" said Ryman, taking the purple-rimmed plastic cover off his sashimi.

"That's what I'm hearing, Martin. Then you go to a different Internet café this afternoon. Maybe you can do them all from the same one. You figure it out. Sign in as an amateur low-roller. You're an Australian physio who dabbles online between clients. Anything you like. You saw the waiter's posting. You make some comments. Seems a good fit. So now's a good time to buy ARB shares. Simple stuff. Tomorrow morning, see how it's going and if necessary do five or six more places. Then at lunchtime tomorrow, you drop it to Magnus Darke. Have you booked the table?"

"Yes. Darke bit my hand off. Said he's very short of material. You know, silly season, Christmas coming. We're going to a place run by that chub-faced TV chef. Darke's column is on Friday, so he can get in tomorrow fine. It's perfect timing for him."

"Good. But today at lunch at Saggiorato's, have a word with Tony the barman. Give him this." Veals passed two £50 notes along the counter. "You know Dougie Moon, the boring red-faced money broker, the guy who always sits in the window?"

"Yes, it's his canteen. I've never not seen him there."

"Tell Tony to tell Moon in the strictest confidence that he saw our man at ARB having dinner in a private room with the chairman of First NY."

Ryman licked his lips. He seemed less keen on this aspect of the plan; without the anonymity of the Internet, very little stood between him and the FSA—or the police. "And then tomorrow. With Darke?"

"There was a tiny thing in the *FT* the other day about possible future bank mergers. Ask if he saw it. Talk about good fits. Remind him of Robert Fleming and the Chase Manhattan/J. P. Morgan sale: Old Empire and New America. Give him the reference of the chat room. Say there could be some corroboration there. Don't start a rumor, you can't do that, but point to what's already there. These journalists get most of their stuff off the Internet these days—they haven't got the time or the resources to do any research. Most of the paper's written by kids on work experience and they're just recycling one another's material via the Web. But tell Darke to be careful how he phrases it. He should just pass it off as a thought that occurred to him as he was looking back on a difficult year. 'Doesn't it look a natural fit?' he might say. If the credit crisis gets worse there's going to be pressure on all the banks and it's natural that a lot of them will want to get extra security. Let him float it as a sort of positive, seasonal thing. Something good in your Christmas stocking. Got it?"

"Yes. I think he'll like it. It goes against the grain, against the doom and gloom. Good for the shareholders."

"Good for the pensioners," said John Veals.

"Sometimes," said Martin Ryman, tasting a bit of wasabi off the end of his chopstick, "I think people could mistake you for Father Christmas, John."

"Well, at this time of year," said Veals, not smiling at Ryman's sarcasm, "all of us in our world try to put a bit back."

192

*   *   *

Gabriel Northwood spent Wednesday morning with his feet up on the desk reading the Koran.

"What a bastard," he muttered under his breath from time to time. "*What* a bastard . . ."

He had always thought of the Old Testament as giving the most implacable and unsympathetic portrayal of a divinity. Jahweh, or Jehovah, the god of the Jews and their Exodus and their dietary laws and bloody battles against the other Semitic tribes; Jahweh the god of exile, punishment, bloodshed, plagues and slaying of the firstborn . . . He had surely set a standard of intransigence. Yet compared to the Koranic divinity, he was beginning to feel, old Jahweh was almost avuncular.

The god of the Koran brought with him neither the great stories of the Old Testament (though he referred back to them) nor the modern life-guide of the New. What he did offer was his own words, *ipsissima verba*, mouthed by the Angel Gabriel, remembered and transcribed verbatim by the Prophet. And over nearly 400 pages, the principal message seemed a simple one: believe in me or burn for all eternity. Page after page.

Woeful punishment awaits the unbelievers. Shameful punishment awaits the unbelievers. For the unbelievers we have prepared chains and fetters, and a blazing Fire. Would that you knew what this is like. It is a scorching Fire. Woe betide every backbiting slanderer who amasses riches and sedulously hoards them, thinking his wealth will render him immortal! By no means! He shall be flung to the Destroying Flame. But if he is an erring disbeliever, his welcome will be scalding water, and he will burn in Hell. We shall sternly punish the unbelievers. The Fire shall forever be their home.

You could open the book at random. It was the same message on any page. "Consider the fate of the evildoers." The phrase tolled like a stuck muezzin.

For the believers, on the other hand, there awaited "dark-eyed virgins in their tents whom neither man nor jinnee will have

193

touched before . . . Virgins as fair as corals and rubies . . . They shall recline on couches ranged in rows. To dark-eyed houris we shall wed them."

The life choice laid down by the Prophet was what Delilah in the clerks' room called, to Eustace Hutton's irritation, a "no-brainer." Anyone, Gabriel thought, would take the virgin option over hellfire—any man, at least; it wasn't clear what was on offer to women. What the book lacked was any reasoning or evidence to support its depiction of this radically divided afterlife.

Jehovah had parted the Red Sea. He had destroyed the cities of the plain. He had spoken in the ears of the prophets. He had visited plagues on the enemies of the Israelites. Jesus had performed miracles to demonstrate his own divinity; he had invented a revolutionary manner of behaving—kindly. He had walked on water. He had risen from the dead. Allah, on the other hand, had not condescended to intervene on earth or to argue his case. He didn't bother to persuade; in his single apparition he had offered only warning. Believe in me or die.

After 200 pages, Gabriel found a great weariness come over him. And there was also something in the self-grounded and unargued certainty of the Koran that reminded him of something else, of someone he knew. A voice. He couldn't at that moment put a name to it.

He had read somewhere that the Arabs had felt excluded from monotheism because, several hundred years into it, they had still had no directly instructed prophet of their own; it appeared that their Jewish and Christian trading partners even taunted them for this lack. When the Prophet finally arrived, it was 600 years after second-placed Jesus Christ had been and gone: a lapse of time as great as 1400 to the present day. That was an awfully long time in the short history of monotheism, Gabriel thought, to be viewed by your neighbors as backward. And sometimes the fierce iterations of the book seemed to show the effect of those pent-up centuries of hope and silence. Here is the god at last. And after all this time, he'd better be emphatic.

But perhaps, Gabriel thought, his view of the book was too legalistic or pedantic. After all, there was a lot of rubbish in Deuteronomy and Leviticus: "A man who has had his testicles cut off cannot be admitted to the presence of Jahweh . . ." But the Jews had moved on. They and the Christians accepted that their holy books had been written by humans, albeit inspired by God, and the great majority were happy to see the words in the context of their time and had little trouble in squaring them with modern knowledge, provided they could just be left with a comforting sense of a higher power who took an interest in their affairs before and after death.

But as far as Gabriel understood it, Islam had never yielded that ground. Once an early theological debate had decided for all time that the Koran was literally and in every syllable the unmediated word of God, then all Muslims became by definition "fundamentalist." It was by its nature unlike Judaism or Christianity; it was intrinsically, and quite unapologetically, a fundamentalist religion. There was, of course, a world of difference between "fundamental" and "militant"—let alone "aggressive"; but the intractable truth remained: that by being so pure, so high-minded and so uncompromising, Islam had limited the kind of believer it could claim.

After lunch, Gabriel went to meet Jenni Fortune for a ride on the Circle Line.

He'd been once before, when he was preparing the case for the first trial, but felt it would be helpful for him to do it again, so he had a true feeling for her work. The supervisor was waiting for him at the barrier and took him down to the platform to wait for Jenni's train.

When she pressed the button to open the door for him, Jenni's face came as close as Gabriel had seen it to a smile.

"Hop in," she said. Because they'd done this once before, he thought, perhaps she felt more confident; there was nothing new for her to fear.

Gabriel folded out the dickey and sat down. The interior of the cab was painted sky blue, and in front of Gabriel on the dashboard was an instructor's emergency brake. Jenni checked her rearview mirror, pressed the two buttons to close the passenger doors, depressed the driver's handle in front of her and turned it slowly anticlockwise. The train moved off.

"How have you been, Jenni?"

"Not bad, thanks. You?"

"Fine, thanks." Was that mascara on her lashes? It was hard to tell in the darkness.

"What do you want me to tell you?" she asked.

"Oh . . . Well, let's just have a chat, shall we?"

"OK."

"Do you feel cut off from things down here?"

"Yeah, I s'pose so. But I like it."

"It's your own world."

"Yeah."

"What do you do in the evenings?"

"Go home. Look after Tony. He's my half brother. Watch telly. Play Parallax."

"Is that the alternative-reality game?"

"Yeah, it's brilliant. My maquette's called Amanda. She's a beautician." She pronounced the word "mack-wet" and it took Gabriel a moment to understand what she meant.

Jenni moved the lever back to six o'clock, then round to about four to bring the brakes on hard, then back to five to let the train decelerate more gently as it ran into the station. When it had stopped, she let the lever rise up on its spring.

"And what about reading?" said Gabriel, as they moved off again. "You like reading, don't you?"

"Yeah, I do."

"Why?"

"Dunno. I s'pose it's an escape from the real world."

"But surely it's just the opposite," said Gabriel. "Books explain the real world. They bring you close to it in a way you could never manage in the course of the day."

"How do you mean?"

"People never explain to you exactly what they think and feel and how their thoughts and feelings work, do they? They don't have time. Or the right words. But that's what books do. It's as though your daily life is a film in the cinema. It can be fun, looking at those pictures. But if you want to know what lies behind the flat screen you have to read a book. That explains it all."

"Even if the people in the book are invented?"

"Sure. Because they're based on what's real, but with the boring bits stripped out. In good books anyway. Of my total understanding of human beings, which is perhaps not very great . . . I'd say half of it is from just guessing that other people must feel much the same as I would in their place. But of the other half, ninety percent of it has come from reading books. Less than ten percent from reality—from watching and talking and listening—from living."

"You're funny."

"Thank you, Jenni. Why are you waving?"

"Driver coming the other way waved at me. They always do. Unless they're District. They just turn the cab light off."

"What? Is there a rivalry between Circle and District?"

"You bet. The five-a-side footie's a bloodbath."

"All right. We'd better talk about your work. Tell me about the stations. Are they all the same to you, or do they have different characters?"

He watched Jenni while she answered. She had quite delicate hands, not really right for a manual job, he thought, even though working the lever and the door buttons was not demanding. The palm was paler than the back of the hand, and the fingers were long, with neatly trimmed nails; that much at least must be necessary for the job, he thought.

". . . and Baker Street's a nice station. Always busy with Madame Tussaud's and that. And the brickwork's just like when it was built all those years ago. Embankment's always busy with the theaters and the Strand. Temple's quiet, usually."

"I know."

Gabriel noticed the care with which Jenni checked the mirrors at the station even as she was talking to him. She was wearing her black hair tied back with a ribbon; the lamp on the platform threw a shaft of light across her face, over the pale brown skin, across her mouth where the pigment changed in her lip from blackish-brown to pink. She seemed to sense him staring at her and turned her head suddenly to look at him.

He looked back into her deep, dark eyes. She held his gaze and said nothing. He felt he mustn't look away, that while their eyes were locked he could transmit belief to her. She didn't blink or move her head, but the light of fear and challenge slowly dimmed in her eyes. She pressed the door-close buttons, her eyes still on his, leaned on the lever and pushed it away to the left. It was not until the clattering train had reached twenty miles per hour that she finally looked ahead of her, through the windscreen, and Gabriel thought he could see in her face the beginnings, or possibly the remnants, of a smile.

"And Aldgate, since you ask," Jenni said. "There's the ghost of a woman there. But it's a friendly one. One of the P. Way guys, he touched the live rail and—"

"P. Way?"

"Permanent Way. The people who maintain the track. He touched the live rail by mistake but the other guys saw this woman put her hand on his shoulder and move him away. He was completely unhurt. He should have fried."

The train hurtled on through the darkness, slowing and speeding at Jenni's simple left-hand command. She was standing up, as she did every other circuit, she explained, to ease her back from the brutally uncomfortable seat. Gabriel was silent. There was something he found harshly poignant about this gruff girl at her work; you didn't need to have read very many books or to be much of an observer to see that she was someone who'd been rebuffed or bruised and now relied on her job as a measure of her own value. He was torn by a desire to lead her into a more ambitious way of looking at her life, and a simple admiration for the pride she took in doing something useful. In any case, what could he offer, broke and alone as he was? What did he know from his precious books that he could teach this busy, thoughtful woman? And what if she was hiding from something underground? Wasn't he, really, doing the same with his crossword puzzle and his French novels?

"We're coming to the end of the circle," said Jenni.

"That was quick. How long's it been?"

Jenni looked at her watch. "Fifty-six minutes."

"Right. I suppose I'd better—"

"I'm going round again, though."

"So I could stay and . . ."

"Yes, you can come round again. If you like. I mean—"

"Yes, I'd like to. I think there are more things I should know. We talked too much about books and stuff that time round."

Jenni was smiling. "Go on then. Sit down. Fire away."

In the darkest section of the Circle, just before Victoria, Gabriel suddenly said, "Maybe I could come and play Parallax one evening at your house."

"Would that be right? If we was like, you know, clients?"

"We could talk about work. I could take you out to dinner maybe. Somewhere local you like. Then I'd go home. We couldn't talk about anything else until after the case comes on in January."

"So just work."

"Exactly." Gabriel was wondering how he was going to pay for dinner.

"Well, that'd be fine then. Maybe tomorrow. I'm off by six."

"Tomorrow would be . . . Perfect. OK." Where the hell was he going to get the money? "Tell me, Jenni. That woman's voice. The recording that says, 'We are now approaching King's Cross. Change here for the Piccadilly Line' or whatever. Is that one of your colleagues? Or an actress, or what?"

"I dunno," said Jenni. "We call her Sonia."

"Why?"

"Because she get s-on-yer nerves."

"And how does she know when to come in? What cues the recording?"

"The number of wheel revolutions. It's different between each station. It works fine unless there's been a lot of rain. Then you get wheelspin. Then she thinks you're in Blackfriars when you're only just pulling out of Mansion House."

"What do you do then?"

"Turn the bugger off."

At 5:30, Knocker al-Rashid was waiting for his penultimate visit from R. Tranter. He had squeezed in one for Wednesday in addition to their regular Thursday morning slot, which would be the last one before his visit to the palace on Friday. They had agreed to put that aside for "revision," so today's was almost the last time they would cover new ground. Knocker looked at his watch. He had become impatient with his teacher lately. How different it had been at the start.

Before Tranter's first visit in the spring, Knocker had felt unpleasantly nervous.

"Nasim," he said. "A distinguished literary man is going to arrive any minute. We'll go to my office to discuss books and reading. Could you bear to arrange for some fruit and tea to be served to us in about twenty minutes?"

"Of course, love," said Nasim. She smiled at her husband's way of speaking; the larger the successive houses they had lived in, the less Knocker had come to sound like a Bradford Paki, as she'd once heard him called, and the more like David Niven.

In the course of her long and happy marriage to Farooq, Nasim herself had lost her Yorkshire accent and now spoke in a way she fancied was pretty close to the BBC—the old BBC, since nowadays so many people on the radio seemed to have come from Bradford.

"What sort of man do you think he'll be?" she asked Knocker.

"An old-style English gentleman, I think."

"A bit of a Prince Charles?"

"I expect so. He was at Oxford University. Do you think my suit is smart enough?"

"Don't be silly, Knocker. Don't be shy of him. He's just a trades-man who's got something you need. Like the lime farmer in Mex-ico."

"Rodrigues! You promised never to mention him again."

The bell rang, and Knocker crossed the enormous tiled hall to open it, braced to see an intimidating guardsman in a Savile Row suit.

"Hello? Mr. al-Rashid, I presume."

The door had revealed a slight, gingery man in a blue anorak with a green tie, brown shoes and forty-eight hours of stubble on his chin. His eyes were a little pink.

He held out his hand. "Ralph Tranter. Most people call me RT, though."

Knocker had not traveled to every continent of the world (bar Australasia) without concluding that the outer wrapping of a man was insignificant. Even so . . .

He rose to the occasion. "I'm very pleased to meet you. Please come this way, Mr. Tranter."

They crossed the hall, then went through the giant drawing room with its views over open countryside, out through the double doors, down a paneled passageway and into Knocker al-Rashid's study, whose long shelves were lined not with books but with Japanese ivory figures, porcelain boxes, framed photographs of Nasim and Hassan and a handful of work mementos—a gold-plated lime, for instance, presented by his workforce and a drive wheel from his first production line mounted on oak with an inscribed plaque. There was a new thirty-six-inch-screen computer on the desk; it was of a make not available in the usual retail outlets.

"Very nice," said Tranter.

There was a faintly sneering edge to his voice that Knocker chose to ignore; some people just had an unfortunate manner. He settled Tranter in an armchair and went to sit behind his desk.

He smiled broadly. "Let's get down to business, Mr. Tranter, if we may. I've got a simple proposition to put to you. I need what you might call a crash course. I shall shortly be meeting Her Majesty the Queen and I feel that I'm not well prepared conversationally."

"Really?" There was a skeptical note to everything Tranter said, though Knocker found it hard to tell whether Tranter thought he had made up the bit about the Queen or was being modest about his readiness.

"I come from a simple family, you see. My family were farmers and didn't read books. My education was in a state school that prepared the pupils to be electricians or plumbers. I think I may also have suffered from dyslexia, though it wasn't a complaint we knew anything about in those days. What I'd like is for you to make me familiar with the great works of English literature of the past and bring me up to date on the writers of today, so that if Her Majesty steers the conversation toward books, I can have something interesting to say."

Tranter's mouth opened and closed a couple of times. "Yes, I can do that," he said eventually. "But do you think it's likely that she'll talk books? She's not famous for reading, is she?"

Knocker frowned. This had not occurred to him.

"But of course," Tranter went on quickly, glancing round the opulent room, "you'd better be prepared. And it'll still be knowledge that'll stand you in good stead. At other times."

"Yes, indeed. That's a good way of looking at it. Now I've done some homework on the most respected writers of today, and I sent my assistant Mrs. Hine out to the bookshop. Come and tell me what you think of this little collection. Tell me which one to begin with."

Knocker pointed to two piles of books, about fifteen in all, that were ready on his desk. Tranter came and stood beside him.

"This author's very famous, I believe," said Knocker, holding up a moody-looking hardback with a belly band that said it had been listed for the Café Bravo award.

"Famous," said Tranter, "but hopelessly overrated. It's what we call OT."

"What's that?"

"Oirish Twaddle."

"I don't understand."

"It doesn't matter. Forget him."

"What about this one?" said Knocker. "It says she's twice won the Allied Royal prize."

"No, no. Awful 'creative writing' sort of stuff. Terribly illusionist and overwrought. Poor man's Somerset Maugham, with embarrassing improbabilities at key moments."

Knocker looked taken aback. "I see. I think perhaps I was misinformed. I took some guidance from the Internet."

Tranter gave a short laugh. "God, that goons' rodeo. Nutter central. I mean, if only they could get a green-ink detection device and use it as a filter the Web'd lose ninety percent of its traffic."

Knocker looked at the sharp, foxy face next to his. He couldn't understand much of what the man said. It struck him as odd that Tranter, who was supposed to be a man of words, wouldn't alter the way he spoke so that Knocker could follow what he meant.

"This one?" he said, holding up another novel heavy with praise.

"Oh God," said Tranter. "The man who put the 'anal' into 'banality.' Costive little stories that beg to be called significant. His tragedy is that he was not born 'European.' Should have worked in advertising."

And so they went down through the pile. "Overblown and sentimental . . . You just wish he'd come out of the closet and stop pretending that his little queens are women for heaven's sake . . ."

By this time, there were only three of the books that Mrs. Hine had bought remaining on the desk, and Knocker was beginning to lose patience.

He held up a book by an author whose name was familiar even to himself.

Tranter took it from him, shook his head and tossed it back on the desk. "Barely animated TV scripts," he said.

The last two he didn't even bother to pick up. "Barbara Pym and water . . . Writing by numbers . . ."

"Well, Mr. Tranter," said Knocker, "I seem to have made a pretty bad start to my project."

"It's not your fault," said Tranter. "These are just the usual suspects favored by the literary establishment."

"Yes," said Knocker, "but are there any living British authors that you do recommend?"

Tranter scratched his chin, and his fingernails made a slight noise in the stubble. "No, not living," he said. "But quite recent. Modern in their way."

Nasim came in with a tray. Normally, she would have asked Lucy, the Brazilian girl, to do it, but she was curious to meet the literary man.

"My dear, this is Mr. Tranter. This is my wife, Nasim."

Tranter and Nasim had a moment of being uncertain whether to shake hands, though it passed when Knocker put his arm round his wife and escorted her to the desk.

"Mr. Tranter says I'm wasting my time with all of these writers," he said. "He says none of them are any good."

"But what if Her Majesty likes them?" said Nasim. "You should still have read them so you can talk to her about her favorites."

Knocker smiled. "A very clever woman, my wife, isn't she? These writers may all be as bad as you say, Mr. Tranter, but I need to have some knowledge of them. Even if they are all a big con trick."

"Well, I can give you that all right," said Tranter. "A sort of bluffer's guide if you like."

"We also need to find out who her favorite authors are," said Nasim.

Knocker looked at Tranter. He scratched his chin again. "I seem to remember she likes Dick Francis."

"Who is he?"

"He writes racing thrillers. You know, horse racing."

"I shall ask Mrs. Hine to buy some tomorrow. Has he written many?"

"Thousands."

"Good. But I should also like to read some great literature. I want to learn for my own sake, not just for Her Majesty. I want to start the habit of a lifetime."

"Then I suppose we should look at the Victorians," said Tranter. "Dickens, Thackeray, Trollope. George Eliot."

"You won't tell me they're a 'busted flush' or 'writing by numbers'?"

"No, no. Not Thackeray anyway."

"I've heard of all those people," said Nasim.

"My wife is very well read," Knocker explained. "Tell him who you've read."

"For our exam," said Nasim, "we could choose between a book by Iris Murdoch—"

"Oh yes," said Tranter, "an excellent example of the higher bogus."

"Or *Howards End . . .*"

"Mmm . . ." said Tranter. "Which Howard? I think we know which end."

"Or Virginia Woolf."

"God. Chick-lit meets psychosis. Which one did you end up doing?"

"We did *Portrait of the Artist as a Young Man.*"

Tranter laughed. "Nothing like a bit of Irishry if in doubt," he said. "A bit of OT always goes down well."

Nasim looked crestfallen. There was a slight flush under her skin.

"There's another Victorian novelist I rate very highly," said Tranter quickly, as though sensing that he might have gone too far. "In fact, I've written a biography of him."

"How exciting," said Nasim, recovering her poise. "And is it published?"

"That's the general idea," said Tranter. "In fact it's a finalist for the Pizza Palace Book of the Year at Christmas."

"Congratulations. And who is this author?"

"Alfred Huntley Edgerton," said Tranter.

"I've never heard of him," said Nasim.

"He's not as well known as the others. But he's very good."

"I think I should like to try him," said Knocker.

"Then you'd be one up on the Queen," said Nasim. "I mean,

thanks to Mr. Tranter you'd have a special knowledge of . . . What was his name?"

"Edgerton."

By the time Tranter left half an hour later, Knocker al-Rashid had his first homework reading list: *Shropshire Towers* by Alfred Huntley Edgerton and *Whip Hand* by Dick Francis. The over-praised "moderns," it was agreed, would have to wait for another day, when Tranter would begin the bluffer's guide.

In Pfäffikon, Kieran Duffy was moving cautiously forward. It was none of his business how John Veals intended to introduce some life into the market for ARB shares, but while he was waiting for it to happen, he turned his attention to the foreign-exchange leg of the trade.

On the grounds that a British bank crisis, even if confined to one bank, would adversely affect the pound when the government had to borrow abroad, Duffy intended to sell forward £10 billion against a mixture of euros, Swiss francs and U.S. dollars. Even twenty years before, such a large trade would have been the talk of every bar in London, New York and Paris, which was still then a financial center. Now Duffy could complete it in privacy in ten minutes on the FX screen installed on his desk by High Level's prime broker. It was the one part of the trade that he himself man-ually instigated.

Foreign-exchange trades required that the trader put up two percent collateral, but High Level could automatically borrow the first £400 million of any margin requirement; this was one of a number of facilities offered by the prime broker when they were pitching for High Level's business. What it meant in practice was that Duffy could place a trade of £20 billion without putting his hand in his pocket, though he preferred to go in at only half that level for the time being.

He keyed in the last of his strokes, less elegantly than Victoria would have done, with a defiant stab. The desktop system he was using rationalized every bid and offer from every trading system in the world, working all day, six days a week. As he sat back in his chair, he knew that risk and settlement systems around the globe were almost instantaneously digesting his trade.

It was no fun anymore. The typical foreign-exchange trader in London had once learned his business in a fish or meat market where he'd been able to do rapid calculations while withstanding a barrage of shouted information. Duffy was old enough to have seen them in action once, these Leadenhall and Smithfield men, on a visit from New York. He'd been taken out to lunch at a place called the Paris Grill, where the steak and chips was served by waitresses in black negligees. He'd been amazed at how much the Brits could drink at lunch before returning to work, where, in the absence of sufficient foreign-exchange activity, they placed huge bets on how long the Pope or Emperor Hirohito was going to stay alive.

When it was confirmed that his currency trade had gone through, Duffy turned his attention back to Allied Royal. The share price had begun to rise—not dramatically, and with one or two blips, but with what looked like a steady underlying confidence. By late afternoon there was enough activity for him to be able to start making some more calls to obtain prices for puts and calls in the stock. He didn't know what part Veals might have played in the rally, and he would never ask, but when the day's trading was finished he was able to send a message to Veals's black mobile number: "Rheumatism definitely easing. Expect full movement tmw."

IV

Sophie Topping's taxi drew into Dover Street at seven o'clock. She'd arranged to meet Lance at 6:30 and some women from her book club at 6:45, so her timing, she felt, was just right.

She had never been to the auctioneers' headquarters before, though she'd seen it on the television news when a suave man in a double-breasted suit extracted £10 million from an absent buyer for a smudged pot of Impressionist flowers.

Tonight, however, was a special gala and Sophie found herself giddy with pleasurable excitement. Here were no Van Goghs or Monets, no Old Masters or Cubists or Moderns; tonight, as the catalog had it, was "a unique artistic event." The forty-two-year-old Liam Hogg had taken over the entire first floor of the auction house. Hogg, with the blessing of the Blank Slate Gallery in Stoke Newington, to whom he had remained brashly faithful through the boom years, had decided to "turn art-world convention on its head."

Sophie walked through the long downstairs lobby, past the coats, and turned to climb the marble stairs. She spotted Lance halfway up, talking to Vanessa Veals and Amanda Malpasse.

"Glad you could make it, Soph," said Lance, looking at his watch.

Sophie wasn't listening; she was taking in what clothes the others were wearing. Both had gone to considerable efforts. Vanessa must have spent thousands on her outfit—not that money was of any consequence to the Vealses; but Sophie recognized the couture dress from a page in a fashion magazine and the shoes from a designer whose work she considered too delicate for her own sturdy ankles. The brassy handbag was another three or four thousand pounds' worth that would appear on Vanessa's arm perhaps twice in its life.

A waiter was offering cocktails of a violent blue, and Sophie opted for the safety of champagne. Amanda also had a new dress from the top end of a Knightsbridge rail and her hair had the slightly dry look of the salon about it. Both declined the morsels of food—raw shark, carpaccio of suckling pig or something equally scary-sounding to Sophie—that were offered on a Perspex tray.

The four of them mounted the stairs and entered the main gallery, which was crammed with people. Sophie's eye ran over the organdies and devorés, the faux-fur and the fox, the taffeta and cashmere, the demure black cocktail dresses with a confidently simple row of pearls; the carefree pinks and golds with bouclé curls and tailored waists; the knee-length slashed satin and two or three instances of carefully ripped denim. The men wore hand-finished suits—some with ties and some without, but none with the shine of chain-store cloth. The only outfits that had cost more than the Savile Row three-pieces, in Sophie's rapid *tour d'horizon*, were the rebel biker outfits with the predistressed boots. The guests were packed in so tight that it was hard to see the art. Sophie sighed happily. She felt the investment in her own dress and shoes had been not only justified but had proved essential. Over the lovely, lively throng she could make out a sort of nimbus, where the muted beams from tracked ceiling lights bounced off the gold and diamonds below to form a thin, vapid haze.

Liam Hogg and his studio had, according to the press release, been "working round the clock" for six months to fill the august space, through which had passed the work of Rembrandt and Turner, Caravaggio and Vermeer. The walls had been stripped of their paper for the occasion and covered with a white distemper. The maroon carpet over which so many Bond Street shoes had slid since the Second World War had been prised up, rolled and stored. The revealed floorboards had been sandblasted by men in masks.

Smoking, at Liam Hogg's insistence, was encouraged by the provision of several freestanding wrought iron ashtrays, in the shape of upright male organs, stationed about the room like collateral damage from an explosion on a porn film. It had been rumored in the gossip columns that the artist had used his own member to make the first cast from which the blacksmith had, *mutatis mutandis*, manufactured the rest.

"All traces of the gallery's normal atmosphere have been purged," according to the catalog introduction. Certainly, the walls bore no reminder of the last two money-spinning sales—of brightly cleaned sixteenth-century Flemish flower paintings and of flat, shy abstracts by Peter Lanyon and Ben Nicholson.

Instead, there were the images that had made Liam Hogg the richest English artist of his time. Here was *Anagnorisis V*, his take on consumerism that was made up of repetitive patterns of bar codes, cut from the back of supermarket goods. Here, too, was his famous pink and turquoise silk-screen print of the Muhammad Ali–Sonny Liston photograph. And at the end of the gallery was the installation *Everything I Know About Life I Learned From Not Listening*, which was a pub table with an empty beer bottle, glasses and a full ashtray.

"I've yet to meet a single person not in finance," grumbled Lance Topping. "Half the bloody hedge-fund industry seems to have pottered over from Mayfair after work."

"Look," said Sophie, "there's Nasim al-Rashid. She's not in hedge funds. She's in pickle."

"I suppose I'd better be nice to her," said Lance. "Her old man did bung us fifty grand."

"Go on, then. And don't forget they're coming to dinner on Saturday."

Nasim had seen the Toppings and crossed the room to speak to them; she didn't know anyone else there. Knocker had refused to accompany her, so she'd had to come on her own. She wore a sari of an intense indigo that looked more Belgravia than Wembley; she also had a gold necklace of flat, concentric hoops like those in a pharaoh's tomb. It was lovely, Sophie admitted to herself, though Nasim seemed unaware of the impression she made: probably something to do with her religion.

"What does this mean?" Nasim was saying. She was pointing to a caption on a large piece behind them. It said "*Arbeit Macht Frei*."

"It's German, isn't it?" said Sophie.

There were black and white news photographs of people in a concentration camp, possibly Belsen or Auschwitz, on which Liam Hogg had drawn in some additions. One skeletal man on a bare bunk had been given a needle and thread to make him look like a tailor; another had a pickaxe over his shoulder and a miner's lamp drawn onto his skull. A third had been given a lawyer's curly wig, while a naked woman on the ground, who looked as though she might be dead, had a nurse's cap and a stethoscope over her bony ribcage.

At the far end of the room, a queue had formed and was waiting, cocktail in hand, to go behind a screen into a room with a low light, like that reserved for the *Mona Lisa* in the Louvre.

210

Consulting her catalog, Sophie saw that it contained something called *Cash Cow, 2007*. "Arguably the most daring piece undertaken by a contemporary artist, *Cash Cow* is a mixed-media piece made from sterling banknotes and lutetium, the rarest metal in the world (symbol Lu, atomic number 71). The materials alone cost in excess of £4 million. 'I wanted to challenge people's preconceptions about art,' says Liam Hogg.

"Please note. Guests may spend no more than thirty seconds each in front of this exhibit."

Sophie Topping was determined not to miss *Cash Cow*. When she had queued for twenty minutes, Lance told her he was going home and she told him she'd catch a taxi later.

Eventually it was her turn in the pink half-light, and she stood alone at last before the exhibition centerpiece. It was a life-size model of a cow in a glass case. It was colored pink and had flaky silver-colored horns and silver eyes, which gave it an odd, blinded look. This was the lutetium, presumably. Sophie peered through the glass and could make out the Queen's face several times on the animal's barreled flanks. The cow itself, she recognized from a semi-rural childhood, was of a shorthorn dairy breed with painfully full udders.

It didn't seem to do anything, other than stare blindly out. Sophie wondered if she should press a button and get it to moo or poo or chew the cud or something. She turned to her catalog for help: "The piece is made from papier mâché of which the paper element consists of 60,000 £50 notes and is coated with new notes of the same denomination.

"The horns and eyes are coated with lutetium, the world's most precious metal, the heaviest and hardest of the rare-earth metals. It is too expensive to obtain in any quantity and therefore has few, if any, commercial uses. Although nontoxic, its dust is a fire and explosion hazard."

"Time's up, madam," said the attendant. "Move on now, please."

Back in the main gallery, Sophie finished the catalog entry. "*Cash Cow* was sponsored by Allied Royal Bank, Salzar-Steinberg

Securities and Park Vista Capital. It is for sale tonight at £8 million."

Sophie went to find Nasim. Perhaps she would be able to explain the point of *Cash Cow*. She understood why it was so expensive, because Liam Hogg had to cover his costs, but she wondered if she was missing something else about it. Unfortunately, Nasim had taken the limousine back to Havering-atte-Bower, leaving Sophie to go down alone into the cold of Dover Street.

As she stepped out to hail a taxi, a bicyclist with no lights on came shooting in the wrong direction up the one-way street and swore at her as she leapt back onto the pavement, her heart thumping.

At 7:45, John Veals had a chance meeting with his son on the stairs of their house in Holland Park. As each shifted from foot to foot, trying to think of something to say, one of Veals's six mobile phones let out a message bleep, and he took it into his study to read. The identity of the sender, according to Veals's personal encryption, was "Kayad," which spelled "Dayak" backward—a reference to a tribe of East Indian headhunters. The number was therefore Stewart Thackeray's and the message said: "Our Mutual Friend says yes, def." The question had referred to the debt covenant at ARB. By the time Veals had finished his small but intense celebration, Finn, to his relief, was no longer on the landing, and the awkward moment had passed.

John Veals fired up the screens in his study and checked a variety of prices around the world. Everything was in order; everything was behaving in the way that it should, and he felt the satisfaction of an engineer who has carefully tested all the parts of a moving system. And yet, he thought, there was only one thing so mournful as a battle lost, and that was a battle won . . . The planning, the precision, the sheer skill of his and Duffy's trades seemed to be bringing Veals the overwhelming victory he had craved; but when he thought about Ryman's part in it, the rumor that had been necessary to inflate the price of Allied Royal, he felt . . . not guilty, exactly; but, well . . . It was, as a matter of simple fact, the first time since his days of front-running as a young futures trader that he had done anything that contravened the guidelines of the regulatory bodies. He had thought himself better than that; he had believed so much in his own superior ability that he had not deigned to do the kind of thing that others in the Bank did almost every day. It was a pity that this trade had needed a preliminary fluffing up before it could be placed; it was just a small maneuver necessitated by the complex nature of the quite legitimate trade he had envisaged; it was no big deal, but still when he thought about it, John Veals felt . . . What was the word? he wondered. Wistful, perhaps. A little wistful.

Upstairs, Finn was watching a football match on his flat-screen television, propped in his favorite position against the end of the bed. It was between his own team, whom he'd supported since he was seven years old, and the club which, like Finn himself in Dream Team, had just signed Spike Borowski.

Open on his thighs with their skinny jeans was a laptop where the latest stats and news from Dream Team were unfolding. Three of Finn's fantasy eleven were in real-life action, so it was a big night.

"And I see the new signing Spike Borowski warming up, Frank," said the commentator about an hour later. "Do you think we might get a look at him in the last twenty minutes?"

"Aye, it looks like it, John. I think he'll take off the big Bulgarian. He's run his socks off but he's not had much change out of their defense. Borowski could be the man to break the deadlock."

"Yes-s-s-s," Finn heard himself hiss, and his fist made a piston movement in the air.

Spike, now fully stripped off, was bending down and touching his toes, jogging on the spot and getting an earful of instructions from Mehmet Kundak. The manager was wearing an ankle-length sheepskin coat that made him look like an Anatolian shepherd, and his transitional lenses had turned to black under the floodlights. Spike nodded at intervals, though Finn wondered how much he really understood. Kundak made emphatic movements with his arm, then quick rotations of the wrist. Finally he tapped his temple with his finger. It looked a complicated way, Finn thought, of telling Spike to score a bloody goal. Then the official—the man who apparently did this job at every football match, seeming to pop up at places 200 miles apart within minutes—held up the illuminated board where the bulbs formed a number 9; and off trotted Vlad the Inhaler, head down, straight past Spike without a look or a handshake. Kundak gave Spike a good-luck slap on the rump, and his English career began.

Finn was rattling between websites and television stations in order to keep abreast of the progress in the games that would affect his fantasy team's progress. What he really needed, he thought, was a third resource: double-screening didn't really give him all the information he required.

During a temporary lull for treatment to Ali al-Asraf, Finn rolled a small joint with the Aurora/Super Skunk Two mixture. He had secreted Simon Tindle's outsize stash in a suitcase deep within his fitted closets and transferred a manageable amount into a zipped sandwich bag for immediate use. There was no risk in lighting up. He'd checked his mother was watching a costume drama—*Shropshire Towers* by Alfred Huntley Edgerton, "adapted" to include scenes of oral sex—on television in the sitting room, her hand clamped round a bottle of Léoville Barton 1990, and his father never came upstairs.

He sucked deeply and settled back against the bed. The smoke made his throat constrict for a moment as it rasped its way down into his lungs; but, as Tindle had predicted, the effect was almost instantaneous. His eyes watered for a moment, and a tear ran out of the corner.

There was a free kick that Danny Bective was lining up at the edge of the penalty area. Finn could see Spike being heavily marked on the far post by the center half, who had a handful of shirt to keep his man from jumping too high.

If Spike should score and lead his team to a victory, then the result would push Finn's own club down into the relegation zone.

214

On the other hand, given that the other three players from his fantasy team had all done well for their respective real-life clubs that night (a goal and an assist from the forwards, a clean sheet from the fullback), it was possible that his fantasy eleven would go top of the league-within-a-league that he and his school friends were running.

Which meant more to him: his real team or his fantasy? The Aurora/Skunk Two made such a nice call hard to make. Then Danny Bective hit the free kick straight into the wall in any event, so the dilemma was unresolved.

Finn sucked in the remainder of the joint and lay back. His eyes took in the poster of Evelina Belle, gazing down at him in an almost caring, almost maternal way.

There were three minutes added for injuries, despite the protestations of both managers in the "technical" area, the small white marked box in front of the dugout, so called, Ken had told him, "because, *technically*, inside it you can call the opposing manager an aunt." Ken always swore in predictive text.

Finn's mouth was dry from the skunk and he was finding reality hard to cling on to.

Then Ali al-Asraf made a run down the left flank. He was quick, you had to hand it to him. He looked up, passed and—bloody hell, Borowski was clean through the offside trap: the center halves who'd kept Finn's team up in the Premiership for three seasons—he'd sprung them like a cheap padlock; and the assistant's flag was pointing at the ground . . .

Finn stumbled to his feet. And now there was no doubt at all, no choices to be made between a lifelong loyalty and a momentary gain in an imagined world—no difficulty in choosing between the real and the fantastic . . .

"Go o-o-o-n-n-n," he yelled, as Borowski took al-Asraf's pass in his stride, steadied for a moment and buried the ball in the lower right-hand corner.

"Oh y-e-e-s-s-s." Finn fell back against the bed, more than one tear now running down his smooth cheeks.

At midnight, Nasim al-Rashid knocked at her son's bedroom door.

"Come in."

"Can I sit on the bed?"

"If you like."

Hassan was reading a book: *Milestones* by Sayyid Qutb.

"You've read that before, haven't you?"

"Yes. So?"

"Hass, darling, we're worried about you. Your father and me."

"Why?" Hassan's voice had the surly edge it had developed at the age of about fourteen—as though he were being persecuted.

"You seem so . . . angry. And we'd like you to have a job. It's not good for you to spend so much time at the mosque."

"I thought you wanted me to be a good Muslim."

"Of course we do. No one's more devout than your father, as you know. But sometimes young men can get too wrapped up in religion. Not just Muslims. Others too. It's not healthy to spend so much time in your room."

Hassan said nothing.

Nasim looked down at the duvet and pinched the edge of it in her fingers. "Where were you today?"

"I had to see some friends about a project."

"You left the house very early. You were away all day."

"I know. And what did you do?"

"Me?" said Nasim. "Oh, you know, the usual. Things in the house. Then I went to the West End to see an art show. A man called Liam Hogg. Have you heard of him?"

"Everyone has."

When Hassan was a child, Nasim believed he would do the things that had been denied to her and Knocker because their families had been immigrants. The education both of them received had been rudimentary, and the job prospects grim for people of their background in postindustrial Bradford. But Hassan . . . Born speaking English, and born beautiful, too, with his long black lashes and his bowed upper lip: the only son of a family that cared for him so deeply and had somehow stumbled on the money to provide for him—surely with his natural intelligence he was destined for greatness, or, at the very least, great happiness. He was a curious and gentle little boy, not rambunctious and aggressive, as so many others were, but not weak or retiring, either—just interested in the world, in how it worked, in stories people told about it, all of which he approached with his head on one side, ready to listen, keen to know the answers. He had something else the other boys didn't have: an ability to sympathize with others, even grown-ups. Sometimes he patted his mother's hand in consolation when he saw she was upset, and Nasim thought he had inherited his father's simple kindness.

The mother's love for her boy was intense; and if there was sometimes a trace of sentimentality in it, then that was necessary, she thought, as a kind of protection or socializing of the dangerously visceral passion that underlay it.

Nasim had found it hard to accept the changes that came over Hassan as he grew older. When he hung out with the bad boys at school she could see how artificial was the veneer of disdain he'd applied to himself, how thin the self-defense. And then the ridiculous student politics. She knew little about these things herself, and some of what he said about what America had done in the Middle East seemed quite likely to be true; but what worried Nasim was not the detail of what he proposed or the old-fashioned Communist language, but the degree of self-dislike that it suggested.

By giving Hassan all the advantages that she and Knocker hadn't had, she believed she would remove him from friction, place him in a comfortable mainstream where he could use all his energies to flourish and waste none of them, as his parents had, on the attritional business of surviving.

She was cut to the heart to see it wasn't so. The boy didn't seem to rejoice in the place that had been carved out for him by the sweat and love of his parents. He became distrustful, separated from them and from their beliefs and alienated too, in some way Nasim couldn't start to understand, even from himself. She asked advice

217

from friends and she consulted parenting manuals. They all stressed that children were their own creatures; that while genetically they were a half each of their parents, this input was of relatively little importance because what they chiefly were was something else: themselves. And there was almost nothing you could do to influence this hard, unknowable core. One of the self-help books compared the mother to a gardener who'd lost the labels on her seed packet. When the young plant grew up you didn't know if it would turn out nasturtium or broad bean; all you could do was encourage it to be as good a flower or pulse as it could be.

Whatever Hassan was, whatever the true nature that he was growing to fulfill, Nasim thought, he wasn't happy. She had to nerve herself for these conversations because she found his abruptness so upsetting and because she feared that by interfering she would make things worse. She approached his bedroom door, therefore, only when she was certain that not to do so risked causing greater damage.

"My love, if there's anything wrong, you would tell me, wouldn't you?"

"What sort of thing?"

"If you were unhappy? People get depressed. It's not a weakness. And boys of your age. Everyone knows that puberty is hard, but in fact it was fine for you, wasn't it?"

"Yup."

"I mean, it's quite fun, growing up, going out and so on. But for young men I think your age is harder. The early twenties. I don't know why. Anyway, all I want to say is, you'd always come to Mummy, wouldn't you? If I could help."

"Aye. Thanks."

Nasim stood up. She felt saddened by her inability to reach the heart of Hassan's problems and bruised by his coldness. Her offer of help if he needed it, to be "always there" for him . . . Pathetic, really, she thought, when once, when he was young, they had had this majestic intimacy . . .

But what more could you do?

Five

Thursday, December 20

I

The Pizza Palace Book of the Year prize, somewhat controversially, was awarded to either a children's story, a travel book or a biography. Excluding all fiction was a bold thing to do, but it was felt that novelists already had enough prizes of their own not to need the £25,000 on offer from the restaurant chain that claimed to have put the "pizza" into "pizzazz."

None of the board of PP was much of a reader (three out of eight voted against sponsoring the prize), but the finance director knew the man who ran the Zephyr public relations agency, which had some connections in the arts world. Trevor Dunn was his name, and his biggest arts client had been a theater company that specialized in putting on musicals adapted from television programs. Dunn asked Nadine and Tara, his two most recent trainees, to help him do a preliminary sift of all the entries and gave them lunch at a hotel in Covent Garden for their trouble.

There wasn't time to read the books, but by studying the jackets and the blurbs, Trevor, Nadine and Tara got the list down to about twenty in each category and sent them off to the preliminary judges: reviewers or trade insiders who were willing to look through twenty books for an "honorarium" of £400. After the category winners had been chosen, Trevor earned his own larger fee from Pizza Palace by luring in some names for the final three-book judging. As early as June, he had been able to announce his panel for the December showdown. They were a junior transport minister from the second Major government who was said to be one of the few politicians who read books; a lively woman presenter on children's television; the "esteemed literary critic" Alexander Sedley; the "well-known reviewer and biographer" Peggy Wilson; and—Trevor's coup—the "former Girls From Behind singer and now TV personality in her own right," Lisa Doyle. In its mixture of gravity and showbiz, Trevor thought it was the best panel he'd yet managed, and the board of Pizza Palace, counting the newspaper column inches his agency mailed to them, was inclined to agree.

One person violently dissented, and that was R. Tranter. His biography of the Victorian novelist A. H. Edgerton had earned him £1,000 as category winner and he had reasonable hopes that it could see off a challenge from *Bolivia: Land of Shadows* by Antony Cazenove in Travel and *Alfie the Humble Engine* by Sally Higgs in Children. And then he had seen the list of judges one morning in the newspaper and his cereal had turned to cotton wool in his mouth. The transport man would be all right, the girl singer would be keen to show off and he'd been nice enough to old Peggy Wilson at the books-page party where Patrick Warrender had introduced him. But Sedley . . . Christ.

All day long, phrases from his review of *A Winter Crossing* two years earlier kept coming back into Tranter's mind. "Moribund and ham-fisted." Could he really have said that? "Watching Alexander Sedley fumble with the English language is like watching a drunk in boxing gloves trying to pick up his front-door key." It had seemed rather good on the afternoon he wrote it. Every time Tranter convinced himself that Sedley would have taken his review "like a man" and would bear no grudge against him, another terrible phrase came stabbing into his mind. "A prose tone-deaf to its own self-importance." God. There was really no way back from that.

There was only one thing to do. A week after Sedley's appointment was announced, Tranter, with Septimus Harding on his lap, sat down to compose what he could only describe to himself as "the hardest letter I have ever had to write." "Dear Alexander . . ." No, that sounded too friendly, too obsequious; it might also send out some sort of gay message to a private-school type like Sedley. "Dear Mr. Sedley . . ." Too hostile, too gas board. "Dear Sedley" was of course what a posh tit like Sedley himself would probably have started. He settled in the end for the bland, tautologous "Dear Alexander Sedley." It would do. "You may remember we met briefly at that weird do at the Natural History Museum, then again—also briefly—at your excellent reading in Hampstead (sorry I had to dash off in such a hurry that night, incidentally, as there was much I wanted to ask you about *A Winter Crossing*—but duty called!). Anyway, I just wanted to say that I've recently had the opportunity of rereading it . . ."

Was "opportunity" a bit strong? After all, anyone could pick up a paperback. But if he said "the pleasure" it gave away too soon the volte-face he wanted to prepare more carefully.

"Anyway, I just wanted to say that I've recently had the opportunity of rereading it. I must say that it was a thoroughly pleasurable experience. One's first reading of such a book is necessarily influenced by the cultural baggage one brings to it; and prose as many-layered as your own really requires a second, closer reading. I relished your lightly worn learning and the playful references to other first novels, ranging from Camus to Salinger and, if I am not mistaken, Dostoevsky, no less! All this done with an enviable lightness of touch . . ."

Bloody hell. This was laying it on a bit. The trickiest part of course was whether to refer to his own review. It was conceivable that Sedley might not have seen it and the letter would then have the catastrophic effect of making him look it up. On the other hand, it was pretty unlikely that someone so far up himself would not have read the papers. Perhaps then he should go for a sort of generic retraction on behalf of all the bad reviews. Yes.

"I don't really recall its reception at the time, but I suppose not all the reviews were able to rise to the occasion straightaway. History tells us—Katherine Mansfield on *Howards End*, Henry James on *Our Mutual Friend*, almost everyone on *Ulysses*—that it's not the first journalistic reaction that matters, but the second and third and, in the case of a novel such as yours, the subsequent responses over many years that really count. I have now had the pleasure of reading it three times and I have no hesitation in saying that it's not only an extraordinary debut, but in its own way is an <u>important</u> novel.

"I look forward eagerly to whatever you care to give us next.

"Yours in haste—"

The hardest thing was to get the dashed-off feeling of one great, distracted mind in a generous hurry to commune with another; but after three hours he was pretty sure he'd nailed it. In the life-shaping straits that Tranter found himself, anything was worth a shot.

Ralph Tranter had been a novelist himself, once. It was a natural aspiration for someone who enjoyed books and had read English at Oxford, though it wasn't one he felt confident to talk about. His first job had been with a large insurance company in High Holborn on their graduate trainee scheme, and he had been dismissive of the various "creative" types he'd known at college who seemed to think the literary or artistic world was agog for their arrival. Three years down the line, he was the only one with a job.

Living at that time in two rooms in a former Peabody building near the BBC, Tranter would get back from work at 6:30, put a large potato in the oven to bake and sit down at his typewriter. He had the modesty to know that he must pay the rent first and buy himself time to write; he had the self-discipline not to go out or watch television; he had read so many books that he also had a prose style that was plausible for most purposes. Most of the prerequisites were in place; all that he lacked was something to say.

But how important—really—was that lack, he wondered? When he looked at the novels he'd read and studied, not much seemed to happen in them. The main characters moved from position A to position B. Plot—at least in the sense of any real action—was the province of the genre writer: the sadly misnamed "thriller," the clockwork detective puzzle or a "disaster" epic of mutant crocodiles in the sewer system. Meanwhile, middlebrow newspaper interviews and highbrow literary biographies focused almost exclusively on the extent to which the contents of a serious novelist's books were drawn from his own experience and the characters "based on" people known to him. After two years of torn-up pages, false starts and sober late nights, Tranter convinced himself that—compared to finding a reputable publisher, choosing a catchy title and looking interesting in the author picture—the actual content of his novel was not that important.

So it was that he began yet again, with a main character not unlike himself on a life path that bore a fraternal relationship to his own. This thing about "inventing" characters that some novelists banged on about; really, when you came down to it, why bother? Very few people knew him, or any of the acquaintances he planned to include, so what was the point of conjuring and molding new people from the void? At least he and his friends came with built-in credibility; they were, by definition, "realistic" . . .

Tranter's hero, John Sturdy, came from a modest Midlands family and his dilemma was much to do with regional issues: whether he should work in the pottery business or go to London with a girl from art school, who resembled Sarah Powell from the street next to Tranter's parents', though with added sexual charisma—a pretty hefty addition in all honesty. Tranter allowed the voices of the English regionalist school to harmonize with his own; there were intertextual references to the novels of Stan Barstow and Walter Allen, for instance. After three chapters, he found his book gaining traction. Every time he felt the need for a new incident, he would throw in an episode from his own life, but with a small twist. In this way, he had eventually spun the book out to 200 typewritten pages. The death of Sturdy's grandfather could occupy another ten, and then he was only forty short of 250—the critical mass, he'd been told, that could be leaded-out by the publisher to cover 200 printed pages.

At the same time, Tranter wrote to small magazines, enclosing copies of articles he'd written at Oxford and unpublished reviews he had written "on spec" of new books. Eventually, *Outpost* printed one; a month later *Actium* followed suit, and Tranter was quick to reinforce success by sending them more. He didn't require to be paid, but when he'd built up a scrapbook of half a dozen cuttings, he began to hawk them round the bigger magazines and even newspapers. Many papers had almost given up reviewing books, but then, following an outbreak of new supplements in the late 1980s, suddenly found their space quintuple overnight. Instead of half a page shared with ads for furniture warehouses, book review editors were suddenly expected to fill three entire pages on a Saturday. They searched frantically through the papers on their desk for R. Tranter's phone number.

At this point Tranter played with the idea of inventing a second initial—calling himself R.G., perhaps. The precedent was auspicious. There were the poets Auden, Yeats, Eliot, cummings and Hilda Doolittle, who was known *only* by her initials, H.D.; in the critical field where Tranter proposed to earn his daily bread, there were the fathers of Cambridge criticism F. R. Leavis and I. A. Richards; more recently there were the prolific A. N. Wilson and D. J. Taylor, the last two, he believed, not much older than himself. How many more copies might A. V. Woolf have sold if so called? In the end, however, he decided it was more original as well as more honest to stick with one.

Then, at the *Outpost* Christmas drinks party, Tranter met a literary agent and persuaded him to look at the novel, now finished and entitled *The Potter's Tale*. A publisher, not one he would personally have chosen, accepted the book and paid him £2,000 for it. It received some friendly reviews but sold only 221 copies in hardback, including fifty-eight to libraries and twelve to the author's mother; no paperback offer was forthcoming. There was a rumor that it was going to be on a long-listing for the Handivac, but this turned out to be false.

Tranter experienced the disappointment at first as an intermittent wave or spasm, but over the following months it changed into crystalline, insoluble bitterness. This was the life event that was exactly the right, or the wrong, shape to fit into a recess in his character. As a child, he had been cheerful and reasonably benevolent in the playground and classroom. He lacked the confidence to be outgoing, but he had friends enough, he was good at schoolwork, he liked pop music and football; if he wasn't in with the cool set, he wasn't quite out of it either. It was no surprise to his teachers or family when he won a place at Oxford; he was good at lessons and had a particularly sympathetic feeling, even at the age of eighteen, for the Victorians.

He found that university, although he liked it, made him develop a defensive layer. He thought he was as clever as the other students, but many of them had a social ease that baffled him. He bought a tweed jacket and a tie from a shop in Turl Street, but they didn't do the trick and he went back to jeans and a safe donkey jacket. He joined societies, went to meetings, spoke up in tutorials; he hung out in the King's Arms. It was not a disaster, but he never seemed to be asked to anything enjoyable or glamorous. He knew these people and they weren't unkind to him; they remembered his name, in either pronunciation; they allowed him to attach himself to the fringe of their pub or college bar sessions, they smiled when he made a joke and they let him buy them beer; but they never condescended actually to invite him to anything. He changed from drinking lager to gin and tonic; he took up smoking, and chose the brand most popular with his friends. He gave up supporting West Bromwich and switched to Arsenal or Liverpool, depending on who he was with; he even considered dropping English and taking up philosophy. But over three years he found that whatever he did, he remained peripheral. This disappointment generated a low but resilient anger in him. One day, without actually putting it into words, he swore that however long it took, he would have his place in the light. Until then, in the short term, so far as university was concerned, he discovered one consolation: he could use what he'd learned from the people who shunned him to discomfit in turn those—and there were many of them—more ill at ease than he was.

Tranter's final session with Farooq al-Rashid was a revision course of all that they had done thus far. A minicab, paid for by Knocker, picked him up from the station and dropped him off at eleven o'clock. Lucy, the Brazilian girl, opened the door and showed him down the passageway to Knocker's study.

The genial old fool rose up from behind his gigantic computer screen and held out his hand in greeting. Tranter felt glad that this was their last encounter. Mr. al-Rashid may well have been a billionaire for all he knew, but he had very little feeling for books.

"How did you get on with *The Secret Agent*?" said Tranter.

Knocker frowned. "It wasn't as exciting as I'd expected. I found it rather difficult to get through."

"That's Conrad for you. You can take the Pole out of the Ukraine, but you can't expect him to write English."

"Do you think Her Majesty will have read Conrad?"

"Probably not. Let's not stress about it. What about *A Maid's Revenge*?"

"Ah yes. Your friend Alfred Huntley Edgerton again. I preferred *Shropshire Towers*."

"Yes, I suppose that's his *Sergeant Pepper*. And what did you make of 'Fra Lippo Lippi'?"

"I liked it," said Knocker. "Was that right?"

"Yes, that's right. Some people think Browning's what you put in gravy, but I think he's the authentic voice of Victorian England."

Lucy came in with some tea, apple juice and a box of dates. Tranter suspected that Knocker had looked at no more than a couple of pages of most of the books he'd recommended. He was far from certain that Knocker could actually read.

"All right," said Tranter. "Let's do a role play, shall we? I'll be the Queen."

"Shall I go down on one knee?"

"You're not being knighted, are you?"

"No, I . . . But I don't know how it'll be."

"Have you read any good books lately, Mr. al-Rashid?"

"Oh yes, Your Majesty. Very many. The winner of this year's Café Bravo prize was especially good, I thought."

"Oh really? I thought it was typical subcontinental, sub-Rushdie, look-at-me-aren't-I-refreshing and tragically not copy-edited bollocks."

"She probably won't say—"

"Not bollocks, probably. But what do you say to the rest?"

Knocker coughed. "The vitality of the modern British novel owes a good deal to the way that it has been energized by writers from the former colonies who have brought a fresh eye and a multicultural sensibility to—"

"It sounds as though you're reciting it," said Tranter.

"I thought you told me to learn it by heart."

"I did. But you could make it sound a bit more, you know, spontaneous."

"Shall I try it again?"

"No. Let's do some quick-fire opinions."

They had been practicing this exchange for some weeks; it involved Tranter royally saying "D'you like *x*?" and Knocker coming back with a swift and polished reply.

"D'you like Hardy?"

"I find him overdeterm . . . determinas—"

"Deterministic."

"Overdeterministic," said Knocker, "but one must admire his true feeling for his native Wessex countryside."

They went through the classics, some foreigners and then came up to date with recent authors. It gave Tranter pleasure to see Knocker repeat his own dismissals.

He asked about a much-liked modern.

"Should learn the difference between 'may' and 'might' if she wants to be taken seriously," said Knocker with confidence.

"Good." Tranter next offered a venerated American.

"Prose so muscle-bound you need a forklift truck to turn the page. Is that right?"

"Spot on," said Tranter, and dangled an African laureate.

"Hmm," said Knocker confidently. "Do you think he took a pledge at school never to use an adjective?"

The final part of the lesson was a recitation. Tranter had guessed that the Queen's favorite poet might be John Betjeman, and he had made Knocker learn a couple of his poems.

Knocker found it easier to remember the lines if he stood up and walked about.

"'From the geyser ventilators/Autumn winds are blowing down,'" he began.

As he stood in the window, the light came through from the hills beyond, going up toward Epping Forest, illuminating the pale brown of his face and the dark pools of his concentrating eyes.

"'On a thousand business women/Having baths in Camden Town.'"

As he watched Knocker's thick black eyebrows spliced with thin gray wires and saw the Adam's apple drag up in his throat, Tranter, for no reason, found himself suddenly thinking of where this man and his ancestors had come from—an agricultural valley in Pakistan, he presumed. He had an involuntary picture of bloody British partition; of religion and greed and the violence, over centuries; and of millions of the rural poor like the al-Rashids—bullied by Arab Muslims pushing east and by raiding Mongols forging south and west, then exploited by their own people.

"'Waste pipes chuckle into runnels,/Steam's escaping here and there,'" Knocker's voice went on, proud and even. "'Morning trains through Camden cutting/Shake the Crescent and the Square.'"

Betjeman's words, and their thoughts for the businesswomen in their baths, had a strange effect on Tranter, as they issued through Farooq al-Rashid's mouth. The vision he had was no longer of the Mirpur Valley but of the city of London—of himself and this Pakistani illiterate as cells in a giant body, celebrated by the verse of a second-generation Dutch immigrant. What a pair of old frauds we are, he thought.

Tranter looked out at the long view and pictured Havering, then Epping to the northwest, then round to Edmonton, where a local

228

stablemaster, Thomas Keats, had fathered a rambunctious boy called John; and south to Camden Town where in *Dombey and Son* Dickens had described the terrifying steam trains as they emerged snorting from the burrows of the old city while the cuttings were blasted out through Chalk Farm . . .

"'Early nip of changeful autumn,'" Knocker went on, as though in a trance, "'Dahlias glimpsed through garden doors,/At the back precarious bathrooms/Jutting out from upper floors . . .'"

. . . And the stone tenement steps that led to Orwell's flat in Canonbury where he was smoking himself to an early grave, the dreadful common at Clapham over which Greene had driven his narrow, loveless characters; and, more than this, the grimy streets of Lewisham and Catford that, so far as Tranter knew, still waited for a voice.

As Knocker's baritone with its Yorkshire vowels and Kashmiri consonants ("*v*aste pipes") came to an end, Tranter's vulpine features began to soften in the short December light.

He coughed and looked away. It was only a little light verse; but in his long bitterness he had almost forgotten what words—the stuff from which he'd made his life—could really do.

Through the morning John Veals stayed in his office with the door shut and his eye on the Allied Royal share price. Occasionally he would rest his gaze on Olya, as she smiled at him from the laptop on his side table. He tried to look at her for as long as possible in the hope that while his eyes were off the ARB screen the price would rise again. Steve Godley had the same theory with the Test match, which he kept going silently on a small television in the summer: if England desperately needed to take a wicket, he would leave the room; when England were batting, he could exercise seven-hour bladder control.

Olya, her knees for once drawn up demurely beneath her chin, cast her spell on ARB. The price rose through the morning, like an air mattress being gently inflated; and by eleven, Veals could see the beginnings of a surge. He wondered if the FSA could tell from his hard drive how much time he'd spent with the Allied Royal figures up on his screen; but even if they could reconstitute his viewing history, he'd done nothing wrong by merely watching.

He began to feel the mixture of emotions he had first experienced as a teenager: the elation of money coming his way, the self-congratulation that followed—because the gain was all down to his inspired decisions—and then the almost equal counter-emotion of sickening anxiety: a fear that there was some aspect of the trade he hadn't covered, some twist that even he had not foreseen.

In many ways the happiest, most stress-free part of John Veals's career had been the first. He had fared badly at his uninspiring North London school, but his maths results had got him a place at what he called a "graybrick" university to study law. He stood it for two years, then left to work as a stockbroker's clerk. It gave him a sense of the market, but the work bored him and he thought the fixed commission system antiquated. Then in 1982, when he was twenty-two, something much more congenial appeared in the City: the London International Financial Futures Exchange. He told his father, who, like his own father, ran a funeral parlor in Hendon, that he was throwing up his job as a Blue Button to go into futures trading. Morris Veals was appalled. John was only the third generation of the family to be British, and Morris was delighted to see him among the bowler hats of the Stock Exchange: that could be a job for life, and John's sons would go to private schools and Oxford. But John sidestepped his father when his uncle Harry, who ran the bookmaker's, said he knew an independent trader starting up at LIFFE after twenty years at Billingsgate; this man, said Harry, might need a runner.

"Is your nephew numerate?" the wet-fish salesman asked.

"Is he numerate?" said Harry. "He could give you the square root of the next prime number they haven't yet discovered!"

LIFFE was rudimentary and slow, and not English, but based on the Chicago exchanges, and full of hard-faced Americans come to make a fast buck; but Veals loved it from the first day he spent there. The trader for whom he worked was called Jimmy John-ston; he was a Gentile, from a line of fishmongers, and was excited by the new challenge. Veals watched how Jimmy was able to keep a huge amount of shouted information in his head and never make mistakes when writing tickets. It was Veals's job, in his trainee yellow jacket, to run them back to the admin booth, where the input clerk would stamp them.

What Veals liked about it was the brashness. Where once the City had been equities, bonds and discount houses, here there were men in brightly colored jackets trading new products with fat margins, making real money. American investment banks, which wanted access to the European time zone, began to move in and to hire trading teams. Their basic trade was to buy interest-rate options and futures on behalf of large clients who needed to hedge their exposure to interest-rate fluctuations—dull enough, thought Veals; but what he liked much more was the way that banks traded not just to service clients' needs but with their own money, as a bet.

After a year working for Jimmy Johnston, Veals was hired by one of the main American banks to execute trades for its clients. His ability to calculate at speed and the tightness of the spreads he offered brought him respect and a degree of fear on the floor of LIFFE. His salary from the bank was not large, but the bonus he earned in his first January pushed him over £250,000 for the first time. After some research among the independent traders, or "locals," he found a reliable clearing company who agreed to back him if he himself began to trade in dual capacity—both for his bank and as a local, on his own account.

Some of the red-jacketed locals were Rabelaisian figures, itching to square up to the might of the American banks. They arrived at 6:30, breakfasted in a Cannon Street tea bar on bacon sandwiches and started trading at eight. At eleven they went for a champagne break and if it had been a good day, some even went home there and then. Others were so in love with the system of open outcry, the clamor of trade, that they stayed till closing time at 4:30, come what may. Most of the traders were young men. The physical demands of rising in a house in Essex or Pinner at five o'clock and then to be in a merciless fight, on their feet, till 4:30 every day were too much for older people.

John Veals didn't mind getting up early to leave Highgate, where he'd bought a bachelor mews house with woodblock flooring and numerous electronic gadgets. He relished the challenge, physical, mental and financial; the hand signals and the head- and shoulder-tapping were second nature to the nephew of a bookie. He had more work than he could handle. Banks wishing to unwind a large position didn't want their recognizable trading teams in cherry and white striped blazers to start selling all at once so the price collapsed; instead, they called John Veals and asked him to unwind for them, softly, bit by bit, so no one knew for whom he was working. And of course, knowing that he had an order to sell 10,000 gilts on behalf of Allied Royal, for instance, it would have been insane not first to unload a few on his own "local" account, before his ARB trade began to depress the price . . .

He was playing with two decks of cards. Everyone did it, and it wasn't the traders' fault that it was so easy. The tickets were time-stamped and there were primitive video recordings in action, but they never seemed to catch anyone out; no one seemed quite sure whether it was even truly illegal. In any case, you'd have to be less than human, Veals thought, not to take a little personal profit up front before the bank paid you at the back end of the trade as well.

There was a nasty term for this, "front-running," but since all the proprietary bank traders were doing it—using client information they had accidentally overheard from their colleagues—Veals was doing no more in his own mind than making sure he didn't lose the hard-won edge.

Then, as volumes started to take off, Veals saw a problem looming: regulation. In 1987 there came word that a plodding army of legislators was on its way; so when the bank asked if he would transfer to New York, where, at a much larger salary, he could lead their team at NYMEX, the mercantile exchange, it took him less

232

than a minute to say yes. When regulation struck, John Veals headed for the airport.

It was in New York, at a weekend in Long Island, that he met Vanessa Whiteway. He was staying with Nicky Barbieri, a metal trader with a house overlooking the dunes in West Hampton, and there was an old-money barbeque party at a colonial mansion half a mile away that Nicky talked them into. Veals was twenty-eight and was earning, with bonus, into seven figures from the bank; he had bought an apartment on the Upper East Side to add to the mews he had let in Highgate. Vanessa was of Anglo-American family, but very much preferred the Anglo aspect after she'd been jilted by her American fiancé. She had never been a warm person, but this reverse had given her a permafrost coating that even the most dedicated skirt chasers, such as Nicky Barbieri, found chilling.

Veals, however, was intrigued by her. She was like a market he had yet to crack, and he wanted to know her risk—her yield, her beta and her delta. She suffered his attentions over the weekend without encouraging him; she made it clear that she thought NYMEX a vulgar place to work. Veals agreed, but the difference was that the vulgarity was what he liked: it went with money, drive and profit. He asked Vanessa out to dinner in Manhattan and took her to that week's hot place in SoHo, but could see at once that the postindustrial decor and zingy fusion food were not to her taste. Next time, they went to a French restaurant with fluttering waiters and velvet-covered banquettes, on Park and 80th, not far from the Met, and Vanessa thawed, a fraction.

Although he had exercised his libido from time to time in London, joining in at strip clubs and stag parties, taking his turn with occasional female City staff who seemed to have made up their minds to work their way through every member of certain trading teams (Brenda-the-overnight-lender: dear God), Veals was not interested in women. He did the deed, as they called it, to stop his colleagues gossiping and because he thought it might be good, in some undefined way, for his health. His heart was never in it.

He had nothing to say to these painted creatures, and anyway he found it hard to hear in noisy bars in Moorgate and London Wall. He watched with some respect as fellow traders unfolded bricks of twenties, bellowing inanities with champagne breath into the faces of their prey, but personally found the dividend of carnal pleasure a brief and poor return for the hours of tedium he'd invested.

Vanessa Whiteway was different. She was good-looking enough, Veals thought, that other men would envy and respect him: slim, with shoulder-length chestnut hair, large blue eyes, and no hint of cellulite beside the Long Island pool in her black one-piece. She drank vodka with lime and mint and smoked a packet a day; she had a private income from her American industrialist father that would be enough for there to be no irritation over dress allowances or occasional women-only holidays if she wanted them. Veals calculated that even if in cash terms she would be expensive to run, the maintenance of Vanessa would in other ways be low: she wouldn't sap his energy; he wouldn't find himself in the position he'd seen with a lot of promising traders: having to spend so much time servicing or reassuring his wife that it would take his mind off making money.

At lunchtime, John Veals made a rare sortie across town. He had arranged to meet Peter Reynolds, an investment manager with Shields DeWitt, the Vatican, not because he had anything in common with the unbearably upright Reynolds, but because he wanted to see if any rumors were circulating among the Barolo and the £35 plates of pasta at Saggiorato's, a few yards from the back end of the Burlington Arcade.

"Are you going to the HOPE bash tonight, John?" asked Reynolds, cracking a breadstick.

Hope was the nickname of an acronym: Hedge funds for Old-Age Pensioners. No one seemed to remember the organization's real name, but it financed a charity evening in which the richest people in financial services competed with one another to raise money in loud open auctions, with an emphasis on helping foundations for old people. In 2005, they had taken over Tate Modern and raised £18 million.

"I did my usual deal," said Veals. "Took three tables at double the going rate on the grounds that I didn't have to fill the seats or go to the event."

"That's the spirit, John."

"No, that's the cash."

"I see Dougie Moon's at his usual table."

"Yes," said Veals. "Wouldn't you hate to be a money broker? Like being a fucking speed-dating bureau or the teaser for a stallion, always trying to maneuver someone into position to shaft someone else."

"Plus you have to entertain every lunch and every dinner. I don't know why he doesn't go somewhere else occasionally."

"I suppose it's so people know where to find him. Mind you," said Veals, picking over a bite of crab and taglioni, "he does seem to get people into bed with one another."

"Bit of a plonker all the same."

"Total," said Veals.

Nevertheless, it was next to Dougie Moon's noisy table that he allowed himself to linger on his way to the cloakroom after lunch. He could tell from the volume of the conversation and from the color of Moon's face that he would be in expansive mood, but feigned surprise when Moon greeted him. Among Moon's lunch companions was a Frenchman called Guy Desplechin who had worked for an American bank in Paris, where, so far as Veals could see, his main job seemed to be advising his colleagues on how they could tastefully part with some of their bonus dollars on houses, art and wine. He certainly had little head for finance, as Veals had discovered when Desplechin came to try to sell him his bank's services as a prime broker.

As they stood, raffle tickets in hand, waiting for their coats, Desplechin gripped Veals's arm and whispered that he had some information so new and so searingly hot that he'd have to tell him outside. Veals said goodbye to Peter Reynolds and Dougie Moon and sauntered with Desplechin to the corner of Cork Street, where he found himself pushed up against a shop window with the Frenchman's face close to his.

"Swear on your children's lives."

"Yeah, yeah, Guy. Whatever."

"No, no, John. Say 'I swear on the lives of my wife and children.'"

"I swear on the lives of my wife and children."

"'That I will not tell a soul what I am about to hear or where I heard it.'"

"All that. What is it?"

"No. Say it, John."

"That I will not tell a soul what I am about to hear or where I heard it."

Desplechin put his lips to John Veals's ear. "First New York have agreed to buy Allied Royal. The chief execs dined together two days ago. It's a perfect fit."

Veals nodded. "Interesting." He began to walk away.

"Remember the oath."

"Sure."

"And . . ." Desplechin had to raise his voice to reach the departing Veals. "We can do business! Call me! Lunch!"

Without turning round, Veals raised a hand in affirmation. He was almost smiling. God, some fucking people.

In Pfäffikon, Victoria Gilpin's fingers were going rapidly over the keys in her stealthy style. She was finding it hard to keep up with the volume of trades that Kieran Duffy was putting on.

Duffy didn't know what Veals had done and would never ask, but the shape of the ARB graph had a familiar look: it was the initially gentle but then accelerating rise that went with a well-based rumor. Duffy could picture something being said or written in London, exaggerated later in New York, then calmed but basically accepted by the soberer heads of Asia. The market across the world had convinced itself that Allied Royal shares were going up;

a move to buy, orderly at first, was by three o'clock beginning to look like a frenzy.

Duffy knew that he and Veals couldn't be the only people who'd noticed a marginally sick edge to ARB over the last nine months or so; but as the price rose Duffy could sense that many fellow bears had lost their nerve. It was a short squeeze: a question of buy now while you still can.

He waited till about three o'clock before putting on the bulk of his own trade.

"Steady as we go, Victoria," Duffy said, trying to conceal how much he was enjoying himself. "Tell Simone to bring me some tea, will you?"

With the puts and the calls bought and sold, it was time to put on the commodity leg of the trade. It was delicate in Duffy's opinion, and a little risky, but it was clever; it was the sort of thing that made working for John Veals tolerable.

In 2001, Allied Royal had bought the "African assets" of a French colonial bank fallen on hard times, and this, together with its own historic presence in the region, meant that ARB effectively financed two thirds of the cocoa crop.

"Well, that much is GCSE geography," Veals had said. "The good bit is this. The warehouse which stores the cocoa before it flogs it on to the chocolate people in the West, they have to borrow money to buy the stuff from the farmers. And who do they borrow from?"

"ARB."

"You got it. A hole in one, as Godley would probably say. Twat. But it gets better. ARB has the whole market sewn up from the seed in the earth to the paper export docket. There's a network of financial relationships among thousands of not only farmers, but agents, brokers, shippers, insurers across the whole of Africa. No bank or group of banks, even the World Bank, could replace it overnight."

"So no one can buy the crop," said Duffy.

"Yes. So the price of what's already in the warehouse goes through the roof. This is not just Belgian chocolate, this is the last fucking Belgian chocolate you'll eat for six months."

Duffy sipped the milkless tea Simone had brought him. What he fancied was trading with some MIT-trained geeks who believed in "rational markets" and relied on fancy formulae to back them up. If one price—cocoa, coffee, whatever—went what they called "off campus," these guys would buy or sell enough of it until it obeyed the rules of their formula again. It was what Veals called the Long Term Fallacy—a reference to the beliefs espoused by Nobel Prize–winning economists that had caused a single hedge fund, Long Term Capital, to blow a trillion-dollar debt hole in the American economy. The next generation seemed not to have learned the lesson.

"Bring on the geeks, Victoria!" called out Duffy, rubbing his hands together.

There would be public recriminations when the world saw others profiting while African farmers watched their crop rot in the earth; but such attention would focus on the regulated futures markets, rather than the twilit world in which Duffy was trading. It was great, just great, that hedge funds were not regulated. The legal counterparty to the trade was not even High Level Capital, but its prime broker—the American investment bank in London.

It was true, Duffy thought as he hung up the phone to New York, that several million Africans would go hungry, but that was nothing to do with him; it was the fault of an imminent banking failure at Allied Royal.

He scrawled details of the trade onto a ticket and called out to Victoria. Back at her desk, it took her some moments to decipher Duffy's writing before she carefully booked the trade and pressed "Send."

II

In the summer of 2006, Salim asked Hassan if he would like to go on a study trip that the Muslim Youth Coalition had organized to visit Pakistan. He would meet like-minded people and do some "training." Hassan was suspicious, and didn't know how he could swing it past his parents; even they had not suggested he return "home" to find a wife, but seemed content that he would marry someone English. He declined the offer, not without a qualm, and Salim accepted his refusal with equanimity.

Six months later, Salim put a further request to him: to meet the Special Vanguard Force. "The others who are going have all trained in Pakistan or Somalia, but you're such a clear thinker, Hass, that I want you to go anyway. You're brainy. Don't be alarmed. It's nothing specific. We're just looking for the leaders of tomorrow. People who understand the territorial challenge."

Salim gave his most Baloo the Bear–like grin. The Vanguard Force was the penultimate tread on the escalator and Hassan was intrigued by the way it carried an English not an Arabic name; attendance involved no flight to Karachi, no long journey to the hills, but a simple train trip of less than three hours to Bradford from King's Cross. "Territorial" was an interesting word, too.

In a bare room above a bingo hall off Lumb Lane, Hassan heard the speech that, together with the British invasion of Iraq, made him believe he was ready to act for his beliefs. It came not from a cleric or rabble-rouser but from a junior welfare officer in the town council with a soft voice and a friendly look in his eyes. First they said a prayer, then, as his audience of twelve young men sat cross-legged, politely passing round fruit juice and biscuits, the man, who gave his name as Ali, set to work.

"Brothers. May I begin by welcoming you. The Vanguard Force will not detain you long. You'll go back to your homes the day after tomorrow. All of you bar one, I know, have already received some training overseas. The message I would like you to take home is this. That life is simple."

Hassan looked round and saw the surprise on the faces of the others. Presumably in Pakistan they had been lectured by frothing bigots and paramilitaries; they had not expected to encounter at this late stage someone who spoke in the cadences of a university lecturer.

So often in the last three years Hassan had felt torn between the rhetoric of purity that came from the mosque and the subversive laughter that came from daily life in a self-mocking country. It was like an enfilade of machine-gun fire: on one side the passion and the grandeur of Islam with its insistent, emotional speakers, loud and inspiring in his ears; and on the other side, the crawling minutes of his every day in a country that could never take itself seriously. He logically believed, he spiritually believed, and he had a young man's thirst for action; on the other hand, he was a Kilmarnock supporter.

What inspired and comforted him that evening when Ali spoke was that the tensions disappeared. All seemed inevitably unified: Hassan could be a *Toad*-reading "unillusioned" Briton who had taken the trouble to understand the truth of human life and was now prepared to act upon it. Ali made final sense of it all.

"Do you ever imagine what an educated *kafir* thinks when he lies down to sleep?" Ali asked. "Let me tell you. He wonders how it can be that of all creatures in the world, he alone, a man, is cursed with consciousness. He loves his children dearly. He yearns for the flesh of women—or of men. He'll try to do well in his life tomorrow. He is not, in so many ways, a wicked man. But he faces this contradiction. He knows his story is futile, because the end is already written. He will die, and all his love will come to nothing. He will not be there to see his children live. It's pure pain, it's a tragedy for him. And his *kafir* books and plays explore almost nothing but this brutal contradiction.

"You and I are free of it. God has set us free. When God declared himself to the Prophet and offered his 'uncreated' word in the Koran, all doubt went out of human existence. If we submit ourselves to God's will and live by his laws we will survive forever in paradise. A place is promised to us by the one true God. There is no mystery, no contradiction. Everything has been explained.

"However, there is one difficulty. Did you spot it? 'If we submit ourselves to God.' Well, that's not so very hard. 'A place is promised to us by the one true God.' That isn't hard at all! The difficulty is this: 'If we live by his laws.' That is why you are here: to learn how hard that is—and yet, how possible, how straightforward in practice.

"Islam is not a religion like Judaism or Christianity. It is the sublime, single and transcendent truth. To compare it to the other two religions is like comparing a decision to lower your hand to the immutable law of gravity. Both cause movement, but they are not to be seen on the same scale. Islam is the one truth, revealed by God himself to the Prophet. It pervades every second of your life. God is in your breath, your hand, your thoughts, in the flame in the grate, in the petal of the flower and in every atom of air. Islam is not a 'religion' that means you go to the mosque twice a year and forget in between; it is all-pervasive—in every second of your life, in every cell of your body. It has freed mankind from the bondage of the earth, from suffering and poverty. It has freed us from the contradictions of being alive—with death awaiting. Because it has revealed the truth, it has freed us from death. Islam is living. Islam is life. Or, to put it a better way, life is Islam.

"How then do we live this life, and where? This is the challenge and the battle. At first, the Prophet was told to establish the proper Muslim community, which he did in Medina. Then God told him to spread the word—to free the world from fear and from all the bad practices of superstition and the false gods that enslaved people. This he was to do by the sword. Islam did not conquer people, it freed them. This was not 'imperialism'; it was the gift of liberation. Through Africa, Persia and Asia the Muslim armies brought the good news that God was all-powerful and that from now on life had meaning.

"Arabs, Persians, Indians, Africans and Asians joined together in freedom. Islam was not defined by race or nation or color. It was never an Arabic civilization, not for a single day. It was never a nationality, always a community of belief. Islam raises no man above another; it has no truck with kings, or tyrants, archbishops or dictators. But it recognizes the spirit of the human as transcendent. Remember our poor *kafir* lying in bed, cursing his consciousness—cursing the fact that by giving him knowledge of his imminent death his god has made him lower than his dog? Islam, on the contrary, knows that humans are higher than all animals, blessed and liberated by Allah. We recognize only two sorts of people: true believers and the others. Either you live in harmony with God or you live in the unreformed world, the *Jahiliyya*.

"Now the fight that never ends is this. Some empires, such as the Christians and the Zionists, were not like ours—free brotherhoods of the spirit, armed by eternal truth. They were narrow, racially bound nationalists who were interested not in the spiritual life on earth and the eternal life hereafter, but in power, territory and money.

"While the Muslim empire flourished and gave to the world all it needed of science and art for a thousand years, it was driven from its physical locations by these worldly forces. We became a glorious spiritual entity, guardians of truth and freedom, but without a country or a geographical community that we could call our own. There was no place on earth in which sharia law was properly enacted; there was no place on earth that would have pleased the Prophet. Medina and Mecca now found themselves located in a country of corrupt and brutal kings, with licensed slavery. Baghdad, the seat of the caliphs, was no longer in a country the Prophet would have recognized.

"The science and the art we gave the world was based on what God showed us. All things in the believer's mind emanate from God because submission to His will means that our thoughts work in harmony with His plan. The mercenary armies of the West stole our science and then detached it from its divine inspiration. Science from then on became not the work of God but the work of atheists bent on power for commercial or nationalist ends.

"I want you to be very clear on this point. The fact that a country calls itself 'Muslim' doesn't mean that it is shaped in God's will. A so-called 'Muslim' country can be as *jahili* as an atheist or Western one. That is the burden, the grief of Islam—that the countries that use the name 'Muslim' are in fact *jahili*. Egypt, Sudan, Somalia, Iraq, Saudi Arabia . . . All these offer examples of government profoundly offensive to Islam. Even Iran. We do not believe in 'theocracy' more than any other 'cracy.'

"That is why the task of the Vanguard Force is a simple one. It is exactly the task that faced the Prophet when he set out from Mecca. We are here to liberate the world: to bring to human beings the wonderful news that their lives do have meaning, purpose, beauty and immortality. But whereas the Prophet began alone, we begin with more than a thousand million believers! So our task is simple: to set up a city, a country, then a world that is run according to the will of the Prophet, and of God.

"Some of our forerunners have tried to do so in so-called 'Muslim' states—in Egypt, for instance, where they met only repression and torture. The belief of the Vanguard Force is that we must begin at home, as the Prophet himself did, in his home in Arabia. God did not at first license the Prophet to use force. Once he had secured a base, however, further verses were revealed to him. Muslims were permitted to fight. Next, they were commanded to fight—to defend themselves against aggressors. And finally, when the time was right, the verses were revealed that ordered the spread of the truth through force of arms: they were commanded to fight all nonbelievers. The truth had to be brought by war to those who did not spontaneously welcome it.

"And so we must begin again. What we do, like the first Muslims, is not 'imperialism' or 'terrorism' or any such thing. What we are doing is liberating the *kafir* in his bed from fear. We are proclaiming that life has meaning and is eternal. We are soldiers of the truth. We are the messengers of immortality.

"When you return to your homes, your group leaders may assign you to another organization: a practical one, the final step. Like Islam itself, it will not have a home. It may not even have a name. Do what they tell you. Trust me, they have access to the truth in the same way that you and I have access to it—through the uncreated and immortal word of God in the Koran, through the Sunna that tell us of the daily life of the Prophet and the Hadiths that describe the proper life. And remember what I said at first.

243

It is so simple. There is no fear. The harshness of life has been taken away from us by the words of the true and only God."

Ali stood up, and he was laughing. He was a small man, handsome and elated. He raised his hands in the air. "Be light on your feet. Be happy!"

III

At about four o'clock, the black phone on John Veals's desk rang. It was his secretary.

"John. There's a lady called Caroline Wilby for you. She's from the Financial Services Authority."

"Hold her for a minute."

Veals stood up. Shit. Fuck. Shit. The blood seemed to have run out of his brain and he felt light-headed. He sat down again, heavily.

His mind began to clear. Nothing wrong. He had done nothing wrong. He was at arm's length from everything. All his deals were under—no, over the counter; O'Bagel would have processed them all properly. There was nothing they had done—let alone done wrong—that came within the remit of the FSA; it was all unregulated. As for the ARB rumor, he didn't even know whether Ryman had done what he suggested in the chat rooms, whether he had spoken to the barman at Saggiorato's—he knew nothing. And Darke would protect his source; that much had been sworn. Anyway, he'd just pointed Darke to an article in the *FT* about possible bank mergers, he hadn't planted the idea. Right.

"Put her on."

"Mr. Veals?"

"Yes."

"Oh, hello. My name's Caroline Wilby. I work for the FSA. I'm awfully sorry to trouble you, but I wondered if I might ask for your help."

"Help?"

"Yes, I'm sorry if it's an awful imposition, but would it be possible for me to come and see you tomorrow? To ask your advice?"

"I suppose so. I may be going to Zurich. You'd better come early. Eight?"

"Eight? Gosh. Yes. OK. Fine. Shall I come to your office in Old Pye Street?"

"Yes. Ask for me at the desk. They'll send you up."

"Thank you so much. I do appreciate it."

"You're welcome, Caroline."

He hung up. Was this woman for real? Either she was playing a game, or she was barely out of school.

Veals put his feet up on the desk and stared out of the window at the piebald brickwork of Westminster Cathedral. His previous feeling of wistfulness had turned a notch closer to regret.

At the same time, Gabriel Northwood was sitting at his desk, watching an icy sleet fall on the lawns of the Inner Temple and remembering a summer Sunday morning in his cramped flat in Chelsea.

Catalina was lying flat on her belly across his bed, in jeans, bare feet and bra—a characteristic combination. She said the position and the clothes helped her think. She had at first been shy about her long legs and the freckles on her back; it took her a while before she'd allow him to look at her and run his finger up and down her spine, then saturate his gaze on the shifts of color in her skin: pink, gold, cream, coral . . . He counted them off to her with his finger going over the parts in question. He'd almost forgotten the brown of her eyes, and how he'd expected blue with her pale hair. He stared at her when she lay beside him, making vague Mendelian speculations about recessive eye-color genes.

"What are you thinking about?" she said.

"Banking," he said.

"Why?"

"Because I never thought I'd fall in love with a banker."

"I only did it for five years. It wasn't my life."

"You never told me why you stopped."

"It was so boring. No, that's not the right word. It wasn't always

245

boring, but it was so pointless. So devoid of any intellectual interest." Catalina sat up on the bed. "I'm not saying you didn't need to
be clever or quick to make money. You did. But the actual process,
the underlying thing that you were doing was without any philosophical content."

"So what was that underlying thing?"

"Moving hypothetical sums of money from one of a thousand
hypothetical homes into a different one. And then, the next day,
fighting and scrapping with the same people over the same strip of
turf."

She went on to give an account of her time in the bond department, waving her hands around to emphasize the circularity of
it all. "But it wasn't like that when I started," she said. "After I'd
trained, I spent my first year with this Englishman called Alexander, who was wonderful. The office was in Paris and we were fi-
nancing the restructuring of the railways in Eastern Europe.
Alexander spoke German and Czech. He was very cultured. We
used to go to the opera and things like that. You felt you were doing something worthwhile because without our bank they couldn't
have got it done—they'd still have no proper train system. Of
course we charged a lot, but it was a job worth doing and they
were pleased with what we did."

"So what went wrong?"

"People like Alexander were quite rare. Most bankers just saw
the post-Communist countries as cash opportunities: children with
no knowledge of the capitalist world that they could rip off merci-
lessly. And when I went back to Paris, they put me on the sell side.
And that was like working in a souk in Tangier."

"It can't have been that bad," said Gabriel. "I thought people
killed to get these jobs."

"Well of course, they wore fancy suits and swanked about in first
class on airplanes and dropped the names of their great banks at dinner parties and hoped that people would be impressed. And it could
be great fun. You know, when you suddenly sensed you'd made a

hell of a lot, by making the right call. It was really exhilarating, like watching your horse romp home in a race. But it was really just gambling with other people's money. 'OPM' we used to call it. If you lost half a million, you just shrugged and said, 'OPM.' And in the end I wanted something with a purpose."

"I see," said Gabriel. "So that's when you decided to become a grocer."

Catalina laughed. "We liked to believe the Copenhagen Herring and Salami Company was a bit more than a grocery. It was import and export, it was quite big. I started it with a girl from the bank in Paris who was as fed up as I was."

"And was there a big market abroad for open sandwiches?"

"Stop it. We sold mostly superior ham, you know, like Italian prosciutto, and very expensive salami. Pigs are Denmark's big thing. Then some cured fish, though we could never really persuade people that herring was a delicacy. But our most successful export was feta cheese. We sold huge amounts to Iran and Iraq. And Greece."

"I thought Greece had more or less invented feta."

"They did, but they liked ours better. It was fantastic. The bit I liked best was our own shop in Frederiksburg, which in my mind was based on one of those delis in New York with the best food from everywhere. A lot of it was Italian. It was a showcase. Sometimes I'd even work behind the counter. I think it was a childhood ambition. You know what I really liked? The floor. We had this old wooden splintery floor. And then I got married."

When Catalina talked, she quite forgot where she was or what she was wearing; so all the time she was frowning and gesticulating about the shipping of Tuscan olives, Gabriel couldn't help noticing that her bra had small pink flowers embroidered into the cups or that the color of the handful of freckles over the bridge of her nose exactly matched that of her eyes, and those on either side of the straps on her shoulders. Although she was a married mother of two, there was something unregenerately childlike in her, something that made him feel by contrast inhibited and worn. Giving up banking, for instance: how impulsive was that? Would he ever have been bold enough to do it?

Meanwhile, he had never fully understood what it was in him she liked, why she was so determined from the outset that she must have him. He felt that she had all the cards—the jobs, the charm, the wealthy family, the children, the looks, the enterprise . . .

Once, when they had come back from dinner on a Friday night and were getting ready for bed, he asked her what it was.

"It's quite simple," she said. "You know things. You just know so much. No one else had ever told me the story of Nathan and the Ewe Lamb. No one else ever gave me the life of Darwin in ten minutes. Or explained how Phil Spector built his wall of sound, or that Tamla Motown emphasized the off beat to rise above the noise of traffic on a car radio in Detroit. Or the difference between Monet and Manet, and why I need to know."

"I just read the papers. I'm not that busy. And knowing what's in the Bible—everyone used to know that."

"I suppose so. But it's what you do with all the things you know. You use them to make the world more interesting for me."

"And I thought it was my charm."

"No. Or yes. I mean, that *is* your charm."

"Shit," said Gabriel. "To think old Mr. Sanderson's scripture-knowledge class would one day win me the most lovely woman in London. Roger Topley used to bunk off every week so Sanderson never even had his name on the register."

"Poor Roger," said Catalina, taking off her skirt.

A knock on the door from Delilah, the junior clerk, announcing tea in Mr. Hutton's room, brought Gabriel back to a dark Thursday afternoon in December.

"I think there's chocolate biscuits if you hurry," said Delilah.

Gabriel didn't go home after work, but took the Tube to Paddington and the overground to Drayton Green ("Zone 4," Jenni told him. "Ever been that far out?"). The journey was mysteriously either fourteen or fifteen minutes through the western suburbs. Watching the backs of the Acton terraces slip by, Gabriel felt tense about the evening ahead. The voice that came from his throat in the darkest part of the Circle Line, asking her if he could take her out to dinner: what was that about? It was unprofessional and absurd. He couldn't stop it, though, and he didn't yet regret it.

The station was a rudimentary "halt" from which he climbed up and made his way toward the address she'd given him. There was a road sign that said "Poets Corner" with a twenty miles per hour speed limit. Gabriel had already noticed from the *A to Z* that there were Shakespeare, Dryden, Tennyson, Milton and Browning roads in the area. How had that happened? Maybe it had kicked off with Drayton Green, and only Mr. Smith in the Street Names department of Hanwell Town Hall in 1909 remembered that as well as being a place, Drayton was a poet—Michael, author of the famous Elizabethan "dry-eyed" sonnet, "Since there's no help, come let us kiss and part . . ." So perhaps Mr. Smith had decided to share his knowledge with the speculators throwing up new houses on the adjoining waste ground. Jenni had pronounced the name of her street "Cow-per" and Gabriel certainly wasn't going to tell her that the nervous poet in question preferred it to be said "Cooper."

It was what his mother would have called a "perfectly nice street"; in fact it might even have qualified for her highest praise: "You could live there yourself"—though he doubted whether she could have afforded to swap her damp little cottage for one of these trim houses with their bow windows and steeply pitched roofs. Some were in a terrace, some in pairs; they seemed to have been built at different times, the better ones Edwardian, the cheaper ones perhaps in the 1950s. There was the occasional satellite dish or garish "No Junk Mail" sticker, but most of the houses looked neat and of single occupancy. Jenni's was one of the few to have more than one front doorbell.

Gabriel, with a bunch of garage carnations in his hand, pressed the bell that said "Fortune."

He'd seen Jenni in her TfL uniform and he'd seen her in her best coat when she'd come to his chambers, but the girl who opened the door was different.

She smiled. "Hiya."

He thrust out the flowers, thinking it would help them round the kissing or shaking hands moment.

"D'you wanna come in then? My brother's out, luckily."

The ground-floor flat had been boxed off from the main stair-well with a cheap partition.

"D'you wanna cup of tea? Or are we going out?"

Jenni was wearing a green dress with knee-length leather boots and there was some blusher on her cheeks. It was like seeing a po-licewoman out of uniform, Gabriel thought; she looked exagger-atedly informal, and about ten years younger. She was smiling all the time now, this serious client who'd sat through hours of con-ferences with him and Eustace Hutton with little more than a grunt. Perhaps being on home ground had made her relaxed.

"Shall we have a drink and then I'll take you out?"

"OK, then. Do you take sugar?"

"No, thanks." He should have brought wine instead of flowers, he thought.

They sat on either side of the glass-topped coffee table, sipping tea. Gabriel found himself affected by Jenni's good mood. Catalina she was not; in fact, could two women have been more different? But that was all right; in fact, everything felt all right.

At Jenni's suggestion, they went to a nearby Indian restaurant. Gabriel made Jenni order first—chicken dhansak, spinach, pop-padoms—then did rapid calculations about what he could afford. He'd borrowed £40 from Andy Warshaw and, to his shame, £20 from Delilah. He couldn't stress his credit card any further. He asked for a biryani because the rice was included and when Jenni wanted only a half of lager to drink, flinched with relief.

"Next year," he said, when the beer had arrived, "my career's going to take off."

"How do you know?"

"Well, I have three cases already booked in. I think your case going to the Court of Appeal has been good for me. It'll get some more publicity. It's OK, Jenni, don't look like that. Not that sort of publicity. I mean, it'll be written up in the law reports and people will see my name."

"Why do you think you've started to get work?"

Gabriel shrugged. "Maybe it's just my turn. Karma. Or perhaps the solicitors have sensed that I care. I really found this case interesting and I worked hard on it. Maybe that somehow showed. Or perhaps you're my lucky charm."

"Are we still talking about work?" said Jenni.

"Of course. That was the deal."

"Why aren't you married?"

"Bloody hell, Jenni! What's that got to do with tort law or local authority liability?"

"Dunno." Jenni crunched a splinter of poppadom. "And what's the answer?"

"Do you want the long version or the short one?"

Jenni shrugged. "We got all night."

Gabriel drank some lager. "All right. There was this girl."

"Oh yeah. I thought there might be."

They had finished the main course by the time he reached the end of the Catalina story.

"So she went back to her husband?"

"She never left him. He got posted to America and she had to decide whether to go with him."

"How old were her kids?"

"Still young. Seven and five or something."

"She did the right thing."

"She did *a* right thing. And you?"

"Me what?"

"Why aren't you married?"

"Oh, blimey. Shall we have some wine?"

"Is the story that long? It's just that I don't have a lot of—"

"I got money too. You don't have to buy everything."

251

The story of Liston Brown took them through a bottle of house white, the paying of a bill that was still mercifully just within Gabriel's range, and the short walk back to Cowper Road.

"You don't seem surprised by all that," said Jenni, letting them in.

"I wasn't. I'm sorry about it, but not surprised. You seem like someone who's been hurt."

"Shall we have another cup of tea?"

"Sure. And you can show me Parallax."

"OK. I'll turn it on now. Grab a chair from the lounge. The computer's in the hall there."

Within a few minutes they were in the bland, unreal landscape of Parallax.

"Shall we go to my house?"

"Sure."

Jenni "airlifted" her maquette, Miranda, from where she'd left her in a shopping mall, and back to her beautiful new house.

"See, here's my swimming pool."

"You keen on swimming?"

"No, I can't swim, but Miranda likes it. Look, we'll put her in the pool. She's got a nice bikini."

Miranda splashed up and down, then got out and took Gabriel for a tour round the house, showing him the tiled hallway and the parakeets, then the bedroom with its view of the Orinoco.

"Lovely," said Gabriel. Although he could see that the game's designers had done a good job with the figures, this world as a whole was about as interesting as afternoon television.

Jenni clicked the "Events" tab. "Let's see what's going on. Hmm. Not much. The trouble is, it runs on Pacific Coast time, so a lot of what they do is not up and running at the moment. Do you want to see a film?"

"OK."

Miranda was airlifted to a cinema club, where she was the only customer. By paying 4 vajos, she could watch a film that had been on release in True Life a couple of years earlier. Because it was shown on a screen in a room within the computer screen, the pictures were small, and the soundtrack was indistinct.

"Brilliant, isn't it?" said Jenni. "I never saw this one when it came out."

"Yeah, it's great, it's just like . . . Well. Are we going to watch the whole thing?"

"Not if you don't want to. I can always come back later and restart it where I left it."

"Shall we go back to your house?"

"OK."

In the airy living room, among the palms, Miranda had a desk with a computer.

"Can you do anything on that laptop?" said Gabriel. "Does it work?"

"Yeah, sure, it works fine. And they're developing an Internet."

"You mean you can connect to the Internet in the usual way—though we're already online of course."

"No, it's an Internet that just works inside Parallax."

"God. What on earth is the point?"

"It's fun." Jenni looked affronted.

"And is there a virtual-reality game on your intra-Internet? Is there a game called 'Third Life' or something, where your pretend person Miranda can pretend to be someone else even further from reality?"

"Don't be silly."

"Oh, Jenni."

"And what does 'Oh, Jenni' mean?"

Gabriel put his head in his hands. How could she have lost herself so deep in this stuff?

He knew he was on the verge of saying something lawyerish he might regret, so he stood up and breathed in deeply. "Shall we talk about books instead?" he said. "Can I have a look at your collection? I caught a glimpse when we were coming in."

They spent twenty minutes browsing through her shelves and

Gabriel was careful to show no hint of judgment or even of surprise, even when he found *The Voyage of the Beagle* next to a sex-and-shopping novelette with embossed gold lettering. He tried to draw Jenni on what she liked about books, but she had become guarded.

Gabriel was determined to restore some of the lightness of the early part of the evening. "I loved this book," he said, pulling out *The Great Gatsby*. "Didn't you?"

"Yeah, it was OK."

"Do you think it's important to like the main character in a novel?"

"Probably." It was as though she suspected a trap.

"But sometimes maybe you could have a villainous main character—like a Dracula or something. You don't have to like him, do you? You just have to be interested."

"Perhaps."

"What's your favorite book of all these?"

"I don't know."

"Who's that man staring at us from the other side of the street?"

"What?!"

"Don't look now, but there's someone looking. He's standing on the pavement opposite. He's quite well lit."

Jenni glanced out of the window. "Shit. I don't know."

"Do you want me to go and talk to him?"

"No, no. It might make it worse."

"Shall I draw the curtains?"

"Yeah."

Gabriel pulled the curtains in the bow window, covering his face with them as he did so. "Have you any idea who it might be?"

"Well . . . I don't really know. I never seen him. But there's someone I met on Parallax who seems a bit obsessed. You know, we met online and we had a date. Or rather, Miranda and Jason did."

"Jason being his—"

"Maquette. Yeah. And another time he said he wanted to meet

254

in True Life and I said I didn't and then he got a bit shirty. And he threatened me."

"What did he say?"

"He said he'd find out where I lived and come round anyway."

"Can you do that?"

"Not legally, but there's probably ways round it. From my e-mail address he could maybe find my IP number, and then from the service provider . . . I don't know. You shouldn't, but there's ways round everything. You know, like spies and that. MI5. They can do it."

There was the sound of a key turning in the front door, and Jenni grabbed Gabriel's forearm. "Shit, Gabriel," she said.

It was the first time she had ever used his name.

"Hell-o-o. Jen?"

Jenni began to laugh. "It's Tony."

A tall man with shoulder-length dreadlocks came into the room. "Ooh, sorry. Didn't realize you had a date."

"Gabriel."

They shook hands.

"Hi. I'm Tony. Anything to eat, Jen? I'm starving."

"No. We been out. But there's a moussaka in the fridge you can microwave."

"Cheers."

"I'd better go," said Gabriel. "I can see you're in safe hands, Jenni. What shall I do if I see that man outside? Kick his arse?"

"Yeah! Give him a good kick! And . . . Gabriel. Well, you know, thanks for the meal and everything. Sorry I was a bit—"

"No. I'm sorry. I . . . You know . . ."

"Whatever. It doesn't matter."

"Shall I . . . You know?"

Once you knew how, Gabriel thought, you could convey quite a lot in this way of talking.

"Yeah, you can," said Jenni.

"There's still stuff . . ."

"Work stuff."

"Right," said Gabriel. "Stuff we still need to . . . Shall I take your mobile number?"

"OK."

She gave it to him. "I'm on midmorning till midafternoon tomorrow."

"Cheers, then."

He gave her a peck on the cheek, and it definitely seemed the right thing to do.

Knocker al-Rashid hurled a book across his son's bedroom. "You cannot read this nonsense. You just can't."

"How do you know it's nonsense? You've never read it."

"Everyone knows. All these people you name. That Ghulam Sarwar. Maybe his book is taught in English schools, but they've been conned. He was a lousy business management consultant with his own agenda, not a proper Muslim. And Maududi. He wasn't a scholar. He was a journalist! A rabble-rouser! And as for this Qutb. Everyone knows he was a terrorist. He—"

"He was not a terrorist," said Hassan quietly. "On the contrary, he was imprisoned by Nasser and brutally tortured, then hanged. He never killed anyone. You should read *Milestones*. It's very good, it's very well reasoned."

"I don't need to read any of these vicious men who've twisted things to their own ends. The only book I need is the Koran."

"But you've never even read it."

Father and son had never argued in this open way before and Knocker felt he was almost certain to lose, because Hassan had read more books than he had; but it enraged him that his beautiful religion had been perverted by modern demagogues for their political ends.

It had begun quite amicably, when Knocker called in on his way to an early bed to make sure Hassan was ready for their big outing to Buckingham Palace. He had found him with his nose once more in *Milestones*.

"Anyway," said Knocker, "Islam has never had a political home. It's a state of mind. The beautiful and perfect way of living. To fight for territory is to do what the Christians and Jews have done. We are better than that."

"Once we had an empire," said Hassan.

"Yes, but it was never governed from top to bottom. Sharia law has never been implemented. And anyway, listen, my dear Hass, we have our own little community, our own *ummah*, here, in our home. You, me and Mum. Every family can be a pure Islamic state. Of course it would be better if we had entire countries and—"

"They're the worst, the so-called 'Islamic' ones. The dictatorships, the kingdoms and theocracies. Don't they make you feel ashamed?"

Knocker sat down on the edge of his son's bed. "It is the sadness of my religion and the sadness of living. And since Islam is Life, the only life, then I accept that those are the same things. But I can't change that. I wish that at some stage in its story Islam had developed a practical society we could believe in and that followed the teachings of the Prophet. We don't have a church, like the Christians, we don't even have clerics like the Jewish rabbis. We are, I must admit, rather otherworldly."

"But we don't need to be! We can be part of this world too. Why should we be excluded?"

"Well of course, my dear boy, of course I wish that there were countries in the world—either the so-called 'Muslim' states or the Western countries—that were acceptable to a true Muslim. I wish that we didn't have to live like exiles inside the shell of the family to be righteous. It's a great sadness. But it may also be a little bit our fault. We've had possession of the truth for nearly 1,500 years, but we've never developed ways of living, you know, the practical aspects of state and church and politics and law to bring an Islamic society into being. It's a great sadness, but—"

"But it's not too late! Don't give me all this 'great sadness,' all this weary old man's resignation! You say you believe in every word of the Koran, then—"

"Of course I do."

"Then study it more carefully. Follow the Prophet's example by taking the good news to the *jahili* world."

"But I like America!" said Knocker. "I like its movies and its TV. What was that one with the pretty girl from the TV series? Never mind. I admire its science and its . . . Its friendliness! When I went there on my way to and from Mexico, the people were so kind to me. In New York and Colorado and Los Angeles. They were welcoming and generous to a stranger with brown skin and a funny accent. I don't have to get drunk or grow fat on their junk food or watch their pornography, but I do—"

"America is the enemy. Just as the Persians and Byzantines were to the Prophet. We should be liberating them."

"And how will you liberate them?" said Knocker. "Fly another plane into a building? Kill all their politicians, break their army, then say, 'Now we will create God's true Islamic society from California to New York—though we haven't yet worked out how to do it in practice because we've never done it before'?"

"You're talking like a *kafir*."

Knocker had regained his calm after throwing *Milestones* across the room. He knew that what he said to Hassan now could be important, and he was careful not to raise his voice. "I've read very little, it's true, but one thing I know is that whenever Islam has meddled in politics, it's made a fool of itself. Those Muslim states who took sides backed the Germans in the First World War and the Nazis in the Second. Afterward they allied themselves to the Soviet atheists. We're not good at national politics."

"That's bullshit, and you know it. In Afghanistan we defeated the Soviets. We won the Cold War! America claims it won, but it didn't. The Afghans won. That was the hard part. Now taking on America is easier. Look at their cretinous leader."

"But I repeat, my dear Hassan. How will you do it? Even if someone could conquer America, which they can't, what would you do with it? You don't even have a blueprint for a modern country. The idea that we can set up a perfect state is ridiculous. That time has gone. Be gentle, be accepting. Say your prayers. We are going to heaven, but we must be patient on this earth. That's why I called you Hassan, not Hussein—after the quiet one of the Prophet's grandsons, not the troublemaker."

Hassan stood up and walked round the room. "Listen, Dad, I don't think either of us must say things we regret tomorrow. But the fact is that almost the entire Muslim world lives in poverty and tyranny. And that is simply because America through what it calls 'globalization' oppresses us and supports the awful governments in the 'Muslim' states. We just can't allow our own people to be treated as the wretched of the earth."

Knocker sighed. "I'm sure it's true that people in the Middle East are repressed by their governments—and I've always supported the Palestinians. But that wasn't an Islamic war, a jihad or anything. It was a battle for the land that had been taken from them. And quite a lot of the PLO leaders were Christians anyway."

"You really haven't understood at all, have you?" said Hassan, his voice rising again. "All your wittering about politics. I'm not interested in British politics or any other nationalist politics. We have on offer a politics that is made by God. It's staring us in the face."

"I don't want to talk anymore," Knocker said and got up stiffly from the bed. "Tomorrow is the biggest day of my life. Please don't spoil it for me."

Hassan looked for a moment at the closed door. He had been on the verge of saying things he would have regretted. Thank God the old fool had gone to bed. As so often, he felt the need for purer air, and he went downstairs. His mother was reading in the sitting room.

"Can I borrow your car, Mum?"

"Of course. You won't be back late, will you? It's a—"

"Big day tomorrow. I know."

As he drove, Hassan pulled out his mobile phone and, on a whim, called Shahla. Although he disapproved of her and thought that her punishment for apostasy would be eternal, he admitted to himself that she could think clearly. And he enjoyed her company, he thought, at an intellectual level.

He knew there was hypocrisy in his attitude: Ali in Bradford would have been appalled to see him calling up this atheist girl. But he felt she might clear his mind; she might help him bring certain things into focus.

"Well, it's a bit unexpected," Shahla said, "but I wasn't planning much. Just reading. I thought I might watch a movie on my new little DVD thing later."

Hassan held the phone well concealed in his hand, leaning his head against the cold car window as though in fatigue and resignation.

It had been a long day for him already. In the morning he had delivered, as he had been instructed, all the components for the making of the bombs to "the pub" at Manor House so that Seth and Elton could assemble them. Salim had told him to return the next day, when they'd receive their final briefing from a member of Husam Nar. It would give him time to go to the palace.

He went round the South Circular, steering with one hand, through Catford and West Norwood. It was late and inhospitable enough for the traffic to be light, and in only half an hour he was pulling into the terrace of railwaymen's cottages in Clapham.

"Come in. Use me like a hotel. See if I care." Shahla's smile took the sting from her words. She gave Hassan a chaste peck on the cheek and stood aside for him.

"Would you like a drink?" They went up to the first floor and into her flat. "I'm going to have wine, but you can have something punitive if you prefer. Black tea? Wheatgrass? Jojoba juice?"

Hassan smiled. "Ordinary tea's fine. Thanks."

They settled either side of the coffee table. The room was small but not cramped. Shahla swung her long legs over the side of the armchair. She was wearing a red dress, woolen tights and leather boots with a kind of sleeveless Afghan sheepskin on top.

"Are you warm enough, Hass?"

"I'm fine, thanks. Did I stop you . . . Er, you look as though you might be going out?"

Shahla looked down at herself. "What? No, no. I just like to keep up standards. You never know who might call. What's new from the madrasa? All the girls still in hijab there?"

"Yeah, yeah. I know. Mock if you like."

"Will I burn, Hass? Will it be bad?"

"I'm going to Buckingham Palace tomorrow. With my dad."

"Oh, I love your dad. Do you remember, we met at graduation? Such a nice man. Rather a sexy smile, too, if I remember."

Hassan laughed. "I'm dreading it. I've managed to get out of the lunch, though."

"Have you got the right clothes?"

"I have a suit. My dad's got the full penguin thing and my mum's bought at least three new dresses. Bags, shoes, everything."

"It'll be fun. You should be proud of him. Do they give you lunch afterward in, like, a big garden party?"

"No, no, we all go our different ways. They're going to lunch in some Lebanese place in Knightsbridge. I'm going . . . I've got other fish to fry."

There was a pause. Hassan drank some tea.

"Are you all right, Hass? You seem a bit tense."

"I'm fine." He wondered how she'd noticed. "I had a bit of a row with my dad before I came. Nothing much."

"What about?"

"Religion."

"Well, there's a surprise."

She swung her legs from one side of the armchair, then placed them over the other side. He wished she wouldn't do that.

"Hass, we're all a bit concerned that you spend so much time at that mosque. Some of the people there are not very nice."

"How do you know? You've never been there."

261

"It has a reputation."

"Oh yes. And what's that, its 'reputation'?"

"For being Wahhabi."

"And what's wrong with that?"

"'What's wrong with that?' That's like saying 'What's wrong with Nazism?'!"

"The Wahhabis were hardly Nazis, they were—"

"They executed a lot of people who didn't agree with them, they burned a lot of books. They were a nineteenth-century throwback to the Middle Ages who wanted to pretend scientific advance had never taken place."

"Well, I suppose you could compare them to the Puritans in Christianity, or the Amish, or—"

"The Amish in jackboots," said Shahla. "Can we agree on that?"

"It's hardly a tiny sect, though," said Hassan. "It's the mainstream religious denomination of the richest and most powerful Islamic country in the world, Saudi Arabia."

"But that's exactly the problem, you great twit!" said Shahla. "Tyrannical Saudi kings and the American billions from drilling Saudi oil are sustaining a violent Flat Earth religion from the Stone Age."

"But they have Mecca and Medina in their country, and—"

"I know," said Shahla. "They have the two holy places and they have the oil money. In some Muslim countries, the Wahhabis are the only people with money to set up schools. Islam *is* Wahhabism to those children. That's as though all Christian kids went to schools run by the IRA or the Ku Klux Klan—because there was nothing else."

Hassan was taken aback by her vehemence. "I think you're exaggerating."

"Quite the opposite. It's actually more bizarre than that. Because the money behind the Saudis and Wahhabism is American. It's as though the British government had *paid* the IRA to educate British children."

Hassan stood up. "My mosque is perfectly respectable."

Shahla also got to her feet, where she was a little taller than Hassan. "I'm sorry, Hass. Don't go. Sit down. I'll make some more tea. It's just that your friends are worried. Did you know that?"

Part angry, part wanting to stay, Hassan sat slowly down again. He heard Shahla in the small kitchen, moving swiftly, as though she wanted to be back before he changed his mind. He had almost forgotten how irritatingly knowledgeable she was, even on "his" subject. She came back with more tea for him and sat down opposite, this time with her feet on the floor.

"Shall we watch that movie I mentioned?" she said. "I've bought this tiny DVD player for only £25. It's like a CD thing. Look. You just stick it on the back of the telly."

"OK," said Hassan.

"But promise me you're not getting in above your head," said Shahla.

"Aye."

"I know how much it hurts," said Shahla. "But I'm sure there is a future for true Islam, but in a quiet, religious way. Modernization will come. People will have more choice and will live more individual lives and that will secularize them. They can still be devout in private, but they'll live their lives in smaller units. Fragmented. Atomized."

"I can't bear that!" said Hassan. "When you think of the glory of the Islamic empire, all different colors and races of people bound together by this great faith. Now everyone just broken up— 'atomized,' as you say, with their own silly little earpiece and ringtone and text message."

"I know," said Shahla. "There's nothing grand about the modern world, is there? 'Consumer choice.' It's so small. The Internet just underlines that. It makes the triviality of living instantly available."

"God, yes," said Hassan. "Blogs."

"YourPlace."

"Aaaagh."

"And really, Hass, it can never happen. A revolution. The best Islamist model that I have read about—"

"In your now very advanced studies."

"Indeed. My very advanced studies . . . Islamism can't generate political systems with inbuilt democratic checks. It relies on good men to rule justly. But it's a vicious circle, because good men can only become good in a society that's already Islamic."

"I like that idealism, though," said Hassan. "Don't you?"

"Yes, I do. But somewhere in the last 1,500 years you guys forgot to get your hands dirty. To invent a polity. And it's too late now."

Hassan bit his lip. "Shall we watch that film then?"

Shahla laughed. "OK. It's what you'd call *kafir* nonsense— some sort of romcom, I'm ashamed to say, with Tom Gritt and Evelina Belle."

"Perfect in our atomized modern world," said Hassan. "We don't even have to go to the cinema. Are you sure you don't mind sharing the sound with me? Wouldn't you rather have your own individual headset?"

"Don't! You'll make me cry."

Shahla put the disc into the small player behind the television. "You sure it's not too late? It won't be over till about one o'clock."

"It's OK. I'll drive back then."

"Fine."

Hassan had a moment of embarrassment, as though the idea of his staying had been broached and he had somehow . . . "Of course. If that's OK by you, Shahla. If you don't have an early start tomorrow—"

"No, no. No meetings with the Queen for me. Here we go. Scene selection? No thanks. Play."

Hassan had not intended to like the film, but after fifteen minutes he could no longer stifle his laughter.

*　*　*

At the start of the evening, Vanessa Veals had put five cubes of ice into a Victorian rummer, poured in vodka till it almost reached the brim and added some fresh mint, a slice of lime and a dribble of grenadine cordial. It was her second "proper" drink since six, and after it she would stick to what she called "just wine." She took it into the sitting room, kicked off her shoes and sat on the sofa, where she fired up the television.

She lit a cigarette, an American classic with a toasted wheat aroma, and pushed her hand back through her hair, which had been professionally washed and dried that afternoon on Holland Park Avenue. Before abandoning herself to the evening, she ran a check over everyone and everything for which she felt responsible.

Max, the West Highland White, had had his walk and a solid two hours' barking at the end of the garden under the neighbors' window. Bella, her fourteen-year-old daughter, was having a sleepover at Chloë's or Zoë's house. She had a sleepover most nights, Vanessa had noticed, but it was probably good for her social skills. Bella's school reports were not encouraging, but then she was not a particularly clever child. She was a mystery to Vanessa. She didn't seem to be interested in fashion, for a start. Perhaps that was because she was plump, but Vanessa didn't think so. She didn't seem to care about discos or parties or boys or shoes or money or music or whatever they were meant to be interested in. God knows what they did at these "sleepovers," apart from eat fattening food and wear fleecy pajamas in their sleeping bags. Bella seemed to have come from a different decade; Vanessa had once found her reading about ponies, for heaven's sake.

Then Finbar. Well, he was up in his room and she no longer dared go up there. He could make her politest inquiry look like a gross breach of his privacy. Presumably he was masturbating or something, but he was sixteen and therefore legally an adult—or as near as made no difference anyway—so there was nothing she could do about it. He looked very pale, it was true, and was as thin as Bella was plump, but what was his mother meant to do: make him go to the gym, eat more potatoes? It was best to leave him to find his own way forward in life, up there, on his own. It really was a nice room in any event; the best room in the house, John always said.

And John? Well, guess what, John was working late. And when he came home, he'd work even later. Vanessa knew he had a big trade on. She could tell, because instead of coming to bed at one and lying awake most of the night worrying, he didn't come to bed until some oriental market had opened or closed—and sometimes not even then: she'd find him at seven, haggard and unshaven with the morning papers in the kitchen, still in last night's clothes.

Vanessa lit another cigarette and sighed. She'd married John because he was rich and because she felt he'd make few demands on her. He had happily given up trading on the floor of NYMEX and taken what she considered a more respectable job on the energy desk in the bank's main building in Wall Street; he told her he'd done it for her, though she already knew him too well to think he would do anything unless there was a financial advantage in it. However, it was a useful fiction for them both: she'd taken the rough trader and made him into a suave creature of charity evenings; he had transformed himself out of pure gallantry and a desire to please his wife.

What Vanessa hadn't foreseen was either the narrowness of her husband's life or the peripheral sliver of it that would be set aside to her. He treated her politely and remembered her birthday and their wedding anniversary with small jeweler's boxes and silent dinners à deux in places of terrible expense from which she could barely wait to get home. She had believed that she'd like being left to herself, being independent, but had discovered that it made her brutally lonely. Although she did read books and did have friends, her inner resources weren't great enough to withstand the relentless, remorseless pounding of solitude. It was like the sea; it never stopped.

John Veals had no interests outside the acquisition of money. He didn't play golf or tennis. He didn't support a football team.

He threw all color magazines in the bin. He went to the theater or the opera once a year if there was a certain and measurable financial advantage in doing so. He never went to the cinema and he thought television was a waste of time. A personal shopper bought his clothes. His idea of dinner was sausages and frozen peas, though he was prepared to sit it out over foie gras and Japanese beef if there was a purpose to the tedium. He disliked alcohol, though kept the cellar well stocked for Vanessa; he had an arrangement with a wine merchant in St. James's to make a fortnightly delivery to the house.

He hated holidays because they kept him from the markets and he had nothing to do beside the pool because he didn't read and had never learned to swim. He disliked traveling and claimed he'd done more than enough of it in the course of his job. The cultures, languages, art and buildings of other countries were of no concern to him. Vanessa had once forced him into a weekend in Venice where the only thing that piqued his interest was the thought that Jewish usurers had first begun to trade beside the Rialto; he declined to enter the Scuola San Rocco to see the Tintorettos because he had to take a call on his cellphone. In any case, he was allergic to anything that smacked of the religious. His family was Jewish, but he had no interest in their God or their traditions; in fact he was himself consistently anti-Semitic in what he presumably imagined was an inoffensive way, talking freely of "Hooray Hymies"— Jews who in his view tried to ingratiate themselves with upper-class Gentiles—or referring to his chief trader as O'Bagel or O'Shlo and even once dismissing a cautiously dull investor as "bog-standard Edgware Ikey." "My granddad came from Lithuania," Vanessa once heard him say at dinner. "So fucking what? Vanessa's grandfather came from Pittsburgh, PA!" It amused him colossally that Steve Godley, a Surrey Protestant, had at one point found his progress barred at the Jewish-owned bank for which he worked. Veals claimed that before the partners' golf day at Pebble Beach Godley had been circumcised at the age of thirty-nine and walked naked up and down the changing room for half an hour after finishing his round. The only thing that tickled him more was the thought of Bob Cowan, who had been promoted to the main board because people thought he *was* Jewish. He wasn't, but the Americans weren't allowed to ask—on the grounds that even to pose the question was in some way "racist." John Veals loved that joke; it somehow really spoke to him.

John had never, so far as Vanessa was aware, read a novel. He found all forms of music irritating and immediately instructed cab drivers to turn off their radios. He disliked art galleries, though thought the financial aspect of modern British art to be of minor interest; he admired the way that the collectors had first created the market for an artist such as Liam Hogg, then cornered it; such manipulation would not, he explained, be allowed by the FSA in any other commodity but "art." Although he understood horse racing and its odds as well as any man in Britain, he never went racing or placed a bet; he disliked the animals themselves because they gave him asthma. He had no social life outside the office, and Vanessa knew that he privately disliked his closest "friend," Stephen Godley.

The only activity, the only aspect of human life, that interested John Veals was money. The odd thing was, Vanessa thought, as she lit another cigarette, that he'd made enough to last a thousand lifetimes—or, with his modest taste in sausages, with no hobbies, booze or entertainment, perhaps two thousand lifetimes, without ever getting out of bed again. Sometimes she pictured her husband's money: the millions, the tens of millions, the hundreds of millions, in neat bundles, in their original bank packaging, the faces of George Washington and Queen Elizabeth II staring into the void, sitting in a vault somewhere in the dark, doing . . . Doing nothing, nothing but just being there, promising to pay the bearer on demand . . . But what bearer? What demand? And in what life on this planet or one yet to be discovered?

Little Sophie Topping had told Vanessa once in great excitement how Lance, her husband, had been told a banking secret—not "inside information," Sophie was quick to stress, but a sensitive and deadly secret. Before he could be included, he'd had to swear to the man who told him that he wouldn't mention it to a soul. And Lance had sworn on the lives of his wife and his children. Sophie was flushed with shock and solemn excitement. "That's what they do," she said. "When something's really, really, deadly secret and important. On the lives of their children."

And Vanessa had laughed. A solemn vow for John would have been for him to make a promise about his children's lives with his wealth the thing on which he swore; that really might have been an oath worth witnessing.

"Why are you laughing, Vanessa?" said Sophie.

"I was thinking about John. I'm sorry. If you lost all your money, Sophie, and you came home in the evening and Lance said, 'Look, at least we're all safe, we're all well, we've got each other, we can start again'—well, you wouldn't be very happy, but it would be some consolation, wouldn't it?"

"I suppose so. But why were you laughing?"

"Because with John it wouldn't. Losing all his money would be worse to him than losing all his family. So swearing on them is no big deal to him."

Vanessa stood up from the sofa and went down to the kitchen. Max was asleep in his basket, Bella was out, Finn was in his room and John was working. *Plus ça change.* She'd eaten salad at lunchtime so didn't need dinner; instead, she took two bottles of Meursault from the fridge, a corkscrew and a clean glass. Up in the sitting room, she closed the floor-length shutters, lit the wood fire, poured some wine and searched the television hard disk for the stored episode of *Shropshire Towers*. Then she lay back and tipped the glass to her lips, feeling the edge of loneliness recede.

Upstairs, in his beautiful room, beneath the ever-watchful eyes of Wireless Boys and Evelina Belle, Finn rolled a three-paper joint of Aurora/Skunk Two and made sure he had everything ready for what looked like being a decisive evening in the Barking Bungalow. He hit the speed-dial button for a pizza delivery and placed his usual order. In a moment of responsibility he also asked for apple slices in sugar-dusted doughnut crust. Fruit, as Ken always said, is for fruits—but you had to think of your health.

As the credits rolled, Finn lit up and inhaled deeply. There was an air of excitement in the studio. It was not the usual set with its celebrity dinner party and damask table linen; for this episode, Terry O'Malley and Barry Levine were, as they put it, "in the lions' den": on stage in front of a live audience.

"It's Bedlam here tonight," said Terry. "This is as edgy as it gets. Ladies and gentlemen, before we go over live to the Barking Bungalow, let's welcome our special guest for tonight, someone who knows more about live TV than just about anyone on the planet, yes, it's the lovely, the irresistible Agneta King!"

It was felt when Lisa was in the bungalow, the studio needed a bit of glamour and Agneta King's CV as weather girl who'd turned presenter qualified her for the job.

"OK, my love," said Terry, "who's your money on tonight? Remember, only one contestant can win the prize. And let's just remind you what that prize is—in case you could possibly have forgotten! It's free private treatment for their condition for a whole year in Park View, England's top hospital, plus a fabulous four-by-four Sherman Pathfinder, worth more than £50,000."

"Well, I think Alan's got to be the favorite, hasn't he?" said Agneta.

"That's what the bookies are saying," said Barry Levine. "But there's been some punters splashing out on Sandra too. And talking of girls that we'd like to splash out on . . . Let's go over live now to the Barking Bungalow and join our very own . . . Lisa!"

Lisa was shown huddled in a heavy fur coat outside the bungalow holding a microphone close to her face. "Blimey, boys, let me tell you it is fr-r-r-r-eezing here! My hands are literally blocks of ice!"

"We can see you're cold from the bumps in your sweater, Leese," said Terry O'Malley. "Now then, before we get down to business, let's have a recap on how everyone's done with the therapeutic challenge. Yup, it's time for TC Update. OK, boys! Roll it!"

Finn dragged deeply on the skunk. This looked like developing into a classic episode. The five finalists were, in his judgment, evenly balanced; the result might come down to how much they really wanted to win. First for the update was Preston, the old man suffering from dementia. When he could bring himself to focus on the prize, Preston was a strong contender, but, as Agneta put it when they showed clips of his behavior, "He's not that sexy, is he?" The jury was out on Channel 7's experiment of going with an old person.

Next was the chronically depressed Sandra. She didn't appear to understand the nature of her therapeutic challenge, which was to try to go for two days without medication. However, she insisted that she was "dead excited" about winning. Valerie, the bipolar patient, seemed euphoric about the bungalow experience. She could hardly stop talking or fidgeting, and frequently interrupted her own train of thought. The other contestants tended to make their excuses when they saw her heading their way.

The person who seemed to be struggling most was the schizophrenic, Alan. Despite constant urging from the judges, he didn't evince as much desire to win as they would have liked. Most of the time, he seemed to be conversing with people no one else could see. He talked loudly and reasonably to them and seemed to resent the real-life intrusions of Lisa and the other judges. Despite this perversity, there was an integrity to Alan that commanded respect.

"Yeah, you gotta hand it to him," said Barry Levine, "he's got something, has Alan."

Agneta King agreed. "You can't take that away from him, Barry."

At that moment the front doorbell rang, and Finn went down to collect his pizza. His father's study door was open, but there was no one inside. Through the glass-paneled door of the ground-floor sitting room, he could see his mother lying on the sofa with her shoes off. There was an empty wine bottle at her side and her eyes were closed. Finn gave the delivery man a £5 tip (he didn't

271

have to pay for the pizza itself as they had an account) and ran back upstairs.

He fast-forwarded through the advertisements as he bit into the unfailing margherita. Although he personally was devoted to it, the popularity of *It's Madness* had always surprised him. A few people of small intelligence, with no conversation and serious personality problems, were banged up together in a house where their witless exchanges were monitored. They shared living and sleeping quarters, though there was nothing entertaining in the rooms themselves: the flat lighting and the textured video recordings stripped out any visual interest. There was an element of competition, it was true, and that could give anything a little drama, though Finn had never worked out what the competition was for—what you were supposed to be better than the others *at*. Sometimes it seemed that what decided whether you won was not something you said or did, but just how much you cared, or said you did; convincing the judges of how very much you wanted to win could itself make you a winner.

Now a group of people, not much favored by nature, would be asked to share a private sexual fantasy with the public. They were to go into the bathroom and speak directly to the camera. Originally, the idea had been to have a sequence called "Solitary Pleasures" in which they were asked to masturbate in a shower cubicle. This idea came from an incident in an earlier show when a beefy young man had "accidentally" been shown touching himself through a half-steamed glass door. However, the resistance to this development had been strong. "A one-off spontaneous gesture made a historic moment in 'reality' TV history," wrote one journalist, "but surely to embed it in the routine of the series is to rob that gesture of its iconic status."

Digitime's board met and discussed the issue. They decided they were not yet ready to "push the envelope," but would reconsider for a future series. "Our medical experts have advised us, however, that the sharing of an intimate fantasy is a standard procedure in most forms of therapy. Taste guidelines will be strictly adhered to."

First into the bathroom was Valerie, or "Scotty." She was wearing a tracksuit and pink trainers. She perched on the edge of the bath and settled herself.

At the top of the screen there was a small inset of the studio where Barry, Terry and Agneta were shown looking at their monitors.

In the early days, they hadn't commented much on the appearance of the contestants, but Terry had broken the ice and Agneta King was always ready to jump in.

"Blimey, with a bum like hers I should think fantasy's all she's likely to get!" said Agneta.

"Seems chirpy enough, though," said Terry.

"Lisa," said Barry, "we're not getting the sound from the bathroom. Has she started yet?"

"OK, Tel," said Lisa. "I'll go and see what the matter is. Wish me luck!"

The handheld camera that followed Lisa everywhere now showed her hopping over one of the long cream leather sofas and going toward the bathroom.

At this moment the audio track picked up what sounded like a scream. The picture skewed from side to side as though the cameraman had lost his footing.

When it steadied up, it showed depressed and red-faced Sandra screaming and sobbing, her face close to Lisa's.

"Nice to see Sandra showing a bit of animation," said Terry, in the top left corner of the screen. "I thought she didn't really want it enough anymore."

Sandra was holding on to Lisa's arm and trying to drag her somewhere.

"I'm going with Sandra. Follow me," said Lisa to the cameraman.

They swayed down a corridor with Sandra screeching and babbling incomprehensibly, and then they were in a prop or storage room. It was not intended as a scene and was not professionally lit; but by using the ordinary ceiling lights, Lisa was able to share with millions of viewers what she was seeing, and what had brought Sandra screaming to her side.

Finn leaned forward, pizza in hand, heart thudding, and peered at the cloudy screen. There seemed to be a huge doll in the middle of the picture, dangling.

The handheld camera pushed in and it became clear that it was not a doll but a man, and that he was hanging from a beam in the storeroom.

The television soundtrack went quiet. The camera moved closer and then up into the man's face. It was Alan, the schizophrenic, and he had hanged himself.

Lisa began to scream. The pictures swayed and went black. Then it cut to the studio where Terry and Barry were shown peering in disbelief at their monitor. Then Agneta also began screaming.

Then the screen went completely blank.

Six

Friday, December 21

I

Eight o'clock saw another freezing start to the day in Ferrers End, where R. Tranter watched a murky sun appear in the distance over Loughton and Chigwell. He had been up since six, unable to sleep for thinking about the Pizza Palace prize dinner that evening at the Park Lane Metropolitan.

He had rehearsed his speech a hundred times, but still wasn't happy with it. He'd begin, he thought, with feigned surprise—even though *Flyleaf*, the trade magazine, agreed with the bookies that neither Cazenove's travelogue nor the children's thing had a chance against Tranter's authoritative work on A. H. Edgerton. Then he'd move on to thank his agent, lazy cow, and his editor, who had told him the book was too long and that the budget could run to only eight pages of illustrations. The thanks were routine, he gathered, from the dinners he'd been to and newspaper reports he'd read. Winners, however, were then supposed to say something important about literature, or their work. Tranter's problem was that he had nothing positive to say. His opinions had been fully discharged in his years as a reviewer and the single thing he felt most passionately about books and writing was that it was wrong that Alexander Sedley, among others, had enjoyed more success than he had.

As he lay in bed, with Septimus Harding curled up beside him, Tranter found various phrases popping into his mind. "Edgerton, a writer of lasting value . . . Striking contrast . . . Today's media

275

darlings . . . Hands out of your pockets at the back, we're talking about you . . ." All these trusty little turns that would have hit the mark in one of his *Toad* pieces sounded, in the context of a prize-giving dinner with champagne, just . . . Snippy. Defensive. People would laugh at him. He was meant to celebrate his book, his subject or himself. And how was he supposed to do that without sounding conceited?

As he stood in the kitchen making tea, Tranter heard the flap of the letter box in the hall below. One of the good things about Mafeking Road, perhaps the best thing, was that it was at the start of the postman's delivery round, and while other parts of London waited till midday or later, Tranter could have read, binned or answered his mail by eight o'clock daily. He put down a saucer of milk for Septimus and went downstairs in his dressing gown. Among the usual bank statements and circulars there was a clean white envelope on which his name and address had clearly not been spat out of a ten-gigabyte mailing list, but had been boldly and individually typed.

Up in his kitchen, he opened it. It was from the head of Humanities at the University of South Middlesex, a Professor Nancy Ritollo. "Dear Mr. Tranter, I am writing with the authority of the board here to invite you to interview for the post of Visiting Professor of Critical and Creative Writing, tenable for one year, renewable annually by agreement for a maximum of five years. The post pays £22,500 per annum and the teaching requirement is two hours each week on our Walworth campus, comments on student work and a termly 'open forum' lecture. I must tell you that, should you be interested in the position, the interview is somewhat of a formality. We are not considering other applicants at this time. Please reply to my assistant Ms. Melinda Asif at masif@smiddle sex.ac.uk to fix a time convenient to yourself to come and see us.

"The University of South Middlesex is a relatively new but thriving university which welcomes students of all backgrounds and is building a strong postgraduate program of which if you accept our offer you would be a part. Yours sincerely."

Tranter laid the letter down on the melamine work surface. Was this some kind of joke? Was someone trying to trick him? He read it again. No, it seemed genuine enough. He would answer carefully, noncommittally, offering no hostage to fortune; but so far as he could see, this letter had, with a single offer, made him financially secure. And surely good things did sometimes happen?

Although it had only just grown light, John Veals had been at his desk for an hour by the time security rang up at eight to say, "There's a Miss Wilby here to see you."

"Tell her I'll meet her at the lift."

Veals watched the indicator lights as the regulator rose to meet him. G, 1, 2, 3 . . . He was waiting for her; he was quite calm now, ready to draw on all his experience—futures, banking, trading, managing: everything and anything to protect what was dearest in the world to him.

The doors parted, and out stepped a young woman in a gray suit and black tights, carrying a briefcase. She had fair hair tied back in a businesslike way, wore metal-rimmed glasses and was slightly flushed.

"Caroline Wilby." Her hand was moist, and Veals could feel a tremor in it.

"Come this way."

He took her into his own office and pointed to the chair opposite his own, the one in which Simon Wetherby had sat while Veals divested him of his innocence on the subprime loans issue.

"Coffee?"

"Thank you. I'd better give you this." She pushed a business card across the desk.

"Coffee," said Veals into the phone. His four screens were blank. "What was it you wanted to ask?"

A secretary knocked and entered with coffee and a plate of rectangular chocolate biscuits with a soft chocolate filling.

"Thanks. FSA favorites!" said Caroline Wilby, biting into one.

Veals watched her. She composed herself a little, settled into the

277

chair, then said, "Do you mind if I record this meeting?" She took out a small digital device from her bag.

"Not at all."

There followed a minute or so of battery checking, of buttons being pushed and released. "Difficult to know if it's actually working . . . Let me see . . . Just going to do a test. 'Testing one two three. High Level Capital . . . December 21st.' Now let's see. Oh, God, sorry. Try again. I think if I hold this down . . ."

Veals gazed out of the window until she was ready.

"First of all, I'm so grateful to you for seeing me at such short notice. I really do appreciate your help. I'm going round a few senior people seeing if they can give me any guidance. As you know, we're trying to improve all our systems, especially at such an awkward time."

Veals nodded.

"We're interested at this time in rumors and how they start. And I know this is going to sound rather naïve and I hope you'll forgive me asking, but do you ever trade on rumors?"

Veals stroked his chin and looked across at her. She had crossed her legs and he noticed the chubby calves and the scuffed edges of the black court shoes. It was utterly quiet in the office.

"Of course," said Veals.

Caroline Wilby looked a little surprised.

"When rumors are widespread they can affect the way a market moves. If people believe, for instance, that a company is to become the subject of a takeover, even though the board has denied it—if that's the rumor, it'll obviously push the price up. And if it's a company we're interested in, we may need to take appropriate action to protect our position."

"Well, naturally, I . . . I do see that."

"We're obliged to look after our investors' interests."

"Yes, I can see that you—"

"Equally, we would never want to be at the beginning of any such word on the street. If I heard some gossip and felt I was one of the first to hear it, I would disregard it. My view is that one should trade on the basis of analysis and information, not rumor. However, if the persistence of a rumor over a period of time begins to alter prices, then the price change becomes a fact—and on that fact we may sometimes be obliged to act."

"So what you're saying is, that it depends at what stage you hear the rumor."

"Often we have no way of knowing whether we're second, third or twenty-fifth to hear something. But it's the one area in which it's best to be behind the game. Unlike analysis, where we try to be ahead."

"So it's a question of being reactive to rumor, not proactive."

"Exactly," said Veals, in such a way as to suggest that Caroline Wilby had been unusually acute.

She smiled. "So I think I've probably answered my next question already, and that is, have you ever deliberately started a rumor?"

Veals tried to smile. "Indeed. See my previous answer."

Caroline Wilby frowned. "Can I be completely frank, Mr. Veals? I really need your help."

"Of course."

"It seems that a particular rumor started about Allied Royal Bank a couple of days ago. That it was going to be taken over by First New York. Did you know about that?"

"I saw something on one of the cable channels."

"Yes, it was denied in New York last night by the chief executive of First New York."

"So I heard. These things happen. Perhaps they might have made a good fit, but I suppose people are scared of overexpanding at the moment."

"Have you any idea where such a rumor might have started?"

"It sounds to me like routine speculation. Bankers talk about this kind of thing all the time. You can't stop people theorizing out loud. But is there a problem? No one can have made anything out of it in such a short time, can they?"

"No, we've no reason to think so. It's just that we're trying to tighten up on all these areas."

"Good idea."

"Have you traded on ARB stock recently?"

"We have a small short position which we put on some months ago. I've been bearish ARB for a while. So actually I was surprised to see the price go up. The first I heard of the takeover rumor was when it was denied. The price'll go back down again now, I imagine."

Caroline Wilby nodded. "Yes, I quite understand. There are two other things I'd like to ask if I may. Do you have a continuing education program to ensure that your staff are up to speed with the latest rules on insider trading? And are they fully conversant with the rules about rumors?"

"Yes, we have a very good new compliance officer. He makes sure everyone's up to date, and I double-check it. We send them on courses. It's not very onerous, but it's worth keeping up."

"That's marvelous. Thank you. One last thing." Caroline Wilby ran her hand back over her hair. "I . . . I don't quite know how to put this . . . Um . . . We're under huge pressure to get to the bottom of this ARB thing, but, to be honest, I just don't know where to look or what to ask. And then how to verify whether what I'm being told is true. Now, you're a very experienced and senior person, if you don't mind me saying so. If you were in my position, what would you ask? And who would you ask?"

Veals looked at her for a long time. "Before I answer that, Caroline, can I ask you a couple of questions?"

"Yes, of course."

"How old are you?"

"Twenty-six."

"What did you do before this job?"

"I worked as a trainee at an investment bank, I'd better not say which. Not one of the American ones. A big European one."

"And?"

"Then I had a trial."

"And?"

Caroline Wilby looked down. "I . . . I didn't get taken on."

Veals stood up abruptly. "I've got an idea. I know one of your top guys from way back. Why don't I give him a call today, tell him you've been, tell him you're a very sharp girl and that I really want to help. I won't mention your last question."

The flush intensified on Caroline Wilby's face. "Would you? Would you really do that?"

"Yes, I would. I wouldn't say so otherwise. Then I'll ask if I can go and see him on Monday, maybe take him out to lunch and really see if I can help him get to the bottom of this."

"God, that's so kind of you. I really do appreciate it."

"I guess it's not easy, your job."

"It's not easy at all. I'm not sure I'm really cut out for it, to tell the truth." Caroline Wilby put the voice recorder back in her bag. "You know, asking all these questions. I'll do it for a bit, I suppose. But what I'd really like is to work for a hedge fund. Obviously, I'd be well placed to work in the compliance department. I don't suppose you ever . . ."

"Not at the moment," said Veals, showing her to the door. "But I'll bear it in mind."

At 8:30 the chutney-colored limousine pulled out of the gates at the al-Rashids' house and started the trip west to Buckingham Palace. At Knocker's insistence they had put aside an hour and a half for the journey. He was sitting in the front alongside Joe, the driver, checking for the third time that he still had the parking permit for the forecourt of the palace. Joe's tabloid paper, stuffed under his seat, bore the huge headline "Bungalow Suicide Shocker." In the back sat Nasim, who had finally settled for an intense blue sari with ivory and saffron embroidery, jettisoning the knee-length beige dress at the last minute.

"I feel a bit of a fraud," she told Knocker. "I'm just a Yorkshire lass and I've dressed up like a maharani."

Knocker grinned. "You look beautiful. It's good to honor the land of our ancestors. After all, today is about lime pickle."

"Which you once told me was a British invention."

"Ssh. Don't tell Her Majesty, she might change her mind."

Knocker's excitement was making him unusually frivolous. Hassan had shaved for the occasion and wore a dark suit with narrow trousers and a navy blue tie. He stared out of the window as the streets of East Ham went by, thinking as he saw the drapers and the greengrocers, the stallholders and the small-business frontages, of how far the people had come to be there. What a struggle was still theirs. The *kafirs* wore trainers and thick anoraks, but there were numerous people in the clothes of the North-West Frontier or those of Arabia, padded against the cold. He had hated it when Shahla was so defeatist about what she called the Muslim "polity," saying an Islamic state could never exist, condemning as she did so his people to a life as visitors, second-class people—squatters, really, in the countries and systems of others.

At the gates of the palace, Knocker withdrew his several pieces of printed instruction and handed the parking permit, a single white letter "M" on a red background, to the driver. After leaving the car, they were shown up some wide stone steps covered in crimson carpet. At this point, Knocker was separated from Nasim and Hassan, who were escorted by a flunkey to their seats in the ballroom, where they would witness the investitures being made.

Knocker watched them disappear with a pang, then stepped forward, as instructed, into the palace itself. At the top of some more steps he found himself in a huge rectangular room with numerous old paintings—Dutch, French, he didn't know. Here, a woman in a black skirt and cardigan, rather like a caterer, Knocker thought, asked him which decoration he was to receive. The KBEs and CBEs went one way, the OBEs and the MBEs another; each then regrouped in a holding pen, cordoned off by a scarlet rope, such as you might have in a post-office queue.

Knocker made desultory chat with a few of his fellow OBEs and tried hard to remember his homework. "Betjeman . . . Indeed. Perhaps underrated. Philip Larkin without the melancholy . . ." Or was that Ted Hughes? A man came and pinned onto his lapel a hook from which the medal would in due course be hung.

A few minutes later, a grand gentleman in a uniform covered in gold frogging and with a scarlet stripe up the side of his trousers came bounding into the room and introduced himself with enormous pleasure.

"Good morning, ladies and gentlemen . . . A few words of explanation . . . Batting order as follows . . ."

Knocker was so nervous he was barely listening. He went over his homework. "Needs to learn the difference between 'may' and 'might' if she is to be taken seriously." But which one was that? Damn it, he had forgotten. Virginia Woolf, perhaps. Or was she the one who'd put the "anal" into "banality"? He tried to summon up Tranter's whiny voice to prompt him.

"Anyone on this side of the room not, I repeat not, for an MBE? Splendid, splendid, you really are fast learners. So by process of elimination, every single one of you on this side must be a C or K. Excellent! You're doing my job for me!"

Knocker licked his lips and swallowed hard. He slipped a mint into his mouth, not wishing to give Her Majesty an unwitting reminder of the industry he had so faithfully "served."

The beaming courtier boomed on: "Now the next thing you need to know is that this morning's investitures will be taken not by Her Majesty but by the Prince of Wales. He does an increasing number these days and the good news for you is that he is extremely good at it."

For six months Knocker had been imagining his interview with the sovereign, the head of state. All his talk had been for her. "T. S. Eliot, I believe, ma'am. A most interesting American poet. Have you read much of his work?" It was difficult not to be disappointed; but it was more than this that he felt: it was a sense of disorientation.

". . . come in from the side, pause next to the gentleman usher, like so, then when you hear your surname called you step forward, like so. Now. The Prince of Wales will be on a dais. Do not attempt to join him on the dais."

Knocker looked round in puzzlement. What was a "day-iss"? Why should he not join the Prince on one?

". . . and finally, can anyone tell me what you should call the Prince of Wales? Yes, sir, you."

"Your Royal Highness."

"Absolutely right. And if that's a bit of a mouthful with your false teeth in, then 'sir' is perfectly acceptable. Now then. Any questions?"

By the time they were ushered out of the room, Knocker found he could barely remember the name of a single English writer. He was toward the end of the OBEs, his surname being deemed to start with R for Rashid, not A for al. They crossed the ballroom at the back and he looked round in vain for Nasim and Hassan. His mouth was dry as he waited in a long corridor and wondered if he had time for another mint, but the last thing he wanted was still to be sucking it when he had to make conversation so that he'd have to spit it out or secrete it in his hand, then shake the Prince's . . . Oh dear.

He looked at the others in the queue. Many of the women seemed to have dressed in a way that Knocker had never seen in any woman except the Queen herself: a dress and a light coat of the same material and a squashed-meringue hat on top. The men looked slightly less ill at ease in their suits, but the people who had fared best were the numerous sailors, airmen and soldiers with shining brass and glowing brown leather belts. These are my fellow countrymen, thought Knocker, people who patrol the seas and skies, defend the shores. I never think of them.

By the time he was in the doorway, two away from his turn, Knocker's mind had gone almost completely blank. He was aware of its emptiness. Indeed, he could picture it: like the huge cauldron in which they stewed the limes, emptied, washed, hosed. He fancied he could actually still hear a slight ringing sound from the final scour of wire wool—but coming from his empty brain.

Some robotic force moved his feet forward and stopped them on the crimson carpet opposite the "gentleman usher." He could see the Prince conversing genially with the man ahead of him, who then took two steps back, bowed, and left the ballroom.

"Mr. Farooq al-Rashid. For services to catering."

The same impersonal force caused one foot to follow another over the strip of crimson to where the Prince stood above him on a dais.

"Catering," said the Prince. "Are you the pickle company?"

"Yes, Your Highness. Lime pickle originally and now a large range of other chutneys and sauces."

"I see. And where are you based? In London?"

"No, we started in Renfrew, Glasgow, now we have other factories in Luton. And . . ." Knocker trailed away, fearing he was babbling.

"Ah yes, I've tried your lime pickle," said the Prince. "Very good it was too. I've traveled a good deal in India and Pakistan, where—"

"Yes, indeed. Have you read A. H. Edgerton, sir?"

"Edgerton, did you say?"

"Yes, Edgerton, sir. He is a very fine Victorian writer. Some people call him the poor man's Trollope, but I think of him as the rich man's Dickens."

"I shall certainly keep an eye out for him. Now I'm going to pin this on you . . . And I hope that if ever times get difficult in your business, you will remember this moment and consider it an encouragement."

"Do you read many good books?" said Knocker.

"As much as time allows," said the Prince.

"I'm also a great admirer of Dick Francis and T. S. Eliot," said Knocker.

"Excellent. So was my grandmother. Of Dick Francis anyway. It was very nice to meet you, Mr. al-Rashid. Many congratulations." The Prince held out his hand, the signal that the interview was over.

Knocker grasped it fiercely and looked into the Prince's eyes. He felt like a small boy. He could feel his late mother and father peering over his shoulder. "What is Farooq doing?" "What are you up to, little menace?"

Their voices were so strong in his ears that he could barely concentrate. His throat closed up and his eyes filled with tears as he stepped back awkwardly, trying not to trip on the bottom of his over-length hired trousers. Somehow he managed to bow and turn away, then walk across the red carpet with the eyes of the ballroom upon him, so that he found it hard to coordinate his arms and legs as he shuffled out.

As soon as he had made it to the far corridor, he was required to give back his medal to be placed in a presentation box. The man doing this gave him a winsome smile.

"Did you have a nice word with the Princess?"

"Pardon?"

"She's ever such a chatterbox once she gets going. There you are, sir. One little gong. Take care now."

Finn slept badly and woke to find life even worse. In order to calm himself after the trauma of Alan the schizophrenic's on-screen suicide, he'd smoked a large joint of Aurora/Super Skunk Two, and he'd inhaled it quickly, leaving no time to gauge its effect. He had fallen deeply asleep, at last, toward dawn.

As soon as he awoke, he fell asleep again, or so he thought. Yet he seemed to be up and moving about in his room. Now this was the dream from which he must awake. He found that he was still in bed. If he fell asleep again, he would never wake, but now he was in the bathroom, the tap was running, he'd turned on the mighty shower that flooded down like a Yosemite cascade, so why was he still lying in his bed? The sheets would be wet from the shower.

"Get up, you're late," said a woman's voice, though not his mother's.

Finn heard his own voice, or thought it was his own.

"I need to go to school."

"It's the last day of term."

"I haven't done my homework, though."

"Get up, you useless fucking lump. Get up."

Finn was on all fours, crawling to the door. The room was full of people, full of voices. He couldn't see the people. Perhaps, he thought, I'm still asleep.

He rested his face on the floor, feeling the tight weave of the gray carpet on his soft skin, abrasive against a new spot forming on his chin.

He called out for his mother, shouting as he lay in the doorway. "Mum! *Mum*! *Mummy*!"

He curled himself up into a ball and gripped his ribs tightly through his T-shirt.

"She's never going to come. She can't hear him."

"Mum-*my*!"

"He's such a sack of shit."

There were too many thoughts in Finn's mind; so much coming in at once that he wasn't able to receive and organize it all. The breakwaters had been washed away.

He wanted to move his body down the stairs to find help, but couldn't mobilize the part of his brain that would have sent the command to feet or legs. He couldn't find it in the chaos. The only movement he could make was a reflexive tightening of his arms around his ribs.

A voice was calling for his mother, but he didn't know if it was his.

Other voices contradicted him.

Eventually, there was a hand on his shoulder. It was Vanessa, though Finn was not sure that she was there.

"What on earth is the matter, darling?"

II

Hassan left his parents at the palace, his father stunned, his mother pink with fussy pride, and walked up over the grass to Green Park Tube station on the Piccadilly Line.

At last, he thought, I am back in real life, back with things that matter. In the train, he took off his tie and stuffed it in his pocket. He was due at "the pub" at 12:40, having asked Salim if he could be the last to arrive. The timing would be tight, but such was his elation that he wasn't worried. It was God's work, God's will.

He'd read accounts of Islamist groups in the *kafir* press and he'd read fine writing about what went on in the heads of "terrorists"; he'd seen a "drama-documentary" in the cinema about the planes that crashed into the Towers. What no one talked about, no one seemed to understand, was the joy—the pure exhilaration of belief!

People like himself were portrayed as madmen, mumbling, but as the Tube train rattled up to Manor House, he had never felt more lucid. It was all, as Ali had pointed out to them in Bradford, so simple. Life did not need string theory, eleven dimensions and a battering of the head against the inherent contradictions of human consciousness. All it required was to follow a simple revealed truth. There it was, on the bookshelf for £6.99. For all time. What was more amazing, the glorious purity of the truth or the bone-headed refusal of people to accept the gift that had been given them?

Hassan went down the lazy street with its outdoor life for what he thought would be the last time, and rang the bell marked "Ashaf." Salim let him in. Upstairs were Gary the Gold Tooth Hindu, Seth the Shy One and Bald Elton.

There were four rucksacks sitting in the middle of the bare wooden floor.

In the corner, with his back to them, looking over the scrap of garden was someone Hassan hadn't seen before. The man turned round.

"This is Steve from Husam Nar," said Salim. "Steve, this is Jock."

Steve was a short, tubby man of African appearance, about thirty years old. "In these bags," he said, "are bomb components. We've used hydrogen peroxide injected into drinks bottles. This is a development of what was due to be used on those aircraft, where you need only a fairly small explosion to bring the plane down. We needed more bang, so each of you is carrying twenty-five drinks bottles. The detonators are in disposable cameras. The battery contents have been replaced by HMTD, or to give it the proper name, hexamethylene triperoxide diamine. This works as the primary explosive, or primer. It's unstable enough to go off easily, but stable enough to transport. Next to it in the battery casing is a small light bulb. When the camera is turned on, the charge to the light bulb is enough to detonate the HMTD which in turn sets off the main explosive. All clear?"

They all nodded. Steve had a thick East African accent, but his words were easy enough to follow.

"Listen carefully. You each go separately to the target. There are no trial runs. At the target you reassemble. You choose exactly where in a minute. One of you will carry all the detonators because we can't risk traveling on the train with the detonators in the same bag as the explosive. They're in this fourth bag here. Once you're at your assembly point at the target, the detonators are given out and the man who brought them is given his share of explosive by the other three. You've chosen?"

"Yes," said Salim. "Jock will take the detonators."

"OK," said Steve. "The timing is that you meet at 11 p.m. tomorrow. You travel alone. You make your own travel plan. If you're on the same train and happen to see one another, ignore it. The target is fifteen minutes' walk from a busy railway station so there's no problem about getting there. You need to leave plenty of time, but not too much. Hanging around can be dangerous. Give yourself half an hour leeway but no more."

The atmosphere in the room had become tense. Hassan no longer felt elated. Something about the charmless, practical way that Steve drove onward made him feel, for the first time, extremely frightened.

From inside his coat pocket, Steve took out a folded piece of paper. When he opened it out fully, it was the size of a lecturer's flip chart. He laid it flat on the table.

"This," he said, "is Glendale Hospital. The local railway station is fifteen minutes this way. The map is not to scale because you need to see the layout of the different units in detail. The first three will be detonating here, here and here. The greatest density of patients is in this building here. It's possible that the first blast will be such that it will detonate the second without you needing to use the camera. Because of the long corridor that joins this outbuilding with the main hospital, the blast should be funneled through into the main building, which is where the fourth and largest bomb will be placed. The outbuildings form a specialized psychiatric unit, but the main building is a general hospital, and the wing attached here, where the fourth blast will be, has 'long-term' units on the first floor—people who are dying, basically—and then the maternity unit on the floor above. Our experts chose this site because of its particular vulnerability. The psychiatric clinic has quite low security, only two porters on the main gate, just here, and simple signing-in at a desk inside. But my ballistics man in Pakistan told me that this joining corridor, which is really there for catering trolleys and things, this bit here, will magnify and funnel the blast and so help with the bomb in the main building. We don't need to go into all those details now. What we do need is for each of you to have a very clear picture in his head of this layout and of where your rucksack is going to be put down. So come and have a close look. Once you've got the overall plan clear I'll show you photographs of the interiors."

The four men gathered round beneath the eye of Steve and Salim.

Hassan inspected the red-felt outlines of Collingwood, Beardsley, Arkell . . . He tried to be businesslike and cool, but a question kept shaping itself in his mouth. He was glad it wasn't him but quiet Yorkshire Seth who finally spoke.

"So . . . Are you saying we're attacking a hospital?"

"Yes."

"I . . . I . . ."

Seth seemed unable to continue.

None of the others spoke. Perhaps, Hassan thought, by not acknowledging that there might be an issue, Steve and Salim were hoping to kill any hesitation at birth. They merely gazed at Seth.

Eventually, Steve spoke. "It's an ideal target. It ticks all three boxes. News impact. Density of population. And third, though this is less important, scarcity of Muslim victims. You may or may not know that the Muslim population is underrepresented in hospitals. There are no alcohol-related illnesses, fewer obese people with diabetes and so on. The figures are even better in psychiatric care. As far as density of people is concerned, it's not as good as the Tube, but security on the Underground is now so tight that it's become impossible. For news impact a hospital is even better than the transport system. Personally, I don't feel that Muslim presence or absence is of great concern considering that any believer who dies will be assured of his place in paradise. But there were some people who felt uneasy about the Edgware Road Tube bomb going off in such an Arab area, where so many passers-by were likely to be Muslim. All clear?"

"Yes," said Seth. "But . . . You know . . ."

"No, I don't."

"For fuck's sake," said Gary, the ex-Hindu. "If we're trying to build a just world by undermining what is unjust, what difference does it make if someone's having their appendix out?"

"I know, but—"

"Having a sprained ankle doesn't make them any less a part of the *Jahiliyya*."

"I just . . . No, you're right."

"You're not thinking some *kafir* shit about 'fair play' or something, because—"

"No, no, stop it. I understand. Stop it. I'm sorry I mentioned it."

When the silence had been left for about twenty seconds, Steve said, "All right. Four bombs. You number from one to four. One, two, three, four." He prodded them each in the chest with a number. "Now we'll look at the photographs of the interior. Memorize them."

Finn was sitting at the kitchen table in the basement, shaking wildly. On the floor were shards of broken crockery where he had thrown cups and saucers round the room, screaming at his mother, screaming at invisible tormentors in his just-broken voice. Vanessa, with a throbbing shin where he had kicked her, had her arm round him and was trying to make him eat some yogurt and cereal while they waited for Dr. Burnell.

Vanessa stroked Finn's hair back from his forehead with her spare hand and murmured comforting words. He seemed, for the moment, to have pulled back from the edge of violence.

"It'll be all right, darling, it'll all be all right."

She had no idea what "it" was, but felt profoundly that it was her fault. She had let Finn live as he chose because he seemed to like it that way and she didn't want to be intrusive—forever knocking on his door or nagging. So she had thought. Now as the child trembled in her arms she could see that she had left him alone because trying to understand him had been too difficult: teenage heart-to-hearts required too much bracing of herself, too much tension, too much effort to make contact with the boy who still existed beneath the gravelly, spiked exterior; too much time away from the cool wines of Burgundy and the TV remote control.

The front doorbell rang and she heard Marla go to answer it. She ran upstairs to the hall herself.

Burnell was a youngish man who had recently joined an established private practice in Arundel Gardens. Although he could be offhand and less sympathetic than his older colleagues, Vanessa liked him because he prescribed her powerful sleeping pills without question.

Downstairs in the kitchen, he examined Finn, taking his pulse, shining a torch into his eyes.

"So, tell me what happened."

"I heard him calling me from upstairs. He sounded desperate. I thought he must have fallen over and broken his leg or something.

When I got there he was lying on the floor, just sort of whimpering and holding himself. The awful thing is I can't seem to get through to him. When he speaks it seems to be to someone else. And then he began attacking me and throwing things around down here."

Burnell nodded. His freshly shaved face had a small cut, to which a piece of bloodied cotton wool was still attached. He made Finn hold out his hands in front of him. They were shaking. Then he shone the torch into his eyes again.

"Finn, I want you to tell me everything you did yesterday. I need to know if you drank alcohol or took drugs of any kind."

He slapped Finn, not unkindly, on the cheek. "Did you hear me, Finn?"

Finn did not respond.

"Drugs?"

Again, Finn seemed not to hear.

"What kind? Ecstasy? Acid? Skunk?"

This question seemed to be beyond Finn. He covered his face with his hands.

"I think we should go and look in his room," said Burnell. "Is that all right?"

Vanessa nodded, shamefaced. She dreaded to think what needles and tourniquets they might find.

Burnell glanced at the boy. "I don't want to leave him. Let's all go up."

In the ashtray on the floor, among the cigarette ends, were the butts of three joints that Burnell lifted to his nose and sniffed.

Vanessa smiled. "Thank God. I thought it was going to be something serious. You know, like heroin or—"

"Doesn't this seem serious enough?" said Burnell. "Look at him."

Vanessa said, "But I thought, you know, soft drugs, marijuana and so on . . ."

"Perhaps in the sixties. Not now. It's brutal. Genetically modified for impact. One of these today may be like thirty from your day." He turned to Finn. "How long have you been smoking this stuff? Do you have any more? Where do you keep it?"

Finn turned away and gripped his mother's arm. "They can't come. They told me they can't come. It's not my fault," he said.

"All right," said Burnell. "I'm going to give him a sedative. Then I think we need to get him into hospital."

"Hospital?" said Vanessa. "Surely there's no need for that?"

"Not in the long run, I hope. But he definitely needs to see someone in a detox or psychiatric unit. I don't feel happy about leaving him without specialist supervision. When I've given him the injection, he should calm down quite a bit. You stay with him here, and I'm going to go outside and make a couple of calls to a place I know. Glendale. It's a National Health hospital, but in my view it offers better care than any private clinic. You may have to go private to get him in at short notice. I'm assuming that's all right?"

"God, yes. Of course," said Vanessa. "Whatever's best."

III

I love him, thought Jenni Fortune. That's the word for it.

She was between Westminster and Embankment, having to remind herself to be vigilant—to watch for office workers coming out of lunchtime Christmas parties. Men often walked down the ramp at the end of the platform to relieve themselves on the rails. Sometimes there was clearance between their shoulders and an arriving train; and sometimes there wasn't.

Is this the first time I've felt love? Maybe for Mum, Jenni thought, never for anyone else. Not her father, not Tony and not Liston Brown. What was that feeling with Liston? Frightened. That's really all it was, when she looked back on it. She had wanted his protection, his power. There was the promise of safety there, but it had never materialized. All she had had was disappointment and anxiety, thinking she wasn't glamorous enough for him—too white, too black, too poor, too young, too ignorant, not knowing whether sex was what he wanted more or less of, where exactly it figured in his opinion of her. And having no one to turn to for advice, the other women cautious, not confiding, and the men eyeing her with a knowing look, a bit contemptuous, she always felt, as though they were thinking "We know her game," but also impressed that she was Liston's girlfriend. She hadn't wanted to impress anyone.

But with this guy . . . There was a moment when it had all changed, perhaps when she saw him struggling not to let her pay in the restaurant; maybe when she felt him staring at her when he went round on Wednesday in her cab; possibly long ago, when he tried to spare her Mr. Hutton's heavy-handedness, that touch of kindness—God knows, perhaps as early as the first time she saw the newspaper sticking out of his wastepaper basket with the squiggles in the margin. He was so thin that she wanted to hold him close to her. There was something sad in him she wanted to put right. And for some ridiculous reason she felt that only she could do that. No one else.

It made her smile. How likely was that? That only she . . . And yet she knew that it was true. No one but her could make that man come truly alive, put on weight, flourish and be happy.

She closed the doors, depressed the lever and moved it gently to the left. Of course, he wasn't just a patient or a case. There was so much that she could take from him, so much he knew, so many thoughts he'd had . . . Things that had never crossed her mind— though when he talked about these things, she seemed to have been aware of them all along. And they would laugh, she knew. He made her laugh already and when she'd got more confidence, she'd do the same for him.

There was something comic in it all, admittedly. To have a feeling like this, right down close to her ribs, right in the intimate center of who she was, not for her mother but for a barrister . . . A man who probably spoke Latin.

And while she still hadn't told him, it was more exciting. She herself was the only one that she'd confided in. One part of her mind had stumbled on it, named it, and the other part had confirmed it with memories, with the details of all their meetings. One part said, I've just this moment understood; and the other part said, Yes, and I've known all along.

They'd been stopped twice by a red light while the train in front cleared the station, and at Mansion House Jenni knew she had time to jump out of the cab and run over to the Ladies'. Her feet in the latest regulation safety issue shoes seemed to fly across the grimy platform. She also took her mug to the tea point behind the brown door, filled it up and slotted it into the cup holder on the dashboard. She checked the rearview mirror, closed the doors and moved off.

Stored in her mobile phone was a message she'd had at 8:30 that morning. "Need more background on safety. Can u come tea not chambers but my flat today? Work only. G."

So after her shift, she'd go to the address in SW3 that a further text had given her. Meanwhile, she pictured what his flat might be like. She knew he was short of money, but thought anywhere in Chelsea must be smart. His lounge would have antiques in it, perhaps, or a grandfather clock. There'd be a dining room with a long shiny table and a dozen of those old-fashioned chairs. And then maybe two or three bedrooms, one of which would overlook the river and would be his with all his clothes in a mahogany wardrobe. Would he ask her to move in with him? That would probably be best, Jenni thought. It wouldn't really work having him in Cowper Road. She'd have to boot out Tony for a start. Perhaps Gabriel would let her have one of his spare rooms for her clothes, but she'd want to spend each night, all night with him. She could easily move her shifts around to suit his working hours, so she'd be there when he came home. She'd cook real food not just twice a week, as she did for Tony, but every night. And with her salary and with his work picking up in the new year, they'd have tons of money—enough to go on foreign holidays where he'd show her all the interesting things. It was not so much a future, it was more like a second chance of living.

At twelve o'clock, the PetJet bound for Zurich was at the end of the City Airport runway, with John Veals one of sixteen passengers on board. Before turning off his phone/e-mailer, he had one last look at the ARB figures. They were still strong, he was pleased to see. The price had come off a little when the market opened in response to the denial of the takeover rumor by the CEO of First New York, but Magnus Darke's article, a gratifyingly word-perfect regurgitation of what Veals had suggested Ryman feed him, had given the rumor new impetus when the paper came out that morning.

As the plane crossed the Channel and the steward came down the aisle with champagne, Veals reviewed the situation. Every piece of the Rheumatism jigsaw was in place. The fancy part of the trade, the bit that Veals really liked, was the commodity leg. He wasn't sure how Duffy had done it, but he was confident it would be off-radar, as they didn't want to be seen to be making a huge profit while many Africans neared starvation. Some other bank would step into ARB's place sooner or later because there was money to be made there; and if not, that was scarcely High Level's problem.

Veals sipped an orange juice as he looked down at the forests of Verdun. When he had told Caroline Wilby that his fund had a "small short position" on ARB for some months, it was not exactly true. He had an enormous short position of recent origin; but in principle he had long thought the bank's prospects poor. The fact was, however, that he did intend at this late stage to short-sell the stock of ARB directly; he had a nice little curlicue in mind to finish off the Rheumatism position.

It was almost three o'clock when the fat German car Kieran Duffy had waiting for him at the airport dropped Veals at High Level in Pfäffikon. He found a confident calm in his offices. Duffy was having a late tomato sandwich and a glass of blood-orange juice; he was chatting to Victoria, who was sitting on the edge of his desk eating a slice of walnut cake. She went smartly back to her office when John Veals arrived. It was an effect he often had, he knew: his lack of small talk made people nervous.

"Everything all right, John?"

"Yes. Pretty much, Kieran. There was a story in the paper this morning. A hack called Magnus Darke. Saying ARB was in talks with First New York."

"Yes, I saw it," said Duffy.

"This Darke may be pissed off that his column appeared after the chief exec denied the whole thing in New York," said Veals.

"Yes, but the price is still holding up." Duffy typed the abbreviation for ARB on his keyboard and a graph showed only a slight decline in the share price.

"Well, Darke's done his job for us, and we may want to give him a little reward for being so helpful."

Veals's voice had the low, suppressed tremor it carried when a coup was ready to be executed.

Duffy, who knew Veals's tightness with information and fear of being overheard, merely looked at him interrogatively.

"Maybe next week," Veals said under his breath, drawing a chair up next to Duffy. "Or the week after. Maybe something will come out through him."

The two men looked at the ARB screen together, like pilots in a cockpit.

"Do you know the people on ARB's stock loan team?" said Veals.

"Not personally. But I can get to them."

"OK. Call them. Borrow $500 million of ARB stock from them."

"Their own stock?"

"Why not?"

"I doubt I can get that much. Even if they play ball. I'd have to go elsewhere as well."

298

"Fine. But get as much as you can from ARB itself."

"OK. Then what?"

"Be prepared to dump it at four o'clock London time. That's five here, right?"

"Yup."

"Know where you dump it?" said Veals. "Call ARB's own equities trading desk."

"Will they do it? D'you think they'll make us a price?"

"Do bears shit in the fucking woods, Kieran? They're bankers. They can't help themselves."

"And I dump all of it?"

"Yes. All of it. I think $500 million sold at teatime on a Friday is enough to give ARB shareholders an interesting weekend."

"What if the price has collapsed by then?"

"Sell anyway. If the price is already falling we still need to sell. It's only got one way to go now."

"OK. And this other thing? Through the journalist?"

"His main column's on Friday. But they've had so many cutbacks at the paper that he has to do a 'Notebook' on Wednesdays now as well."

"So we expect it the first Wednesday of the new year?"

"I'm not saying anything. But the price will be heading due south by then anyway."

Kieran Duffy got up and walked round the office. It was snowing again outside on the gray streets of Pfäffikon.

Duffy sighed. "You are one evil bastard, John. Their own stock loan team. Their own equities desk."

"Our fund could double in value. I think it's only right that the last leg of the trade should have a small flourish."

"But their own—"

"It's called irony, Kieran. I wouldn't expect you to understand."

At five o'clock, Jenni rang the bell of 5 Flood Street Mansions. The door buzzed open and she went into an echoing hall with a caged lift.

299

"Up here, Jenni. You can walk. It's only one flight."

He was at an open door in shirtsleeves with his tie off.

Seeing him for real, Jenni felt embarrassed by how far ahead of the facts she'd let her imagination run. She could barely look him in the eye as she bumped her cheek painfully against his in greeting.

"Come in. I'm sorry, it's all a bit of a mess. I didn't have time to tidy up. Drop your coat on this chair if you like. Would you like some tea?"

"Thanks. I'd love some."

"Come on, then. You can help me make it."

The kitchen was what they called a "galley," Jenni thought: a narrow slit with no room for sitting or relaxing.

"Excuse me," he said, squeezing past. "Sorry it's a bit cramped. I don't do much cooking."

"I can see that."

Gabriel's "flat" was really two rooms, plus galley and bath. The sitting room had dark green walls and bookshelves. There was a desk with a laptop and piles more books and magazines on the floor. There was a set of golf clubs in the corner.

"Do you play golf?"

"Only very occasionally. I hate it."

"So why do you—"

"A friend of mine gave me his old clubs when he got some new ones. What are you smiling at, Jenni?"

"It's all so . . . It's just not how I imagined."

"And what did you expect?"

"I don't know really. I thought, you know, being in Chelsea it'd be like really smart."

"People think all barristers earn a lot. They don't. A few commercial silks make a fortune, but most of us earn about what a teacher makes and the young ones much less."

"Sorry, I didn't mean to say that—"

"No, no. I know what you mean. It is a bit of a tip, really. Catalina was always ticking me off about it. She once sent round a cleaner. At least I keep the bathroom clean. And the bedroom's nice. But in here. Well, you know. Life's short. I've only got another two years on the lease anyway, so there's not much point."

"What'll you do then?"

"I don't know. There were seven and a half years left when I bought it. It was quite cheap, but I suppose it was a bad investment. I just liked the street. I couldn't see further than seven years ahead anyway. Who can?"

Jenni felt a little confidence returning. She had forgotten how easy he made it for her.

"You're still laughing inside, aren't you?" Gabriel said. "It's a hard thing to explain. I just don't notice what it looks like. I don't see it. I notice if it's too warm or too cold and I adjust that. Otherwise it's just a question of how it works. If the television has a light reflecting on it or not. If there's somewhere I can put my feet up when I'm watching."

"Just how it works, then."

"Exactly. Not how it looks."

Jenni put down her teacup. "Why did you want to meet here?"

"I thought, you know, after I'd been to your flat you should come to mine."

"I see." Jenni didn't in fact see the logic of his reply, but was glad that it at least seemed friendly. "And why teatime?" she said.

"I haven't got much on at work, so I could leave early. And this evening I won't be free because I'm going to see my brother in hospital."

"Has he had an operation?"

"No, he's in a psychiatric hospital. He has schizophrenia."

"Is that split—"

"No, it isn't. That's a common misunderstanding, because of the silly name. They're trying to rechristen it, I believe. DPI. Delusional Psychotic Illness, or something like that. What it means is that he's seriously deluded. He hears voices which give him instructions. And these voices are real and loud, louder than mine is in your ear now. So when you meet him he sometimes can't hear you. He lip-reads me. And even if he can accurately lip-read

301

what I'm saying it often doesn't seem important to him by comparison with what the voices are telling him. I'm saying things like 'How's it going?' or 'Would you like some tea?' and the voices are giving loud instructions about life and death."

"Shit," said Jenni.

"Yes, Jenni."

"How long has he been like this? What's his name?"

"Adam. He started being a bit odd in his teens. He read the Bible a lot in his room. Then he began to talk about being tailed by MI5 because they thought he was a drug dealer or something. And we all had a laugh about it. We thought he was just having these fantasies for fun. And he didn't seem particularly upset by them. But then when he was about twenty he seemed just to drift away from us. His system of beliefs became very fierce and very structured. He would draw diagrams for me that showed the emanation of power from some remote force in the cosmos. It was like a mixture of religion and advanced physics."

"Couldn't you explain to him that it wasn't true?" said Jenni.

"No, that was the trouble. His belief in his world was more secure than my belief in ours. I mean, I feel pretty sure that you are sitting here and that your name is Jenni and my name is Gabriel and that this is London, that's a window and so on. But I do have room for doubt. It could be that this is some dream and we'll both wake up. Or that our idea of physical reality is somehow misleading. I mean, after all, we don't really understand the nature of physical existence, do we? Maybe Stephen Hawking does, but I certainly don't. How does time bend? What really is antimatter? What happens at the edge of the expanding universe? So if it turned out that my grasp of all this was not only incomplete, which it certainly is, but also almost delusional—in the sense that a dog or a mouse has only a minute understanding of what the world is . . . Well, I wouldn't be altogether surprised. I know more than a mouse, but not much more. I may be working minute by minute under the same gigantic limitations of understanding as a woodlouse. I score five where the louse scores one and the cat three. But a full understanding may require a million. So I do have room for doubt."

"And what about Adam?"

"That's the difference. Adam has no doubt. His cosmos is fully understood. He receives instruction from voices whose reality is stronger than mine is to you. I forget the name of his supreme power. Axia or something. But he or she is self-grounded, beyond reason or doubt."

"Does it make him unhappy?"

"I can't always tell. I don't think the way that he appears to be is always a guide to what's going on in his head. But I do believe that he is really dreadfully unhappy. Not in quite the same way as you or I can feel unhappiness. In a darker, weirder way. To do with the very roots of conscious existence."

Gabriel stood up and turned away from Jenni. She saw him surreptitiously push his sleeve across his face as he looked out of the window.

He turned back. "Anyway, that's where I'm off to this evening. It's not that I do him any good, but I suppose it makes me feel better."

"Can he ever be cured?"

"I don't think so. Not now. But the drugs take away some of the worst of it. The trouble is they seem to take away something of him as well. Part of him, the person he was, seems to have died."

Jenni nodded. "I suppose we all live in our different worlds, don't we?"

"I guess so." Gabriel smiled. "Shall we have a drink? A glass of wine?"

"I'd better not. I'm driving tomorrow."

"But didn't you . . . When we went out to dinner?"

"Half a glass." Jenni laughed. "You drank the rest. Anyway, I took a chance. It was the first date I'd had for a long time. I mean—"

"I know what you mean. Even though it was work, it was a bit like a date in that . . ."

303

"Yup."

Gabriel went to the kitchen, leaving Jenni to catch her breath. Her feeling of embarrassment had ebbed. It didn't matter that she'd got so far ahead of herself, planning how they'd live together and everything. She hadn't blurted anything out. What she wanted to do now, though, was to get an idea of how far behind he was in his feelings.

He came back with a glass of wine for himself and some orange juice for Jenni. He sat down heavily on the sofa. "So, Jenni. The case. January 18th. Anything you want to ask me?"

"Yes. How come you know so much?"

"About the case?"

"No. Everything. Is it just because you've read so much?"

"I hardly know anything."

"Don't be modest. I want to know. Tell me. I drive a train."

"Well . . . I suppose I was lucky enough to be educated at a time when teachers still thought children could handle knowledge. They trusted us. Then there came a time when they decided that because not every kid in the class could understand or remember those things, they wouldn't teach them anymore because it wasn't fair on the less good ones. So they withheld knowledge. Then I suppose the next lot of teachers didn't have the knowledge to withhold. Was it like that at your school?"

"My school was pretty shit. You didn't really think about learning, you just thought about getting through it."

"Where I went there was still this assumption that each generation would know everything its predecessors knew—and more. So school was to bring you up to the level of your parents' knowledge and then university maybe would take you on past them. But when you come to think of it—when you come to think of how much people already know—that's very ambitious. Also very modern."

Jenni wanted Gabriel to tell her more about himself, but if he wanted to talk about learning in general, she would have to go with it and wait for an opening. "What do you mean by modern?" she said.

"Well, I think that in premodern societies the aim of people was simply to preserve what had been learned, not to lose it. It would have taken far too much training and money and infrastructure in, say, Iran in AD 1300 to bring all children up to speed and then push them on further. If they could feel they'd had no net loss of knowledge from one generation to the next, that they hadn't actually gone backward, they thought that was a good result."

"But wouldn't kids find out new things anyway?"

"In agrarian Iran? I doubt it. And they would have been strongly discouraged from doing so by their elders. In Muslim societies, they learned the Koran by rote and that was it. There was no printing, and few people could read. Just to keep hold of knowledge at a steady level was a success."

"And what happened here?"

"We had more money, and not such an overpowering religion. Avenues were open. But it was only the twentieth century in Europe that had universal education and the belief in progress—a net gain of knowledge among all. And that's now been abandoned as a goal."

"Why?"

"It was too difficult. People weren't prepared to put in the hours on the donkey work—you know, dates and facts and so on. I think in retrospect my generation will be seen as a turning point. From now on there'll be a net loss of knowledge in Europe. The difference between a peasant community in fourteenth-century Iran and modern London, though, is that if with their meager resources the villagers occasionally slipped backward, it was not for lack of trying. But with us, here in England, it was a positive choice. We chose to know less."

Jenni laughed. "You sound like a dinosaur. An old guy in a cave."

"I think so." Gabriel laughed too. "Imagine him. He knew his main subjects at school and then his degree and then his professional thing. But he would have expected as of right to have a knowledge of art, music, French kings, all the Bible and so on. He wouldn't necessarily love music, but he could tell you within twelve bars if it was Brahms or Mendelssohn. The difference between Tintoretto and Titian. Maybe he didn't care much for either, but he could tell you because he was required to know. He's probably still alive somewhere."

"You could sell tickets to him," said Jenni. "In his cave."

"I think you could. I suppose it was a dream that lasted really about fifty years. By the time universal education had begun to work properly, say 1925, and the time the first teachers started to hold back information, say 1975. So a fifty-year dream."

"But does it really matter?" said Jenni. "As long as somebody knows these things. There's always going to be a geek somewhere who understands."

"Yes. Maybe it doesn't matter. I think what's happened is that because they themselves know less than their predecessors, innovators and leaders today have remade the world in their own image. Spellchecks. Search engines. They've remodeled the world so that ignorance is not really a disadvantage. And I should think that increasingly they'll carry on reshaping the world to accommodate a net loss of knowledge."

"Though that in itself is quite clever. Isn't it?"

"Yes. In a way. It's a perverse form of natural selection. People might have been selected against on the grounds that they had lacked the mutation of knowledge. But they actually changed the environment, so that it was they who were selected, while the people who had what looked like a helpful mutation—knowing stuff—could actually be selected against."

"I think you've lost me," said Jenni. "Are you talking about the Internet?"

"In a way." Gabriel inhaled. There was a pause, as though he was changing the subject. "You know that Internet game you play?"

"Parallax?"

"Yes. I mean . . . I can see that it's well made. But don't you think you should be engaging more with the real world?"

"Is that what you meant when you said 'Oh, Jenni'?"

"I'm sorry about that. But, yes, I suppose it was."

"And what is real?"

"Other people."

"And what about you?" said Jenni. "Your crossword? Your books?"

"Yes, the crossword's an escape, I admit. It's silly. But the books. Well, as we said once before, they're not an escape, they're the key to understanding. The key to reality."

Jenni suddenly saw her moment. She breathed in deeply, then plunged. "You know your big escape, don't you?"

"No. What?"

"Your big alternative-reality game. You know what your Parallax is?"

"What?"

"It's her."

"Who?"

"Catalina."

There was a silence, and Jenni feared she'd gone too far. Gabriel stared down at the coffee table, with his face between his hands.

Eventually, he looked up and sighed. "Would you like to see a picture of her?"

"All right." Jenni couldn't bring herself to sound enthusiastic.

Gabriel went over to the desk and took an old mobile phone out of a drawer. "There's one in here," he said. "I took it in Stockholm."

"Show me, then."

"I can't. The battery's dead and they don't make this model anymore."

"You should have downloaded it."

"I know. It's too late now."

"You should throw the phone away, then. It's no good to anyone."

"All right." Gabriel dropped it in the wastepaper basket.

"But you'll just pick it out again when I've gone."

Gabriel stared out of the window again, toward the gray river. "I suppose I would be tempted. It's hard to terminate these things. These dreams. Forever. I'll tell you what I'll do. If you give up Parallax, I'll chuck the phone in the Thames."

"But I like Parallax," said Jenni.

"And I liked Catalina. Maybe we've both lost touch with something, though. Perhaps we all have. Adam, you, me." He looked down at the evening paper on the table, whose front page spoke of mounting Wall Street losses. "Bankers trading bets on bets on bets."

Jenni stood up. "Do you ever take anyone with you to visit Adam?"

"No, there's no point. He wouldn't appreciate it. He'd hardly notice."

"What about you, though? Wouldn't you like some company?"

"Are you—"

"I don't have anything on. I'd like to go with you. It might make it nicer for you. And afterward we could go to a restaurant. My turn to pay."

They caught a train with two minutes to spare, but it was full and they were forced to stand between two carriages. The train picked its way through Pimlico, on the same track that Hassan al-Rashid had taken two days earlier. Then, as it went slowly over Grosvenor Bridge, Gabriel suddenly pulled down the window in the door, took his old mobile phone from his pocket and hurled it out, as hard as he could.

Jenni watched as it cleared the low rail of the bridge and soared on for a moment or two, before dropping into the waters of the Thames.

At 6:30 John Veals was on his way home from the airport, sitting in the debris of giveaway newspapers on the Tube. One last time, just to be certain, he checked the messaging inbox of his green mobile phone. There it still was in bald sans serif glory. In large letters it said "O'Bagel," the name of the sender; in smaller characters, underneath, were the first words of the message: "Confirm rheumatism sell . . ." Veals pressed "Open" to read the rest of the message ". . . completed at agreed time. All dumped."

Veals felt an intense exhilaration at the thought that he had pulled off the greatest financial coup of his life. The fund could double in size. His name would become even more venerated. He was rich beyond his, or anyone else's, dreams. Against the elation there was still a niggling fear that he had overlooked some small but vital detail that even at this late stage could derail him. But he hadn't. He'd run through every angle a thousand times. He'd tested it for hours on Godley and Duffy. He'd even talked it through with Bézamain in New York. It was bombproof.

And then there was the slight Wellingtonian melancholy of the battle won, almost as haunting as the battle lost. What fresh worlds now remained for him to conquer? But, as the train rattled through the tight-fitting tunnels, there was above all the sense of satisfaction—of having fulfilled the purpose of his life. Billions of pounds and dollars had been diverted from other destinations and rerouted into the bank account marked "Veals." He sat back against the plush of the seat and sighed.

At seven o'clock R. Tranter walked up from Hyde Park Corner, a station he had never used before. He wore a dinner jacket from an outfitter in Holborn; it had wide lapels and a faint smell of old banquets and mothball. Just as he was approaching the revolving doors of the hotel, a bicycle with no lights shot past him along the pavement, making him leap to one side.

Tranter swore shortly, then recomposed himself before going in. The rider, briefly visible in the light from a ground-floor room, wore fizzing earphones so wouldn't have been able to hear the curses that followed him.

The Park Lane Metropolitan was one of the newer hotels, and

of an impressive size. It had already attracted a number of well-dressed but clearly available women on the plump semicircular sofas in its atrium. Tranter managed not to catch their eyes as he pushed on, head down, to the lifts at the back, where white letters stuck to a black felt board announced: Pizza Palace Book of the Year Prize, Sir Francis Drake Suite, Fifth Floor.

He ascended silently, his mouth dry, his palms wet. Double wooden doors gave on to the sight of about 400 people standing round in small groups, drinking. Tranter felt the reflexive panic of the King's Arms in college days, but his literary agent, Penny McGuire, was for once on time and waiting for him. He braved her garlicky embrace, congratulating himself on having splashed out on a new razor blade.

"Are you all right, RT? Not nervous, are you?"

"No, I'm fine."

Tranter looked round the room. It was filled with people he disliked, simpering confidently, tossing back the cheap champagne.

"What does Antony Cazenove look like?" he said.

"He's the chap over by the window, there," said Penny, a large woman in a blue dress with a small bunch of flowers on the bust. Tranter followed her pointing finger to where a man of about forty was talking to two good-looking women, one dark with an oriental look, one with tumbling blond hair. He was wearing a green velvet smoking jacket.

"Would you like to meet him?" said Penny.

"Fuck no," said Tranter.

He withdrew a few paces so that his back was near to the wall, a position from which he could more safely survey the room. He raised his glass to his lips and held it there while his eyes swiveled inquiringly from side to side above the rim. They were scheduled to sit down at eight, with the prize announcement no later than 9:15, to give the newspapers time to get the result into their first editions. Once he was seated, Tranter felt, the evening would be all right; it was getting through the next forty-five minutes that would be the problem.

"Which one's Sally Higgs?" he said to Penny.

"The children's writer? I'm not sure she's arrived yet."

"Hello, Ralph."

Tranter knew without turning round that it was Patrick Warrender, the only person to use his first name.

"Hello, Patrick. Do you know Penny—"

"Of course. How are you? Everything all right, Ralph? It's in the bag, I gather. Your Edgerton thing. I looked at the Cazenove. Absolute drivel. 'Land of contrasts.' Lots of conversations with random people on trains repeated word for word. Tedious beyond all parody. You've got no worries. You'll be fine."

"I hope so."

"And if it doesn't come off this time, you can always go back to writing fiction. More prizes there."

"Not my thing."

"You did write a novel once, didn't you?"

"Just one, yes."

"Why didn't you do a second?"

"Writer's block, I suppose."

"There's no such thing as writer's block," said Patrick. "Don't you agree, Penny? Writer's block is God's way of telling you to shut the eff up."

Tranter wasn't paying attention, however. Over by the huge picture windows with their view above the traffic of Park Lane, Antony Cazenove and the two fawning women in backless dresses had now been joined by the person R. Tranter most detested in the world: Alexander Sedley—on whose judgment his life now depended. "Of all men else have I avoided thee," he thought, the line remembering itself from some teenage revision notes. He wondered what Sedley had made of his letter of recantation; of course the smug bastard hadn't bothered to reply.

The backless vamps were draping themselves all over Sedley's expensive dinner suit, Tranter noticed through narrowed eyes; now the blond one, on the pretext of picking up something she had dropped, was virtually fellating him. But worse than that was the body language between the two men. Sedley's hand was on Cazenove's laughing shoulder in a familiar way that made Tranter freeze. It was the attitude of the prefect to his personal fag. Shit, he thought. Of course. School friends. Some awful posh freemasonry of shared studies, tuck and sodomy. Just look at them. Fuck.

"Couldn't get through it myself," Patrick was saying. "Did you read it, Ralph?"

"What?"

Tranter never discovered what, because a young woman came up and introduced herself as being from the diary column of a newspaper.

"Can I just ask you a few questions?"

"OK." He glanced at Penny. She shrugged. His call.

"Is this the first time you've won a prize?" said the diarist.

"I haven't won it yet."

"Oh, sorry. So, is it a novel or what?"

"No, it's a biography."

"Oh, I see. And what gave you the idea for it?"

Tranter gawped. "What 'gave me the idea' for it?"

"Yes, you know. Is he a relative, the person you've written about?"

"Edgerton? No. He was a great Victorian writer."

"OK. Can I ask you a couple of personal things?"

The journalist was only about twenty-five. Tranter thought he should say no, but he didn't want her to write anything disobliging, saying he was standoffish or unhelpful, so he agreed. "All right," he said.

"You were educated at Cambridge, right?"

"No, Oxford."

"And this chap . . . Edgeworth?"

"Edgerton."

"Right. Edgerton. Is he still alive?"

"No. He died in 1898."

"Pity," the journalist said. "I wanted a quote from him. And is your wife happy that you've won a prize?"

"I'm not married," said Tranter. "Where do you get your facts from? Your research?"

"Off the Internet. Encyclotrivia dot com mostly."

"Aren't you going to write anything down? Take notes?"

"No, no, it's OK, I can just remember it. Do you know which one's Mr. Cazenove?"

IV

At 7:30, Gabriel and Jenni walked the fifteen minutes from the station to Glendale Hospital. Dave was in the porter's cabin and gave them a wave as they went up toward Wakeley. Gabriel could sense Jenni silently taking in the NHS signs—Long-Stay Unit, Electroconvulsive Therapy—and a slight tension coming over her as she did so. A psychiatric hospital was a daunting place to go if you'd never visited one before.

"You all right, Jenni?" he said.

"I think so."

"It's nothing to worry about. Just some unhappy people watching television. And smoking." He was starting to wish he hadn't accepted her offer to accompany him. As second dates go, this was about as unromantic as he could imagine.

When they arrived in the hallway, Rob, the charge nurse, asked them to wait.

"Sorry," he said, "there's been a bit of a kerfuffle. Young lad came in. Very distressed. It'll be all right in a minute. Trouble is, it upsets the others. It's like a fire going through a field. They seem OK, but they're on a knife edge half the time."

The corridor leading into the main part of the building was dark. There were dim lights from one of the dayrooms used for group therapy; otherwise the vista was one of shrinking darkness. Jenni licked her lips. They could hear soft moaning from inside.

They silently looked at the "art" displayed around the small entrance hall. Gabriel smiled tensely. "Sorry, Jenni. It's not normally like this."

There was a sound of running feet, never a good sign in a hospital, as Gabriel knew from years of visiting his brother. Then the awful quiet resumed.

The window off the square hall had curtains of orange and brown squares. There were half a dozen hard chairs with their backs to the wall and a cheap whitewood coffee table with some old magazines.

Gabriel had let nothing slip, he felt, in his long conversation with Jenni at his flat: he'd maintained a professional facade, but he liked the way that Jenni had played along with him, tacitly acknowledging that it was a game by making no effort to discuss the court case. The fact was, however, that in the last few days he had felt the constellations of his world, which had for so long been fixed, begin to tilt and alter their positions.

Sometimes he felt his life was not a narrative or a sequence of events, but a succession of disconnected images, fragments of a larger dream. And Catalina had been such a fragment, torn off from the gulf. Everything that made life tolerable derived from a premise that you could expect reward or permanence: that you could build. It had been too difficult for him to accept that Catalina and the feeling that he had for her were not like that at all; that she had been a bubble on the surface of a stream, held in perfect tension—no less real because translucent, temporary—then reabsorbed by the element that had made her, carried on by the current of time. And all the years he'd known her, believing that he loved her, it hadn't really felt like that: his awareness of time passing had made it feel less like loving than like dying. The only way that he could be with her truly would be after death, in some other place, in some other manner of being.

What he'd read in the Koran had also troubled him: the strange—yet to him naggingly familiar—violence of the assertions, and the lack of much else other than assertion. The widespread historical explanation, that this simply reflected the desperate social and commercial need of the Arabs of the Peninsula for a modern

314

monotheistic god—and their relief at having found one—was appealing, but inadequate. He sighed. Perhaps the hallucinatory reality of the book with its sequence of "heard" instructions was no more bizarre than the alternative realities inhabited by people of the twenty-first century.

The double doors opened onto the corridor and three people came out from the ward into the hall. There was a smartly dressed woman in her forties and a teenage youth, presumably her son. The boy had curly hair and a handful of pimples on his chin. His eyes seemed fixed, and Gabriel imagined he must be sedated. He stared across the hall, unseeing. But it was not the son's eyes that struck him; it was the mother's. Her face was stretched tight in anguish; someone had scraped a deep vertical between her eyes and torn her mouth downward into a grimace. She put her arms round the boy and held him to her breast.

"Don't worry, Finn," Gabriel heard her whisper. "We'll look after you."

"All right, Gabriel," said Rob, emerging from the darkness. "You can come and see him now."

"Thanks, Rob. This is Jenni, by the way."

"Hi. Don't fret if Adam seems a bit odd. They were all upset by the boy who came in. It may take Adam a while to settle."

They went down the dark corridor, through the dining area, in whose unlit air Gabriel could just make out the figure of Violet, still standing at the window, her arm forever raised in greeting, or farewell.

Adam was called from the smoky dayroom and the television's roar. Rob showed him into the visitors' lounge where Gabriel and Jenni sat.

"Hi, Adam. This is a friend of mine I've brought to see you—Jenni. We got you these." He held out some cigarettes and chewing gum, which Adam took without speaking.

Far from being upset, Adam seemed cogent and relaxed.

"Who sent you?" he asked, eyeing Jenni.

"No, no. She's . . . She's a friend," said Gabriel.

"You should marry," said Adam. "It's permitted to marry two or three people."

"Is it?" said Jenni.

Gabriel tried to catch her eye, to warn her not to engage too literally in conversation.

"Oh yes," said Adam. "But the penalty for adultery is severe."

"Is this in the Bible?" said Jenni.

"No. Axia told me."

"Who's Axia?"

"The ruler." Adam spoke as a teacher to a slow child.

"And you know this Axia, do you?" said Jenni.

"Of course. There is also the Disaster Maker. You can't understand the Disaster Maker. When he comes to us, you'll be scattered like flies."

"Like some tea, Adam?" said Gabriel.

"If your life's been wrong, he will punish you."

"Who?" said Jenni. "Axia?"

"The Disaster Maker. You can't know what it'll be like. Shall I tell you what it's like?"

"Yes," said Jenni.

"It's a scorching fire."

At that instant Gabriel knew what the relentless voice of the Koran had reminded him of: it was his brother.

While Adam went on to explain his eschatology to Jenni—who was saved and who would burn, how power and the chance of salvation rained down upon the world and how he alone was the channel of the truth—Gabriel cast his mind back over what he'd read, and saw in all of it a common thread. He remembered the awesome nature of the Prophet's experience as he received the visitation in the chapter named "The Star." And when he had stressed to Jenni how the difference between his reality and Adam's was that Adam's was so much more confident and secure, he could have been speaking equally of the Prophet's experience—in its intensity and its vehement exclusion of all doubt.

The same certainty was there also in biblical leaders—in Abraham instructed by a voice to sacrifice his son, instructed by another voice to save him; Abraham had never doubted the reality of the voice, as Adam had never doubted Axia, it was only the detail of the order that was a worry. All the great Jewish prophets heard voices and were led by them. Three times in the night the infant Samuel went to the prophet Eli, having heard his name called by the old man; three times Eli was asleep. John the Baptist, raving, all but naked, unkempt, eating insects . . . He was like the poor man Gabriel had seen wrapped only in a black bin bag one winter night near Waterloo Bridge soon after the psychiatric hospitals had been closed and their patients thrown out to "care in the community." It was a brutal shame. And then, in the Bible at least, the hearing of voices had become less common, so that when Christ arrived he was welcomed as the first true prophet in generations, the first man to have heard God's voice clearly. How badly the Arabs of the Peninsula had needed a voice-hearer of their own, and how long their 600-year wait must have seemed. And then, when God came . . . he came with hard threats, saying: It is so because I say so.

Shortly after eight o'clock, Hassan secured his rucksack for the final time. It had eight disposable cameras whose batteries had been hollowed out and their contents replaced with HMTD; four were "operational" and four were spares. He had checked and rechecked them and there was nothing left to do. They had agreed on a place to make their rendezvous at Glendale, at the maintenance shed some 200 yards from the building called Wakeley. Two of them would enter through the front door of the main hospital, which had the typical laissez-aller attitude of all large NHS buildings, with staff, visitors, trade, maintenance and outpatients coming and going unchallenged, at least in the communal downstairs areas. Just in case of difficulty, one of the four, Seth, would approach from the open-plan psychiatric side of the site and one, Hassan, would scale an eight-foot perimeter wall. He was chosen for the climb because his load was the lightest.

317

He sat down on his bed. This was to be the last night of his life.

There seemed nothing he could do that was momentous enough to mark such an event. He smiled. Should he reread a favorite book? Telephone a special friend? Or even an old girlfriend. Dawn! He laughed out loud. Or Rania—though she'd never technically been his girlfriend. Or Shahla, maybe. Why had he suddenly thought of her? She was an apostate, she was worse than a *kafir*.

He opened his laptop and went to babesdelight.co.uk. He checked Olya for any last message, but her spread legs showed only pink. He looked at one or two of the other girls, then closed the screen down.

Hassan held his face in his hands. This was going to be a little harder than he'd imagined, to leave behind everything in the world.

He picked up the paperback Koran, and it fell open at a marked passage.

"Never think that those who were slain in the cause of God are dead. They are alive, and well provided for by their Lord; pleased with His gifts and rejoicing that those they left behind, who have not yet joined them, have nothing to fear or to regret; rejoicing in God's grace and bounty. God will not deny the faithful their reward."

Hassan knelt by the side of the bed and held his head tight between his hands.

At 9:15 exactly in a room full of old-master paintings, the chairman of HOPE rose to his feet to begin the auction of prizes to the assembled members of the financial world. Hire of the famous gallery had cost £250,000, with HOPE further agreeing to cover the extraordinary insurance premium incurred by the risk that a futures trader lighting up a crafty smoke might accidentally ignite a Titian.

"Ladies and gentlemen, may I have your attention, please. We have thirty lots to get through in this year's auction, so as usual we must begin promptly. Do enjoy your dinner, but please be as quiet as you can so that the auction can run smoothly. I know you'll be delighted to hear that it's not me who'll be conducting the auction, but a mystery celebrity I shall be introducing to you at any moment. And he's going to introduce you later to tonight's surprise star guest."

The chairman was the chief executive of a bank, whose television advertisements featured black and white footage of a Pennine town, while their investment arm had bought billions of pounds' worth of febrile derivatives in new Asia. The head of the department responsible for helping the bank avoid tax had been paid £42 million in salary and bonus that year. Being domiciled abroad, he did not pay income tax on this sum.

Beneath a fifteenth-century painting of the Return of the Prodigal Son sat the London chief executive of the financial services division of a giant American insurer. Of his own $30 million annual remuneration, the CEO had earmarked $500,000 for spending, con brio, at the HOPE auction. He could probably reclaim it on expenses, he thought, if the year-end results were good (not likely as of that moment). A colleague had set his previous year's bid off against tax, but that was of no interest, the chief exec pointed out testily, if you didn't *pay* tax.

". . . outstanding support from the financial community," the chairman continued. "I would especially like to thank John Veals of High Level Capital, who has been a longtime supporter of our work. John can't be here tonight, but has made a most generous gesture in booking three tables at twice the going rate and then releasing them to us to sell again. John has always shown great commitment to pensioners' causes."

Some tables were growing restive. It was amusing enough to dress up in black tie and diamonds, to drink the champagne stipulated by petulant rock stars for their dressing rooms, but the attention spans of the assembled guests were short and they needed the stimulus of action: they wanted to see large sums of money changing hands, soon. The equities division of one of the brasher banks began to rattle its table, making a cacophony of china, glass and cutlery. A young sell-side analyst with a lapel badge saying "Call Me Gus" raised his head from his lap, where he had snorted a line of cocaine from the back of the stiff printed menu, wiped his nose with the back of his hand and, in a burst of chemical exhilaration, shouted, "Show me the money."

". . . without further ado," the chairman swiftly concluded, "I would like to introduce you to your host for the evening, fresh from the travails of the television studio, Mr. Terry O'Malley!"

From behind a wide black screen that held a fragment of a fresco under glass, Terry, with gray curls and ruddy jowls, came bounding out in a green velvet bow tie.

"All right, you fat capitalist bastards," he began. "Time to put your hands in your pockets. Quiet now. Honestly, you lot, you're worse than the nutters in the Barking Bungalow. I'll have the whole lot of you under sedation if you're not careful. And just so we can get the question of what happened last night out of the way: yes, it was unfortunate, no it's not our fault, and yes we are insured . . . I'll tell you about Lisa's reaction later. Poor girl, you'd think she'd never been face-to-face with a stiff before . . . All right. First up. It's a cultural package. You get two tickets for one night at Bayreuth. No, sir, it's not the capital of Lebanon, it's the capital of Wagner. You get a behind-the-scenes tour of the Royal Ballet, plus two tickets to the performance of your choice. You have a signed print by one of Britain's most famous artists, Liam Hogg. And finally you get to have lunch at the award-winning Green Pig restaurant, as featured on TV, with the leading novelist and critic—it says here—Alexander Sedley. Let's start the bidding at £25,000. Come on, you tight bastards. I warn you, the early lots are the bargains. You'll look back and think, Why did I miss that when I've ended up paying twice the final amount for something half as good? Over there. Table five. Thirty thousand? Good. With you, madam."

For the sum of £95,000, the lot was won by "Call Me Gus," who started to make his way to the podium to receive his envelope.

"Before you come up here, mate," said Terry O'Malley, "I'd like to introduce our surprise star guest. You've no idea how much it cost to fly her here all the way from Hollywood. But expense is no object when it comes to HOPE, and in fact I'm pretty sure this is a girl the boys on table fourteen wouldn't mind blowing their whole wad on . . . Yes, it's the one and only . . . Evelina Belle!"

There was a roar from the diners, many of whom rose to their feet, as the shy-looking actress, so small and pale in reality, was led on by two shaven-headed thugs with curly wires behind their ears.

She stood beneath a mighty oil of Judith and Holofernes, painted by the inhabitant of one of the new county lunatic asylums in 1862.

"Why, thank you, everybody," Evelina said, her huge red mouth opening to show her blinding white teeth. "I hope y'all will consider it an incentive to bid higher knowing that you get to shake my hand."

"Ah, go on, Evelina," said Terry. "Give the man a kiss."

"Congratulations," said Evelina, offering Gus a cheek. "Are you an opera kinda guy?"

"No, I never 'eard of any of these people," said Gus. "I was just hoping to impress my date."

"Well, good luck, honey," said Evelina.

"And if your date won't put out for ninety-five grand," said Terry, "don't come crying to me!"

At 9:45 in the Sir Francis Drake Suite in the Park Lane Metropolitan, a man in a maroon nylon jacket with a black bow tie placed a microphone in front of the chief executive of Pizza Palace, Nigel Salisbury, and banged it a few times with his finger, making the noisy diners turn their heads and concentrate.

R. Tranter felt a tightening in his belly and a loosening in his bladder. His palms spurted moisture, while Penny McGuire laid a calming hand on his forearm.

Nigel Salisbury had originally voted against sponsoring a prize for books, as he couldn't see what it had to do with selling more pizza. Over the last few years, however, he had come round to thinking that the publicity was good value. Each year, his head chef devised a new topping somehow connected to the winner of the prize. A travel book about the Australian outback had naturally given birth to an "Ozzie Hot," featuring slices of barbecue-seared meat (allegedly kangaroo) on a dark brown vegetable-extract base; a biography of Hitler had led to a vegetarian layer. Neither had sold well, but the publishers had been pleased.

From behind his raised glass, Tranter surveyed the room. Dinner had seemed never-ending, and he had long ago tired of explaining to Mrs. Jones, the wife of Mr. K. R. Jones (regional development), who Alfred Huntley Edgerton was. The collar of his shirt was too tight and he had become aware during the rack of lamb with over-reduced jus and string beans that his body heat was starting to call up the ghosts of banquets past from the serge of his hired jacket.

After a speech about the sales growth of Pizza Palace and the number of new outlets in the northwest, Nigel Salisbury handed over to the chairman of the judges, the former transport minister who allegedly read books.

After telling his audience how honored he was, the Literate Politician went on to describe how extremely difficult the task faced by the panel had been.

Tranter dug his fingernails into his palms. Dear God, he had begun by thinking, please bring this to an end; but after a bit, he found to his surprise that, mixed with the extended agony, there was a kind of exhilaration. It was as though everything in his life had been leading up to this moment and he didn't mind prolonging it. He knew now that he was going to win. His diligence as a schoolboy had been the start of it all; although they didn't rank the kids officially it was obvious that Tranter had been top of the class. Secondary school, Oxford, the early years . . . He had stuck firmly to what he believed. His excoriating reviews in newspapers, magazines and in *The Toad* had served a high critical purpose: to purge the world of the "higher bogus," to rip the scales from readers' eyes, to attack the lazy assumptions of the "literary establishment." He had sought neither fear nor favor—if that was the expression he wanted. It had taken real courage to write—albeit anonymously—and explain why this year's darling of the press was an empty hype, a hollow vessel; why that old fool, laden with honors, was just one of the old gang of mutual . . . mutual . . . Whatever. Tranter took another swig of the Metropolitan house rioja.

And his critics said he had nothing to offer but derision. Well, he had shown them. He had found a real writer, examined his life and presented it to the public with a full commentary on the novels, explaining in detail how *Shropshire Towers*, for instance, was a work hugely superior to anything published in the last twenty years.

He heard a falling note in the Literate Politician's voice that suggested he was about to end his speech and name the winner. The man took an envelope from his pocket. Tranter looked down at the half-eaten crème caramel on his plate. There was a ringing in his ears, a pounding of blood. Every particle of his body was now straining and craving for the desired vowel sounds that made the name of Alfred Huntley Edgerton. His inner ears were flaming with desire. "And the winner is . . ." And then, all at once, the longed-for vowels were his, laying their soft blessing on his ravenous hopes. He pushed his chair back and clambered modestly to his feet; he had gone no more than two paces when he felt his coattails being vigorously pulled by Penny McGuire, hissing, "Sit down, you idiot." Resuming the seat of his banqueting chair, openmouthed, Tranter looked up toward the Literate Politician in time to see him hold out his hand to a flushed woman of a certain age, and in a moment of terrible clarity Tranter replayed the announcement in his mind and heard almost the same vowels form not the name of his subject, but of *Alfie the Humble Engine*, and gathered from the loud and standing ovation that Sally Higgs was the winner of the Pizza Palace Book of the Year prize and that the 400 people gathered in the Sir Francis Drake suite were mightily pleased for old Sally, a much-loved toiler in the garden of that humble genre, the children's picture book.

* * *

It was 10:30 by the time Gabriel and Jenni boarded the train back to Victoria, having eaten at the local Pizza Palace. It was either that or the Everest Nepalese, and they had had Indian the night before. Jenni insisted on paying, though since she drank water because she was driving the next day and Gabriel tactfully had only one glass of wine, it was not expensive.

Jenni was shocked by what she'd seen in Glendale, but was wary of upsetting Gabriel by asking him too much. He seemed very resigned, she thought. If this tragedy had come to her brother, she would have been outraged, appalled, distraught. It intrigued her that Gabriel could seem so detached.

"Don't you find it depressing?" she'd asked over her pizza.

"The institution? Yes, I do. But there are things that you can't understand in life. There are things where your sympathy, however passionate, is not going to make a difference. It's terribly frustrating because I feel that Adam, the Adam I knew, is still somewhere inside that body. Occasionally I catch a glimpse of him, but I can't reach him. And then he's gone again."

"I've never met anyone like him before. What was he like when . . . before it all happened?"

"Just a normal kid. He had a bit of a temper. He could be quite intense. But he was good at work, good at games. We had fun together."

"Was it just the two of you?"

"Yes. We grew up in a village in Hampshire. My father had a farm. He was the tenant at any rate. Then he entered into some crazy scheme to buy the farm and breed racehorses. It didn't work out. But it was all right. There was a good school in the town and a teacher there pushed me on toward university."

"Were you, like, a geek then?"

"No, Jenni, I was not a geek. I was just naturally brilliant."

"Oh yeah, tell me about it!"

"And you?"

"I grew up in a tower block in Leyton with my mum."

324

"Shit. As you would say."

"Yeah. But it wasn't that bad. I didn't know anything else. Mum was nice. It was OK till the lift broke down."

"What did you do for money?"

"Mum worked at the post-office sorting depot. I was left to myself."

"That's how you became so independent."

"I s'pose it is. I never thought of it like that. But with Adam . . . I'm just curious. Of course I knew there were people who were like, mad. But not, you know, ordinary people."

Gabriel finished the rough Italian wine. "That's the trouble with psychosis. It picks on ordinary people. One in a hundred. No other animal has it, so far as we know. When the horse stands alone in the field he doesn't hear the neighing of three horses who aren't there. He doesn't believe he's being hunted down by other horses. Actually, it's stronger than that. It's not a question of believing. Adam doesn't 'believe' that Axia and the gang are broadcasting his thoughts on Channel 7 at prime time. He *knows* they are."

"One in a hundred," said Jenni. "That's unbelievable."

"But true. No one wants to know. It's shameful, it's hard to take in. It's as though one in a hundred eagles was blind from birth. Or one in a hundred kangaroos had no hop. It's that weird."

"And why does no one want to know?" said Jenni. "I want to know. I care about Adam. And . . . you know, people like him."

Gabriel looked at Jenni. Her eyes were shining, with tears or with excitement or with indignation—he didn't know her well enough to say. There was something about this girl, though . . . She had touched a susceptibility very deep in him.

"I think it's just too shaming for humans to admit that we are basically fucked," he said. "Sorry, Jenni. Sorry about the language."

"I drive a train, Gabriel. I work with men. You can swear about it, you're allowed to be angry. Why are we fucked?"

"Genetically."

"Go on."

"Do you understand natural selection?"

"I think I was off school the week we did that one."

"It's like this. Species change because, as they breed, minute errors occur in cell duplication which give minor variations to the offspring. Usually the change dies with the individual. But once in a million times this tiny change gives the individual an advantage in his world, so he's favored in breeding. The change is passed on and becomes embedded. The species has evolved. To survive better than your competitors, you need only minute advantages. But some freak change happened in human ancestors. It was not microscopic, it was gigantic. We needed only to keep half a step ahead of other primates and carnivorous land mammals with strong incisors. But instead of that, we produced Shakespeare, Mozart, Newton, Einstein. We only needed a slightly more agile gibbon and we ended up with Sophocles. And the flip side of this colossal and totally unnecessary advantage was that the human genome was, to use our favorite technical term, fucked. It's unstable, it's flawed, because it's so ahead of itself. One in a hundred pays the price for everyone else to live their weirdly hyper-advanced lives. They're the scapegoats. Poor, poor bastards."

Jenni said, "So it's passed on, this problem? Schizophrenia. It's, like, hereditary?"

"Yes. Well, mostly. If one of your parents has it, you're much more likely to. It runs in families. But it's not completely hereditary. You have identical twins with identical genomes and one will develop the illness and the other one won't. So they figure there's something else too, what they call an 'environmental factor.'"

"So it's part hardwired and part not? That's really strange."

"I know. But this is what Adam's doctors have told me. Sometimes the wiring's such that you just get it. When your brain circuits finish growing and the last connection's made, that's it. You're psychotic. Others are delicately balanced. The circuitry's complete but it still needs a push."

"And what pushes it?"

"Drugs are the commonest cause. Skunk, acid, amphetamines.

LSD was actually synthesized in a lab by chemists asked by psychiatric researchers to come up with a drug that would induce temporary psychosis. So acid can work pretty well. Or alcohol. Or extreme stress, which can release similar chemicals in the brain."

"And the chemicals cause the electrical circuit to join up?" said Jenni.

"Pretty much."

"I guess it's like when they throw the switch on the Circle Line."

They didn't talk much on the train. Jenni was puzzling over what Gabriel had told her and was hoping that, however much she sympathized with Adam, the evening wouldn't make Gabriel forget about her. But he was looking out of the window, seemingly lost in his own thoughts.

"Tell me something from your childhood," said Jenni, determined not to let him drift away from her. "Tell me the best thing that happened. Maybe before Adam got ill."

Gabriel turned his head, rather wearily she thought, toward her. "The best thing? Well, I think we were happy most of the time. But I do remember once, a summer evening. A tiny thing, just a moment really. I suppose I wasn't a child, though, because I could drive a car. Maybe I was eighteen. I'd worked all summer to save up to buy this old deathtrap. It cost £200. I was working on a farm on the other side of the county. And I'd got up at seven on a Sunday to drive miles and play cricket somewhere and I'd persuaded this girl to come with me. She was someone I'd met at a party. She was so pretty, she was really out of my league. Luckily I was out first ball so I could sit and talk to her, so she didn't get too bored. And when we were fielding I was worried she'd just disappear. But she didn't. She stuck it out. And we all went to this pub afterward and drank beer, and I had this thought that I hadn't been home for a long time, a month or so, because I'd been working, and I telephoned from the pub and my mother said if I could get there

327

within the hour, she'd keep supper. And I knew there'd be all these fresh vegetables from the farm garden. And this girl said she'd like to come and although it was nearly nine it was still light. And I just remember driving down these narrow lanes with the windows open and the overpowering smell of hawthorn and cow parsley coming in and seeing the sun go down and driving a bit too fast and eventually I recognized where we were and told her to put the map away. And we arrived in the village and the headlights picked out all the moths and midges in the air. And nothing had happened. I hadn't even kissed her. And that was what was so wonderful. Everything was just beginning. Everything was in perfect equilibrium, it was unimprovable. My father was alive. Nothing had gone wrong."

Jenni smiled. "I can see that."

"And you?"

"When my father came back once and said he'd stay forever."

"But he didn't."

"No."

"How old were you?"

"Five."

Gabriel sighed. "I'm sorry."

At Victoria, Jenni said she would take the Circle Line to Paddington for Drayton Green.

"I'll see you home," said Gabriel. "It's late."

"Don't be daft. I'm not sixteen."

"I'd like to."

She barely hesitated. "All right, then."

They reached Cowper Road just before midnight and Gabriel said goodnight at the door.

"We never talked about your case, I'm afraid," he said.

With her key in the lock, Jenni turned back to face him. "Better fix another meeting," she said.

"Maybe tomorrow evening?" said Gabriel, forgetting he was due at the Toppings'.

"Whatever," said Jenni. Or at least that was what Gabriel thought she said, but it was hard to be certain because her lips were pressed against his as she spoke. He ran his hands down the back of her chain-store coat and pulled her toward him by the hips.

From the corner of his eye, he saw a man watching from the other side of the road. He put his lips to Jenni's ear. "Will you get Tony to come out here a second?"

"What's the matter? Is it that man again?"

"Ssh. Just get Tony."

While he waited, Gabriel tried not to let the other man see that he knew he was there. He stared at the closed front door, consulted his watch and stamped his feet in the cold, as though waiting for someone. Eventually, Tony put his head out.

"There's someone watching the house," said Gabriel. "Watching Jenni. Shall we get him? The man who was here last night."

"You bet. Let's go."

As they ran across the road, the man emerged from the shadows and took flight. There was enough of the 400-meter runner still left in Tony, however, and he scragged him at the corner of Dryden Avenue. Gabriel arrived a moment later and they shoved him up against a lamppost.

"What do you want?" said Tony.

"Nothing. I just—"

"What's your name?" said Gabriel.

"Jason."

"I thought so. It's not a game. Whatever your real name is. This is not a game. Miranda, the girl you want, she doesn't exist."

"I know."

"She's really an old man. She's not even a girl."

"Whatever."

"If you come round again, I'll knock your fucking head off," said Tony.

"Get back to reality," said Gabriel. "Get a fucking grip."

"I'm sorry. I promise I won't come back."

"You'd better fucking not," said Tony.

"Chuck out the game," said Gabriel. "Just bin it. Miranda's not real."

They let him go, and he ran off toward the station.

Tony and Gabriel walked back down Cowper Road.

"Why are you coming back?" said Tony.

"Just . . . I . . . Don't know really."

"You want to kiss my sister again, don't you?"

"Maybe," said Gabriel.

"All right, but you're not coming in, mate."

"I don't want to come in," said Gabriel. "I just want to kiss your sister one more time."

"Go on, then," said Tony, as he let himself into the house. "I'll send her out."

Seven

Saturday, December 22

I

During the morning, the cold weather disappeared from the capital. By 2:30, the matinee-goers in the stalls of the Theatre Royal, Haymarket, were fanning themselves with their programs; below them, in the tunnels of the Bakerloo Line, shoppers on their way from Charing Cross were pulling at the collars of their now unnecessary overcoats. Chefs in the Chinese restaurants of Queensway were driving their sleeves across their brows to keep the sweat from falling on the carrots they were dicing for the evening service; the mosaic tiles in the Regent's Park Mosque glistened with condensation and there was steam in the windows of the last bespoke tailor in Tulse Hill. In the department stores of Oxford Street, the atomized perfume spray hung static in the ground-floor fug, as people carrying folded coats pushed their way through the crowd, leaving piles of woolen scarves and gloves unbought, emblems of Christmas past.

At ten o'clock, Roger and Amanda Malpasse left their Chilterns house and set off for London and the Toppings' party. Amanda thought she could probably do all the shopping that remained and still have time to have her hair done before they went out. She had booked lunch at one in an Italian restaurant in Fulham Road; it was near their flat in Roland Gardens and had been run by the same people for twenty years.

Roger was reluctant to leave the country on a Saturday, as his routine was one to which he'd grown attached. An early dog walk, then an hour's vigorous gardening and a game of doubles on the all-weather tennis court of a village neighbor gave him a righteous thirst that beer, gin and tonic and a half bottle of white burgundy, in that order, exactly satisfied. In the afternoon, he liked to listen to the football commentary on the radio in the "snug" with his feet up on the sofa, some of the many dogs snoozing by the fire and the colorful nonsense of the newspapers spread about him. At about four, he closed his eyes; at five Amanda usually came in with tea.

Amanda, on the other hand, took every opportunity to visit London. In the redbrick mansion blocks off the Brompton and the Gloucester roads, in the boutiques and museums and cafés, she could still just recapture the lightness of her youth; she walked down Brechin Place and Drayton Gardens pretending to be twenty-three again. It wasn't difficult, because nothing much had changed there, and it wasn't too depressing because she wouldn't want all that passion and fatigue again. Not really.

"Just don't drink too much, Roger," she said, cracking a lunch-time breadstick and sipping her aperitif. "I don't want you getting pissed and making a scene at the Toppings' tonight."

"Would I ever?" said Roger.

At noon, the removal van arrived at Sophie Topping's house in North Park. They took out all the furniture from the first-floor sitting room, then brought in a series of tables long enough for thirty-four guests and set them up on the ground floor. The normal furniture would be stored overnight and returned the next day; Sophie was fairly sure it stayed in the back of the van, but so long as it came back safely didn't like to make a fuss.

It took her two hours to finalize who should sit where. She was always torn between the need to keep two people known to get on badly as far apart as possible and a mischievous desire to put them next to one another; the same applied to men and women known to have what Lance called "the hots" for one another. One way round this dilemma was to move people halfway through the evening, so they had both a hot and cold seat; but which was the better way

332

round? Prudence suggested that the hot seat should come first; then, at halftime, the man would move on, wrathful or aroused, and take his vigor with him . . . But Sophie wasn't feeling prudent: she was feeling proud of Lance, and playful and ambitious; so she did the placings with the cold seat first—to give the evening what she hoped would be a high-temperature finish. The footballer, Borowski, had telephoned only twenty-four hours earlier to say he was bringing his girlfriend, a Russian called Olya, which had caused Sophie a panic as she searched for a last-minute man. She had plumped for someone she'd met at a literary fund-raiser for talking books: Patrick Warrender, a seemingly civilized journalist. Shortly after securing Patrick, she'd had a call from Radley Graves, the schoolmaster, saying he had flu and wouldn't be able to make it. And this time she decided to let the numbers stay odd.

In all social matters, Sophie was motivated by a desire to win the competition with the other wives and mothers of North Park. It was an all-female, all-consuming endeavor; the husbands or partners were involved, but were not themselves participants. What the competition actually consisted of was unclear: there were no rules, no definitions of success and no prizes. In Sophie's mind, however, there was a virtual league table from which people were promoted and relegated. Money, naturally, played a part. Having the clear blue water of £10 million in cash (what the bonus-bankers called their "nuts") squirreled away was a sound start. Next came good looks, notably appearing younger than your age. Having brilliant or—since exam grade inflation had made it hard to discriminate between them—charming children was vital. Their number also counted in your favor: four or more showed confidence, an unruly sexual life and impressive organizational ability. Perhaps the single most valuable factor in Sophie's mythology was the appearance of your house. Again, it was more than size and value; it was to do with the degree to which visitors were impressed by its decor and atmosphere—by its veneers and surfaces. Sophie was fairly sure that while she and Lance were in no danger of relegation from the premier division, they were not exactly pushing for the top places either; a glance at the football tables on Lance's back page suggested they were a social Everton.

The objective success of Lance Topping in becoming the party's newest MP didn't count for very much. In North Park, politics was rated below banking, broking, business or even "creative" things, such as advertising. There was also the awkwardness of ostentation, of being too obviously in the spotlight, because this made it look as though you were trying too hard. The first rule of the competition was not to be seen to be competing; the second rule, so far as Sophie had worked it out, was not to be fat. There had been a chubby woman once, but she had moved—had to move, Sophie sometimes thought. As one who enjoyed three meals a day, not eating had been the toughest North Park discipline for Sophie to master. Most of the women she knew suffered low blood pressure, hypoglycemia, stomach cramps or gastroenteric disorders from having no lunch, no carbohydrates—but occasional cheesecake orgies. All of them thought it worthwhile, however, as their slimness belied their age, and in their own minds they edged a place or two up the fantasy league, displacing someone who had fallen prey to "bar mitzvah" arms, love handles or cellulite.

There were no fatties tonight, Sophie noticed, though Micky Wright, one of her singles repertory, had always been broad across the beam—ever since they'd met at school in Epping. Amanda Malpasse was like a breadstick, lucky thing. Gillian Foxley, the agent's wife, was plump and motherly, but she didn't really count because she wasn't local; ditto Brenda Dillon, who'd obviously spent too long in the House of Commons tea room. Vanessa, John Veals's wife, was irritatingly slim and good-looking. Cold, though, Sophie thought; she doubted Vanessa ever went facedown into a Pizza Palace family-size American with a two-liter bucket of Toffee Double Gush ice cream.

The thought of the evening ahead made Sophie Topping feel light-headed with apprehension. She decided to spend an hour in the gym before going to the hairdresser at two o'clock: that would still give her time before the caterers arrived at four and might calm her down a little. It was going to be a memorable night; of that alone in her competitive anxiety, Sophie felt convinced.

Vanessa Veals, far from thinking about food or competition, was wondering if she would ever see her only son again. A sword of guilt was driven up through her entrails as she sat by the orange and brown curtains, flicking through the out-of-date magazines in the reception area of Wakeley. It wouldn't have taken so very much courage, would it, to have gone up to Finn's room from time to time and have a talk with him? Suppose he'd been surly, and had made it uncomfortable for her. Suppose he'd been abusive and had hurt her feelings. Discomfort, hurt feelings . . . These would not have been much to put up with if it might have meant saving him from whatever psychiatric black hole had swallowed him.

She put down the plastic cup of tea on the table and gazed through the window, where some of the patients were walking aimlessly over the bare lawns. She had never been to a psychiatric hospital before and had the unreasonable idea that the patients were kept in pajamas. What could be the point of that, though, unless they were in bed all day, like physically sick people? Perhaps to make them conspicuous if they escaped.

Vanessa checked herself. "Escaped"? What sort of word was that to use of an institution that suddenly contained her son? She knew nothing of this world, she was gradually having to admit; she had even been slightly surprised that such places still existed, vaguely believing they had all been closed down by the government. When people heard that Finn was in Glendale Psychiatric, she would be blamed. It showed either some hereditary weakness, unstable ancestry, or was a damning verdict on her motherhood; it was a public shame as well as a private devastation.

"Mrs. Veals? I'm Dr. Leftrook. Sorry to keep you waiting. Would you like to come this way?"

Dr. Leftrook was a woman in her sixties with wiry gray hair; she reminded Vanessa of the old type of severe schoolteacher, possibly lesbian, with a hint of the arty in her John Lennon glasses and ecological sandals.

"Can I see Finn?" said Vanessa, taking the indicated chair.

Dr. Leftrook sat on the other side of a desk. "Yes, I don't see why not. But I expect you'd like to know what the problem is first."

"Thank you." Vanessa felt rebuked.

"Your son has something we are seeing increasingly often with young people. It's a disturbance caused by drugs—usually by genetically modified cannabis or 'skunk.' He's had a psychotic episode."

"What does that mean?" Vanessa felt her mouth go dry. It sounded terrible.

"Psychosis is the name we give to the serious illnesses, such as schizophrenia or bipolar disorder. It entails a more or less complete severance with reality."

"My God."

"What we don't know yet with your son is whether this will be a one-off episode, from which he should make a complete recovery, or whether it will be more serious and long-lasting."

"When will we know?"

"Over the next ten days or two weeks we'll get a good idea. I'm sorry I can't be more positive at the moment. We know that schizophrenia has a strong genetic component, but we also know that other factors can be involved. A very large number of schizophrenics are heavy cannabis users in their teens, but the profession is divided as to whether there is a causal link. It may well be that people with the schizophrenic makeup are just more likely to indulge in drugs and alcohol. They already feel less attached to reality, they're naturally careless of their health. In fact, that's the majority medical belief at the moment."

"And what do you think?"

"I would like to know if there are instances of serious mental illness in your family or your husband's."

"None that I know of. But my husband's family only goes back three generations. Before that I don't know."

"Well, that's helpful," said Dr. Leftrook. "That's a good sign. You may also hear people talk of something called 'cannabis psychosis.' I'd ignore that if I were you. It's not an established condition. But heavy use of the drug by teenagers is definitely very dangerous because their neurodevelopment is undergoing its final, infinitely subtle changes. It's like plunging a large spanner into those delicate works."

Vanessa put her head in her hands and began to cry.

Dr. Leftrook said nothing, for which Vanessa was grateful. Eventually, having taken a tissue from her bag and recomposed herself, she said, "You'd better tell me what's the worst thing that can happen."

"The worst is that your son has a schizophrenic inheritance and that his drug abuse has provided the catalyst to activate that inheritance. We can manage schizophrenic symptoms with modern drugs, but we can't cure the disease."

"Ever?"

"No. But some patients can live a reasonable life."

"That doesn't sound good."

"No."

"And what's the next worst?"

"That your son remains ill with psychotic symptoms which, while not strictly schizophrenic, are so similar as to make little difference. But if there's no genetic inheritance he may well recover completely."

"After how long?"

"A year, perhaps. Two years."

"And what's the best outcome?"

"The best hope is that your son has suffered a one-off psychotic episode and that with the right treatment and support from us and from his family, he will resume a full and healthy life within a matter of weeks."

"And which do you think is most likely?"

Dr. Leftrook paused and looked out of the window; Vanessa felt Finn's life hanging on the thread of her silence. "I think," the doctor said at last, "that he'll be all right. I think we'll have him out of here and back to you within six weeks. But that's not a promise and it's not a prediction. It's my best guess."

"But why has no one ever warned us of all this? Why have you people never—"

"Some of us have tried," said Dr. Leftrook. "But I think it's a case of the profession being a little too scientific, almost too precise. Until a causal link is established, it's only correct to assume it's absent and that the coincidence of high use with psychosis is exactly that, a coincidence, and so—"

"But for God's sake," said Vanessa. "Just some clear warnings, just some bloody common sense would have helped, wouldn't it? Surely when you've seen all that you've seen and all the stuff you've told me."

Dr. Leftrook stood up. "I have to admit, it hasn't been my profession's finest hour."

Vanessa was silent.

"Shall I take you to see him now?"

Pushing back her chair, Vanessa said, "Can I quickly telephone my husband first?"

"Of course. I'll wait in the lobby."

Outside Wakeley, on the tarmac beneath the cedar tree, Vanessa rang the house in Holland Park. "John? I've talked to the doctor and I'm going to go and see him now."

"Great. What did they say?"

"It's a bit long-winded. Basically, on balance, they think he's going to be OK. But—"

"That's great news."

"But they don't know yet because it's all a bit—"

"Darling, do you mind calling back a bit later? I'm expecting a call from Duffy in Zurich."

"All right, John. Goodbye."

Spike Borowski was also saying goodbye: to Olya, in their hotel suite. He told her he would not be back before 7:30, as he would need to spend time rehydrating, "warming down" and stretching with the physiotherapy team for at least two hours after the match. They'd leave at eight for dinner with the politician-man he'd met when his team turned on some Christmas lights.

"Look beautiful," he said.

"I try," said Olya, shaking her black hair, then pushing it back from her face. "I buy a new dress, yes?"

Spike drove his disappointingly small German car to the hotel where the team were assembling for an early carbohydrate lunch. Mehmet Kundak took him to one side over the fusilli with ham and cheese. "You start today, Spike," he said. "Play good."

This was the first time Spike had been asked to start a game and the first time he had played at home. The training ground with its offices and medical backup was the players' base; the stadium was for show, and for the fans. At two, the team coach parked flush against the main building, with security guards appearing at either end of the vehicle, so the players had to run a gauntlet of only two or three paces before they were inside, away from any taunts or missiles of the visiting supporters.

Spike was accompanied by Archie Lawler, the first-team coach.

"Not there, laddie," he said. "That's for the away team."

"It is nice," said Spike.

"Aye. Used to be a shitehole. Tiny room with only two showers. The new sports psychologist reckoned it was giving the visitors a goal start. Now they have heating, air con, the lot. And we've lost at home only once this season."

The home team dressing room was almost large enough for an eleven-a-side game. Russian death-metal music was pounding out of concealed speakers from Danny Bective's private collection. There were large chill cabinets with selections of sports drinks, and the extensive shower area was stuffed with shampoos, body lotions and conditioners of the same brand as those in Spike's five-star hotel bathroom. His own locker, handmade in walnut and ash, had hanging space, a socket for his personal music player, a lockable "bling box" for his jewelry and, unless his nostrils misled him, rose-scented air conditioning being blown gently from a grille in the rear panel. A new green and white shirt, number 39, hung on the outside with his surname curving over the number. Inside the locker were three new pairs of shorts and socks of slightly different sizes. Max the bootman had already laid out his preferred boots, with scarlet flashes, and had two reserve pairs in his bag.

Trying to look bored, as though all this was standard in Kraków, Spike did a few stretches and examined the studs of his boots. He waited till the others began to change, then put on his support shorts and cotton undervest beneath the man-made fabric of the club kit. This was the fourth professional club he had played for, but the thrill he experienced as he slid the green and white shirt over his head made him feel like a small boy: it was all he could do not to grin with glee. In tracksuits, they went out onto the pitch to warm up, and Spike went to the penalty area to hit some shots at Tomas Gunnarsson, the big blond goalkeeper, who caught them disdainfully in giant gloved paws.

At 2:40 they went back inside, where Mehmet Kundak came to join them. He pulled Danny Bective's music player out of the system and handed it back to him.

"We see the video yesterday," he said. "Now you play. Vlad and Spike, you get in those spaces I tell you. Stop the keeper rolling it out to those two guys. Yes? I want you, Sean, Danny, put a foot in straight off. Fucking let them know. OK? Any questions? You win. You fucking win. OK?"

It was not too technical for Spike. He'd been surprised at how much emphasis had been laid on his and Vlad's defensive duties—disrupting the other side's smooth distribution from the back. Almost nothing had been said about attack, but that, Archie had explained, was because all the teams from the Youths upward used the same essential movements, so that any of them could slot in at any time in the event of injury. Most of the moves were diagonal, played off the two small English pivots, Bective and Mills, in midfield.

At 2:50 they gathered in a circle with their arms round one another while the club captain Gavin Rossall, a bloodthirsty central defender, offered his final encouragement. Then they fell into line to leave the dressing room, with Spike being elbowed by one player after another until he took the only position in the order—eighth—not of superstitious value to someone else. They were on a purple carpet in the hallway when the opposition emerged. There were some halfhearted handshakes as they went downstairs, under the glass-roofed tunnel and up three rubberized asphalt steps into the "technical area," still below ground. The marked camber of the pitch at eye level made it look narrow for a moment, but as they climbed the last step and ran out onto the grass, Spike saw that it had been an illusion. To dispel his nerves he sprinted hard toward the penalty area, riding on the enormous wave of sound. He felt the need to remind himself that everything was normal, that it was just a game with a leather ball. He trotted over and put his arm round Vlad's shoulder.

"Is OK?"

To his relief Vlad didn't tell him to fuck off, but patted him reciprocally on the back, and Spike could see that Vlad, too, had felt the effects of the noise.

The referee, a paunchy little man in a tight shirt, blew his whistle and waved his hand; Spike wondered if his stubby legs would allow him to keep up. He himself scuttled back and forth for eight minutes before he had a pass—a slightly short one from the fullback he was happy to lay off without mishap. After twenty minutes or so, Spike, his shirt damp and his hair dripping, had received no useful pass despite having taken up positions at the far post, the near post, on the edge of the offside trap, in behind Vlad and, on two or three occasions, out wide. Bective and Mills seemed automatically to look to play the ball to one of the fullbacks on the overlap or to one of the wide players. The consolation for Spike was that Vlad had received an equally meager service. Then, finally, as one of the fullbacks escaped his opposite number and hit a long ball across, Spike was able to get above the Croatian defender who was marking him and meet it firmly with his forehead. The keeper, perhaps unnecessarily, palmed it over the bar for a corner; but the crowd roared its approval and Spike felt he had arrived at last in the English Premier League. A pat on the back from Gavin Rossall as he came up from the corner confirmed him in his belief.

Shortly before halftime, the opposition, who had been content to defend and hit occasional long balls hopefully to their front players, had a piece of good fortune. Ali al-Asraf was undone by a high punted clearance which slid off the top of his head, allowing the opposing center forward time to gather the ball, steady himself and guide it simply beneath the advancing Tomas Gunnarsson. Spike found the furious silence that greeted the goal more unnerving than the roar that had met the appearance of his own side.

At halftime he asked the manager if it was all right for him to come further back to find the ball.

"Yes, is OK if Vlad stays up," said Kundak, half tripping on the step going up to the pitch as his transitional lenses darkened.

The second half was a rerun of the first, with the home team increasingly frustrated by trying, at one end, to beat the offside trap and, at the other, to make sure the lone opposition striker didn't latch on to one of the many hopeful long-ball blasts from his beefy defenders. Spike sweated and panted. In his experience, the one thing that managers, coaches, commentators and supporters never understood was how extraordinarily draining a ninety-minute football match was for the players. He personally might cover 10,000 meters, with three quarters on the run and maybe a tenth at a sprint, as well as twisting, leaping, stretching and occasionally kicking the ball. In the second half he went deeper to find it, offering himself to the midfield when they were under pressure, and after an hour managed to work a ball through to Vlad, who was in the space between the center backs. As Spike took the return pass, he heard his name screeched by Danny Bective and pushed the ball into his path. Nothing he had seen in training had prepared him for the force of Bective's sidefooted shot inside the far post to make it 1–1.

The pace of the game became more frantic as they pushed on for the win. The visitors' Texan goalkeeper, however, seemed untroubled by the half dozen shots they managed to get on target. After eighty-one minutes, Spike saw his number, 39, being held up at the side of the pitch and trotted off to make way for Xavier, an aging Spaniard who had once been prolific in front of goal. Kundak patted him on the shoulder as he went off, and Kenny Hawtrey wrapped a thickly padded parka round his shoulders. He sat behind the manager and shouted for his team until the final whistle went for a 1–1 draw. It could have been worse.

At five o'clock, the football results were read out on the radio, but for once Finn didn't hear them. His own team had won, and the performance of the players in his fantasy eleven, including Spike's "assist," had been good enough to move the team a place or two up the imaginary league in which they played; but Finn was asleep, alone in a four-bed dormitory, where he was to stay until a bed came free in Collingwood, the young people's block.

Rob, the charge nurse, put his head round the door. It was dark in the room where Glenys, the junior staff nurse, had drawn the curtains and switched off the lights when Finn had gone upstairs earlier. Only a night light glowed blue in the skirting board as Rob went over the lino and sat down on the edge of the bed. He could hear Finn's breathing, as he sucked in long drafts of peaceful air. The longer he slept, the better it would be, Rob knew. It was heartbreaking sometimes to see them wake—to lose unconsciousness, the only happiness they knew.

Rob searched for a pulse in the wrist and checked it against his watch. Then he lifted the eyelid of the sleeping boy. All was well. He would listen for him in the night and if necessary give him enough sedation to get him through till morning. Then they could begin to have a look and see what needed to be done.

Poor kid, Rob thought. What on earth had his parents been thinking?

At six o'clock, Olya returned from a shopping trip to Sloane Street and started to run a bath in her hotel suite. She poured in three bottles of free gel to let them foam beneath the pounding water and plugged her music player into the sound system, where it played the "Best Of" Girls From Behind, her favorite band. She knew they were meant for younger kids, but she didn't care; and in any case, she was only just twenty herself.

Olya chucked her jeans and underwear onto the king-size bed and walked naked to the bathroom. It sometimes felt a little strange to take her clothes off without a photographer present. She instinctively felt herself flex and smile a little for the camera; she had put on three or four pounds since she'd been in London and thought it suited her. She would have liked to see how it might have looked in the hands of a good snapper—these slightly fuller hips and thighs. Olya had never understood why men wanted to photograph her. Her anatomy was no different from that of the other girls in her village, nor of those she'd met when she joined an agency. Everything was in the right place, and there was no extra fat on her, but more than that . . . It was merely youth, she had eventually concluded; it was no more than the fact (not much prized by the eighteen-year-old she then was) that she had no lines, no looseness, and that the legs and breasts, so ordinary to her, were, in the eye of the photographer, teeming with some sort of priceless vigor. She felt disappointed by this understanding, as though she had been sold short; and it had made her a little vain, she had to admit, as now she tried to convince herself that she was not just young but truly beautiful.

The important thing, meanwhile, was to keep hold of "Tad," as she called him. She had had lovers before him, but never a boyfriend. She had slept with her first boy when she was only fourteen and had later been persuaded it was necessary to oblige the head of the model agency and most of the photographers who had shot her. But Tadeusz Borowski was the first man who seemed to think it necessary to pursue her, as if she had the absolute power to reject him. They had met at a party in London, during the weekend he had been summoned from his French club for his medical; she was a hostess on behalf of the car company that was sponsoring the evening. He telephoned the next day, sent flowers and, when the club wanted to meet his wife/partner/girlfriend, he asked Olya if she would come along. Spike had thought the club wanted proof he wasn't gay; in fact, Mehmet Kundak just liked to check he was not taking on, through marriage, some prima donna like Sean Mills's endlessly tiresome Zhérie.

Olya, unaware of either the gay or the bitch issue, thought Spike already loved her. She dressed in a new coat, chic and restrained, and made sure that Mr. Kundak understood how devoted she was to her boyfriend. Her attitude, and Spike's enthusiastic gratitude after he had signed up, had kick-started their affair in passionate terms. Olya had not known that sex could be so enjoyable, or frequent. She had initially seen Tad as the next male rung in a longish ladder that would take her step by step from poverty in the Ukraine to some sort of comfortable life in a European capital. His gallantry confused her. She hardly knew what to do with his affection, or with the troublesome feelings it awakened in her.

She sang along with Lee and Pamilla and Lisa in the bath. She had no idea what was happening to her, but it was exciting. Who were these people whose house they were going to? An MP? What did that mean? What did it matter? Her Tad would look handsome and would have the best clothes, because she'd bought some for him that afternoon. And in case she felt shy because she didn't speak much English, there was a small bag of top-quality cocaine on the dressing table.

As Olya rose from her bath, Sophie Topping slipped into hers, careful to keep her newly washed and dried hair away from the water.

Sophie closed her eyes and pictured all of London under the winter sky. In her mind's eye, she focused on individual rooms throughout the capital where people were now starting to turn their thoughts to the evening ahead. John and Vanessa Veals in their stucco-fronted, pillared mansion, John probably on the phone to some market out of hours, Vanessa thin and alone, applying makeup in their giant bedroom ... Poor Clare Darnley, counting her money for the bus fare ... Gabriel Northwood in his chambers, surrounded by wigs and dust (she didn't know where he lived but pictured him always among the red-ribboned briefs) ... Simon Porterfield, grandly deflecting questions on the home phone from some impertinent journalist about the suicide on *It's Madness*, with Indira gazing on regally in a sari ... R. Tranter, emerging from some grim burrow the wrong side of the North Circular ... The al-Rashids, facing Mecca on their knees for a bit of Allah-bothering before calling up the chauffeur ... Richard Wilbraham, the Leader of the Opposition, perhaps just back from being an unlikely man-of-the-people for the press cameras at a football game ...

And all the babysitters, all the baths and showers; all the useless gifts of chocolates and candles and bath oils they were readying to bring her; all the blow-drys and the hairdos and the party dresses ... From Havering to Holland Park, from Forest Hill to Ferrers End, from Upminster to Parsons Green, the individuals would shortly leave their flats and houses, fragrant and hopeful, bang the doors, and go like invisible cells into the bloodstream of the city, whose heartbeat tonight was beyond all doubt in one place only: in the North Park home of the country's newest Member of Parliament.

Roger and Amanda Malpasse were almost ready to go. Roger was checking that the French doors onto the terrace were locked, while Amanda was settling two whippets and a pug in the kitchen of their flat in Roland Gardens. These three were her responsibility; the lurchers and the yellow Labrador—Scholes, Butt and Beckham, Roger's dogs—were too big for London and were left in the Chilterns under the vague supervision of a housekeeper.

"Time for a primer, darling?" said Roger, pouring himself some gin, adding a drop of bitters and, on reflection, a dribble of dry martini. He took it into the kitchen to fetch ice.

"Not for me, thanks," said Amanda.

"You sure? Just a pub one maybe?"

"No thanks. Do you like this dress?"

"Yes, lovely. Have you seen a lemon?"

In Roger's vocabulary, there were many different kinds of drink. A "primer" was a preparation for a social event, or ordeal. Essentially philanthropic, its aim was to render him benign, so that from the moment he arrived he could be a good guest. A "phlegm cracker" would be the first of the day, and not a serious one—a small glass of white wine, perhaps, left over from the night before, taken after mowing the huge lawn in the country. A "heart starter" performed the same function, but a shade more vigorously; it often entailed gin. A "sharpener" preceded food.

Roger's favorite drink was a "zonker," and his evenings at home would consist of two zonkers before dinner, then wine with. The zonker itself might be a champagne cocktail—a finger of three-star cognac, a lump of sugar, a single drop of bitters and a tumblerful of very cold biscuity champagne; or it might be a dry martini or a straightforward whisky with ice and soda. The zonker was the king of drinks; its opposite was the dismissive "just a pub one," which involved barely dampening the bottom of the glass.

"Do we know who's going to be there?" Roger said, taking his drink through to the sitting room, and checking his pockets to make sure he had his keys.

"It'll be a show-off do with the Wilbrahams and that education woman. What's her name?"

"Dillon. I'm missing the football."

"I'm sure you can record it, darling."

"Easy for you to say. Have you seen the zapper? Don't say Bumble's had it again."

"Plus the usual book-club people, I imagine," said Amanda. "I think Sophie will've pulled out all the stops. She'll try to impress Wilbraham and suggest that Lance is a natural for the shadow cabinet. He's very good on immigration and all that."

"Yes," said Roger, "but do you think we could ever really have a Home Secretary called 'Lance'?"

He patted the keys in his pocket again.

Amanda Malpasse, tightly slender in her green satin sheath, was staring out of the window at the street. She liked this time of day, when the traffic subsided and the restaurants and pubs had not yet filled. You could almost sense the capital breathe in and brace itself. This part of London had barely changed since she first glimpsed it on a daring weekend out from school in Hampshire. She and her friends had eaten hamburgers in the Fulham Road and drunk wine from straw-covered bottles. From where she stood at the tall window she could see two restaurants with swarthy waiters in red shirts who might have stepped out of the same decade. They were poised now for the evening's work: attentive, flirtatious, looking after racy couples no longer in the first exuberance of youth—men who'd clawed back just enough from a divorce to raise a glass to lined blond consorts: women with what Amanda's French friend Hélène called *"des heures de vol"*—hours of flight time, like just-serviceable airliners decommissioned by their European owner and bound for Air Congo.

With a sigh, Amanda turned back. They'd go home, these paired-off people, to a flat and then, and then . . . wake to a London morning, congratulate themselves on sex, on living, nose the car out of its slot in the residents' bay . . . None of them could know, in their routines, what she had known. Her youth. One day, it would come again.

"Come on, then, you bony old mare. Are you ready?"

"Yes, I'm ready," said Amanda. She was happy enough with Roger, really.

"Have we got an address for these crashers?"

"Yes, it's in my bag."

"Right-ho," said Roger. "Hang on, have you got the keys?"

They were still in his pocket, it transpired, and a few minutes later, as they drove up Gloucester Road, Roger said, "God, I can't believe it's almost the C-word again."

"I know," said Amanda. "I remember when I was five and we moved house. I thought Christmas would never come. There seemed to be about a decade between each batch of presents and reindeer. I did love it, though."

"Me too."

"Now it seems I barely have time to get the decorations up into the attic before it's time to get them out again. It seems to come round every three or four months."

"I know," said Roger, wistfully, as he slowed for a pedestrian crossing. "I think I preferred it when it was an annual event."

Roger always drove the car when they went out, on the grounds that Amanda would drive it back; this arrangement, while appearing to be a modern and equitable division of labor, enabled Roger to drink as much as he liked.

As they turned up Campden Hill Road, he said, "Right. Now fill me in. It's Lance and Sophie, isn't it? How do we know them?"

"Sophie," said Amanda, adjusting her makeup in the mirror of the sun visor, "I met at Judith's Christmas fund-raiser last year. She asked me to sit on the committee of the children's hospice thing. We met them both that night at the Simpsons'."

"Is she the one who looks like Mr. Gorbachev?"

"No, that's Elsa Thingy. Sophie's a bit plump, animated, tends to wear pink or turquoise. Always has a lot of bangles on."

"Oh, I know," said Roger, "the one with the Edward Heath vowels. I had an absolute basinful of her after dinner."

"Yes. And he—"

"I've seen him on television, haven't I? Earnest but a bit dim."

"Yes, he worked for Allied Royal for a long time. I don't think he was ever a high-flier, but he put away his ten million or whatever and then started some little 'boutique' fund with a friend."

"I see," said Roger. "And what have they got on the children front?"

At this moment, they had reached the foot of Ladbroke Grove where the traffic lights at the junction with Holland Park Avenue had a double phasing to allow right turns. As Roger maneuvered into the Grove, he found a bicyclist with no lights coming toward him through the box, going against not one but two red traffic signals, balancing his almost-static bicycle with smart pedal work as he forded through the twin stream of green-lit cars and lorries, then, as death brushed either shoulder, fishing a mobile phone from his pocket and initiating a call. While the traffic braked and swerved round him, he put both feet down so he could shake his spare fist more vehemently against them.

"Wouldn't it be easier for him just to throw himself under a Tube train?" said Roger. "Anyway, the Toppings' children."

"There's a boy who was supposed to be very brilliant and was going to Cambridge to read maths and philosophy, called Thomas, I think. And then it turned out he got a B in one of his A levels."

"Shit!" said Roger. "I didn't know you could still do that."

"Yes, I know," said Amanda. "So I think he's off somewhere else. And then there's a girl. I can't remember her name. Bella maybe."

"They mostly are. If in doubt, Bella."

"And then a nice little boy called Jacob or Jake."

"Any subjects I should steer clear of?" said Roger.

"Lance is thought to have had an affair with his secretary, so better not mention that."

"I thought politicians were allowed to do that."

"I don't think so," said Amanda, folding back the sun visor.

"But the Deputy Prime Minister, what's his name. He use to have her on the table, zip up, then chair the meeting. And that was considered absolutely fine."

"Was it?" said Amanda.

"I believe so. They didn't bat an eyelid. He didn't resign, didn't lose a week's pay, nothing. The PM said it was fine. Maybe it helped the fellow gather his thoughts. Such as they were."

They crossed the Harrow Road, and London came at them through the car window: the pavements and the shopfronts washed in gray by the color-flattening effect of the sodium street lamps, then a flash of muted red from the tire dealer and the universal yellow of the Chinese takeaway. The army-surplus supplier had gone from the corner after two decades, and in its place there was a white-goods showroom with a chilly cut-price display. Two used-furniture stores were unlit; the redbrick church was dark, though the poster for salvation was illuminated: God Said, I Shall Return.

The years of statistical "boom" had left no visible mark on the modest shopfronts or the long orderly terraces that ran up to Kensal Rise. It might have been the night the FTSE peaked or the day the early 1990s' recession touched its nadir; there was no way of knowing from tidy streets that hadn't really changed since 1945.

Or, as the Malpasses' car moved carefully over the cold black surface of the road, past the Golden Coin Laundromat, it might even have been the precise moment at which the final straw, laid twenty-four hours earlier by a nervy trader in New York, had broken the back of the world's banking system.

In Havering-atte-Bower, Hassan al-Rashid locked the door of his bedroom and fired up his computer. It was time for one last look through babesdelight.co.uk. He clicked on "Olya" and went to the final picture, number ten. He opened "Stegwriter" and double-clicked "Scan." The membrane displayed by Olya's separating fingertips was devoid of messages. It was just a young woman's flesh framed by white-painted fingernails. No word, and no chance of turning back now, Hassan thought.

He was surprised by his own response. Had he really hoped for a last-minute cancellation? He felt ashamed of the possibility. Surely his dedication to righteousness was strong. He did then what he always did when he thought he might waver: he thought less about eternal truth—the unprovable word of the invisible God—and

351

more about Iraq. Those British politicians who had invented an excuse to invade a Muslim land, sending back their own spies' professionally accurate report and telling them to rewrite it so it said what they wanted; then cutting and pasting a student essay from the Internet in the hope that it would give some spurious backing to their predecided course of action . . . Surely this was the most despicable deceit that even the West had yet descended to?

It made him almost sympathetic to the Americans. They had been so shaken by the Twin Towers that they no longer knew what they were doing. The country had had a nervous breakdown with the wrong man at the helm; their hapless president was an ex-drunk without a map and almost, it seemed, without an education. That was the American tragedy. But the British . . . They had been entitled to hope for better things. Their leaders had at first seemed better educated—though each had later been found out. In what seemed to Hassan a morality tale of almost crude simplicity, a fatal arrogance had convinced each that he was infallible, and neither had understood the lessons of history—neither the political lesson, in the case of former Mesopotamia, nor, as it now turned out, the financial one, when they had boasted that they alone in history had tamed the market. And then to justify their invasion of Iraq, they had just lied and, knowingly, lied and lied.

Remembering this, Hassan felt stronger again—strong enough to let his eyes linger on the rest of the page of babesdelight. After all, he was allowed to "look": the book said so. And he would see no more women's bodies now until he entered paradise.

He stared with valedictory affection at the green eyes of a girl who looked back over her shoulder as she stood on a step outside a barn and thrust her rear toward the lens. Her hair had that shine of recent shampoo and her eyes a friendly look, neither cowed nor anxious; the round swell of her right buttock, not model-thin but healthily plump, had minute red dots in one place, as though she might have received a friendly smack or kept on a wet swimsuit a minute too long. In another shot she held her breasts up to the camera, smiling, as a peasant girl might hold up apples from her father's orchard at market. He would miss girls, he thought, whatever the nature of the afterlife the Prophet had promised him.

Surely, though, the promises that God had made through the Angel Gabriel and whispered in the Prophet's ear, the assurances of paradise, would take into account all that he must forgo. It was written. "God will not deny the faithful their reward."

Hassan clicked shut the window, selected "Wipe Personal History" (not that it much mattered now) from the drop-down menu and turned off the computer.

His parents had left for the Toppings' dinner party.

He called a minicab to take him to Upminster station. "Aye, twenty minutes'll do just fine."

While he waited, he flicked through an old copy of *The Toad*.

II

Gabriel Northwood emerged from the Tube and looked at the local map near the station exit. As he walked the three blocks to the Toppings' house, he could see the other guests converge by car. The al-Rashids' chutney-colored limousine drew up outside the front door and double-parked, hazard lights blinking, while Joe held the door for his employers. The Vealses' four-wheel-drive off-roader just beat Spike Borowski to the best remaining parking place on the other side of the street. Impoverished Clare Darnley had arrived half an hour early by one of the six articulated buses she'd found waiting empty, throbbing, pumping fumes into the air of Shepherd's Bush.

On the hall table inside, Gabriel saw the pile of unwanted offerings that would be recycled through Sophie's compendious "present drawer." Spike Borowski had brought the only thing that would be used: a football signed by his teammates for Jake, the Toppings' eleven-year-old son.

Gabriel followed a caterer upstairs to the sitting room. To his relief, he remembered Sophie Topping when she greeted him with a kiss on the cheek. Her skin snagged a fraction on his as she withdrew, and he wished he hadn't economized on razor blades.

A tray of fizzing flutes was offered to him and he took one, holding it by the base.

"Now then," said Sophie. "You're not to talk to Nasim because you're sitting next to her at dinner. Clare Darnley's on your other side, so you're not to talk to her either . . ."

Allowing himself to be led by the arm, Gabriel caught the elbow of a waiter and hungrily took a classy-looking canapé; only as he swallowed did he recognize it as raw fish. Something about Gabriel's appearance made other people talkative. He had never understood what it was, but women stood close and confided in him; men prodded him in the chest as they explained their triumphs. Both sexes seemed anxious to inform him, to keep him in some all-important loop. Perhaps there was something in his eyes, he thought misanthropically, that they mistook for sympathy.

He overheard, at that moment, a man with a face like a fox terrier and a reedy voice: "It's hard to know which is more baffling, the sales or the critical acclaim."

A pace or two away from him was an exuberant, paunchy fellow in his forties, saying: "In six months Digitime is going to offer you the complete service—television, broadband—the whole kit and caboodle. We won't just be a program maker but a full service provider. We've gone into business with an ISP and one of the old franchise holders. You'll be able to tailor-make your own package through opt-ins, then vary it online each month at no extra cost . . ."

Despite the nature of what he was saying, Gabriel thought, the man sounded like a wing commander from an old war film.

A demure woman in a gray woolen dress squared up to him: "So, will I still get the BBC?"

"Of course, if you opt in," said the wing co. "But not as a default."

A regal, brown-skinned woman, Indian probably, interrupted:

"What Simon isn't telling you—are you, darling?—is that the only free programs, the only defaults in his packages, are pornography he's bought from Richard Branson."

The demure woman: "So if I don't upgrade my package, I can only get pornography?"

The wing co: "Public service broadcasting—all those gorillas, heritage and news analysis stuff—that's increasingly niche. So you would expect to pay for that, yes."

"So it's a porn package," said the woman, growing steely, "with respectable add-ons as options?"

"We already have a ten percent market share," said the wing co—or the television magnate Simon Porterfield, as Gabriel now deduced him to be. "À la carte viewing is the future of tele—"

"But it's just a porn package," said the woman, "which I—"

"Not *just* that. The starter pack, which is only a few pennies a month, includes all our big hit shows for Channel 7. *It's Madness*, for instance, which is pulling six million viewers on 7 even as we speak . . ."

"But that's a catastrophe," said the woman. "It's a disgusting program and somebody took his life on it two days ago."

"It's far from catastrophic," said Simon Porterfield. "It's more or less single-handedly kept Channel 7 afloat."

"Better to have let it sink. And what about this poor man who killed himself?"

"It was very unfortunate, I admit. But I think in the long term, in the history of television it'll be remembered as . . ." Simon Porterfield looked round for a moment, as though searching for the perfect word, then beamed in triumph, like a retriever dropping a prized bird at its master's feet. "Iconic," he said.

Gabriel moved on past a small man with unblinking eyes and shiny skin, whom he had overheard being introduced as John Veals: "Yes, we dropped six bar on that one but we'd made it up by the end of the week. That's life."

"Bar?"

"Million."

"Million?"

"Yes. U.K."

"Isn't that rather a lot?"

"It's not nothing. But this is not the fucking soft-toy business."

And behind him, in the window, was an eager-to-please man Gabriel recognized as the Leader of the Opposition. He was leaning toward a slender woman in a green sheath dress: "That's exactly right," he was saying. "What we have to fight against is the low expectation of so many parents. It's no good just getting little Johnny . . . or, er . . . Joanna—"

"Or Wazir."

"Especially not Wazir, no use getting *any* of them through with half a dozen meaningless exam passes. We have to raise the bar. Raise the standards all round . . ."

The removal of all the furniture meant the guests could move freely without falling over chairs and tables, but unfortunately the empty room had developed an echo that made it difficult for people to hear unless they bellowed or stood close.

Gabriel noticed a small man with a dandruffy collar he thought he had heard introduced as "Len" leaning close to make himself heard. He saw the Indian princess, presumably Mrs. Porterfield, politely lower her head toward him, then recoil.

Olya was holding tight to Spike's arm. Spike stood with his back to the fireplace, in which a superfluous log fire raged. He wore a new white shirt, designer jeans and expensive black suede trainers. He looked younger than the other guests, exotic, aglow with vascular well-being and recent sex. His lightly gelled hair, black and curly, and his unmarked dermis made the others look old and defeated, their eyes red from staring at computer screens, their skin shining only from applications of expensive snake oil, said to rejuvenate.

Spike was talking to Roger Malpasse, who was in some difficulty—fascinated by what Spike could tell him about the Premier League, but unable to keep his eyes from Olya, so much of whom was revealed by her sleeveless, almost (it seemed to Roger) top-less, yet at the same time curiously demure dress in deep red satin.

"This thin person is your wife?" said Spike, pointing toward Amanda in her emerald sheath.

"Yes, yes, that's her all right. So, now, what do you reckon? Man United. Think you'll beat them?"

Roger had had a crafty second primer (technically almost a zonker) before leaving home, and he felt bold.

"Man U is a very good football team," said Spike. "I learn much when young from the celebrated quartet—Beckham the stylish icon, Keane, the Hibernian man of war, Scholes in the hole and Giggs, the wizard of dribble."

Roger laughed. "Me too. I have some dogs at home called after them. Well Beckham, Scholes and Butt anyway. Butt's a lurcher."

A frozen egg-timer appeared above the links of interbabel.com in Spike's mind. Lurcher? Lurch: *v* stumble, walk unsteadily . . .

"Why you call your dog Butt?" said Spike.

"Because I didn't want to call him And," laughed Roger Mal-passe. "No, no, just kidding. Should've called the bugger Rooney. Bloody ugly enough."

"I think you like dogs?" Spike said.

"Oh yes. We have six. Amanda's got two whippets and a pug. We've brought them to London."

Whip it? Pug? . . . This was impossible. "I like dogs," said Spike. "My bitch is in doghouse waiting to come into England. She is four years old. Bernese Mountain bitch."

"Ah I see," said Roger. "Thought you meant . . . Careful now. I see the other half making her way over."

Spike glanced over to where Amanda was coming to talk to them.

"Other half . . . What? I see. Very beautiful person."

"Yes, that's no dog," said Roger, on a roll. "That's my wife."

"Tad," said Olya. "There is man over there who is looking at me in strange way."

"Which one?"

357

Olya pointed.

"Who is that man?" said Spike.

"That one?" said Roger. "That's John Veals. The hedge-fund manager. He looks at everyone in a strange way. I wouldn't let it worry you. Look, here come the drinks again."

Patrick Warrender arrived late, and, after having made his apologies to Sophie, went in search of R. Tranter, whom he found quite easy to detach from a group that included John Veals.

"I've got something for you, Ralph." Patrick took his elbow and guided him through the door and onto the landing, where he withdrew an envelope from his inside pocket. "I hope you'll like it. Open it now if you want."

"What is it?" Tranter's first response was to fear that he was being fired from his never-ratified position as a reviewer for Patrick's newspaper.

Patrick smiled. "Go on. It won't bite. Open it. I had Arabella on the Sunday paper type it up this afternoon. I went in specially."

With his hands shaking a little, Tranter ripped open the envelope. It appeared to be an offer of work: a formal monthly retainer for his services. His eyes went rapidly down the page till they snagged on the crucial detail: £25,000 a year.

He tried to conceal his amazement. "Looks fine. Thanks. But why now? I wasn't expecting anything. I was happy with the arrangement we had."

"I know," said Patrick. "I just thought it might make up for your disappointment with the Pizza Topping thing."

"Pizza Palace, you mean."

"Pizza Whatever." Patrick laughed. "I seem to have elided two evenings there. You'll see that we're offering to pay you monthly in return for three reviews a month. If there aren't three suitable books, you just keep the money. If for some reason you do more, then you're paid pro rata."

"Sounds fine."

"Just one thing, Ralph." Patrick was walking round the landing with his hands behind his back, like a headmaster explaining something to a favored pupil. "From now on, you can only write about the nineteenth century."

"What?" Tranter was suspicious again.

"No more stuff about today." Patrick coughed. "It's not really your thing, is it? But biographies, letters, poetry, travel, anything from long before you were born, that should be all right, shouldn't it? I mean, be honest, Ralph, the work of your contemporaries is . . . It's an affliction to you, isn't it?"

Tranter looked down. He had the strange feeling that his life had reached a turning point. What was even odder, he thought, was that he should be aware of it as it was happening; normally such things were clear only in retrospect. But he was light-headed with relief and financial exhilaration: £47,500 a year had fallen into his lap in little more than thirty-six hours. Who cared about the Pizza Palace anymore? The giddiness tempted him into honesty. This was not a response he knew well, so he trod carefully.

"Well," he said. "I, er . . . I think you may be right." He stopped to see if the ceiling would fall in or if Patrick would laugh, but nothing happened. Tranter felt emboldened to go further. "The truth is," he said, "I can't bear contemporary stuff. Excuse me a moment. I just need to get some air."

Tranter went abruptly downstairs to the hall, down again to the kitchen, bypassing a number of caterers hard at work, then opened the French doors onto the patio, where the chef was having a cigarette, and went past him onto the lawn.

He sat down on a knee-high brick border wall at the end of the garden, struggling with his turbulent emotions. Almost £50,000 a year to live only in the nineteenth century . . . What joy, what fun, what larks! Perhaps he'd get another cat, some company for Septimus. He'd go on holiday, he'd accept that trip they'd offered him, to lecture on a cruise ship in the Baltic. "Trollope: the Writers' Writer"; "Alfred Huntley Edgerton: The Unknown Victorian."

No more Sedley, no more Oirish Twaddle, no more the poor man's Somerset Maugham with his embarrassing improbabilities at key moments. No more the higher bogus, Pym and water, the busted flush and the woman who wrote by numbers . . . From now on, just Browning and Thackeray and Edgerton, George Gissing and dear old William Harrison Ainsworth.

He kicked the last of the autumn's leaves with the toe of his brown shoe and dashed his sleeve across his damp cheek. In a minute, he'd go back inside and face all those sneery people with the fire of forty-five grand in his belly.

Upstairs, Nasim al-Rashid was talking to someone called Mark Loader. He was under the impression that she had recently arrived from the other side of the world, and she hadn't the heart to tell him she was from Bradford.

"And do you like it here?" he said, looking candidly over her shoulder for someone more interesting.

"In London?"

"Yes."

"We haven't been here long. But yes, I do."

"Very big. Crowded," Loader said, his eyes still roving in search of a native. "Many people in London," he added loudly.

"Yes indeed. But we live just outside town. At Havering-atte-Bower."

"Where's that?"

"On the way to Ipswich," said Nasim.

"Oh, I see," said Mark Loader.

"Are you a politician, too?" said Nasim. "Like Lance?"

"God, no."

Since Loader offered no more, Nasim continued. "So what is it you do?"

"I'm a mathematician." The way he pronounced it made it sound like "methemetician." He seemed very pleased by his calling.

Nasim smiled. "I used to love maths at school. It was my favorite subject. Where do you teach?"

"I don't *teach*." Loader looked as though he'd been accused of a minor but disgusting offense. "I run a fund."

"What are you raising money for?"

Loader's face creased with impatience, then relaxed, as though he had decided to give the wetback one more chance. "To be precise," he said, "I run a fund of funds."

"A fund of . . . ?"

"I've been very lucky." Loader took a passing canapé and focused briefly on Nasim. "I worked for an old mate in a hedge fund for some years. I did the heavy lifting. The analysis. Then we had an offer we couldn't really refuse from one of the American banks. So we sold it. Johnny's still a consultant. So I sort of retired." Mark Loader took a sip of his drink. "But I was only thirty-six. And after a couple of years, I got rather bored. You know. Had the Georgian rectory, swimming pool, blah blah."

"So what did you do?" said Nasim.

"Well, me and a couple of mates started a fund. Or to be precise, a fund of funds. You know, some people think hedge funds lose their touch after a short while. Style drift. So you want to keep moving. Even the best hedgie can't really cover all the bases. So it's quite usual to have money in a fund of several different funds. It's an obvious way of maximizing your profit. Keeping fresh."

"I see," said Nasim.

"It's just a little thing," said Loader. "Very few investors. But it keeps me out of mischief. I do a couple of days a week on it. I've been awfully lucky."

Gabriel was standing next to them. He introduced himself.

"Oh dear," he said, when Nasim told him who she was. "Sophie told me I was not to talk to you because I'm sitting next to you at dinner."

Nasim smiled. "Perhaps you should talk to Mr. Loader, then. He was telling me that he runs a fund of funds."

"Really?" said Gabriel. "What's that?"

"I'm just going to have a word with our host," said Loader. "Excuse me."

"It's a way of keeping fresh," said Nasim. "Of avoiding style drift. Do you have money in a fund of funds?"

361

"I keep all my wealth there," said Gabriel. "Mad not to. But I'm thinking of moving it to a fund of funds of funds."

Loader lingered for a moment as Sophie Topping joined them. "You can laugh as much as you like," Loader said. "But if you were in work between 1986 and 2006 and you failed to bank fifty million, then your children are going to wonder whether you bothered to get out of bed. There's never been a time like it and there never will be again. Even al-Qaeda couldn't derail it. Look over there. That's Jamie 'Dobbo' McPherson. He was at school with me. Left with two exam passes, and one of those was in woodwork. Even Dobbo made it in the end. God knows, we thought he'd never manage it. But finally, finally, he flogged his share in Café Bravo, then made a pile in commercial property. Christ, he even made money backing *films* for heaven's sake! He's made north of a hundred million. And if *you* haven't, your children and grandchildren are going to want to know why."

"Is it too late now?" said Gabriel.

But Loader had gone. Gabriel put his empty glass back on a tray and, taking a fresh one with him, slid from the room and went downstairs to look for a way outside. He needed air. He was also very hungry, and the raw fish had not sat well on his empty stomach. At the back of the house, he pushed open a door onto what appeared to be a study. There was a wall full of photographs of Lance Topping, taken over many years, shaking hands with famous people. Here was Lance with a fierce economist, once tipped as party leader, now teaching in the University of the Third Age; Lance with the then party leader, latterly delusional in a care home; Lance with a former Chancellor who'd lost his seat and turned to writing detective stories. Among them all, Lance was now the only serving MP.

Gabriel felt that he had wandered into a world he didn't understand. People like Mark Loader and, in his different way, Lance Topping were playing by different rules. And somehow money had become the only thing that mattered. When had this happened? When had educated people stopped looking down on money and its acquisition? When had the civilized man stopped viewing money as a means to various enjoyable ends and started to view it as the end itself? When had respectable people given themselves over full-time to counting zeroes? And, when this defining moment came, why had nobody bloody well told him?

Next to the desk was a glass door that gave onto a small balcony. Gabriel undid the security locks at top and bottom and let himself out. He lit a cigarette, sucked in the smoke and swilled down some cold champagne. He saw a man sitting on a low raised brick wall at the end of the garden, all alone.

Without thinking, Gabriel took out his mobile phone and wrote a text message to Jenni. "Stuck at party. Tossers. Meet tmw? Still important aspects of case 2 discuss . . . G x."

Having pressed "Send," he felt dizzy. Perhaps it was the unaccustomed nicotine—there was hardly anywhere you could smoke these days and he didn't allow himself cigarettes at home. Or maybe it was just that the whole world had tilted and he was out of kilter with it, doomed to feel forever seasick. Was Jenni the answer? At least she seemed real. She seemed grounded, earthed. He smiled: almost all the ways in which he thought of her seemed to evoke trains or electricity. But something about that girl filled him with a sense of urgency—with a desire to live that he hadn't known before.

He could hear a steady, fulsome braying from upstairs. "There was a sound of revelry by night . . ." he thought.

Byron. "The Eve of Waterloo." The words brought back with almost painful clarity the feel of a book, *Poetry Worth Remembering*, the yellow cloth on his eleven-year-old fingers, the schoolroom on a hot afternoon and his striving to force the words into his memory.

"Sir. Excuse me."

The caterer was in the study staring out at Gabriel on the small balcony with the look of a sympathetic police officer about to run in an old lag, but who, almost regretful that the long pursuit is over, has decided to give him a few more minutes at large.

"Dinner is served, sir."

Gabriel ground out his cigarette. The man was waiting, and watching him.

"It's OK, Super." Gabriel could imagine him speaking into his lapel. *"Chummy's not going to give us any trouble this time."*

He came quietly. Out in the hall, he saw women picking their way carefully downstairs in high heels and going across into the brightly lit dining room.

"If anyone needs the toilet," called out Sophie, "it's down at the end of the hall."

There was a tailback on the stairs as the guests went down to dinner, and John Veals found himself standing next to a tall, debonair man in a chocolate-colored corduroy suit with a purple tie.

"Hello," he said, holding out his hand. "Patrick Warrender."

"John Veals."

"I saw you just having a word with one of my star reviewers in there. Ralph Tranter."

"Yes," said Veals. He paused. "Vindictive little cunt, isn't he?"

Patrick coughed. "That's rather a quick summing-up."

"It's what I do," said Veals. "Sum things up. And I see you don't deny it."

"Well it's fair to say that Ralph may have a slight problem with the . . . er, the contemporary," said Patrick.

"Christ, you can say that again," said Veals. "If he was a chocolate drop he'd fucking eat himself. Even in my business . . ."

But Veals didn't complete the sentence, as Patrick had slipped through a gap on the stair below and made his escape.

The cleared rooms opened onto one another through an arch, where once there had been a wall. A long table ran under it, swathed in floor-length white linen with clusters of candles and bowls of cut flowers at intervals. Sophie's voice scraped against the hubbub as she ordered her dilatory guests to their places. A second, much less sympathetic caterer hovered by her elbow; this man was not so much deserving plod as supercilious schools inspector, who watched more in sorrow than in anger as the head-mistress struggled with her charges.

The shrill insincerity of the conversation was acting like a drug. No one wanted to sit down for fear it showed that they were not entranced by what was being bellowed at them. Almost all the guests had overcome strong competition in their fields of work, proving keener, greedier or more obdurate, so none would yield in the game of conspicuous gaiety.

Gabriel pulled back the hired banqueting chair for Nasim (it reminded him with a brief stab of the one he'd sat on when he first met Catalina), and introduced himself to the woman on his right, Clare Darnley, who'd been the one confronting Simon Porterfield about his new TV package.

"You gave him a good going-over, I thought," said Gabriel. "You should be in my job. You'd be good with witnesses."

Clare didn't seem amused. "But do you ever watch this stuff? It's absolutely appalling. Posh people think it's chic to say they like it. You sound like a snob if you say what you really think."

"But you're not afraid to?"

"God, no," said Clare. "Someone has to tell the truth. This kind of television is the vicious exploitation of stupid ignorant people by cruel rich shits. It's a disgrace to our society."

Gabriel bit his lip. "You should write a newspaper column."

"That's the second job you've offered me. Do you work for an employment agency in your spare time?"

"No, I do the crossword and read poetry. But I'm beginning to think that not enough clues have been devised and not enough lines of verse written to fill the deserts of vast eternity that make up my spare time."

"Marvell," said Clare.

"Yes."

"Why've you got so much spare time?"

"Because I have so few cases."

"And why do—"

"I don't know. I'm not fashionable. My chambers are not fashionable. No one apart from the head of chambers has much work. And one other person, a commercial silk."

"It can't be just that."

"No, I think you're right. I think there's something deeper. I think that solicitors sensed my lack of enthusiasm. But that's changing. I think I've turned the corner. I've already got four cases booked in next year. I have a case coming up in the Court of Appeal in January and I think it's going to change everything."

"And did you vote for Lance in the by-election?" said Clare.

"No. I don't live in his constituency."

"Neither does Lance."

"Anyway, I don't know what he believes in," said Gabriel. "I always think of him as someone who could be in any party. He probably chose the wrong club to join at university. The flip of a coin. I think he just wants to be in power. He wants to run things."

"Well, perhaps his day will come. He's certainly trying his socks off with Mrs. Wilbraham."

"I hope it comes soon. For his sake."

"White wine or red, sir?" The schools inspector was leaning over his shoulder, his eye taking in the half-eaten salad, the messily torn slice of walnut bread.

"Red, please," said Gabriel. He thought it was time he spoke to the woman on his left, Nasim al-Rashid. The subject moved naturally from why she had no wineglass to the question of religion.

"Are you very devout?" said Gabriel.

Nasim smiled. "Not really. My family wasn't at all religious. I was just an ordinary Yorkshire girl. Knocker—my husband—his family's very religious. So is he. And my son, too. He used to sing and recite in the mosque, until he discovered politics. Now I think he's coming back to Islam."

"Are you happy about that?"

"Of course."

Nasim didn't look happy, though. Gabriel watched her knitted brow, her big brown cloudy eyes. She was a fine-looking woman, he thought, though somehow she seemed sad—marginalized, perhaps, as though she felt her life was one of watching others, not participating.

"Anyway," he said. "The Koran's a funny book, isn't it? I mean, not farcical, but odd."

"Funny peculiar, you mean," said Nasim.

"Yes. It's so unstructured."

"He wrote it down as it was revealed to him."

"I know. By the Angel Gabriel. But my namesake didn't have much narrative discipline. It kind of just comes at you, doesn't it? There's so weirdly little story. Just assertion."

"More red wine, sir? The next course is lamb."

"Yes. Still red, thank you."

Gabriel felt his school being marked down as "problematic" by the inspector, who allowed him a bare half glass more of Lance Topping's burgundy.

Gabriel turned back to Clare, but she was dealing with a man on her right; Nasim's attention was switched to her left, so Gabriel was given a few minutes' respite. His hearing was unusually acute, and even in the noisy dining room he could tune briefly in and out of many conversations.

Magnus Darke was leaning across to Richard Wilbraham. "So what sort of limit might you set on immigration?"

Wilbraham smiled uneasily. "I assume that Chatham House rules apply tonight?"

Darke shrugged and looked pained, as though his honor had been doubted. "Just a rough figure."

Sophie Topping: "Don't be naughty, Magnus."

Wilbraham: "Well, you have to understand that seventy-five percent of births in London last year were to mothers who were not themselves born in this country."

Indira Porterfield: "Speaking as someone also not born in—"

Spike Borowski: "You want beautiful football, you cannot make team from all English players."

Olya: "Yes, Tadeusz is paying much taxes."

367

Roger: "Yes, I'd love some more. Lance, where d'you get this burgundy?"

No one was prepared to listen; and a look of quiet relief came over Richard Wilbraham's face as the clamor of received ideas made it impossible for Darke to pursue his questioning.

In the rear carriage of a westbound District Line train, Hassan al-Rashid was sitting with a packed nylon rucksack on the floor between his feet. He wore a navy blue woolen hat, anorak, jeans and climbing boots with thick socks underneath. He had shaved in order to look less threatening and he held his right hand firmly in his left. What could that hand desire, he thought, that he gripped it so tight?

Now that the end was approaching, now that he had actually put himself on rails toward his destination, he felt calmer. The train would carry him to Waterloo, and then a second train would take him on to Glendale, where the others would be waiting. They'd be excited, he imagined; they'd punch each other on the shoulder, touch flesh and reassure, like rugby men before a game. He was looking forward to seeing his friends. It was a fine thing they were doing: a clean deed in a foul, befuddled world.

He clung to the words of the Koran that promised eternal life to all martyrs for the simple reason that the words of the Hadiths, the collections of traditional wisdom from the Prophet's life, were considerably less comforting. They made no bones at all about the fact that suicide was a sin and that the sinner would be doomed to repeat the act forever in the afterlife. Hassan tried not to think about the Hadiths.

In order to attract no suspicious glances, he stared straight ahead, though not too fiercely. He tried to look tired without being zonked; unwilling to engage with others but only because that was the way of the city. Above all, he tried to look unconcerned. He was sure his clothes must help: everyday, anonymous, but clean and of decent quality, chosen for their ability to make a curious glance bounce off them. He was Mr. Londoner personified, a transient in a private daze whose every pore said, Leave me to my own small world, my virtual life: respect, and don't come near.

The train went so fast. Who was driving this thing? They were already out of Essex and rattling through the old East End—Stepney, Bow, Mile End, once the cockney, now the Muslim, heartland. Hassan breathed in tightly as he thought of the narrow streets above his head with the halal grocers and the market barrows, loan sharks and hijab drapers. Could they form the hard-core base, the foundation, of a second caliphate? Would they be strong enough?

This driver was pitiless. Why such a rush? On, on, now into the financial world at Monument—then Cannon Street and Mansion House where the *kafirs* worked at fever pitch twelve hours a day, shouting into telephones, hoping by their frantic betting to transfer some coins from one fund to another . . . Woe betide every backbiting slanderer who amasses riches and sedulously hoards them, thinking his wealth will render him immortal! By no means! He shall be flung to the Destroying Flame . . .

For three years at college, Hassan had changed train onto the Northern Line at Embankment, but a glance at the *A to Z* told him the best stop for Waterloo Bridge was Temple, a pleasant station with flower sellers outside and the river just across the road. Salim had told them not to enter Waterloo by Tube as the mainline stations had too many CCTV cameras.

Ready to walk the final ten minutes of his journey, Hassan passed his Oyster card across the reader, replaced it in his pocket, though he'd have no further use for it, and emerged into the night.

John Veals was not enjoying the Toppings' dinner party. He spent most of the main course sending and receiving text messages from Kieran Duffy, holding his phone beneath the tablecloth. It had always vexed him that the New York and London markets were closed at the Christian weekend. How many traders were bloody Christians anyway?

He was also made edgy by the presence of Magnus Darke. This

Darke was not a financial specialist; his column was a general current-affairs commentary with two or three different items and he could quite simply be squared away by being given a second, more reliable, piece of information by Ryman in due course. His article had been pretty well phrased and had done Darke no lasting damage. It still made Veals uneasy, though, to see this man across the table. As he pushed the lamb and ratatouille to the edge of his plate, he felt a dyspeptic unease, and it would last, he knew from experience, until the trade was successfully completed. But why the fuck would Lance Topping invite such a grimy little hack? Was Lance trying to wind him up?

As if this was not enough to spoil his dinner, there was the further irritation of the Russian bimbo. When he first saw her across the room, Veals found he had given an automatic nod of acknowledgment; but no such answering gesture came from the girl. She looked at him as though they'd never met, raising an eyebrow that seemed to question his motives for even looking at her.

It had taken twenty minutes of memory ransacking before Veals suddenly saw that he was searching the wrong disk. This girl was from another world. She wasn't real; she was a screen fantasy, a laptop dancer. Fuck me, he thought. He'd never quite believed that such women lived and breathed and had existence. She was younger than she looked with no clothes on and considerably more three-dimensional. Had she put on weight? he wondered. It rather suited her. It was bad enough that Lance Topping had invited Magnus Darke, bringing worlds of rumor, lies and abstract prices into painful collision with what was tangible; but to have plucked this digitally pixelated tart from cyberspace and animated her to spite him . . . He couldn't tear his thoughts from the shape of her slightly-too-large breasts, which were as well known to him as the backs of his own hands.

Veals looked back below the tablecloth to the safety of his phone's illuminated screen.

*   *   *

Sophie Topping leaned back in her chair and let them all scrap it out. There did seem to be a gratifying roar of conversation. Magnus Darke had given up on Richard Wilbraham and now seemed to be locked in some intimate exchange with Amanda Malpasse. Roger couldn't take his eyes off Olya's cleavage. Farooq al-Rashid, genially exuberant on fizzy water, was making a good fist of being interested by Brenda Dillon's plans for failed comprehensives. R. Tranter was telling a baffled Gillian Foxley about the novels of Walter Allen.

John Veals, she noticed, was surreptitiously looking at his phone beneath the table. Like Roger, he seemed fascinated by Olya, though not necessarily in the same way. Simon Porterfield was hitting on Jennifer Loader, not something Sophie had ever seen attempted before. Perhaps Simon was interested to meet someone who had almost as much money as he did. Not that Jennifer alone could match him, but if you put her income along with her husband Mark's . . . They weren't known as the Loadeds for nothing. Mark had offered to fund a new wing for a gallery in the city of his birth, and when they had demurred he said he'd also buy them a starter collection of paintings to put in it.

It was a funny thing, Sophie thought, how everyone you met these days seemed not just to be wealthy but insanely, ineffably, immeasurably rich. Hundreds of millions of useless pounds slopping out of their accounts and into hedge funds and private-equity companies who could no longer find anything worth buying with it. She used to think Lance was rich on his salary and bonus, a couple of million a year; but now she looked at him and knew for sure that by comparison he was a failure: relatively, they were almost broke. It didn't bother her particularly. They had enough for this lifetime and half a dozen more, and it was good not to lose touch with your constituents, many of whom, she knew for a fact, did their household sums in thousands.

Sophie Topping, born Sally Jackman in Epping forty-two years earlier, had never imagined as a diligent, contented child going to the local primary school that life would turn out so bizarre—in England of all places. Her father had been an RAF wireless operator and her mother a hairdresser; when the old fellow died and his debts were paid off, it turned out he had left his wife £28,000. Mrs. Jackman had a small building society account, no mortgage, the state pension, few expenses, and it was enough. She did the occasional cut and blow-dry for pocket money, about £50 a week, visiting the houses of friends and neighbors. It all worked out fine. Sally had done well at school and left at seventeen to work as a secretary in the City, where five years later she'd changed her name to Sophie after meeting Lance, who was struggling in the public relations department of a stuffy bank and trying to get on his party's list of candidates.

Looking down the table at her guests now, Sophie tried to calculate their worth. The Loadeds: countless; hundreds of millions of pounds. The Porterfields: said to be more than a billion. The al-Rashids: tens of millions. Dobbo McPherson: "north of a hundred million," she'd heard Mark Loader say. Jimmy Samuel, the debt packager and seller-on: likewise, north of a hundred. The Margessons, the teenager-website couple: certainly tens of millions. John and Vanessa Veals: billions in the fund. But apart from Farooq al-Rashid, who'd shifted tons of limes from the groves of Mexico and Iran via the steaming vats of Renfrew down the gullets of the masses and thence into the sewers underground, none of them had engaged with anything that actually existed.

Gabriel Northwood and Clare Darnley, on the other hand: zero. They didn't do their sums in thousands, perhaps not even in hundreds. They were in negative-equity land; and the contrast with the others was this: a billion or bugger all.

The other thing that perplexed Sophie was that, with the exception of the al-Rashids and Spike Borowski, she hadn't deliberately sought out rich people as her guests. All the others, the mills, the multis, the bills and the trills, were people she had met—a simple cross-section—at the school gates over the last ten years in North Park.

Sophie pushed her chair back with a squeal and clapped her hands. It was time to move people round.

III

Adam Northwood was standing alone in a dark corridor of Wakeley.

Alone was not how he felt himself to be, however. Three voices spoke to him loudly: Axia, the Disaster Maker and the Scissor Girl.

His own voice was audible as he debated with them, though the only person there to hear it was Violet, who kept her vigil by the darkened window of the dining room, looking out over the lawns.

More than six feet tall, handsome once, now run to fat round the belly, stooped and unkempt, Adam saw himself as the leader of Wakeley, its chosen and most senior inhabitant. With his beard and shaggy hair, he might have been a prophet.

On him fell the responsibility of making sure the building did not burn. By touching every third tile in the hallway, he might placate Axia and spare the fire this time; but a failure to count precisely, or a failure to touch would most assuredly signal the end.

With a heavy step, he began his task, the sound of the Scissor Girl so loud in his ears that it was hard to concentrate. And the names she called him . . . the things she said . . . She imputed to him desires so disgusting he barely understood what she meant . . . Where did she get these things from? Not from him, that was for certain, because he'd never even heard of half the things she talked about, let alone told her about them . . .

Earlier that day he'd thought for a second about Gabriel, his younger brother. He wondered how he was doing at school and why he never came to visit. Perhaps he was busy on the farm.

Axia's voice was now louder than the Scissor Girl's. "I destroyed the generations before them and I will destroy you in the same way," said Axia. "The fire is your home. Believe me and follow what I say or you will surely burn. I will cut off their heads, I will cut off the tips of their fingers."

373

Adam breathed in tightly as the volume rose. It was always hard to concentrate, and sometimes he thought his counting the tiles just infuriated Axia and made him shout more loudly.

He was halfway down the passage, where it widened out into the dining room. The cacophony in his head made it hard to think a thought.

Oh, if only he could go round himself, go round his brain and turn off the noises one by one, then he might concentrate long enough to hold a single thought, pure and soothing to his mind. Then he might stop the Scissor Girl from plucking out his thoughts and broadcasting them so all the people in the dayroom saw them on the television, even his worst thoughts about women.

Seventy-nine, eighty . . . He had almost reached the doorway of the dining room, almost done his duty for the night. But Axia was angry with him. "I have power over all things and if anyone denies it he is lying and I will make him burn for all time."

At one end of the corridor was the entrance hall, dark now except for a bar of light that came from under the night porter's door. At the other end, in the bowels of Wakeley, was the closed door of the dayroom, emptied now for the night, the television having been switched off at 10:30.

In between stood Adam, roaring to keep out the sound of Axia and the Disaster Maker as they shouted their cataclysmic warnings in his ears; and beside him now, in the silence she had kept for twenty years, was Violet with her bent arm still raised in greeting or farewell as her eyes gazed over the dark and empty lawns.

Moving people round the long table at the Toppings' had been almost too successful, to judge by the liveliness of the conversations that ensued.

Roger Malpasse was shifted so that he was no longer distracted by Olya and no longer within football-chat distance of Spike. The schools inspector had made a special friend of Roger, hovering at his elbow through the evening and diligently replenishing his glass. Roger had promised himself to drink no more than three glasses, but since the level had never dipped below halfway he could technically say he was still on his first. But whatever the exact volume of wine that sat on top of the double-zonker base and half a bottle of champagne before dinner, it filled him with exuberance and geniality.

He now found himself opposite John Veals, whom he knew slightly through old corporate connections from his time in the law.

"Well, John. How much more of these bank problems, do you think?"

Veals looked up from his screen. "A lot. I think all the American banks are in trouble."

"Why?"

"You have a pile of shit—these bundles of CDOs that are starting to default. Banks have sold them round the world, so everyone's infected. They've also sold them to hedge funds they themselves manage. That's what Bear Stearns has done. But Merrill Lynch is clearing Bear's trades for those funds. Merrill doesn't like what it sees. So it makes a margin call on Bear's hedge funds. Bear hasn't a clue what the thing's worth anyway, because it seldom actually trades. Like your house. It's worth what someone will pay and you only need one buyer. But they're leveraged ten times over and Merrill's telling them it's worth only 75 cents on the dollar. So without their ten percent equity Bear's now at minus 15. They're fucked. Mind you, so's Merrill."

"So they're all going to go broke? All those big shiny American investment banks?"

"I shouldn't wonder. There seems to be a trillion-dollar hole."

"At least a trillion," said Roger. "Thanks. Just a half glass. Thanks."

"But John," said Sophie, "where's all the money gone?"

"It's gone into John Veals's back pocket," said Roger.

"The money doesn't exist," said Veals.

"It existed until you trousered it," said Roger genially.

"Fuck off," said Veals. "You don't know what you're talking about."

A spasm passed over Roger Malpasse's face as he drained his

glass of burgundy; it was like a very dark cloud, the only one in the sky, going across a midsummer sun. "As a matter of fact," Roger said, "I do. You forget that I was a partner at Oswald Payne for twenty years. One of my colleagues—a guy in the capital markets or finance group, I forget which—he was responsible for helping you people design these absurd products, CDOs and so on, in a way that was at least nominally legal."

"Congratulations," said Veals.

"What happened," said Roger, "is that investment banks and hedge funds created ever more arcane instruments which they could flog to one another in a completely false market. Because it was over the counter, in private, the regulator couldn't see it. Then they could sell an inverted iceberg of bets on the likelihood of the original instruments defaulting. They were able to account a notional profit on the balance sheet on all this Alice in Wonderland crap and so pay themselves gargantuan bonuses."

Other conversations along the table were dying out as people began to sense drama or blood.

Veals smiled thinly. "I'm afraid it's rather more complicated than that."

"Do you know what?" said Roger. "It really isn't. It's a fraud as old as markets themselves. The only difference is that it's been done on a titanic scale. At the invitation of the politicians. Behind the backs of the regulators and with the dumb connivance of the auditors. And with the fatal misunderstanding of the ratings agencies."

"That's a cute story," said Veals. "But financial life is more—"

"No, it isn't," said Roger, his voice growing louder. "Do you know how high a million dollars in $100 bills would come up off the table, tightly packed? I'll tell you. Four and a half inches. And do you know how far a trillion reaches?"

"Yes. I can work it out." John Veals paused only for a moment. The whole table was now watching and listening as his fabled mental arithmetic went to work. "Seventy-one miles."

"Correct," said Roger. "That's how much has been misappro-

376

priated or mislaid. And all of it will have to be paid back before the world can move on. Every inch of the tightly packed seventy-one miles. Over a period of—how long would you say? Five years? Ten? And it won't be paid back by people like you, John, you or the bankers, because I don't suppose you pay tax, do you?"

"I pay what I'm legally required to pay."

"I think we can take that as a no," said Roger. "And the misdemeanors of the bankers will be paid for by millions of people in the real economy losing their jobs. And in paper money, the trillion will be repaid in higher tax on people who have no responsibility for its disappearance. And the little tossers in the investment banks who've put away their two and three and four million in bonuses each year over ten years . . . They'll hang on to it all. And they of course will be the only ones who won't pay back a coin. Which is bloody odd when you come to think of it. Because really they ought to be in prison."

"That's enough, Roger," said Amanda.

"Why, darling?" said Roger, sitting back in his chair, rather red in the face. "Is there something fundamentally wrong with that analysis?"

Jenni Fortune was on the last circle of her evening shift. All day long she had thought of him and wondered why he hadn't telephoned or texted her. Perhaps he went to dinner with all his clients, then invited them to his flat and took them to see his brother in hospital on their second date . . . Perhaps he kissed them all on the doorstep, then came back shamelessly for more . . .

There had to be an explanation; she was not prepared to abandon trust in him. Not yet. People were busy, even on a Saturday. There was perhaps a football match he had promised to take some kid to . . . There was tidying up his flat . . . No, there wasn't that, obviously. But there must have been a trip to the launderette at least.

She would just have to concentrate on driving, going round and round. It seemed such a disappointment, the dirty black of the tunnels, the same old names of the stations, the circles of hell, when only a day ago everything had been lit with hope and possibility.

Then, as she handed the keys to the next driver and went wearily upstairs to the canteen, lonely Jenni, back where she'd begun a week ago, her mobile phone was able to receive a signal and bleeped twice in her pocket. Her hand was shaking as she pulled it out.

She flushed with pleasure as she read Gabriel's text. But she should punish him. She ought to make him wait, play hard to get. She should . . . Oh, what the hell, she thought. I love him.

IV

Once up on Waterloo Bridge, Hassan began to walk south. Halfway across the river, he came to a halt with a strange, panicky feeling: there was no sign of Waterloo station on the other side. He stopped and tried to regain his bearings. Behind him, he remembered a huge building with a courtyard. He thought it was Somerset House. Ahead, he could see a cluster of equally large buildings in a brutal modernist style, but he didn't know what they were. Theaters, galleries? He looked, in vain, for the arched roof of a railway station. It wasn't there.

He didn't know whether to go on or turn back; he had no way of orientating himself. Then he remembered how this had happened to him once before, when the GPO Tower appeared to be in the wrong place. His mother had told him it was because he had been too long without food and his blood-sugar levels had crashed; this led to mental confusion and could be dangerous, Nasim had read, because he might faint and his brain could be damaged by lack of oxygen. She insisted that he see a doctor, who told him it was called "hypoglycemia" and could be cured at once by a simple bar of chocolate. It was true he'd eaten nothing today since a piece of toast with his parents at about nine—more than twelve hours ago. But how could you lose an international mainline station, however low your blood sugar? How could it just disappear?

Hassan found sweat on his upper lip despite the increasing cold of the night. His hands were both shaking now, though whether from fear or from hypoglycemia he didn't know. Then he had an idea. His rucksack had a compass sewn into the top flap; it was part of the kit. He knelt down on the pavement and fumblingly undid it. If it showed north behind him and south ahead, across the bridge, then surely all he needed to do was carry on.

When he had finally obtained a reading, it told him he was heading southeast. Yet surely the Thames ran west–east, so he could only be going north or south across it. The compass had simply made things worse.

Someone was coming toward him on the footpath of the bridge and Hassan decided to ask him the way. But as he came closer, it was clear that the man was plugged into loud music from his earpiece and couldn't be distracted. A woman was crossing the other way, but she was talking into a mobile phone and didn't see Hassan when he waved at her.

Above the almost freezing Thames, Hassan stood, trying to persuade a passing Londoner—anyone—to engage with him.

A strange memory came to him in his light-headedness. Waterloo station was not at the foot of Waterloo Bridge; perplexingly, it was at the foot of Westminster Bridge. No. That was irrational, impossible. And anyway, when he looked upstream there was a rattling railway bridge—Hungerford, was it—not the stately Westminster. Where now was Westminster Bridge? Had that gone too? Or maybe the Thames took a sudden turn and ran north–south at this point, in which case he should be going . . . east?

Oh God, he thought, oh God. I mustn't lose it now. He muttered a prayer, then turned back for human help.

Five people he tried to stop on the bridge; five times he moved forward and tried to intercept these passing strangers, and five times he found them wrapped up in private music or talking into hands-free microphones concealed in their coats.

They were talking to the air. All were listening to voices, talking back, but there were no people. His was the only real voice on the bridge, but the only one to whom no one would listen.

He couldn't give up now. He couldn't stop. What he had to do was somehow to make the world hear—not the profane nonsense of rap and rock, not the garbage of *kafir* phone calls, but the truth and beauty of another voice: the words of the unseen God, spoken to the Prophet almost 1,400 years ago. Those were the words that must reverberate in the ears of the people on the bridge, and in the ears of all the world.

At that moment a bicycle with no lights on shot past him along the pavement, making him leap to one side.

Hassan stood back against the parapet of the bridge, with his heart hammering his ribs in a huge lumping rhythm. Shit. He had thought for a second he was going to die.

His body wouldn't return to normal; he couldn't get a rhythm back. It was hard to breathe.

Then he leaned forward on the stone parapet and put his head between his hands. Where was it? Where was the voice, the voice of God that the Prophet had heard in the desert? This was the voice of the truth, the world's salvation. This was what he must die for. What he must kill for. For that disembodied voice only and not for any other, he must go to the station, go to the hospital and kill.

It was all so fantastically, so risibly, improbable.

Hassan hoisted himself onto the parapet so he could see down into the icy darkness of the river below, the oily surface sweating black.

He thought of his mother Nasim's earnest face leaning over his bed, and of his father's dear worried eyes with those little specks of pigment under them.

His heart was still pounding from where the unlit bicyclist had brought him face-to-face with reality.

And as he moaned like a wolf in a trap, a strange thing began to happen in his mind. He found that his pumping heart began to slow, and as it brought him back from the edge of death, his moaning began to soften; and in the bellows of his chest it mutated slowly into something deep and uncontrolled and wholly unexpected that felt like—that in fact turned out to be—laughter.

380

Hassan knelt on all fours and laughed; then he rolled onto his side and hunched up in a ball to try to bring relief to his airless lungs.

When he could stand again and could breathe unimpeded, he slowly unhitched his rucksack and lowered it onto the paving stone. He thought carefully before the next movement. With deliberation, unhurried, he hoisted the bag onto the parapet.

He stood back and looked both ways to be sure that no one was watching. Then, with both hands, he gave the rucksack an unequivocal shove. A moment later, he heard it splash into the Thames and pictured it as it sank into the dark, forgiving water. No explosion disturbed the current.

Then he turned back, pulled his own mobile phone from his pocket and scrolled down the stored names till he found the one he wanted. "Hello?"

Not long after midnight, the first guests began drifting away from the Toppings' house in North Park. Nasim and Knocker went out to where Joe was waiting for them.

Nasim put her hand on her husband's in the backseat. "That was fun, wasn't it?"

"Marvelous," said Knocker. "But I wouldn't want to do it every day."

"I promise I won't make you."

"Who was that man who was so drunk?"

"Roger Somebody. I thought he was funny," said Nasim.

Knocker sighed as he watched the terraces go by. "We've had a big two days, haven't we? You know what, I'm glad I didn't have to talk to Prince Charles about books. I felt confused at the time. I think I made a fool of myself. But I don't care."

"I thought you said the Prince was nice."

"He was. I expect he knew I was nervous. But when you come to think of it, I suppose it was a pretty crazy idea that I was ever going to have a conversation with anyone about books. Let alone the Queen."

Nasim laughed. "I did wonder," she said. "But you seemed so set on it."

She kissed him on the cheek as the limousine turned left and started its journey toward Havering.

Conversation was still continuing at Sophie Topping's table, but the heat was going out of it.

Vanessa thought the moment right to go upstairs to the now empty sitting room, where she checked her mobile phone. There was a message for her, as she had requested, with an update from the hospital. It said, "F is asleep and peaceful. A bed free in Collingwood tomorrow. No cause for concern. Regards Rob."

Tears stung Vanessa's eyes as she slipped the mobile back into her bag. There were going to be changes at home. Such big changes.

Roger slumped into the passenger seat and struggled to fit the seat-belt tongue into its slot. Amanda had already moved the car to the junction and made a sober turn into the traffic.

"Blast this thing," said Roger. "Sorry, I got a bit carried away with old Veals in there. I know I promised not to—"

"Don't worry, darling." Amanda's thin face broke into a smile as they stopped at a traffic light. "To be honest, I was rather proud of you."

Downstairs in the detritus of dinner, Mark Loader was explaining to Olya why it was necessary to pay several million pounds a year to certain derivative traders. If you didn't pay millions, he told her, you wouldn't attract the best talent. When he had started his speech, there had been a wider audience; but as he continued to expound his theory, they seemed to drift away, one by one, leaving only Olya in the end to listen, openmouthed.

R. Tranter had still not given up hope of persuading Brenda Dillon that the winner of the Café Bravo was a fraud; Mr. Dillon was standing up, jangling the keys at his waistband in a meaningful way.

Patrick Warrender had pulled his chair up next to Gabriel and was wondering if he ever fancied writing the odd article or book review on legal topics.

382

Gabriel wasn't sure if Patrick's interest in him was strictly business, but didn't like to seem unfriendly. "I might do," he said.

"I heard you talking to Ralph Tranter earlier," said Patrick, "and I could tell you were pretty well read. Perhaps you'd like to have a bite of lunch one day?"

"Never one to say no to free food," said Gabriel, wondering how free it would be.

"Do bring your wife . . . or . . . Did you bring . . . someone? Tonight?"

"No, I came alone."

"Splendid!" said Patrick. "I'll get your number off Sophie and give you a ring next week."

"That would be great," said Gabriel. What the hell, he thought. It would be fun to write the occasional article; as for the other, he could let Patrick down gently.

When he had said his goodbyes, he remembered that he had turned off his mobile phone to stop it ringing during dinner. He fished it out of his pocket and found that it said "1 message received." "Come for dinner tmw at one. I will cook. Bring booze. Not driving Mon. Tony out all day. J x."

It was far too late to text back, in case Jenni hadn't put her phone to Silent when she went to bed, but in his delight Gabriel couldn't resist. One word was all it needed anyway, so he risked it: "Heaven." He was startled when a few moments later, just before he reached the Tube station, his phone buzzed back and told him: "X."

"Hello," said Hassan again. "Hello?" Don't say there was no bloody signal. "Hello? Is that Shahla? Can you hear me? OK. Great. Look. I'm sorry to ring so late . . . I was wondering if . . . I was wondering if I could possibly come round. What? Yes. Now. I'm really sorry, I wouldn't ask unless . . . You are kind. I really appreciate it. No, no don't go to any trouble. OK. See you in a bit."

He had £100 emergency money from Husam Nar and £40 of his own, so a taxi fare was not a problem. He crossed the river and hailed a black cab at the roundabout.

Hassan sat back and sighed. Now that the laughter had passed, he felt shaken and empty. He had betrayed a cause and left three men exposed to danger. There was in practical terms nothing they could do without the fuses and the primer; presumably when they had waited long enough, they would simply ditch their rucksacks, separate and go home. He himself would be in some difficulties with MYC and Husam Nar; he would have to give solemn undertakings of secrecy to Salim. Two things worked in his favor, however. Many young men went through periods of activism and training without ever engaging in positive action; the organizations were practiced in dealing with them: they knew how to retain their interest for possible future use or how to debrief, deactivate and disown them. The second thing was that the system of cutouts was so well arranged that he knew nothing of value: no names or addresses or personal details of any kind that could be passed on. The "pub" would be relet at once to an immigrant family. As for "Salim," he didn't even know if that was his real name, any more than "Alfie" or "Grey_Rider."

The taxi went down Albert Embankment, and Hassan looked out at the lights along the Thames. He was not a soldier, he was not a jihadi or a terrorist or whatever term people might use. But was he still a believer? Had he failed even in that? It was too soon to say. His thoughts were too turbulent for him to be able to take stock of what he now thought. But something had happened on that bridge. Something more than the shock of almost being knocked down by a speeding cyclist . . . Something profound and real at that moment had changed in him, had shifted on its axis; and it was never going back.

Down Wandsworth Road the taxi went rapidly through a sequence of green lights, making Hassan worry that Shahla wouldn't have time to prepare herself; she had sounded confused by sleep when she answered the phone. Now they were outside her house, his taxi the only noise, ticking and throbbing in the narrow street. He paid the driver and watched him disappear before touching Shahla's bell. He heard her on the stairs, coming down to the front door, then saw the anxiety in her face under the 60-watt hall bulb in its paper lantern shade.

He was shaking—with cold, he thought—as he sat down in her living room. Shahla lit the gas fire, then went to the kitchen and returned with two cups of tea. He was in the armchair, and she sat on the edge of the coffee table so that her knees, at the end of those long thighs, were against his.

She was wearing pajama bottoms, a college sweatshirt and what Hassan was fairly sure were skiing socks. Her long, dark hair was tousled from her bed and she smelled slightly of toothpaste as she leaned forward and said, "So what's all this about, Hass?"

He smiled sheepishly. "I'm not sure I know where to begin."

"Try."

"I think I may have been . . . misled."

"Go on."

"It's so kind of you to let me come round like this and—"

"Don't worry about all that now. Just tell me. Misled. How?"

Hassan breathed in tightly. "It's very difficult in life to know what's valuable, what's lasting. Even to know what's real."

Shahla nodded. A slight smile broke through her solicitous expression, reminding Hassan of how much more she always seemed to know than he did.

Slowly, Hassan put together a few words that seemed to come close to what he meant. "Maybe I was not as lonely as I thought. There must be lots of other people like me who feel . . . different. Who feel they don't belong."

"There were people who cared for you. Always."

Hassan nodded, dumbly.

"Your parents."

"I know. I know now. My mother . . . She came to my room."

"And others . . ." said Shahla.

"But it was so glorious, so pure. It was such a beautiful thing. People who have never believed can never know the joy of it. The shining, burning joy of it."

Shahla was holding his hands in hers, but she said nothing, merely gazed at his face.

"And I . . . I was happy for the first time in my life. I had discovered who I was. And now . . . and now."

Tears erupted from him and he fell forward on his knees. Shahla knelt down with him on the floor and wrapped her arms round him. He sobbed against her shoulder, wetting her sweatshirt with mucus and tears while her long black hair covered his head. After a minute or so, when his sobs were subsiding, she lessened her grip, but he was reluctant to let her go.

At last she succeeded in disengaging herself, and he lifted his head, shamefaced. "I'm so sorry, I—"

"Shh. Stay there." Shahla left the room and came back a minute later in a clean sweater with a box of tissues. "There. I'll make some more tea."

When she had put the cups down, she said, "You're going to be all right, Hassan. Did you know that? Everything's going to be all right."

He nodded. He inhaled and seemed about to speak—then to abandon what he was going to say, as though it was too difficult.

"Go on," said Shahla. "Say it."

"Do you . . . Do you know what I feel for you, Shahla?"

"No, I don't, Hass. I never have."

"I think that all along I have had these feelings for you that I couldn't allow myself to admit. All the time we've spent together. As friends. The jokes, the fun we've had. I think I always loved you. Really. Now I know I do. But I can't in the space of one day go from one life to another."

For a moment, Hassan felt weightless with relief at what he had said; but when he looked at Shahla's face, he felt desperate again—desperate with anxiety that he had said the wrong thing and in so doing had forfeited any chance he had.

He was in the armchair, and she was on the edge of the table, looking down, so he couldn't see her expression.

When she finally lifted her head, Hassan saw his future written in her smile.

"My beautiful boy," she said, "I've been in love with you for three years. I can wait another day."

"Oh my God," he whispered.

She took his hands between her own again. "*Il n'y a qu'une vie, c'est donc qu'elle est parfaite.*"

"What did you say?"

"It's from a poet called Éluard."

"Your Ph.D. man."

"Yes. It means very roughly, 'There is only one life; it is therefore perfect.' The key word is '*donc.*' It doesn't exactly mean 'therefore,' it's less assertive. It means 'and so.' It means: it's obvious, it's natural."

Hassan nodded. "'There is only one life; it is therefore perfect.' Yes, I like that. I think I like that. Can I kiss you, Shahla?"

"I think you should. There are no nuns in Islam, Hassan. In Islam, there is no virtue in chastity."

"Thank you," he said a minute later. "I liked that, too."

Shahla stood up, tall, her flowing black hair lit from behind by the light of the fire. She looked, to Hassan's clouded eyes, magnificent.

"And one day," she said, her face flushed and shining, "you'll tell me in your own words just what on earth has been going on."

V

In the car on the way back from North Park, Vanessa made a call on her mobile phone.

"What are you doing?" said John. "It's ten past one."

Vanessa ignored him. "Hello, Sarah? I'm sorry to call you so late at night. Is it all right if we come and collect Bella? Yes, now. No, there's nothing wrong. I just want her at home. What? Yes. We'll be there in about ten minutes. Thank you."

They bundled the sleepy child into the back of the car and then, when they got home, John, on Vanessa's instructions, accompanied her up to her room. She barely stirred as he closed the door behind her.

"There are going to be no more sleepovers for the time being," said Vanessa, when Veals joined her in their bedroom.

"Is this because of Finn?"

"Yes. There are going to be a lot of changes round here, John."

"Well, that's fine. It's your call. It always has been. Who was that drunken jerk at the dinner party? Roger Somebody?"

"I don't really know. I'm going to sleep now."

"When are you going to tell me about the new regime?"

"In the morning. I'm too tired now. But you must come and see Finn with me tomorrow."

"All right. I'm just going to read downstairs for a moment."

When he was sure that Vanessa was asleep, John Veals quietly let himself out of the house.

He started the car as discreetly as he could, drove along the Bayswater Road, down Park Lane, through the deserted streets of Victoria and into the backwater of Old Pye Street. It took him ten minutes to bypass the alarms systems with codes and keys and magnetic cards until he was at last in the secure surroundings of his own office, where he fired up his screens and sat back, gazing out in the darkness toward Westminster Cathedral.

His light was the only one that burned in the tall, blank building.

The Muslim Sunday is a working day, and in a few hours' time the markets in Dubai would be up and running. It was odd to Veals that few people he regarded as competitors even had facilities there; the weekend traders he thus found himself up against were, to put it politely, unsophisticated. They reminded him of the excitable young Gulf Arabs who'd come to Park Lane in the 1970s, clamorous for whisky, women and clothes with the designer's label on the outside. So while his London competitors played weekend golf or did dutiful things with their children, John Veals would be

388

silently separating young men from quantities of their recently acquired cash.

He wasn't ready for the action yet. He went into the private bathroom that opened from the rear of his office; and here, with purposeful calm, he shaved, showered and changed his clothes. It always made him feel better to have a clean shirt on, and there were thirty identical white ones still in their packets, piled up in a warm cupboard where they had been deposited by his "personal shopper." On a rail next to them hung a dozen suits in charcoal gray with additional inside pockets for his six mobile phones. He wore the shirts once only.

Refreshed, Veals went out into the main meeting room of the office and looked down at the city of London below him.

Worlds of which he knew nothing were contained within the darkened streets, where febrile realities competed for attention: YourPlace, Parallax and Husam Nar; True Life, Stargazer and Dream Team . . . The words of Axia and the Disaster Maker, as well as those of the Prophet and Lisa on *It's Madness*, might ring disembodied in the ears of the millions.

What John Veals saw was buildings only, silhouettes on a river, units of economic function.

He went back into his own office to concentrate. The plan was simple; all the work was done. On Monday he would give Martin Ryman a photocopy of the Allied Royal debt covenant, and Ryman would pass it to Magnus Darke, explaining its significance. Following Darke's disclosure, there would be panic.

Allied Royal Bank would fail. It followed that the government would take it over and High Level Capital would make hundreds of millions on its positions. As other banks became infected by the immovable debt on their books, they too would need to be rescued by the payers of tax—the workers, the everyday people. At least one American investment bank would go broke; the others would seek help either from the Fed or by allying themselves to giant commercial outfits. Then several more British banks would need rescue; in fact, in John Veals's estimation, every single one of them would need life support. By shorting them, he could profit from that pain, too.

The commodities gamble was frankly a bit of a stretch. The volumes were disappointing and they might lose money before they gained, but the positions he had taken on British government debt and on sterling would, combined with the profit on the fall of ARB, perhaps double the size of his fund within six months. A profit—or rather a capital gain—of £12 billion would accrue in High Level's books.

When, or rather if, the financial crisis ever stabilized, there would be a recession in what journalists charmingly termed the "real" economy. Millions around the globe would lose their jobs; other millions would go without food, or at least see their modest lives stripped of comfort.

But I have mastered this world, thought John Veals, passing his hand over his newly shaved chin. To me there is no mystery, no nuance and no complication; I am a man alive to the spirit of his time, the one who hears the whispers on the wind.

A rare surge of feeling, of something like vindication, came from the pit of his belly and spread out till it sang in his veins. As he stood with his hands in his pockets, staring out over the sleeping city, over its darkened wheels and spires and domes, Veals laughed.

Acknowledgments

With thanks to:

Gillon Aitken, Rachel Cugnoni, Caroline Gascoigne, Gerry Howard, Chloë Johnson-Hill, Andrew Kidd, Emma Mitchell, Gail Rebuck and Steve Rubin for helping this book to publication in various ways. On finance: Matthew Fosh, Glenn Grover, Will Hutton, John Reynolds, Paul Ruddock. On Internet "reality" games: Tim Guest, in person, and his book *Second Lives* (Vintage). On teaching: Sabrina Broadbent, Tabitha Jay, Rebecca Terry and colleagues. On football: Giles Smith; Roy Hodgson and Jaki Stockley at Fulham FC. On the London Underground: Andy Daugherty, Ben Pennington, Donna Sarjant, Albanne Spyrou. On music, Internet and other matters: my children, William, Holly and Arthur. Also, merci to Jill Lewis.

Particular thanks on finance to Kevin Davis, a friend for over thirty years, from the Lower Fifth to the Upper West Side; and to Dr. Duncan Hunter, for his patience with a frequently slow pupil. Any errors or inconsistencies of fact in the financial or other detail are entirely my responsibility.

Thanks also to my wife, Veronica, for literary and many other kindnesses.

Quotations from the Koran are from the Penguin edition, translated by N. J. Dawood. *Milestones* by Sayyid Qutb, referred to in the novel, is published by Islamic Book Service; I am also indebted to *The Crisis of Islam* by Bernard Lewis (Phoenix). Karen Armstrong writes affectingly of the eagerness of seventh-century Arabs in the Peninsula to discover a voice-hearing prophet of their own in *Islam: A Short History*.

I would like to acknowledge how much I enjoyed, and learned from, Michael Lewis's writing on finance in his book about the 1980s bond market, *Liar's Poker*, and in a November 2008 *Vanity Fair* article, "The End," on the American subprime loans crisis.

One of the characters in this book reflects that "Newspaper interviews and [. . .] literary biographies focus[ed] almost exclusively on the extent to which the contents of a serious novelist's books [are] drawn from his own experience and the characters 'based on' people known to him . . ."

In view of this, it might be worth stressing more than ever that: Although reference is made to real events and people, and such reference is intended to be accurate, the characters in this book, and their actions, are invented; any similarity between any of them and any real person, living or dead, is coincidental.

S.F., London, 2005–2009.